THE
GERMAN
HOUSE

D0582995

THE GERMAN HOUSE

ANNETTE HESS

Translated from the German by Elisabeth Lauffer

HARPERVIA

HarperVia
An imprint of HarperCollins*Publishers*
1 London Bridge Street
London
SE1 9GF

First published in Great Britain by HarperVia in 2019

Originally published as Deutsches Haus in Germany in 2018 by Ullstein

1

Copyright © Anette Hess 2019
English language translation © Elisabeth Lauffer

Anette Hess asserts the moral right to be identified as the author of this work in accordance with the Copyright, Designs and Patents Act 1988

A catalogue record for this book is available from the British Library

This is a work of fiction. Names, characters, places, and incidents are products of the author's imagination or are used fictitiously and are not to be construed as real. Any resemblance to actual events, locales, organizations, or persons, living or dead, is entirely coincidental.

ISBN 978-0-00-835986-7

Printed and bound in Great Britain by CPI Group (UK) Ltd, Croydon CR0 4YY

All rights reserved. No part of this publication may be reproduced, stored in a retrieval system, or transmitted, in any form or by any means, electronic, mechanical, photocopying, recording or otherwise, without the prior permission of the publishers.

This book is sold subject to the condition that it shall not, by way of trade or otherwise, be lent, re-sold, hired out or otherwise circulated without the publisher's prior consent in any form of binding or cover other than that in which it is published and without a similar condition including this condition being imposed on the subsequent purchaser.

MIX
Paper from
responsible sources
FSC™ C007454

This book is produced from independently certified FSC™ paper to ensure responsible forest management.

For more information visit: www.harpercollins.co.uk/green

PART
ONE

LONDON BOROUGH OF WANDSWORTH	
9030 00007 0303 2	
Askews & Holts	30-Jan-2020
AF	£12.99
	WW19015927

THERE HAD BEEN ANOTHER fire last night. She smelled it the moment she stepped out, without a coat, a thin layer of snow blanketing the quiet Sunday-morning street. It must have happened near her house this time. The sharp odor cut through the familiar smell of damp winter air: charred rubber, burned fabric, and melted metal, but also singed leather and hair; some mothers used lambskins to protect their newborns from the cold. It was not the first time Eva wondered who could do such a thing, who could sneak through backyards to break into apartment buildings and set fire to the strollers parked in the entryways. *Must be a lunatic—or a bunch of hoodlums!* many thought. Fortunately, none of the fires had spread to the building. No one had yet been hurt. Other than financially, of course. A new baby carriage cost 120 marks at Hertie's. No small peanuts for young families.

"Young families" echoed in Eva's mind. She paced nervously up and down the sidewalk. It was freezing out. Although Eva wore no more than her new, light blue silk dress, she wasn't cold—she was sweating with excitement. She was waiting for none other than, as her sister teased, the "apple of her eye," her future husband, who would meet her family for the first time today, the third Sunday of Advent. He had been invited to the midday meal. Eva checked her watch. Three minutes past one. Jürgen was late.

The occasional car crawled by. It was snowdusting. Eva's father had coined the term to describe this weather phenomenon: tiny ice flakes came sailing down from the clouds, as if someone up there were shaving an enormous block of ice. Someone who made all the decisions. Eva gazed up at the gray skies over whitish roofs. She discovered then that she was being watched: standing at the second-story window—above the sign that read "German House," above the letters "ou"—was a beige figure looking down at her. Her mother. She appeared unmoved, but Eva had the feeling she was taking her leave. Eva quickly turned her back on her. She swallowed. That was all she needed right now. To start crying.

The door to the restaurant opened and her father came out, heavy and dependable in his white chef's coat. He ignored Eva and opened the display case to the right of the door, to place a supposedly new menu in it, although Eva knew there wouldn't be a new one until Shrove Tuesday. Her father was actually very worried. He doted on her and now jealously awaited the unknown man making his way there. Eva heard him softly singing one of those folk songs he delighted in butchering, pretending everything was normal. Much to his own dismay, Ludwig Bruhns was utterly unmusical: "While a-clownin' at the gate, a little song comes to meeeee. Under the linden treeeeee."

A younger woman with teased, light blond hair appeared next to Eva's mother at the window. She overeagerly waved at Eva, but even at this distance, Eva could tell she was depressed. But Eva did not blame herself. She had waited long enough for her big sister to marry. Then Annegret turned twenty-eight—her waist-line expanding with every passing year—and following a secret discussion with her parents, Eva decided to break with convention. Before it was too late. She was practically on the verge of becoming an old maid herself. She hadn't had many admirers. Her family couldn't understand it. Eva had such a healthy, feminine presence, with her full lips, slender nose, and long, naturally blond hair that she cut, styled, and sculpted into an artful updo by herself. Her eyes, though, often appeared troubled, as if she were anticipating some impending catastrophe. Eva suspected this frightened men away.

Five minutes past one. No Jürgen. Instead, the door to the left of the restaurant opened. Eva watched her little brother Stefan come out. He wasn't wearing a coat, which prompted a concerned rapping on the window and gesticulation from their mother upstairs. Stefan obstinately trained his gaze ahead. After all, he had put on his orange pompom hat and matching mittens. He tugged a sled behind him. Purzel, the family's black dachshund, scampered about his feet; he was a sneaky dog they couldn't help but adore.

"Something stinks!" Stefan said.

Eva sighed. "You now, too! This family is a curse!"

Stefan began pulling the sled back and forth through the light snow on the sidewalk. Purzel sniffed at a streetlight, circled excitedly, then pooped in the snow. The pile steamed. The sled runners scraped across the asphalt, joined by the rasp of a snow shovel, as their father got to work before the entrance. Eva caught the way he clutched his back and screwed up his eyes. Her father was in pain—something he would never admit. One morning in October, after his back had been "smarting like hell," as he put it, for some time, her father was unable to get out of bed. Eva called an ambulance, and the hospital X-rayed him and discovered a herniated disc. They'd operated, and the doctor advised him to close the restaurant. Ludwig Bruhns explained that he had a family to feed. And what about his measly pension? They urged him to hire a cook and get out of the kitchen. But Ludwig refused to allow a stranger to enter his realm. The solution had been to stop offering lunch, so since that fall, they'd opened only in the evening. Revenue had dropped by nearly half since then, but Ludwig's back was feeling better. Still, Eva knew that her father's greatest wish was to start serving lunch again that spring. Ludwig Bruhns loved his job, loved it when his guests gathered in good company, when they enjoyed the food and went home smiling, satisfied, and tipsy. "I serve up full bellies and happy hearts," he liked to say. And Eva's mother would tease back, "He who can, does. He who cannot, serves."

Eva was feeling a bit chilled now. She crossed her arms and shivered. She hoped fervently that Jürgen would treat her parents with respect. There had been a few times she'd witnessed an unpleasant, condescending attitude toward waiters or shop girls.

"Police!" Stefan bellowed. A black-and-white vehicle with a siren on its roof was approaching. Two men in dark blue uniforms sat inside. Stefan froze in awe. The officers were surely headed for the burned stroller, Eva thought, to collect evidence and question the building's residents whether they'd noticed anything suspicious the night before. The car glided by almost soundlessly. The policemen gave first Ludwig, then Eva a nod. People knew each other in this neighborhood. The car turned onto König Strasse. *Sure enough, the fire must have been in the housing estate. That new pink apartment building. Lots of families live there. Young families.*

Twelve minutes past one. *He's not coming. He reconsidered. He'll call tomorrow and tell me we aren't a good match. The disparity in our families' social standing, darling Eva, is just too great for us to bridge.* Pow!!! Stefan had thrown a snowball at her. He hit her square in the chest, and the icy snow slid down into her dress. Eva grabbed Stefan by the sweater and yanked him toward her. "Are you crazy?! This is a brand-new dress!" Stefan bared his teeth, his guilty face. Eva would've scolded him further, but at that moment Jürgen's yellow car appeared at the end of the street. Her heart leapt like a spooked calf. Eva cursed her nerves, which she'd even seen a doctor about. *Breathe deeply.* It was something she failed to do now, because as Jürgen's car drew near, Eva was struck by the realization that nothing would ever convince her parents of Jurgen's ability to make her happy. Not even his money. Eva could make out Jürgen's face behind the windshield. He looked tired. And serious. He didn't even glance at her. For one horrifying moment, Eva thought he might step on the gas and drive off. But then the car slowed. Stefan burst out, "Gee, he's got black hair! Like a Gypsy!"

Jürgen steered the car a bit too close to the sidewalk. The rubber tires squealed against the curb. Stefan reached for Eva's hand. Eva felt the snow melting inside her bodice. Jürgen switched off the engine and sat in the car for another moment. He would never forget this scene: the two women—one fat and one short—standing at the window above the word "House," in the mistaken belief that he couldn't see them, the boy with the sled gawking at him, and the father, massive, standing in the door to the restaurant with a snow shovel, ready for anything. They studied him as though he were a defendant entering the courtroom and taking his place for the first time. Except for Eva. Hers was a gaze of anxious love.

Jürgen swallowed, put on his hat, and picked up a bouquet

wrapped in tissue paper from the passenger seat. He got out and approached Eva. He was about to smile, when something nipped him painfully in the back of the leg. A dachshund. "Purzel! No! No!" Eva cried. "Stefan, bring him inside. Put him in the bedroom!"

Stefan protested, but grabbed the dog and carried the struggling animal back into the house. Eva and Jürgen locked eyes timidly. They weren't entirely sure how to greet one another with Eva's family watching, so they shook hands and began speaking at the same time.

"I'm sorry, they're just so curious."

"What a welcoming committee! To what do I owe the honor?"

The moment Jürgen released Eva's hand, her father, mother, and sister vanished from their posts, like rabbits slipping into their burrows. Eva and Jürgen were alone. An icy wind swept across the street.

"Are you in the mood for goose?" Eva asked.

"I've thought of nothing else for days."

"You just need to get along with my brother. Then you'll have everyone on your side."

They laughed, neither certain why. Jürgen headed for the restaurant, but Eva steered him to the left, toward the door to the house. She didn't want to lead him through the dim dining room that smelled of spilled beer and damp ash. Instead, they climbed the polished staircase, with its black banister, to the apartment above the restaurant. The two-story house had been rebuilt after the war, having been almost completely destroyed in an air strike. The morning following that inferno, all that survived was the restaurant's long bar, which stood there defenseless and exposed to the elements.

Eva's mother waited by the apartment door upstairs, wearing

the smile typically reserved for regulars at the restaurant. Her "sugar face," as Stefan called it. Edith Bruhns had put on her double-strand garnet necklace, along with her gilded stud earrings with the dangling cultured pearls and her gold brooch shaped like a clover leaf. Edith was wearing all the jewelry she owned, which Eva had never seen before. She was reminded of the fairy tale she had read aloud to Stefan, about the fir tree. After Christmas, the tree was stored in the attic till spring, when it was carried outside and burned. In its brittle branches hung the forgotten remains of Christmas Eve.

Fitting for Advent, at least, Eva thought.

"Herr Schorrmann, what is this weather you've brought with you? Roses in December?! Where on earth did you find these, Herr Schorrmann?"

"Mum, his last name is Schoormann, with two *o*'s!"

"I'll take your hat, Herr Schooormann."

In the living room, which also served as the dining room on Sundays, Ludwig Bruhns met Jürgen, wielding a roasting fork and poultry shears. He offered Jürgen his right wrist in greeting.

Jürgen apologized, "The snow."

"Not to worry. No harm done. It's a big goose, sixteen pounds. It takes its time."

Annegret emerged from the background and fell upon Jürgen. The eyeliner she'd put on was a little too black, the lipstick a little too orange. She shook Jürgen's hand and smiled conspiratorially. "Congratulations. You're getting the real deal." Jürgen wondered whether she meant the goose or Eva.

A short time later, they were all seated at the table, regarding the steaming bird. The yellow roses Jürgen had brought stood to the side in a crystal vase, like flowers brought to a funeral. The radio played unidentifiable Sunday music in the background. A Christmas pyramid powered by three flickering candles twirled on the cupboard. The fourth had yet to be lit. At the center of the pyramid, Mary, Joseph, and the newborn child in the manger stood before a stable. Sheep, shepherds, and the Three Kings and their camels scurried around the family in an endless circle. They would never reach the Holy Family, never be able to offer their gifts to the Baby Jesus. This had saddened Eva as a child. She'd finally snapped the gift from the Moorish king's hands and placed it before the manger. By the following Christmas, the little red, wooden package had gone missing, and since then, the Moorish king had spun empty-handed. The gift never had turned up. Eva's mother told this story every year, when she brought down the pyramid from the attic for the Christmas season. Eva had been five at the time, but she had no memory of it.

Eva's father carved the goose along the breast with the poultry shears. "Was the goose alive once?" Stefan looked quizzically at his father, who winked at Jürgen.

"No, this is a fake goose. Just for eating."

"Then I want breast meat!" Stefan held out his plate.

"Guests first, sonny."

Eva's mother took Jürgen's plate—the Dresden porcelain patterned with fanciful green tendrils—and held it out to her husband. Eva observed the way Jürgen looked around without being obvious. He eyed the worn sofa and yellow checked blanket her mother had arranged over a tear in the upholstery. She had also crocheted a small coverlet for the left armrest. That was where Eva's father, once he'd closed up his kitchen, would sit after midnight and rest his feet on a low padded stool, as the doctor had recommended. The weekly newspaper, *The Family Friend*, lay on the coffee table, opened to the crossword puzzle, a quarter of which had been solved. Another doily protected the precious television set. Jürgen inhaled through his nose and thanked Eva's mother courteously for the full plate she set before him. She positioned the dish to look especially appetizing. Her earrings swung as she moved. Eva's father, who had traded his white chef's coat for his Sunday jacket, sat down next to Eva. There was a small green fleck on his cheek. Probably parsley. Eva quickly brushed it off his soft face. He took her hand and gave it a little squeeze without looking at her. Eva swallowed. She was furious at Jürgen for his appraising look. Fine, he might be used to something else. But he had to see how hard her parents were trying, how good they were, how endearing.

They started eating in silence. As she always did in front of company, Annegret restrained herself and poked at her food, as though she weren't hungry. But afterward, she would stuff herself with leftovers, and then go for the cold goose in the pantry later that evening. She offered Jürgen the salt and pepper caddy and winked.

"Would you like some pepper, Herr Schoooormann? Salt?"

Jürgen politely declined, which Eva's father registered without looking up.

"No one's ever had to season my cooking."

"Eva tells me you're a nurse? At the hospital?" Jürgen addressed Annegret, who was a mystery to him. She shrugged, as if it weren't worth mentioning.

"Which department?"

"Nursery."

In the silence that followed, they could suddenly all hear the radio announcer. "From Gera, Grandma Hildegard sends her regards to her family in Wiesbaden, especially her eight-year-old grandson Heiner, on this third Sunday of Advent." Music started to play.

Edith smiled at Jürgen.

"And what do you do professionally, Herr Schoooormann?"

"I studied theology. Now I work in my father's company. In upper management."

"Mail-order business, isn't that right? Your family runs a mail-order business?" her father chimed in.

Eva elbowed him. "Daddy! Now don't pretend to be dumber than you are!"

A short silence, then everyone laughed, including Stefan, although he didn't understand why. Eva relaxed. She and Jürgen exchanged a glance: *It'll be fine!*

"Of course we receive the Schoormann catalog too," Eva's mother admitted.

Stefan sang the jingle in falsetto. "Schoormann's got it, Schoormann gets it—to you. Ding dong! Dong ding!"

Jürgen feigned seriousness. "And have we also ordered from the catalog? That is the question."

"Of course," Edith responded solicitously. "A blow-dryer and a raincoat. We were very satisfied. But you should start selling washing machines. I'd rather not go to Hertie's for such a big purchase. They always talk your ear off. With a catalog, you can consider your options in the comfort of your own home."

Jürgen nodded in agreement. "Yes, you're right, Frau Bruhns. I happen to have several changes planned for the company."

Eva gave him an encouraging look. Jürgen cleared his throat.

"My father is sick. He'll not be able to run the company much longer."

"I'm so sorry to hear that," Eva's mother said.

"What has he got?" Her father passed Jürgen the gravy boat.
Jürgen wasn't prepared to say any more, though. He dribbled gravy
on his meat.

"It tastes delicious."

"Glad to hear it."

Eva knew that Jürgen's father was growing increasingly se-
nile. Jürgen had only spoken about it once. There were good
days and bad. But his unpredictability was only getting worse.
Eva hadn't met Jürgen's father and his second wife, yet. After all,
the groom was supposed to visit the parents of the bride first.
Eva and Jürgen had argued about whether he should ask for her
hand today. Jürgen was against it. Eva's parents would think
him unserious if he stormed in with such a request. Or—even
worse—think that there was something else going on. The quar-
rel went unresolved. Eva studied Jürgen's face, trying to detect
whether he planned to ask her father today. But his expression
revealed nothing. She looked at his hands, which clenched the
silverware tighter than usual. Eva hadn't experienced an "in-
timate encounter," as Doctor Gorf called it, with Jürgen. She
was ready to, considering she'd already lost her virginity two
years ago. But Jürgen had clear expectations: no intercourse
before marriage. He was conservative. A wife was to submit to
her husband's authority. From the first time they met, Jürgen
looked at Eva as though reading her from the inside, as though
he knew what was best for her, better than she did herself. Eva,
who most of the time didn't know what she really wanted, had
no objection to being led—whether dancing or in life. This marriage would also allow Eva to move up in society. From the innkeeper's daughter born and raised in Bornheim, to the wife of a

distinguished businessman. The thought made Eva dizzy. But it was a happy dizziness.

Right after lunch, Eva and her mother started fixing the coffee together in the spacious kitchen. Annegret had left. She had to work the late shift at the hospital, had to feed her infants. Plus, she didn't care too much for cake with buttercream icing.

Eva sliced thick pieces of Frankfurt Crown Cake while her mother ground coffee beans in a small electric grinder. Edith Bruhns stared at the growling appliance. When the noise stopped, she said, "He's not at all your type, Evie. I mean, I can't help but think of Peter Kraus. He was always your heartthrob. . . ."

"Just because Jürgen's not blond?"

Eva was shocked by how obviously her mother didn't like Jürgen. And she considered her mother a great judge of character. Working at the restaurant, Edith had met countless people. At first glance, she could tell whether a person was decent or a lout.

"Those black eyes . . ."

"Mum, his eyes are dark green! You just need to look more closely."

"I mean, it's up to you. His family is certainly above reproach. But I have to be honest, child, I can't help it. He will not make you happy."

"Would you just get to know him first?"

Eva's mother poured bubbling water into the filled coffee strainer. The coffee smelled like the expensive kind.

"He's too withdrawn, Eva. He's spooky."

"He's thoughtful. Jürgen did want to become a priest. . . ."

"God forbid!"

"He had already studied theology for eight semesters. But then he met me and started rethinking celibacy."

Eva laughed, but her mother remained stony-faced. "Surely he left school because of his father? Because he needs to take over the company."

"Yes." Eva sighed. Her mother was not in the mood to joke. They watched the bubbling water seep through the coffee filter.

Spooky Jürgen and Eva's father sat in the living room with cognacs. The radio played untiringly. Jürgen smoked a cigarette and studied the ponderous oil painting hung above the cupboard. It depicted a marshy landscape at sunset, the red sky flaring up beyond the dike. Some cows grazed upon a lush meadow. There was a woman hanging laundry beside her cottage. A short distance away, on the right edge of the painting, stood another figure. It appeared out of focus, as if sketched in after the fact. It was unclear whether this was the cowherd, the husband, or a stranger.

Stefan crouched on the rug and prepared his plastic army for battle. Purzel had been let back out of the bedroom, and he lay on his belly and blinked at the soldiers gathered before his nose. Stefan assembled long rows. He also had a tin wind-up tank. It lay waiting in its box.

Meanwhile, Eva's father was sharing a general outline of the family history with his future son-in-law. "Yep, I'm an old sandworm. Grew up on Juist, as you can probably hear. My parents owned a shop. Supplied the whole island. Coffee, sugar, window glass—we had everything. Actually, Herr Schooormann, just like you. My mother died early. Father never really did recover. He's been gone for fifteen years now, himself. Edith, my wife, well, I met her at the school of hotel management in Hamburg. That was in '34, and boy were we wet behind the ears! My wife comes from a family of artists, if you can believe it. Her parents were both musicians in the philharmonic. He played first violin, she played second. It was the other way 'round at home. My wife's mother, she's still alive. Lives in Hamburg. My wife was meant to play violin too, only her fingers were too short. So her hope was to become an actress, which her parents nipped firmly in the bud. At the very least, she wanted to see the world, so they sent her to study hotel management."

"And what brought you here?" Jürgen asked with friendly interest. He'd enjoyed the roast goose. He liked Ludwig Bruhns, who was giving such an enthusiastic account of his family. Eva had inherited her sensuous mouth from her father.

"'German House' had belonged to one of my wife's cousins, and he wanted to sell it. Boy, if that didn't fit like an ass on the can. Pardon the expression. We seized opportunity and reopened in '49. We've never looked back."

"Sure, Berger Strasse is worth it. . . ."

"The decent part, I'd like to point out, Herr Schoormann!"

Jürgen smiled reassuringly.

"Anyway, since the episode with my back, my doctor's been saying I should close up shop! So I spelled out my pension for him. Now we don't open till five. But there will be an end to this decadent lifestyle, come spring!"

They fell silent. Jürgen sensed there was more Ludwig wanted to say. He waited. Ludwig cleared his throat and did not look at him.

"Yes, well, my back issues. They're from the war."

"An injury?" Jürgen asked politely.

"I served in the field kitchen. On the Western Front. Just so you know." Eva's father polished off the rest of his cognac. Jürgen was slightly perplexed. He didn't sense that Ludwig Bruhns had just lied.

Pow pow pow! Stefan had released his tank. It made a tremendous racket struggling over the rug, as though the pile were eastern marshlands. It ran over one soldier figurine after the other.

"Young man! Take it into the hallway!"

But Stefan had eyes only for Jürgen, who feared children's directness. Then he remembered Eva's advice, to win over her brother.

"Can you show me your tank, Stefan?"

Stefan stood up and handed Jürgen his tin toy.

"It's almost two times bigger than Thomas Preisgau's," he said.

"Thomas is his best friend," Ludwig explained, pouring more cognac.

Jürgen admired the tank with due care. Stefan snatched up a figurine from the floor. "Look, I painted this one. It's a Yank! A Negro!"

Jürgen glanced at the small plastic soldier with the painted face Stefan was holding out for him. It was blood red. Jürgen closed his eyes, but the image remained.

"And I'm getting an air rifle from Father Christmas!"

"An air rifle," Jürgen repeated absently. He took a long draft from his glass. The memory would fade in a moment.

Ludwig drew Stefan close. "You don't know that for certain, little one." Stefan squirmed loose.

"I always get everything I ask for."

Ludwig looked at Jürgen apologetically. "It's true, I'm afraid. The boy is spoiled rotten. My wife and I, well, we certainly weren't expecting anything to come after the girls."

The telephone rang in the hallway. Stefan reached it first and flatly recited his lines: "Bruhns family residence, Stefan Bruhns speaking. Who's there, please?" Stefan listened, then called out,

"Eva, it's Herr Körting! For you!" Eva came out of the kitchen, drying her hands on her apron, and took the receiver. "Herr Körting? And when? Immediately? But we're all here—"

Eva was interrupted. She listened and looked through the open door at the two men sitting at the table. *They look quite comfortable with each other already,* she thought. Then Eva spoke into the phone, "Yes, all right. I'll come in." She hung up.

"I'm so sorry, Jürgen, but that was my boss. I have to go to work!"

Her mother emerged from the kitchen with the coffee tray.

"On Advent Sunday?"

"Apparently it's urgent. There's a trial date scheduled for next week."

"Well, it's like I always say, you can't mix duty with pleasure." Ludwig got to his feet. Jürgen stood too. "But you stay here! You've still got to try this cake!"

"It's made with real butter. A whole pound!" Edith added.

"And you haven't even seen my room yet!"

Jürgen escorted Eva into the hallway. She had changed and now wore her modest business suit. Jürgen helped her into her pale checked wool coat and murmured in comic desperation, "You planned this as a test, didn't you? You want to leave me alone with your family and see how I fare."

"They don't bite."

"Your father's got those bloodshot eyes."

"That's from his pain medication. I'll be back in an hour. I'm sure it has to do with that suit for damages. Those faulty engine parts from Poland."

"Should I drive you?"

"Someone's picking me up."

"I'm coming with you. If you're not careful, you could end up compromised."

Eva pulled on her deerskin gloves, Jürgen's gift to her on Saint Nicholas Day.

"The only client who's ever compromised me is you."

They looked at each other. Jürgen moved in for a kiss. Eva pulled him into the corner beside the coatrack, where her parents couldn't see them. They embraced, smiled, kissed. Eva felt Jürgen's arousal, saw in his eyes, that he desired her. Loved her? Eva stepped out of the embrace. "Would you ask him today, please?"

Jürgen did not respond.

Eva left the apartment, and Jürgen headed back into the living room. There the Bruhnses sat at the coffee table, like actors waiting onstage for their prompt.

"We're not at all dangerous, Herr Schoormann."

"Totally harmless, Herr Schooormann."

"Except for Purzel. He bites sometimes," Stefan called from the rug.

"Well, let's get a taste of that cake."

Jürgen returned to the warmth of the living room.

Eva came out of the house. It was already getting dark outside. The snow cover glowed soft blue. Circles of amber lay beneath the streetlights. A large vehicle, its engine running, stood in the middle of the street. The driver, a young man, impatiently beckoned to Eva. She climbed into the front passenger seat. It smelled of cigarette smoke and peppermint in the car. The young man was chewing gum. He was not wearing a hat, nor did he shake Eva's hand. He just nodded curtly: "David Miller." Then he stepped on the gas. He wasn't a good driver—too fast—and routinely shifted gears either too late or too soon. Eva didn't have a license, but she could tell he was not familiar with this vehicle. He was a bad driver in other ways too. The car repeatedly fishtailed. Eva studied the young man out the corner of her eye. He had thick reddish hair a little too long in the back, freckles, fine, pale eyelashes, and slender hands that gave off a strangely innocent impression.

It was evident Herr Miller had no interest in conversation. As they drove in silence toward the city center, the lights grew brighter and more colorful, with a particular tendency toward red. The lower section of Berger Strasse featured several such establishments. Suzi's or Mokka Bar. Eva thought of Jürgen, who had by now returned to the table, sat, and eaten the Frankfurt Crown Cake she'd baked, barely tasting a thing. Because without question, he was nervously debating whether he could ask of his family that they accept hers, and whether he wanted to spend the rest of his life together with her.

The law offices were in a tall building on one of the city's main streets. David Miller stepped into a small elevator alongside Eva. The doors shut automatically twice. Double doors. David pressed the eight, then looked at the ceiling, as if expecting something. Eva also looked up, at a screwed-shut hatch with countless little holes. A ventilation duct. She suddenly felt confined. Her heart pounded faster, and her mouth went dry. David looked at Eva. Looked down, although he wasn't much taller than she. He felt uncomfortably close. His eyes were strange.

"What was your name?"

"Eva Bruhns."

The elevator stopped with a jolt, and for a moment Eva feared they'd gotten stuck. But the doors opened. They stepped out, took a left, and rang at a heavy glass door. An office girl in green trotted up from the other side and let them in. Eva and the girl swiftly looked each other over. Same age, similar figure. The girl had dark hair and bad skin, but her eyes were a clear gray.

Eva and David followed the girl down a long corridor. As they walked, Eva scrutinized the girl's tight suit and the folds that formed on her rear with every step. The heels on her black pumps were brazenly high. She'd probably bought them at Hertie's. What sounded like sobbing could be heard from a room at the end of the hallway, but the closer they came, the softer the noise grew. It was silent when they finally reached the door. Perhaps Eva had simply imagined the cries.

The girl knocked, then opened the door to a surprisingly cramped office. Inside were three men, surrounded by cigarette smoke and document files stacked on tables, shelves, and the floor.

One of them, a short, older gentleman, sat bolt upright in a chair in the center of the room, as though the entire room—the entire building—had been constructed around him alone. Perhaps even the entire city. A younger man with light blond hair and fine, gold-rimmed glasses was wedged behind a desk laden with files. He had cleared himself a small spot, where he was now writing. He was smoking a cigarette but had no ashtray. As Eva looked over at him, the ash fell on his notes. He mechanically brushed it to the floor. Neither man rose, which Eva thought quite rude.

The third man, a gnarled figure, even turned his back on her. He was standing at the window, peering out at the dark. Eva was reminded of a film on Napoleon she had seen with Jürgen. The general had assumed the same stance at the palace window. In despair over his planned campaign, he had gazed across the countryside. Only they could see that the landscape outside the window was painted on cardboard.

The blond man behind the desk gave Eva a nod. He gestured

toward the seated man. "This is Herr Josef Gabor, from Warsaw. The Polish interpreter was meant to come with him today, but he encountered some difficulties in leaving the country. He was detained at the airport. Please."

Since none of the gentlemen made any moves to help her, Eva removed her coat herself and hung it on a stand behind the door. The blond man pointed at a table against the wall. On it were dirty coffee cups and a plate with a few leftover cookies. Eva loved speculoos. But she refrained from indulging. She had put on two kilos in recent weeks. Eva positioned herself at the table so she could look Herr Gabor in the face, and removed the two dictionaries from her handbag. One general, the other a lexicon of specialized economic terms. She slid aside the cookie plate and set the books in its spot. Then she pulled out her notebook and a pencil. The girl in green had taken a seat at the other end of the table, at a stenotype machine. She fed the paper tape into the machine, the roller chattering. She never took her eyes off the light blond-haired man. She was interested in him, but it wasn't mutual, which Eva detected straightaway. David Miller also removed his coat and sat down in a chair against the opposite wall, as though he weren't involved, his coat across his knees.

Everyone waited, as if for a starting pistol. Eva looked at the cookies. The gnarled man standing at the window turned around. He addressed the man in the chair.

"Herr Gabor, please tell us what, exactly, occurred on the twenty-third of September 1941."

Eva translated the question, although the year struck her as odd. That was more than twenty years ago. They must be examining some crime (although hadn't the statute of limitations expired?) rather than a contract violation. The man in the chair looked Eva straight in the face, clearly relieved to have finally met someone in this country who understood him. He began to speak. His voice was in direct contrast to his upright bearing. It was as if he were reading from a letter faded with time, as if he were at first unable to decipher all of the words. He also spoke in a provincial dialect that gave Eva some trouble. She translated haltingly.

"That day it was warm—almost humid, in fact—and we had to decorate all the windows. All the windows in hostel number eleven. We decorated them with sandbags and filled all of the cracks with straw and dirt. We put a lot of effort into it, because mistakes were not tolerated. We finished our work toward evening. Then they led the 850 Soviet guests down into the cellar of the hostel. They waited till dark, so you could see the light better, I suspect. Then they threw the light into the cellar, down the ventilation shafts, and closed the doors. The doors weren't opened till the next morning. We had to go in first. Most of the guests were illuminated."

The men in the room looked at Eva. She felt slightly nauseous. Something was wrong. The woman tapped away at her machine, unfazed, but the blond man asked Eva, "Are you sure you understood that correctly?" Eva paged through her specialist dictionary. "I'm sorry, I usually translate in contract disputes, regarding economic affairs and negotiating settlements for damages. . . ."

The men exchanged looks. The blond man shook his head impatiently, but the gnarled man by the window gave him a placating nod. From across the room, David Miller looked at Eva with disdain.

Eva reached for her general dictionary, which was heavy as a brick. She had the feeling it wasn't guests, but prisoners. Not a hostel, but a cell block. And not light. No illumination. Eva eyed the man in the chair. He returned her gaze, his expression as if he were suddenly feeling faint.

Eva said, "I apologize, I translated that incorrectly. It was, 'We found most of the prisoners suffocated by the gas.'"

Silence filled the room. David Miller was trying to light a cigarette, but his lighter refused to catch. Chk-chk-chk. Then the blond man coughed and turned toward the gnarled man. "We should be glad we found a replacement at all. At such short notice. Better than nothing."

He responded, "Let's try to continue. What other option do we have?"

The blond man turned to Eva. "But if you're ever uncertain, look it up immediately."

Eva nodded. She translated slowly. The woman typed on her machine at the same trickling pace. "When we opened the doors, some of the prisoners were still alive. About one third. It had been too little gas. The procedure was repeated with double the amount. We waited two days to open the doors this time. The operation was a success."

The blond man stood up behind his desk. "Who gave the order?" He moved the coffee cups and laid out twenty-one photos on Eva's table. Eva regarded the faces from the side. Men with numbers under their chin in front of whitewashed walls. But some in sunny yards, playing with big dogs. One man had the face of a ferret. Josef Gabor stood up and approached the table. He gazed upon the photos for a long time and then pointed at one so suddenly, it made Eva jump. The picture showed a younger man grasping a large rabbit by the scruff, holding it toward the camera with a proud smile on his face. The men in the room exchanged satisfied glances and nodded. *My father used to breed rabbits*, Eva thought, at their garden plot outside the city, where he grew the vegetables for the kitchen. The endlessly chewing animals were kept in little enclosures. But the day Stefan realized he wasn't just petting and supplying his silky soft companions with dandelions, but also eating them, he had thrown a terrible fit. Her father got rid of the rabbits.

Later, Eva had to sign her translation of the testimony. Her name looked different than usual. As though written by a child, clumsy and rounded. The blond man gave her an absentminded nod. "Thank you. Invoice goes through your agency?" David Miller rose from his chair against the wall and said brusquely, "Wait outside. Two minutes."

Eva put on her coat and stepped into the hall, while David conferred with the blond man. She could make out, "Unqualified! Utterly unqualified!" The blond man nodded, picked up the telephone, and dialed a number. The attorney general dropped heavily into a chair.

Eva stepped up to one of the tall windows in the hallway and peered out into the shadowy back courtyard. It had begun to snow. Thick, heavy flakes. Countless dark windows, deserted and mute, in the high-rise opposite returned Eva's gaze. *Not a soul lives there*, Eva thought. *Just offices.* Three mittens had been laid to dry on the radiator under the window. *Who do they belong to?* she wondered. *Who does the single mitten belong to?*

Josef Gabor appeared beside her. He bowed slightly and thanked her. Eva nodded at him. Confused. Through the open door, she noticed that the gnarled man was observing her from his chair by the window. David Miller joined her in the hallway, pulling on his coat as he walked. "I'll drive you." He clearly wasn't happy to.

Neither spoke in the car. The wipers moved fitfully, driving off the innumerable snowflakes from the windshield. David was beside himself. Eva could sense his fury.

"I'm sorry, but I just jumped in. Normally I just handle contracts. . . . It was absolutely horrible, what that man was—"

The car skidded narrowly past a streetlight. David cursed under his breath.

"What was he talking about? An incident from the war?"

David did not look at Eva. "You're all so ignorant."

"I beg your pardon?"

"You all think that the little brown men landed their spaceship here in '33. Am I right? Then off again they went in '45, after forcing this fascism thing on you poor Germans."

It wasn't until he spoke for a longer stretch that Eva could hear he wasn't German. He had a slight accent, maybe American. And he placed his words very precisely. As though everything he said had been rehearsed.

"I'd like to get out, please."

"And you're just another one of the millions of idiot *Fräuleins*. I saw it the moment you got in the car. Oblivious and ignorant! Do you know what you Germans did?! Do you know what you did?!!"

"Stop the car this instant!"

David hit the brakes. Eva seized the handle, opened the door, and got out. "That's right, just run away. I hope your German comfort ki—"

Eva slammed the door. She hurried through the falling snow. Suddenly everything was quiet, the furor behind her. The heavy vehicle swooped off. Eva thought, *That driver, or whatever he is, isn't mentally stable!*

Jürgen's car had disappeared from out in front of German House. Where he'd parked was covered in snow, as though Jürgen had never been there. The windows of the restaurant glowed warmly. The drone of voices inside could be heard from the street. Company Christmas parties. Those meant good business for them every year. Eva watched the silhouettes moving behind the panes. She saw her mother, laden with plates, approach a table and serve the guests swiftly, deftly. Chops. Schnitzel. Goose with red cabbage and the endless dumplings her father, the magician, formed with his soft, dexterous hands and sent into the seething salted water.

Eva wanted to go in, but she hesitated. For a moment, the place seemed like a maw that threatened to swallow her. Then she pulled herself together. Herr Gabor had experienced something terrible, but the question of the hour was: Had Jürgen asked for her hand in marriage?

As Eva stepped into the restaurant—into the human warmth, the haze of sizzling goose fat, the roomful of bodies, all a bit drunk and merry—her mother came up, balancing plates. Edith Bruhns was now wearing her work clothes: black skirt and white blouse, a white apron and her comfortable beige shoes. She whispered in alarm, "What happened to you? Did you fall?"

Eva shook her head indignantly. "Did he ask?"

"Talk to your father!" Edith turned and carried on serving.

Eva entered the kitchen. Her father was hard at work with his two helpers. Her father, in his white coat, dark trousers, chef's hat on his head, his belly always pushed out a little in front, which gave him a funny look. Eva whispered, "Did he ask?" Her father opened an oven, which released a massive cloud of steam in his face. He didn't appear to notice. He heaved a large pan of roast goose—two whole, brown birds—from the oven. He did not look at his daughter. "Nice young man. Decent."

Eva sighed in disappointment. She had to struggle to keep from crying. Then her father came up to her. "He'll ask, Eva, sweetheart. But if he doesn't make you happy, heaven help him!"

That night, Eva lay in bed and stared at the ceiling. The streetlight in front of the house threw a shadow into her room that looked like a man on a horse. A tall man with a lance. Don Quixote. Eva studied him every night, the way he floated above her, and asked herself, *What is it I'm fighting in vain?* Eva thought of Jürgen and cursed her fear that he might leave at the last moment. Maybe women didn't interest him. After all, who voluntarily decides to become a priest? Why hadn't he ever touched her? Eva sat up, switched on the light on her bedside table, opened a drawer, and pulled out a letter. The only letter from Jürgen in which he'd written "I love you." It was, however, preceded by "If I had to settle on a feeling, then I could definitely say that . . ." There it was. In Jürgen's awkward way of expressing emotions, this was an untarnished confession of love! Eva sighed, placed the letter back in the bedside table, and turned off the light. She closed her eyes. She saw flakes swirling, and an indistinct façade with dark windows. She began to count them. At some point, she fell asleep. She did not dream of Jürgen. She dreamed of a hostel, far to the east. A hostel tastefully covered in flowers and grasses to keep out the wind and cold. She had invited many guests. As Eva and her parents served the crowd, the guests reveled heartily till early morning. Till none of them were breathing.

Monday. The city lay under a thick blanket of snow. Those responsible for the roads ate breakfast standing that morning while making phone calls about the precarious situation, only to spend the rest of the day in their overheated offices, being bombarded with complaints about vehicular damage and streets that hadn't been cleared.

Mondays meant that German House was closed. Ludwig Bruhns got in his "weekly beauty rest" till nine. Annegret, who had gotten home from her shift earlier that morning, hadn't made an appearance yet, either. The remaining family members ate breakfast in the big, bright kitchen that faced the back courtyard. The fir tree that towered there was covered in white, a few crows perching motionless in its branches, as though they couldn't comprehend the snow. Stefan had stayed home, supposedly with a "beastly" sore throat. Edith Bruhns had feigned mercilessness and responded, "Well, someone decided to play in the snow without a coat . . ." But then she had rubbed his little chest with eucalyptus salve, which lent the kitchen a gentle aroma. She'd wrapped a scarf around his neck and was now slathering a third slice of bread with honey, which was good for sore throats. Meanwhile, she was also comforting Eva, who paged unhappily through the morning paper.

"Your worlds are too different. I can understand the attraction, child. But it would be the end of you. Just the thought of that estate. I know the ones, up there in the hills. People's properties the size of ten soccer fields . . ."

"Can I play soccer up there?!" Stefan asked with his mouth full.

"After the first flush of love has faded," Edith continued, "you need to represent. You need to keep a smile on your face and stay strong. And don't expect much of your husband. He's got such an important post, you'll barely set eyes on him. You'll be alone. And that's not the life for you, Eva. It'll make you sick. Your nerves always were so delicate. . . ."

"Nerves." The word bothered Eva every time she heard it. It was as though her nerves were something outside of her, cladding her body. As though her delicate nerves were a matter of having chosen the wrong clothing. Eva thought of Brommer's Costumes, by the train station, a store as musty as it was magical, as dark, dangerous, and impenetrable as the jungle. Since childhood, she had loved plunging into their wares every year in preparation for Carnival. She imagined coming across strong nerves hanging among ruffled princess gowns on one of the store's countless racks. A coat woven and knotted out of thick, steely strands. Impregnable, impossible to tear, protection from all pain. "Mum, that's something you can learn! Just look at Grace Kelly. First an actress, and now she's a princess. . . ."

"You have to be the right type for something like that."

"Then what type might I be, pray tell?"

"You are a normal young woman who needs a normal man. Maybe a tradesman. Roofers make very good money." Eva snorted in outrage and was about to voice her disdain for every last type of tradesman, when a small black-and-white photograph in the newspaper caught her eye. It showed two of the men she had spent an hour with in a smoke-filled room yesterday: the younger, blond man and older fellow with the funny windswept hair. They were pictured in serious conversation. The caption read, "Lead prosecutor and Hessian state attorney general holding preparatory discussions." Eva started to read the one-column article. A trial against former members of the SS was evidently set to begin in the city that very week.

"Eva? Are you listening? I'm talking to you! What about Peter Rangkötter? He courted you for such a long time. And tilers never run out of work."

"Mum, do you seriously think I would ever want to be named Eva Rangkötter?" Stefan, his little chin covered in honey, giggled and gleefully chanted, "Frau Rangkötter! Frau Rangkötter!" Eva ignored her brother, pointed to the article, and looked at her mother. "Have you heard about this? This trial? That was my assignment yesterday."

Edith took the paper, glanced at the photograph, and skimmed the article. "It's terrible, what happened. In the war. But no one wants to hear it anymore. And why in our city, of all places?" Edith Bruhns folded up the paper. Eva looked at her mother in surprise. It sounded as though she had some stake in it. "And why not?" Her mother didn't respond. Instead, she stood and began to clear the dirty dishes. She was wearing a tight-lipped expression—her "lemon face," as Stefan called it. She turned on the boiler above the sink to heat dishwater.

"Can you help downstairs today, Eva, or do you have to work?"

"Yes, I can. Things are slow around Christmas. Besides, the boss always asks Karin Melzer first. Because she always wears such pointed brassieres."

"Shhh," Edith hissed, with a glance at Stefan, who merely smirked.

"As if I didn't knew what a brassiere is."

"As if I didn't *know*," Edith corrected him. The water in the boiler began to seethe. Edith stacked the dishes in the sink.

Eva opened the newspaper again and finished reading the article: twenty-one men had been indicted. They had all worked at a camp in Poland. The trial had been repeatedly delayed. The main defendant, the camp's final commander, had already died on them. His adjutant, a Hamburg businessman of excellent repute, had been indicted in his place. Testimony would be heard from

274 witnesses. Hundreds of thousands of people in the camp were allegedly—

"Boo!"

Stefan unexpectedly smacked the bottom of the paper, one of his favorite jokes. As always, Eva was terribly startled. She tossed the paper aside and leaped to her feet. "Just you wait!" Stefan stormed out of the kitchen, Eva on his heels. She chased her little brother through the apartment, finally capturing him in the living room, where she held him tight and threatened to squish him like the lousy louse he was. Stefan squealed in delight, his peals so shrill they shook the crystal glassware in the cupboard.

In the kitchen, Edith still stood at the sink, watching the boiler. The water was now boiling loudly, unsettlingly. The dirty dishes waited in the sink. But Edith didn't move. She stared, motionless, at the big, hot bubbles dancing behind the glass.

At the same time, in the offices of the prosecution, the atmosphere resembled backstage at the theater shortly before the curtain rises on a world premiere. David Miller attempted to appear composed and professional as he stepped into the corridor but was instantly seized by the feverish surge: every office door was open, telephones were ringing, pastel-colored office girls balanced towers of files or wheeled documents across the linoleum on squeaky carts. Ring binders were laid out along the length of the hallway, dark red and black, like collapsed rows of dominoes. Plumes of smoke spilled from every room. The clouds reminded David of greyhounds hovering, as if in slow motion, over the nervous chaos and dissipating before their chance to chase the mechanical hare. David almost laughed. It made him uncomfortable, it seemed cynical—but he was excited. He was there. Of the forty-nine applicants for the clerkship, only eight had been selected. Himself included, despite having passed the bar only a year earlier in Boston. David knocked on the open door to the lead prosecutor's office. He was standing at his desk, on the phone, a glowing cigarette between his fingers. The outlines of a construction crane in the courtyard outside were visible through the foggy windows. The blond man gave David a curt nod and, as usual, appeared to struggle to recall exactly who he was. David entered.

"The length of the trial will depend on the chief judge," the blond man spoke into the phone. "And I cannot read the man. If he acts according to the consensus, then things will be hushed up and relativized and we'll be through in four weeks. But the prosecution will insist upon a thorough evidentiary hearing. Personally, I'm expecting more along the lines of four months." He paused. "Sure, consider it a present. Go ahead and write it." The blond man hung up and used the butt of his cigarette to light the next. His hands were steady. David didn't waste time with a greeting: "Has he been in touch?"

"Who?"

"The Beast."

"No. And I would prefer it, Herr Miller, if you would refrain from using such slanted terms. We'll leave that to the public."

David waved off the rebuke. He couldn't comprehend how the prosecutor could remain so calm. One of the main defendants had been released from custody three months earlier, citing health issues. For the past five days now, they'd been unable to reach him at his registered address. And the trial was scheduled to begin Friday morning.

"But then we've got to get the police involved! They've got to launch a manhunt!"

"No legal basis, I'm afraid. The trial hasn't begun yet."

"But he'll abscond, damn it! Like all the others, to Argentina and—"

"We need that young woman. The one from yesterday. What was her name?" the blond man interrupted him. David shrugged reluctantly, although he knew who he meant. The prosecutor didn't wait for a response.

"They won't let Dombreitzki leave the country."

"Dommitzki."

"Exactly, him. Negotiations are under way, but he's staying where he is for now. In a Polish prison. An agreement could take months to reach."

"I don't believe that a young German woman, of all people, is suitable for such a demanding position. Sir"—David was becoming more insistent—"we are entirely dependent on our interpreters. They could tell us whatever the hell they wanted—"

"She'll take an oath. You could also see it this way: a woman might have a calming effect on witnesses. And that's exactly what we need, witnesses who feel safe! We need to get everything we can out of them—and they have to tell us what happened, have to endure the strain. So drive over there straightaway. You remember the address?" David nodded hesitantly and shuffled out.

The blond man sat down. This Miller fellow was too keen, too dogged. He'd heard a rumor that Miller's brother had died in the camp. It would be tricky if there were any truth to that rumor, because they'd have to replace him then, due to conflict of interest. On the other hand, they needed dedicated young people like him to spend day and night processing the thousands of documents, comparing dates, names, and events, and helping maintain order in this cacophony of voices. The blond man deeply inhaled the smoke from his cigarette, held his breath for a moment, and turned to the window. Outside in the courtyard, the shadowlike crane traced its usual circles.

Eva mopped the floor of the cavernous German House dining room. Her father, who had since risen from his beauty sleep, was in the kitchen polishing surfaces with the radio on. A *Schlager* pop song Eva and Jürgen had once danced to carried into the dining room. Peter Alexander crooned, "Come with me to Italy!" Jürgen was a good dancer. And he smelled so good, like resin and the sea. He held her so tight when they danced. He always knew what was right and what was wrong. Eva swallowed. She pushed him away in her mind, furious and disappointed. Jürgen, who for half a year had called from his desk every morning at eleven, hadn't been in touch today. Eva slapped the wet mop on the floorboards. She resolved never to see him again if he didn't call by two. As for his letters, the white gold bracelet, deerskin gloves, angora undergarments (she'd had pneumonia in November, and Jürgen had been very concerned), collection of Hesse poems, and . . . boom boom boom! Someone was thumping on the locked front door. Eva spun around: a man, a young man. Jürgen, overcome by emotion, had uncharacteristically abandoned his desk to ask for her hand in marriage, right here, right now. On bended knee. Eva set aside the mop, hastily shed her smock, and rushed to the door. Everything was fine. But then she recognized the unfriendly man from yesterday through the glass. David Miller. Annoyed, she opened the door. "We're closed!" David shrugged and looked at her, unfazed. "I'm here on behalf of . . ." Eva was astonished to notice that David hadn't left any tracks in the fresh snow, as though he'd flown up to the door. Strange.

"The lead prosecutor sent me."

Eva hesitantly waved him inside. David entered. They stood

at the bar, while in the kitchen, an Italian tenor sang his heart out. Eva could have joined in. "Seven days a week, I want to spend with you."

"The interpreter can't enter the country, at least not yet. He was deemed politically unreliable, and he's got to get his affairs in order. So we need a replacement. Trial begins Friday."

Eva was stunned. "You mean to say I should translate?"

"I'm not the one saying it. They just sent me."

"Oh, my. And for how long? A week?"

David studied Eva almost pityingly. He had pale blue eyes, and his left pupil was larger than the right. Perhaps it had to do with the light, perhaps it was something he'd been born with. It gave him an unsteady, permanently searching expression. *And he'll never find himself,* Eva thought instinctively, although without a sense of why.

"Have you already spoken with my agency? With my boss, Herr Körting?"

But David appeared not to have heard the question. He recoiled, as though Eva had struck him, and leaned against the bar.

"Are you unwell?"

"I forgot to eat breakfast. It'll pass in just a minute."

David caught his breath. Eva stepped behind the bar and filled a glass of water from the tap. She handed it to him, and he took a sip. As he drank, his gaze traveled to the opposite wall, which was densely hung with autographed black-and-white portraits. There were men and women, mostly local celebrities, he assumed—actors, soccer players, or politicians who had eaten at German House. They smiled at David and showed him their best side. He didn't recognize a single one of them. He straightened and placed the half-empty glass on the bar.

"Call this number." David handed Eva a business card with the name of the attorney general, an address, and a telephone number. "And if you take the job, you'd better start learning the necessary vocabulary."

"What do you mean? Military terms?"

"Every conceivable word for how to kill a person."

David turned abruptly and left the restaurant. Eva slowly closed the door behind him.

Her father had come out of the kitchen in his white coat and dark trousers, chef's hat on his head, a red checkered dish towel slung over his shoulder. *He looks like a clown about to get a cannonload of spaghetti and tomato sauce blown in his face*, Eva mused.

"Who was that? What did he want? Perhaps another suitor, daughter dearest?" Ludwig winked, then got to his knees before the bar and with the dish towel, began polishing the tin facing at its base, which was there to protect the wood from being kicked. Eva shook her head impatiently. "Daddy, can you think of nothing else? It was about a job. As an interpreter in court."

"Sounds major."

"It's a trial against SS officers who worked in that camp."

"And what camp would that be?"

"Auschwitz."

Her father kept polishing the facing, as though he hadn't heard her. Eva studied the back of his head for a moment, where his hair was thinning. Every eight weeks, she trimmed her father's hair in the kitchen. He couldn't sit still for long and fidgeted like a little boy. It was always a tedious process, but Ludwig refused to go to a barber. Eva had a deep aversion to the hairdresser's, herself. She had a childlike fear that getting her hair cut there might hurt. Annegret called Eva's fear "nervous nonsense." Eva reached for the mop, dunked it in the bucket, and wrung it out with her hands. The water had gone lukewarm.

Later that evening, her parents sat in the living room. Ludwig to the left, on his shabby end of the sofa, Edith in her little yellow armchair, whose velvet upholstery had once glowed gold. Purzel was rolled up in his basket. He yipped occasionally as he dreamed. The *Tagesschau* was on television, and small images appeared onscreen as the anchor presented the news stories. As usual, Ludwig provided commentary for each segment. Edith had pulled out some sewing. She was mending a tear in Stefan's orange mitten—apparently Purzel had gotten hold of it again. The anchor was reporting on West Germany's largest dike construction project. After only four months' time, the final section of the three-kilometer-long protective dike on the Rüstersiel mudflats had been completed. The footage showed a great deal of sand.

"Rüstersiel," Ludwig said, with a bit of homesickness in his voice. "Do you remember the time we were there and ate fresh plaice?"

Edith didn't look up, but answered, "Mmh."

"In an art gallery in Detroit, a fire has destroyed thirty-five paintings by the Spanish artist Pablo Picasso. The damage amounts to approximately two million Deutschmarks," the anchor read. A Cubist painting appeared behind him, but on the small black-and-white screen, it had no impact.

"That's almost sixty thousand marks per picture! God only knows why these pictures are all worth so much."

"You wouldn't understand, Ludwig," Edith replied.

"All the better."

"Federal Minister of the Interior Hermann Höcherl has ordered the transfer of former SS Hauptsturmführer Erich Wenger from the Federal Office for the Protection of the Constitution to the Federal Office of Administration in Cologne." The wall behind the anchor remained gray. Viewers did not get to see what Erich Wenger looked like. Eva's parents were silent. They breathed in time with one another. The weather forecast followed, showing a map of Germany covered in white crystals. It would continue to snow.

"She should hurry up and marry that Schoormann fellow," Ludwig said, putting on his thickest Low German dialect.

Edith hesitated. But then she responded, "Yes. It would be for the best."

In the Schoormanns' mansion, Jürgen sat at dinner with his father and his second wife. Like every evening, they didn't sit down to eat until half past eight, a by-product of working in the mail-order industry. Jürgen had worked well into the evening with his staff on the new catalog. Now he watched his father, who sat across from him at the table, warily dissect his bread and cheese. His father was deteriorating noticeably. He'd always been bulky but was now turning into a shrunken little man. *Like a grape becomes a raisin when left in the sun*, Jürgen thought. Brigitte sat close to his father, stroked his cheek, and placed a slice of cheese back on the bread.

"It's Swiss cheese, Walli. You like that."

"At least Switzerland is neutral."

Walther Schoormann took a careful bite and began to chew. He sometimes forgot to swallow. Brigitte gave him an encouraging nod. *She's a blessing*, Jürgen thought. He was certain his mother would approve. The first Frau Schoormann, whose gentle face appeared in soft focus in a photograph on the sideboard, had been killed in an air raid on the city in March of '44. Jürgen, then ten, was living on a farm in the Allgäu region, where his parents had sent him. The farmer's son told him his mother had burned up, that she had run through the streets like a flaming torch. Screaming. Jürgen knew the boy just wished to torment him, but he couldn't escape the image. He began to hate everything. Even the good Lord. He nearly lost himself to it. His father was in prison at the time. The Gestapo had picked him up in the summer of '41 for his membership in the Communist Party. On an early morning two months after the war ended, he appeared on the farm in the Allgäu to get his son. Jürgen shot out of the house and embraced his father, refusing to let go and crying so hard and for so long that even the farmer's son had pitied him. Walther Schoormann hadn't said anything then, and even now, he refused to speak about his time in prison. Since falling ill, however, he had taken to spending hours in the little garden shed, perched on a stool and looking out the barred windows, as though an eternal prisoner. Whenever Brigitte or Jürgen took his arm and tried to lead him out, he fought back. Jürgen was baffled by this, but Brigitte believed that his father was doing it perhaps to come to terms with something he'd experienced. Walther Schoormann swallowed and took another bite, lost in thought. The bread and cheese tasted good. As a former Communist and later businessman, he was a much-respected anomaly. He had always insisted, however, that his social attitudes were the very reasons for his success after the war. He wanted to help those people who had lost everything by offering affordable products. Affordable because he bypassed retailers, saved on sales and distribution, rent, and employees, and delivered straight to households. Within ten years, the "Schoormann Shop" grew into a company of 650 employees, whose proper treatment and social security Walther Schoormann always prioritized. In the mid-fifties, he built a house in the Taunus hills that turned out a little too big. Its many rooms served no purpose, and the pool was only filled that first year. The blue-tiled basin remained drained and deserted after that. Now, five years after Walther Schoormann remarried—one of the underwear models from the Schoormann catalog, thirty years his junior, worldly and ever optimistic—there was at least one person in the house who appreciated the luxury. The pool was filled with water once more, and Brigitte swam her daily laps. The smell of chlorine gently pervaded the house again. *Eva would live here too, and maybe even swim,* Jürgen thought. Eva. He knew she was waiting for his call. But something he could not pinpoint—nor wanted to—was holding him back. Jürgen had wanted to become a priest since childhood. The captivating rituals, numbing smell of incense, magnificent robes, and infinitely towering naves had fascinated him. And God undoubtedly existed. His devout mother supported his inclinations and played Mass with five-year-old Jürgen. She sewed him a purple cassock, and when he stood at the little table in his room and intoned "O Lamb of God . . ." she represented the congregation and humbly responded, "Hosanna." Lit candles and incense were the only things he was not allowed. His father, an unwavering atheist, always disparaged the performances. And when, shortly before his final exams in secondary school, Jürgen expressed his wish to study theology, father and son found themselves at odds. Ultimately, Walther Schoormann deferred to the wishes of his late wife. Jürgen was free to begin his studies. But everything changed two years ago. Walther could no longer be left alone, the company suffered marked losses under a succession of new managers, and Jürgen traded in his life plan for his father's lifework. But if he was honest, the idea of celibacy had increasingly concerned him.

Eva. She had come to the office a few times to translate correspondence with their Polish suppliers. The first thing he noticed was her hair, which she wore in an updo, rather than a more current style. There was something touchingly antiquated and naive about her, he found. She would take direction—she would behave in subservience to her husband. He wanted to have children with her. Only he wasn't sure what would happen when he confessed to his father that Eva's family ran a restaurant on Berger Strasse, of all places. It helped that the Bruhnses were Protestants. But a restaurant in the "merry village" of Bornheim? No matter how innocent Eva was or how vehemently Jürgen stressed that their business was in the decent section of the street—anything on Berger had to be a flophouse! Walther Schoormann was not only a socialist businessman, he was also one of the rare examples of a prudish Communist.

"Jürgen, what's so funny? Can I get in on the joke?" His father looked at him directly, his eyes clear, as though a line in his brain had been reactivated. Jürgen set down his silverware.

"Do you know what Schurick wanted to include in the catalog? An electrical device that pokes holes in eggs. Apparently it's all the rage in America."

His father smiled, and Brigitte shrugged. "I'd buy one."

"Because you'd buy anything."

Walther Schoormann took Brigitte's hand and gave it a quick, but loving, kiss, then held on to it. Jürgen looked past the two into the snowy yard, which resembled a park. The outdoor lamps wore snowy caps. The bushes were still. He had to call Eva.

Eva sat at her desk, an extremely useful piece of furniture, and made an attempt at a letter to Jürgen. She voiced rage and disappointment and threatened blackmail, while also attempting to spark love and desire for her and her body and her virginity (which, of course, he didn't know no longer existed). It was useless. She crumpled up another piece of paper, sat there for a moment, at a loss, and then pulled the business card David had left out of her pocket. She turned it indecisively. There was a knock on the door, and Annegret came into the room. She was wearing her powder pink dressing gown and hadn't put on her face or done her hair. Eva welcomed the interruption. She put the business card on the table.

"Don't you have work?"

"I have off. I worked a double shift yesterday." Annegret dropped heavily onto Eva's bed and leaned back against one of the posts. She'd found a package of pretzel sticks in the pantry, and she pulled them out by the dozen and snapped them off in her mouth.

"We've got a newborn, a boy, two weeks old, who almost died. He was totally dehydrated."

"Again?"

"Yes, it really isn't funny anymore. Someone must be carrying these germs in. The doctors, they can't be bothered about hygiene, but of course there's no talking to them. I sat with the tiny bean for eight hours and kept giving him sugar water, one drop at a time. Little fellow was in pretty good shape again by the end."

Annegret's eyes fell on the balled-up papers.

"Has he still not been in touch?"

Eva didn't respond. Annegret hesitated. She pulled a pack of cards from the pocket of her dressing gown and waved them invitingly. Eva sat down across from her sister on the bed. Annegret shuffled the cards in a quick, practiced manner with her fat but supple fingers. She was wheezing slightly. Then she set the cards on the blanket between her and her sister. "Ask a question. Then draw a card."

"Will Jürgen marry me?"

Eva concentrated and drew a card. Annegret took the stack and laid out the cards following some pattern. It was clear she knew what she was doing. Eva noticed that her sister smelled slightly of sweat. Annegret was excessively clean. Although their parents thought it a waste of water, she bathed daily. Nonetheless, she could never quite rid herself of the faintest whiff of pea stew set out in the sun. Eva was filled with affection as she watched how earnest Annegret was in laying out the cards for her. *I love you,* Eva wanted to say. But they didn't say that to each other. And it would have come across as pity, condescension. She let it go. Annegret pulled another handful of pretzel sticks from the bag and crunched into them. She studied the arrangement of cards as she chewed.

"Queen of hearts, upper left. You will become a queen, the wife of a millionaire. Provided you don't make a mess of it. Here's the seven of spades. That means there's still a chance of botching things."

"That's a real help, Annie. Where is Jürgen? What's he thinking? Does he love me?"

Annegret gathered the cards. "Now you shuffle. Then lay out the cards. The twelfth card is Jürgen."

Eva shuffled as though her life depended on it, and sent a few cards flying. She laughed, but Annegret remained solemn. Eva then laid out the cards and counted under her breath to twelve.

"Why are you counting in Polish?"

"Doesn't that count?"

"Sure it does, but I think it's odd."

Eva paused before turning over the twelfth card. She looked at Annegret.

"Do you know what's really odd?"

"All of life in its entirety?"

"I've always known my numbers in Polish. I mean, even before I began studying translation. Perhaps I was a Pole in a previous life?"

"Who cares about your previous life, little Evie-cakes? Show me your Jürgen. Come on now, show some courage!"

Eva flipped the card. It was the eight of hearts. She looked at it, blind to its significance. Annegret grinned.

"Well, my pretty little sister, be as dotty as you damn well please, because you'll never shake this man off!"

"And why is that . . . ?!"

"The suit is hearts, and eight is the symbol of infinity."

"Or handcuffs," Eva said.

Annegret nodded. "Either way, your days here are numbered."

Annegret collected the cards with her eyes lowered. She looked like a sad lump all of a sudden. Eva stroked her cheek. "Can I have a pretzel?" Annegret looked up and gave her a crooked smile.

The sisters lay beside each other in the semidarkness a while later, chewing on the last of the pretzel sticks and watching the gently quivering Don Quixote on the ceiling.

"Do you remember seeing the film in the theater?" Eva asked. "Where that old man attacked the windmill with his lance and got it caught in the sails. He was carried off and spun 'round and 'round on the windmill, screaming. I thought it was just terrible, it made me sick to my stomach."

"Children always find it unsettling when adults lose control."

"Annegret, should I take it on, this job? Translate in the trial, I mean. It's—"

"I'm aware. I wouldn't do it. Or do you want to help spread these horrifying myths?"

"What do you mean, 'horrifying myths'?"

At that, Annegret stiffened and fell silent, got up, and left without a word. Eva was familiar with this. Her sister would now head for the kitchen and really stuff herself. The phone rang in the hallway. Eva checked the time. Ten thirty. Her heart began to pound. She leaped from her room and reached the phone before her mother. It really was Jürgen.

"Good evening, Eva."

Eva tried to sound nonchalant, casual. "Good evening. A little late for a phone call." But it came out a bit hoarse.

"Are you well, Eva?"

Eva was silent.

"Please forgive me. I'm sorry. But it is for the rest of our lives."

"I realize that."

They were silent until Jürgen asked, "Would you like to go to the movies with me tomorrow evening?"

"I don't have time. I have to prepare for my new job."

"A new job? Did you get an assignment?"

"It's a lengthier engagement. I've got to provide for myself, after all. I can't live off my parents' goodwill forever. I've got to earn money."

"Eva, I will pick you up at seven tomorrow!"

He sounded stern. Eva hung up. Annegret came out of the kitchen, chewing, with a new, dark stain on her light-colored dressing gown, and looked at Eva quizzically. Eva shrugged in mock despair, but she was smiling. Annegret said, "You see? The cards don't lie."

The next morning—without any instructions from the prosecution, without any official permission—David Miller started driving south in a rental car that had cost him half a month's earnings. His destination: Hemmingen, near Stuttgart. One of the main defendants, the head of the political department at the camp—the Beast—was registered there as a resident. David had read all of the interview transcripts and allegations against Defendant Number Four and prepared an analysis for the prosecution. If only a fraction of the accusations were true, this man—now employed as a commercial clerk—lacked the very capacity for human emotion. The prosecution had been trying for days to reach him by phone. In vain. And with so little time left before the trial. As he sped through wintry southern Germany, David felt justified in pursuing his suspicion that the defendant had absconded. He drove in the passing lane and far too fast. The countryside, hills, forests, and odd farm to the left and right of the autobahn hurtled by and looked like a toy landscape compared to Canada's ancient grandeur. David fishtailed, after braking abruptly. He forced himself to slow down. *Imagine the irony if I were to die here on one of Hitler's autobahns*, David thought, and smirked.

David had intended to bypass Heidelberg but found himself in the heart of the city, entangled in a network of streets. He crossed the same bridge three times, and whenever he thought he'd found the way, the towering castle would rise in front of him again, as in a bad dream. David cursed. There was no city map in his road atlas, and he was about ready to surrender. While waiting at a stoplight, however, he discovered himself behind a car with

French plates. He followed the foreign vehicle, in the hope that it would guide him out of the city. His plan proved successful, and after an hour of senseless straying, David's car was once more flanked by forests and fields.

In Hemmingen, a sleepy town, he rolled down his window and asked someone cautiously picking their way through the snow for directions. Moments later, David stopped the car on Tannenweg, in front of number twelve. The house was well tended, a typical single-family home in a working-class area; built before the war, David imagined. Like all of the houses in the neighborhood, it was simple, with white plastered walls and a dark, wraparound balcony with barren flower boxes. There was no car outside the garage. David got out, walked across the snowy yard, and rang at the front door. He couldn't find a nameplate. He waited. Everything was quiet behind the small barred window in the door. He rang again, twice, and looked around. A few shrubs stood naked in the small front yard. Several rose bushes had been covered with old sacks and looked like bony, mummified figures. They seemed prepared to ambush him should he drop his guard for even a moment. David heard a door inside. He rang again, and this time he kept his finger on the button. The door slowly opened a crack—it was locked on the other side with a door chain. "My husband isn't here." David could make out the elegant features of a dark-haired woman of about sixty, who looked at him with dullish, almond-shaped eyes. *A faded beauty*, David thought. "Well, where is he?"

"Who are you?" The woman regarded David with suspicion.

"It's regarding the trial. We can't seem to reach your husband. . . ."

"Are you a foreigner?"

David was momentarily thrown by the question. "My name is David Miller. I'm a clerk for the prosecution."

"Then I know exactly the sort of man you are. You listen to me, Herr David," the woman spat through the crack. "What you're doing is utterly indecent! These outrageous lies you're spreading about my husband. If you knew how engaged my husband has always been, the kind of person he is. He is the best father and best husband anyone could ask for. If you knew my husband . . ."

While the man's wife continued to expound on her husband's virtues, David recalled one witness's account that had been placed on the record for the prosecution. She had had to work as the defendant's secretary in the camp. She described a young prisoner, whom Defendant Number Four had interrogated for hours in his office in the political department. "By the time he was through, it was no longer a human being. It was just a sack. A bloody sack."

"If you don't tell me where he is, I'll have to inform the police. Surely, you don't want him to be picked up by the police, like a criminal—which you've assured me he isn't."

"He's done nothing wrong!"

"Where is he?"

The woman hesitated, then snarled, "Hunting."

THE TWO MEN SLOWLY traverse a rugged mountain landscape on horseback. The sun glitters, waterfalls tumble, birds of prey circle overhead. Screeching. One of the men is dressed in a buckskin suit with fringes. The other wears Indian garb. It's Old Shatterhand and his blood brother, Winnetou. They ride in silence, on guard, scouting the area. Because somewhere in those rocks up there, their enemies are on the lookout, waiting for the perfect moment to shoot them dead on the spot.

Eva and Jürgen sat in the second row of the Gloria Palast cinema, their heads tilted back. They hadn't managed to find any other spot. Every last seat was taken. *Apache Gold* had just opened in theaters. More importantly, Ralf Wolter would be signing autographs after the show. He played Sam Hawkens and was everyone's favorite. Eva's and Jürgen's faces reflected the colorful shadows onscreen. Another screech of the eagle. Or was it a vulture? Eva didn't know her raptors. The first shot was fired with a loud bang. Eva jumped and mused happily, *The gunshots always sound best in Winnetou films.*

The music swelled, and the battle got under way . . .

A LITTLE LATER, after good had prevailed, Eva and Jürgen ambled around the brightly lit Christmas market. The sky was black, the air frigid. Clouds formed in front of their faces when they spoke. They felt far removed from the heat of the prairie. Eva had gone without getting Ralf Wolter's autograph, and Jürgen would rather have seen the new Alfred Hitchcock film, anyway. *The Birds.* Eva had linked arms with Jürgen. She was telling him about her first time at the movies. *Don Quixote.* The way the old man screamed as he hung from the sails of the windmill. She had been frightened. Her father had comforted her quietly: loons like that were very rare. Eva said her father could always calm her down. Jürgen wasn't really listening. He stopped at a booth and bought two mugs of mulled wine. As they stood facing each other, he asked to hear more about this assignment. Eva told him. She lied, though, and said she had already agreed to the job. Jürgen had read about the trial.

"Eva, this trial could stretch on for ages."

"All the better. They pay weekly." Eva was already a little tipsy from the half cup of mulled wine. Jürgen remained stern.

"And I do not wish for my wife to work. Our family is known in this city, and word would get out . . ."

Eva looked at him defiantly.

"And which wife might that be? I thought those plans had been dashed last Sunday."

"You shouldn't drink any more wine, Eva."

"My family isn't refined enough for you! Admit it!"

"Eva, please, don't start with that again. I found your parents very likable. I am going to ask your father."

"And besides, I'm not sure if I like that I'm not allowed to work. I'm a modern woman!"

But Jürgen was still speaking. "Under one condition: that you resign from this job." He looked at Eva with the dark eyes she loved so much. His gaze was calm and secure. He smiled. She took his hand but couldn't feel its warmth, because they both wore gloves.

Not far from where they stood, a brass ensemble began to play "Unto Us a Time Has Come." Others at the market stopped to listen, the mood solemn. But the old men played so unsteadily and off-key that Eva and Jürgen couldn't help laughing. Though they tried to stifle the urge, it was no use. With every new blunder, one of them would start again and infect the other. By the end they both had tears in their eyes, despite its being Eva's favorite Christmas carol.

Later, on the walk home, she quietly sang it for Jürgen.

Unto us a time has come,
And with it brought an awesome joy.
O'er the snow-covered field we wander,
We wander o'er the wide, white world.
'Neath the ice sleep stream and sea,
While the wood in deep repose doth dream.
Through the softly falling snow, we wander,
We wander o'er the wide, white world.
From on high, a radiant silence fills hearts with joy,
While under astral cover, we wander,
We wander o'er the wide, white world.

Jürgen loved the way Eva nestled up and clung to him. If someone were to ask him that very moment what he felt for her, he thought, he could say, *I love her.*

DAVID WAS BACK IN HIS CAR. It bounced down a forest track, wheels spinning, till one of his rear tires slid into a pothole. The Ford wouldn't budge. David switched off the engine and climbed out. The air was still, the sky starless. A cold full moon provided the only light. David looked around and spotted a gleam in the distance. He turned up his coat collar and trudged toward it. Snow filled his oxfords and melted. His socks were soon soaked. David kept walking. He arrived at a simple cabin with shuttered windows. A little light forced its way between the cracks. He heard nothing but a gentle rustling in the treetops. He hesitated, then opened the door without knocking. Three men in hunter green were gathered around a suspended carcass. All three looked toward the door. None appeared surprised. Two of the men were drinking bottles of beer. The third—haggard, with the face of a ferret—held a long knife in his hand. David recognized his face as that of Defendant Number Four. He was gutting a deer. Or whatever it was, it hung from a hook in the ceiling. It could be a person, for all David knew. Either way, it looked like a bloody sack.

The defendant gave David a quizzical but friendly look. "How can we help you?"

"My name is David Miller. I work for the attorney general."

The man nodded, as though he'd expected as much. One of his hunting mates, meanwhile, a red-faced man who was already drunk, advanced menacingly on David, but the defendant stopped him. "What are you doing out here, and at this hour? The trial doesn't start till Friday."

"We've been trying to reach you for days."

"Make yourself scarce, kid!" his other crony joined in.

David trained his gaze on the defendant. "I would like you to come right now, come with me back to the city."

"You couldn't possibly have the authority! Or can you show me some credentials?!"

David didn't know how to respond. The defendant set aside the knife and wiped his hands on a threadbare cloth hanging from a hook on the wall. Then he slowly approached David, who involuntarily recoiled. "I know I've nothing to fear. I'll be there punctually. You have my word." The man held out his right hand to David. David looked at it. A human hand, like any other.

A short time later, David stood outside the hut as though marooned in the moonlit forest. His feet were cold and wet. He didn't remember where his car was. He set out, stumbled through the snow for a while, then stopped. No car. The cabin had disappeared now too. David stood under a thick cover of fir trees, in the middle of

Germany somewhere. A gust of wind blew through the treetops, a quiet sigh. David looked into the canopy above him. Here and there, snow fell from the branches. He was suddenly overcome by the staggering number of crimes to be presented in three days' time. He briefly imagined the number of people they were fighting for and for whom justice was due. As many as were he to gather all of the needles from the fir trees above him. Each stood for one of the persecuted, tortured, murdered humans. David's legs went weak, they began to shake, then buckled. He fell to his knees, folded his hands, and held them high over his head. "God, visit your judgment on us all!"

Half an hour later, he had found his car. He maneuvered it laboriously out of the pothole. The car careened back down the forest track to the main highway, which had since been plowed. David hit the gas. He was embarrassed by his genuflection. Luckily, no one had seen him.

The new day brought with it new record low temperatures and blue skies. Eva, feeling well rested and in love, marched up the street to the newsstand. Her father needed this month's issue of his favorite food magazine, *The Pleasing Palate*. The elderly Fräulein Drawitz vanished into the depths of her stand to look for it, surprised anew by the request, as she was every time. Eva's gaze lingered on the daily papers on display. The upcoming trial was front-page news. One especially thick black headline read, "70 Percent of Germans Do Not Want Trial!" Eva felt guilty: she had never contacted the office of the prosecution. She bought the paper. Along with several others.

EVA HAD THE APARTMENT to herself. Her father was at the wholesale market, as he was every Thursday morning, her mother taking care of Christmas errands in the city, Stefan sweating it out at school, and Annegret tending to her infants at City Hospital. Eva sat down at the kitchen table, spread the papers out in front of her, and started reading. The time had come to draw a line under things, the articles argued. The twenty-one defendants were harmless family men, grandfathers, and good, hardworking citizens who had all undergone the denazification process without incident. That tax money should be invested more sensibly in programs for the future. Even the victors considered the chapter closed. "The moment one believes the grass to have grown back on a thing, along comes some stupid camel and eats it all up." In this case, the camel had the same glasses and hairstyle as the state attorney general. Eva discovered, in a newspaper from Hamburg, that it had been the young Canadian lawyer David Miller who had managed to locate the Polish witness Josef Gabor just in time for him to testify on the first ever use of Zyklon B. That was the gas allegedly used to kill more than one million people in the camp. Eva was sure the number was a misprint. One entire back page was dedicated to photographs of the accused, several of which Eva had already seen at the law office. Now, however, she could study the men closely and right side up. She fetched the magnifying glass from her mother's sewing box and looked at each face individually. One was fat, the next narrow, others smooth or wrinkled. One man grinned like a big friendly ferret, nearly all wore glasses, and several defendants were going bald. One was heavily built, with bat ears and a flattened nose, whereas another had very fine features. There was neither correspondence nor distinction. And the more Eva wanted to find out, the closer she leaned into the images, the more the faces dissolved into tiny squares of black, gray, and white.

The apartment door snapped shut. Eva's mother came in with Stefan, whom she had picked up at school. He was bawling because he had fallen in the street and hurt his knee.

Edith set down her shopping basket and scolded him, "I told you to stop sliding around out there!"

Stefan sought refuge on Eva's lap, and she inspected his knee. His checkered pants were torn, his skin beneath a little scraped up. Eva blew on the harmless wound. Stefan noticed the pictures of the defendants. "Who is that? A team?"

Their mother had come to the table too, and looked curiously for a moment at the sea of newsprint. The moment Edith realized what it was Eva found so interesting, she swept up all of the papers in a single motion. She opened the oven beside the stove and shoved in the entire armful.

"*Mum!* What on earth are you doing?!"

The faces caught fire, turned black, and ash fluttered through the room. Edith closed the oven door. She covered her mouth with her hand and rushed from the kitchen to the bath. Eva got up and followed. Her mother kneeled at the toilet and vomited. Eva watched, perturbed. Stefan appeared beside her in the doorway.

"Mummy, what's wrong?"

Their mother stood up and rinsed out her mouth at the sink.

"You know that Mummy sometimes feels sick when she smells smoke," Eva answered her brother. But that didn't explain why Edith had burned the newspapers. Eva studied her.

Edith dried her face on a towel and said, "Let go of the past, Eva. It's for the best, believe me." Edith returned to the kitchen with Stefan. Eva stayed where she was, in the bathroom doorway. She looked into her own baffled face in the mirror above the sink.

That afternoon, Eva and Annegret went into the city together. Their father had slipped them an envelope containing five hundred marks, amid a flurry of enigmatic hints and indecipherable hand gestures, although their mother wasn't even in the room, and although they had agreed weeks earlier that the sisters would purchase a washing machine for their mother, on behalf of their father. A long-coveted Christmas gift. They submitted to the presentation of one of Hertie's new products, a top-load drum model with both prewash and normal cycles. The salesman opened the lid, closed it, pushed in the detergent drawer, and pulled it back out again. He earnestly described how much laundry could be washed per load (5.5 kilograms), how long that took (two hours), and how clean their clothing would be (like new). Annegret and Eva exchanged amused looks here and there: they both found it ridiculous how well this man knew his laundry. Regardless, they ordered the newest model from Herr Hagenkamp—as identified by his name tag—and took his word that the machine would be delivered and installed before Christmas Eve. As they left the department store, Eva realized that, during the Twelve Nights, their mother wouldn't be doing any laundry. Annegret retorted that the tradition applied only to bed linens, because that's what the mischievous spirits were known to steal between Christmas and Epiphany. They crossed the Christmas market. It was already getting dark. Annegret wanted to get a bratwurst. Eva was hungry too. They went to Schipper's Sausages, although their father had forbidden them from eating at that stall: "Schipper fills his sausages with sawdust, I'm sure of it—especially for the Christmas market! How else could he afford that house in the Taunus hills?" The sisters liked Schipper's sausages best, though. Perhaps it was their forbidden nature that made them so delectable. Eva and

Annegret stood facing each other, chewing happily. Annegret mentioned that she still needed to buy her gift for Stefan, a book by Astrid Lindgren, whom Annegret adored. He was getting too old for those simple fairytales Eva always read to him. The detective at the heart of the story was a boy just a little older than Stefan. A real crime occurred. Their brother was mature enough for that now. But Eva wasn't listening. She had noticed an older bearded man cautiously making his way across the market, as though afraid of slipping in the snow. He wore a thin coat and a tall, jet-black hat with a narrow brim. He carried a small suitcase. He approached a stall selling tropical fruits. A large banner depicting the rising sun hung on its back wall. The man said something to the woman behind the counter, but it looked like she hadn't understood. He pulled a piece of paper from his pocket and showed it to her. She just shrugged her shoulders. The man persisted—he pointed again at the sheet, then at the stall. The woman raised her voice.

"I do not understand you! Get that in your head! No un-der-stand-y! Nix!"

The woman shooed him away, but the man didn't move. The stall owner now appeared beside his wife.

"Scram, old man Israel! Go away!"

Eva wasn't sure if "Israel" was what she had heard, but she left Annegret—who hadn't observed the scene and now watched her in surprise—and went over to the stall.

Eva walked up beside the man in the hat. "Can I help you? *Kann ich helfen?*" She repeated the question in Polish as well. The man reluctantly looked at her. Eva peeked at the paper in his hand. It was a brochure for a boardinghouse called the Sun Inn. Eva noticed that its emblem was a rising sun. She addressed the stall owner. "The gentleman is looking for a place called the Sun Inn. He must have seen your sun there and thought—"

But the two behind the counter didn't care what the man thought. The owner bristled. "Is he going to buy anything? If not, he'd better quit loitering and go back to Israel."

Eva wanted to respond, but then shook her head and turned to the old man. "Come with me, I know where the boarding-house is."

The man responded in Hungarian—that much, Eva recognized. But she understood very little. Only that he had just arrived at the train station and was now looking for the inn. Eva left the man for a moment and returned to Annegret.

"I'm going to bring this gentleman to his boardinghouse."

"Why? How is that any of your concern?"

"Annie, the man is completely helpless."

Annegret glanced at the man and turned away. "By all means, run along and rescue some unknown tramp. I'm going to go buy the book."

Eva went back to the bearded man, who stood waiting for her motionlessly and seemed to be holding his breath. She tried to carry his suitcase for him, but he refused to let it go. She took him by the arm and began leading him toward the inn. The man moved slowly, as though fighting some inner resistance. Eva noted that he smelled slightly of burned milk. His coat was stained, he wore thin, scuffed shoes, and he kept slipping, and Eva held him up each time.

The boardinghouse was on a side street. Eva spoke with the owner behind the small reception desk, a doughy man who had clearly just eaten dinner and was now blithely fishing bits of food from between his teeth with a toothpick. Yes, a room had been reserved for one Otto Cohn from Budapest. The innkeeper eyed the bearded man with aversion. The elderly man then opened his wallet, in which several crisp hundred-mark bills were visible, and pulled out his identification. The innkeeper tossed aside his toothpick and demanded a week's advance pay for the room. The bearded man placed one of the bills on the counter and received the heavy key to room eight in return.

He then started in the direction the owner had indicated. He seemed to have forgotten all about Eva. She watched him stop in front of the elevator and shake his head. *He's at sixes and sevens,* Eva thought. She snorted impatiently, approached the helpless man, took him again by the arm, and led him up the stairs. Eva unlocked the door to number eight. They entered a small room with a simple bed, unadorned wardrobe finished with an oak veneer, and orange curtains bright as fire. Eva stood there indecisively. The man laid his suitcase on the bed and opened it, as though Eva were no longer in the room. A black-and-white photograph, half the size of a postcard, lay on top of his things. Eva could make out the merged shadows of several people. She cleared her throat.

"Very well, then."

The man in the hat did not respond.

"A thank you might be in order."

Eva was about to leave when the man turned to her and said, in broken German, "I beg your pardon. I cannot say thank you to you."

They looked at each other. In the man's pale eyes, Eva discovered a pain more profound than any she had ever seen in a person. She suddenly felt ashamed and nodded. Then she carefully exited the room.

Otto Cohn turned back to his suitcase. He picked up the photograph and gazed at it. Then he said, in Hungarian, "I'm here now. Just as I promised you."

EVA'S FATHER NEEDED her help in the kitchen early Friday morning. The fourth Sunday of Advent was upon them, and he expected triple the orders as usual to pass through the window that weekend. Besides, he had already taken two painkillers with breakfast, because his back was "smarting like hell." The cold crept into his bones, and he wasn't at the top of his form. He hadn't even turned on the radio today. He looked pale as he dressed one goose after the other and gathered the giblets—save the liver—in a pot for the gravy. Frau Lenze, an older employee whose husband was a war cripple and who therefore had to earn a little extra, silently scrubbed vegetables for the stock. Eva shredded cabbage till her right arm ached. Her father combined the red cabbage with cloves and lard in an enormous black enamel pot that no one but he could lift. The stove was fired up. Cooking aromas filled the kitchen. Eva separated eggs and beat the whites to stiff peaks. She mixed up two types of pudding, chocolate and vanilla. These would be served with rhubarb compote her mother had made last summer. All three began to sweat as the air grew impenetrable. Then Frau Lenze cut a deep gash in her finger while dicing onions. Her face went white. The blood dripped on the tile floor, and the water she ran over it from the tap turned red. Eventually they stanched the bleeding, and as Eva put the adhesive bandage in place, she stole a glance at Frau Lenze's watch. The trial was set to begin in three quarters of an hour. Eva took over the onions from Frau Lenze, who removed her apron contritely. Ludwig gave her a nod. "You'll be paid through three o'clock." Relieved, Frau Lenze went home with her throbbing forefinger.

THE AUDITORIUM IN THE MUNICIPAL BUILDING had the ambiguous character of a function hall. A light-colored veneer clad the walls, and the floors were an impervious beige linoleum. Instead of regular windows, big smooth glass panes had been installed from floor to ceiling in the outer left-hand wall. The trees in the overgrown courtyard beyond the wall were distorted into flickering spots and silhouettes, which could give one the feeling of intoxication. The auditorium was typically used for Carnival programs, sports banquets, or touring theater performances. Just last week, a troupe from Braunschweig had presented the comedy *The General's Trousers*. In the play, a rather juicy case was taken to court. The audience had laughed in appreciation of all the double entendres, and the performance concluded to hearty applause. A real trial had never been held in this room, though. Since the city courthouse lacked the capacity for the trial's many participants, this convenient space had been selected. For days, builders had been hammering, tightening screws, and doing what they could to transform the prosaic space into something approximating a hallowed court of law. The gallery had been separated from the action by a balustrade, to underscore that the trial was not intended for entertainment. What was actually the stage had been hung with thick, pale blue drapes. The long, heavy judge's bench had been erected before this backdrop. The prosecution would sit on the right side of the hall. Three rows of individual tables and chairs had been arranged in front of the glass wall, facing the prosecution: the defendants' spots. A solitary table waited somewhat forlornly in the open space between the prosecutors and the accused. This was where the witnesses and interpreters would sit and speak. Every last spot had been equipped with a small black microphone, and yet, half an hour before the trial was set to begin, there were still some that didn't work. Technicians hectically tinkered with connections and taped up the last cords. Staff working for the prosecution trundled carts carrying their precious files and deposited folders on the prosecutors' table and the bench. Two hall attendants carried in a wide, rolled-up screen and began securing it to a map stand behind the bench.

A young man with reddish hair was placing numbered cardboard signs on the defendants' tables. It was David Miller, his expression as rapt as if he were executing a sacred rite. He was reading the seat assignments from a sheet. That chart was the product of lengthy discussion. The main defendants, who carried the most serious charges, were now seated at the front. Behind them, those accused of lesser allegations. *As if you could consider them lesser. Is someone who kills ten, less harmful than one who kills fifty?* David thought. He looked at the clock. It was five minutes to ten. At this very moment, eight of the defendants were being picked up by minibus from pretrial detention. Thirteen had not been detained or had been released on bail, such as the affluent main defendant, who had been the adjutant to the camp commandant. Or they'd been released from custody for health reasons, such as Defendant Number Four, who had given David his word he would be there. Meanwhile, the attendants hoisted up the map stand and unrolled the screen, which immediately filled the auditorium with the smell of fresh oil paint.

"C'mon, Officer, let us in already, will ya?!"

"We've been standin' out here since eight!"

Outside the double doors to the courtroom, a throng of spectators was growing impatient, as all hoped to secure a spot in the front row. Judicial officers in dark blue uniforms prevented them from entering the hall. It was already evident that the seating in the gallery was insufficient. Hall attendants were bringing in more of the stackable chrome chairs, always in threes. Two men in black robes entered the hall through a side door. One of them was the man with light blond hair. He appeared primed for battle—the coat he wore beneath his robe was bulky and looked like armor. The second man was older and rather plump, and his robe billowed out shapelessly around his body. He was partially bald and his strikingly round, pale face provided a sharp contrast to his black horn-rimmed glasses. He stumbled over one of the cables but caught himself. He was the chief judge, the man who would lead the trial. The man who would deliver the sentences. The two men conversed quietly. The blond man explained that they were still waiting for the Polish interpreter, but that they'd received confirmation of his permission to leave the country by next week. The Czech translator could help answer questions till then, although he neither wanted nor was able to translate witness statements. They had therefore postponed the Polish witness testimonies till later in the trial. By now, David had distributed all of the cardboard signs on the tables. He made his way across the room to introduce himself to the chief judge. David was already lifting his hand, but as he drew near, the blond man turned his back on him, as though he didn't recognize him yet again. He blocked David's path. David let his hand fall. The blond man had stopped one of the attendants and was giving him instructions, upon which the man began dragging the witness stand away from the defendants' tables. This pulled at the microphone cord. One of the technicians jumped in.

"Watch it!" he admonished him. "You can't just yank it away like that. D'you've any idea how long I had to mess around with this?!" The technician turned on the microphone on the table and rapped against it with the knuckle of his index finger. A deafening sound popped over the speakers: everyone froze for a moment and traded looks of surprise.

"Now we're awake!" someone called. The speaker system worked, beyond question. Then they all laughed.

At that moment, a haggard man wearing a perfectly tailored dark blue suit appeared among the swarming spectators in the doorway. He presented identification and an official letter to one of the judicial officers. The officer abruptly stood at attention and clicked his heels. David looked over and recognized the man. A feeling of triumphant hatred—if such a combination even existed—surged down his body. The man, unknown to the crowd and consequently undisturbed, entered the hall and oriented himself. He headed for the defendants' tables and took his place. It was Defendant Number Four. The Beast. After removing several folders and notes from his briefcase and arranging them neatly on his table, he looked up. He noticed David watching him. He gave him a nod. David quickly turned away, but the blond man, who had witnessed the greeting, caught his eye and rushed over.

"Are we acquainted?" he asked quietly.

David hesitated, then admitted that he had driven to Hemmingen. "We've got to err on the side of caution!"

"We'll discuss this later!" The blond man stormed over to the haggard man, who politely stood as the prosecutor told him the defendants were all first meeting with their lawyers in another room, then entering the hall together.

Defendant Number Four responded curtly, "I require no legal

counsel." Nevertheless, he gathered up his papers and followed the blond man out the side door. For a moment, David stood alone in the middle of the hall. He studied the screen that had been hung. It was a map the prosecution had commissioned from a painter. The artist had used diagrams and photographs to create a rendering that appeared spatially accurate. Even the lettering above the gate to the main camp had been perfectly replicated. The *b* in the word *Arbeit* was upside down. One of the witnesses had told them this had been a silent protest by the metalsmith who'd had to craft the sign for the SS.

In the spacious, sunny foyer—which seemed newly opened, with a light stone floor that invited rubber soles to squeak—more and more spectators were gathering and surging toward the auditorium doors. English, Hungarian, and Polish could be heard. Drinks and sandwiches were being sold at a counter. The air smelled faintly of coffee and cervelat. A clutch of reporters had formed around the gnarled figure of the state attorney general. Some extended microphones in his direction, whereas other reporters scribbled on small notepads.

"Following four years of preparation . . ." one young man began.

"We could easily say ten years."

"Following ten years of preparation, and counter to public interest, you have managed to force this case to court. Sir, do you consider this a personal triumph?"

"If you take a look around, my good man, one could hardly suggest a lack of interest."

Another reporter had turned away from the group and was speaking into a *Wochenschau* camera: "Twenty-one defendants, three judges, six jurors, two associate judges, and three talesmen are involved, as well as four prosecutors, attorneys representing three joint plaintiffs, and nineteen defense attorneys. The taxpayer may well ask: what is the justification for these efforts and these costs?"

IN THE KITCHEN AT GERMAN HOUSE, Eva peered at the clock again through the steam. It was ten minutes past ten. If she ran as fast as she could, and if she caught the streetcar, she could still make it. She washed the smell of onions from her hands.

"Daddy, the basics have been taken care of for now."

Ludwig Bruhns was just patting dry the inside of the last goose with crepe paper.

"The stuffing hasn't been made yet . . . someone needs to shell the chestnuts for that, Eva."

"But I still need to . . . go into the city. Now."

Ludwig Bruhns turned to face Eva.

"Where's the fire?"

"I can't postpone it," Eva responded evasively. Ludwig gave his daughter a puzzled look, but she didn't elaborate.

"Presents, right? Me and my dumb questions, huh?"

"Exactly, Daddy. It *is* almost Christmas."

"Then by all means, leave your poor, old, sick father in the lurch. Heartless child!"

Eva gave her father a peck on his sweaty cheek and ran out. Ludwig was alone. The red cabbage simmered quietly. He felt queasy. Afraid. And he didn't know why. He looked at the dead bird in his hands, which was now cleaned and dried. It must be those damned pills. They must not agree with his stomach.

Moments later, Eva stumbled out the front door of the restaurant, pulled on her plaid coat as she ran, slipped in the snow, steadied herself, and kept running. She didn't know what was driving her. But she had to be there when they read the indictments. She owed it to someone! But who? She couldn't think of a soul.

THE EXPANSIVE FOYER WAS NEARLY EMPTY, but for a few hall attendants. Eva came in, out of breath, her updo askew. Her chest ached. An electronic gong sounded three times. The doors to the auditorium were supposed to close at the tone, Eva could see, but several people hadn't made it in and continued to block the opening. Two judicial officers pushed them back.

"Now, would you please be reasonable? There is no more room! Clear the doors!"

Eva joined the group, wedged herself in among the latecomers, and jostled her way to the front, something totally out of character for her. "Please, I would like to . . . can I please still get in?"

The officer shook his head apologetically. "I'm sorry, miss, every last seat is taken."

"It's important. I have to be there!"

"You and everyone else—"

"Now, just a minute, young lady! We've been waiting here far longer!" Accusations whirred by Eva's head. She now stood directly in the doorway, but the officer was slowly pulling the doors shut. Then she spotted the attorney general, who was conferring with two men not far from the door. Eva waved.

"Hello! Sir . . . hello, you know me. . . ." But the gnarled man didn't hear.

"Step back, or I will close the door on you!" The officer had taken Eva by the shoulder and pushed her back. Eva ducked abruptly, dove under the officer's arm, and slipped into the hall. She headed straight for the attorney general.

"Pardon me, but I would like to hear the opening statements. I was at your office on Sunday, for the translation. . . ."

The attorney general eyed Eva and appeared to remember. He gave the officer at the door a signal. "It's all right."

The others waiting there protested in outrage.

"Why her?"

"Just 'cos she's blond?"

"I came all the way from Hamburg!"

"And we came from West Berlin!"

The doors closed. Eva thanked the attorney general, who seemed to have forgotten about her already. An usher directed Eva to the edge of the gallery and removed a piece of paper from a vacant seat. It read "Reserved—Press." Eva sat down, caught her breath, and looked around. She was familiar with the auditorium. She had attended many theater performances here with her mother—the most recent had been *The General's Trousers*, a ridiculous play that had nonetheless made them laugh. As usual, Edith Bruhns had criticized the female players' acting as unbelievable and stilted. Eva knew how badly her mother would have liked to be the one onstage. Eva didn't particularly care for the theater, herself; the actors exaggerated their speech and behaviors too much for her liking, as if they wanted to tell her something with violent force. She tried to get her bearings. Where did the judge sit? And the defendants? All she could see were dark heads, gray, bald, black, bluish black, or dark blue suits, muted ties. There was whispering, coughing, noses being blown. It seemed the air in the room was already stale. It smelled vaguely of damp coats, wet leather and rubber, cold cigarette smoke, freshly shaven men, eau de cologne, and hard soap. A hint of turpentine or maybe fresh paint mingled in the mix. Eva eyed her neighbor, a nervous woman in her early sixties with a pointed face and wearing a little felted hat. The woman was kneading her brown handbag, and her gloves dropped. Eva bent down and picked them up. The woman thanked her with a stern nod, then opened her bag and stuffed in the gloves. She closed the bag with a click. At that moment, the bailiff announced the entrance of the judges. All rose noisily and watched as the three men in robes—the chief judge and his associate judges—entered the hall through the side door, with the solemnity of a priest and his acolytes. *Only thing missing is the incense*, Eva thought. The chief judge—his face somehow paler and rounder, the contours of his black glasses more pronounced than before—reached his spot at the middle of the bench and raised his voice, which was carried over the public address system. His voice was clearer and quieter than expected from a man of his proportions. He said, "I hereby declare proceedings in the criminal case against Mulka and others opened."

He took a seat. There was a stir in the auditorium as everyone sat back down. It took some time for the room to quiet, for the seat shifting, rustling, and whispering to abate. The chief judge waited. Eva recognized the blond man seated alongside other men in black robes at a table to the right. The attorney general was not among them. Eva scanned the crowd for David Miller. She thought she recognized his profile at a table behind the prosecutors. The chief judge again raised his voice. "The court will now present the charges." An associate judge beside him got to his feet. He was young, very slight under his robe, and seemed nervous. He was holding several sheets of paper, and more documents lay before him on the table. He adjusted the papers, cleared his throat thoroughly, and took a drink of water. Eva was familiar with the painful feeling that struck when someone was about to give a speech and kept fumbling with their papers: a fear took root that one might shortly die of boredom. Her fear was different this time. Eva was suddenly reminded of the fairy tale in which Brother wanted to drink from the bewitched spring. *Of those who from my waters take, shall I then a wild beast make.* The young judge appeared to become lost in sorting his papers. A short, derisive laugh came from the left. Were those the defendants' tables? Were those the defendants? Those men, so clean-shaven, polished, and civilized, looked no different from the men in the gallery at first glance. Some of them did, however, don dark glasses, like those worn for winter sports. And vertical signs with clearly legible numbers had been set up on the tables before them. Then Eva recognized the partially bald man who'd held up the rabbit in his photograph. There was a fourteen on his sign. He scratched his fleshy neck and gave a quick nod to a short man wearing dark glasses in his row. Number Seventeen returned the greeting. The young judge began speaking so suddenly that Eva and other spectators jumped. He read clearly and intently from the page. His voice was carried by the small black microphone that stood before him on the table. It reverberated in every corner of the hall. Eva could hear every word perfectly. She listened. She tried to understand what the young judge was saying. Seated to the left, she learned, were an importer-exporter, head cashier of a regional savings bank, two commercial clerks, an engineer, a merchant, a farmer, a building superintendent, a stoker, a medical orderly, a laborer, a pensioner, a gynecologist, two dentists, a pharmacist, a cabinetmaker, a butcher, a cash messenger, a weaver, and a piano maker. These men were allegedly responsible for the deaths of hundreds of thousands of innocent people.

Eva folded her hands like she was in church, but immediately unfolded them. She placed them beside each other on her thighs and lowered her gaze, but that made her feel as though she'd been indicted, herself. She looked up at the ceiling, which was hung with spherical glass light fixtures. But then she might come across as inattentive. She allowed her eyes to slowly wander. The mousy-faced woman beside her sat up very straight with her handbag on her knees. She was fidgeting relentlessly with her gold wedding band, which had been worn thin from years of work. The man sitting in front of Eva had a thick neck covered in small red pustules. The woman to his left slumped in her chair, as though drained of all life. The young policeman guarding the door was breathing through his mouth—maybe he had a cold. Or polyps, like Stefan. Eva trained her gaze straight ahead at the map hung behind the bench, the chief judge's face before it like the rising moon. It looked like a cemetery from above: a grid of grayish red tombstones laid out on a soft green lawn. Eva couldn't make out the inscriptions from this distance. Her eyes wandered over to the left, to the wall of glass panes. A black silhouette teetered outside the building like a drunken giant, then abruptly dissipated like smoke, while the young judge's voice continued to fill the hall with words. Eva grasped her wrists. She had to hold on to something. *This can't be true!* Eva wanted to stand up and object, make a plea. Or leave—running away would be best. But she remained seated, like everyone else, and listened. The young judge was now reading the detailed allegations against Defendant Number Four. It seemed the list would never end. The commercial clerk was charged with selecting prisoners, flogging, abusing, torturing, beating them to death, shooting them, killing them with a wooden board, killing them with a rod, killing them with the butt of a rifle, battering, trampling, kicking, crushing, and gassing them. In the barracks, on the streets of the camp, at roll call, at the execution site—known as the Death Wall—in his office, and in the medical block. In the lavatory of Block Eleven, he allegedly murdered a young prisoner secretary named Lilly Toffler with two shots, after days of summoning her to mock executions; the fifth time he called, she fell to her knees and begged him to finally shoot her. Eva searched for Defendant Number Four. He reminded her of Herr Wodtke, a regular at German House, who came in with his family on Sundays and always first made sure his wife and children were happy with their orders. He always treated his well-behaved children to an ice cream for dessert and tipped well—sometimes even too well. Eva didn't want to believe that that haggard man with the face of a ferret could have done all of those things. He listened to the accusations against him without any discernible reaction, the corners of his mouth turned up and frozen. Like the defendants before him, he looked like he was being forced to pay attention to long-winded remarks on a topic that held utterly no interest for him. Bored, impatient, and irritated, but too well bred to just stand up and leave. The litany of accusations fell on deaf ears among the defendants' tables, Eva observed. Here and there, one of the men would cross his arms, lean back in his chair, turn to whisper something to his lawyer, or make a note in his papers. The medical orderly, Number Ten, wrote feverishly in a thick little notebook. Before starting each note, he licked his pencil with the tip of his tongue.

Two and a half hours later, the young judge reached the end of his final document. His face was white as a sheet above the jet-black robe. "The accused are sufficiently suspected of committing these offenses. Upon request by the prosecution, proceedings for the jury's consideration of the charges against the defendants are now open."

The young judge sat down. His voice cut out abruptly, unexpectedly, and was followed by absolute silence. No one cleared his throat, no one coughed. They all sat there, as if life might end at any moment here too. All it would take was for someone to extinguish the big light. Eva felt a drop of sweat running down the middle of her back and into the crack of her bottom. She didn't feel she could ever speak again or draw another breath. The moment did not last long. Whispers erupted throughout the room. The chief judge leaned in to confer with one of the associate judges. The prosecutors discussed with one another in low voices. The defense lawyers quietly answered their clients' questions. The radiators whistled and sang. In one of the front rows, a man was crying—it was inaudible, but his shoulders were trembling. From the back, he looked like the bearded Hungarian man. Only the hat was missing. *But maybe it's in his lap*, Eva thought. The man then pulled a handkerchief from his pocket, and Eva briefly caught sight of his profile and realized it was someone else.

The chief judge now spoke into his microphone. "Defendants, you have heard the charges. How do you plead?" The spectators all leaned forward slightly. Some tilted their heads to the side, and several opened their mouths to listen. David watched as the main defendant, Defendant Number One—a highly regarded Hamburg businessman, dressed in dark gray with a tasteful tie, who was the most important man at the camp, after the commandant—slowly got to his feet. David knew that this hawk-faced man was staying at the Steigenberger Hotel. In a suite, where he had surely taken a hot bubble bath that morning. The trim defendant looked the chief judge in the eye and said, "Not guilty." At the same moment, there came a whisper in the gallery that only Eva could hear: "Not guilty!" She turned quickly toward her neighbor. The woman in the little hat now had red blotches on her face. She had stopped spinning her ring. She smelled slightly of sweat and vaguely of roses. Out of nowhere, Eva thought, *I know her.* But that was impossible. Eva felt hysterical. It was no wonder after those monstrosities. After everything she had just heard. After everything those twenty-one men sitting up there with an air of detachment were said to have done. Although they now each stood and pleaded, "Not guilty." One after the other. Defendant Number Ten, the medical orderly, the only one who—to Eva's eye—looked like a murderer, with his flattened nose and close-set eyes, stood up and yelled toward the gallery, "I am well loved by my patients! They call me 'Papa'! Ask anyone! These accusations are based on mistaken identity and lies!" He sat down. Several of his fellow defendants applauded him by rapping their knuckles on the table. The chief judge called sharply for order and signaled one of the hall attendants, who then scurried over to the wall of glass panes. There was a contraption that allowed some of the windows to be tipped opened a crack. The attendant operated the mechanism, and cold air crept into the room, while the defendants continued to rise, one after the other.

"Not guilty!"

"Not guilty!"

"Not guilty as charged!"

Even the youngest defendant, who—according to investigations conducted by the prosecution—had killed countless people with his bare hands, expressed his innocence. But his face turned red as he spoke. And when he sat back down, he leaned forward, as if trying to devour the microphone on his table, and softly uttered a short sentence. His words rustled over the speakers and were hard to understand.

"I'm ashamed of myself."

Several defendants shook their heads in scorn, and the following suspect, who was second to last, stood up and droned, all the more emphatically, "I have not done anything wrong!"

At that, a woman in the gallery began sobbing loudly. She stood up, forced her way through the seated crowd, and stumbled out of the hall. Eva heard voices growing louder. It was Polish.

"Kłamiecie! Wszyscy kłamiecie!" You're lying! You're all lying!

"Tchórze!" Cowards!

"Oprawca!" Murderers!

The chief judge pounded on his table and cried, "Order!! Order in the court, or I will clear the gallery!"

Everyone fell silent. The final defendant, the pharmacist, now stood and turned to face the court. But before he could break the silence, suddenly a bell sounded, grating and drawn out. It came from outside. Now a jumble of excited, high-pitched voices, screams, screeches, squeals. Eva remembered that behind the municipal building was a grade school. She checked the clock: it was probably their second recess. It was children playing.

"Not guilty," the pharmacist, in his expensive suit, echoed and sat down.

IN THE NURSES' LOUNGE at the hospital, Annegret was taking her second coffee break of the early shift. She sat at a white Formica table and drank her coffee black as she leafed through a fashion magazine. The magazine was tattered—it had served as the nurses' break time entertainment for more than a year now.

This style has already gone out of style, Annegret mused. The closely tailored waistlines on those dresses and suit jackets would look ridiculous on her body anyway. In her free time, Annegret wore stirrup pants and long, shapeless sweaters, and that was that. At work, the blue-and-white nurse's apron was tight around her hips, and the white cap perched on her large, round head seemed tiny. But she looked smart. While Annegret took little sips of coffee, which always tasted bitter and she never particularly enjoyed, the small portable radio atop the tin storage cupboard holding cloth diapers buzzed with the day's news. There was a man speaking about an important day for all Germans. About a trial of the century. About a turning point. Annegret stopped listening. She turned the page and started reading the June love story, although she knew it by heart. A homely secretary with ponderous eyeglasses and ill-fitting clothing is in love with her boss, a rakish bachelor. While out one day, she bumps into an old school friend, who has always dressed to impress, and goes shopping with her, then to the beauty salon, and finally to the optician's. The secretary transforms from an ugly duckling into a beautiful swan. The twist, however, is that her rakish boss doesn't even recognize her the next day—but the messenger who delivers the office mail does. A young man with a good heart, who comforts her as she sits crying in a corner of the corridor. Annegret didn't know whom she despised most in this story. The idiot secretary who couldn't dress herself, the overbearing friend with the perfect hair, the rakish boss who didn't cotton on to a damn thing, or the dopey mailman who was too afraid to speak to the woman till she was crying. Annegret thought of her sister and that filthy rich snob. She was sure the two had not yet slept together. She considered that a mistake. Everything about a person was revealed in the act. Ample and difficult though she may be, Annegret had had several sexual encounters. All of the men had been married. Nurse Heide appeared at the door, a reserved older colleague who sometimes wheeled screaming infants into the broom closet and left them there till they fell asleep from exhaustion.

"Here she is. This is our dear Nurse Annegret."

A younger woman in a winter coat entered the nurses' lounge alongside Nurse Heide. She was smiling from ear to ear and took a large step toward Annegret. In the hall was a dark blue baby carriage, which rocked gently and emitted happy babbling.

"I wanted to thank you!"

Now Annegret understood, and she got up.

"Bringing Christian home today?"

The young mother nodded happily and handed Annegret a flat parcel wrapped in reddish tissue paper.

"It's nothing, I know, compared to what you've done."

Probably pralines. Or brandy beans. Sometimes they gave a pound of coffee or air-dried mettwurst as a thank you for good care. Of all the nurses, Annegret received by far the most gifts. But she was also the one who truly sacrificed herself for the problem cases, the one who ignored her schedule and didn't sleep until the infant was back on the path to recovery. In the five years Annegret had worked in the nursery, she'd had only had four children die. It had been best in those cases, too, she thought, because after an initial recovery, these patients would have led sad lives as cripples or halfwits or both.

Annegret shook the young mother's hand. Then she stepped into the hallway, up to the stroller, and looked down at the little face that was nice and round again. "I wish you all the best, Christian." Annegret placed her hand on his tiny chest in farewell. Christian pedaled his legs and sprayed drool out of happiness.

"I heard you stayed up with him for two nights. We will never forget that, my husband and I."

Annegret gave a crooked but happy smile. "I was just doing my job."

Annegret watched the young mother push the brand-new stroller down the hall and through the frosted glass doors. Doctor Küssner walked up, a tall, somber man with smooth features, early balding, and a prominent gold wedding band. He appeared deeply concerned: they had to get these E. coli cases under control! Annegret assured him that she exercised tremendous care with hygiene protocol at all times. Doctor Küssner dismissed this with a wave.

"I don't mean you. The residents, though, they'll use the bathroom and not wash their hands and then examine newborns. I'll bring it up tomorrow, before the rounds."

Annegret went into the first nursery, where fourteen infants lay in their bassinets. She checked the babies' temperatures by placing her hand on their cheeks. Most were asleep. One little girl was awake and cooed adorably. Annegret picked her up and swayed gently from side to side, humming a song she had come up with herself. She had inherited her father's tone deafness.

TWO HOURS LATER, Eva was on her way home. She didn't even consider taking the streetcar, but set out on foot. She strode furiously through the slush, as though she never wanted to stand still again. Salt crystals and pebbles crunched under her heels or jumped and sprayed away. She was panting.

After the chief judge had adjourned the court until the coming

Tuesday, Eva had watched incredulously as most of the defendants exited the auditorium through the main entrance, their passage unchallenged, as though it were a matter of course. Out in the foyer, her neighbor in the little hat linked arms with the main defendant, who turned his hawkish face toward her, and the two walked out onto the street like any other elegant couple. Eva then spied the light blond-haired man in one of the hallways and ran over somewhat rashly. She impolitely ignored the fact that he was in the middle of a conversation.

"Why are they free to go?!" she blurted out, as upset as a child over some injustice. But the blond man didn't recognize her and turned away without answering. David Miller also passed by Eva without so much as a glance. The men rushed off to their important meetings. And she had been left there in the hallway, an entirely unimportant young lady alone with her questions, most of which she knew were naïve. Walking down the street now in the din of traffic, passed by countless clattering and speeding cars and trucks and mopeds, blasted and enveloped by the reek of exhaust fumes, she regretted having attended the opening at all. What did she have to do with this trial, this bygone world? She was out of place there. Miller and that other fellow had made that abundantly clear! Yet they were themselves incapable of keeping those criminals from walking the city streets!

"In our midst!" Eva exploded. She couldn't remember ever having been so angry. Not even at Annegret, who had an unrivaled ability to infuriate Eva with her scornful obstinacy. Eva was nearly hit by a car as she unbuttoned her wool coat, and she bellowed "Idiot!" after the driver. She had never done anything like that before. Only prostitutes yelled in public. Had Jürgen heard that, he'd have had his worst fears confirmed: Berger Strasse. A barman's daughter. Seedy home life. Something gurgled up in her like a spoiled meal that just had to be expelled and one would immediately feel much better. Eva coughed up bile but forced herself to swallow it. Unthinkable, to let herself go like this in public. She took a shortcut. Her route led through a charmingly snowy park. Upon closer inspection, however, she discovered that the snow was gray with soot. The trees stood there, bare and helpless. Eva slowed her pace and breath. A uniformed man stood on a plinth, wearing a crooked cap of snow. He gazed at Eva with what seemed like pity. A squirrel darted past and zigzagged over the path in front of her, as though playfully inviting her to follow. *Lilly Toffler*, Eva thought suddenly. *Her name sounds so carefree. Like I'd have liked her.* The squirrel scrambled up one of the tall tree trunks with astounding speed. The animal seemed to be laughing at her from up there, at how heavily and lethargically, how clumsily she walked that path, like all the others. Eva stopped. She thought back to the man whose eyes she'd felt on her as she stood all alone in the corridor outside the auditorium. It was the Hungarian man from the Sun Inn, Herr Cohn, who'd been among the spectators, after all. He had looked at her, out from under his black hat, and nodded almost imperceptibly. Or was she just hoping that? That he had recognized and greeted her? Yes. And then Eva knew what she had to do. She rushed out of the small park. But she didn't go home. She boarded a No. 4 streetcar and took it to the office building she had entered for the first time in her life the past Sunday.

JÜRGEN LEFT THE SCHOORMANN OFFICE half an hour earlier than usual, to buy an engagement ring. He drove into the city, or rather, crept forward in an endless, fuming procession of metal. The *Frankfurter Allgemeine Zeitung* had recently dubbed this phenomenon "rush hour," something that had previously been known to occur only in large American cities. Frankfurt had the most cars on the road of all West German cities, that much was undeniable. Jürgen liked his Lloyd just fine, but he still found it ridiculous, all the men in their hats, stuck behind the wheel, on their way home to "Mother." Ready for the weekend. When did spouses begin addressing each other as "Mother" and "Father"? At the very moment their erotic relationship ended. When would his erotic relationship with Eva end? Jürgen shook his head at himself. What a question, when it hadn't even yet begun. As he pulled up to a red light, his eyes fell on Santa Claus sitting in a big armchair in a shop window. It was a life-size figure with some sort of motorized system. Santa nodded kindly and tirelessly, surrounded by piles of gifts of various sizes. A few children were gathered at the window, the little ones spellbound, the older kids smirking: "It's all just a fake!" Jürgen couldn't remember ever having believed in Santa Claus. His mother had only ever mentioned the Christ Child. When the winter skies turned a rosy orange at sundown, she would say, "Look, Jürgen, the Christ Child is baking cookies!" His father dismissed Christmas as folklore, despite the fact that he always made a fortune on it. As they did for every holiday, he and Brigitte would be going to their house on the northernmost island in the North Sea. Jürgen would be alone on Christmas Eve, a thought that didn't bother him. On the contrary: he enjoyed experiencing the miracle of Christmas on his own. He would attend midnight Mass and immerse himself in the festivities. Appearances to the contrary, he could be swept up in the joy everyone always sang about. Jürgen mused that it would also be the last Christmas he'd spend alone. He would be married next year. Eva would presumably be pregnant. Jürgen pictured her with a fat belly. Her breasts would grow too. She would be a good mother. The light turned green. But Jürgen didn't move till the cars behind him began honking impatiently. He passed through the light, pulled over to the right, and double-parked in front of Krohmer Jewelry. The other drivers, who all had to pass him, tapped their temples at him in annoyance.

EVA FELT NERVOUS ENTERING the apartment above German House late that afternoon, because she saw Jürgen's car parked outside. She hung up her coat in the hallway and listened. Animated voices were coming from the living room, then laughter, then swearing. Eva stepped into the doorway. There were Jürgen and her father, groaning and joking as they struggled to put up the Christmas tree. They hoisted the trunk into the cast-iron tree stand that had first belonged to Ludwig's parents. Stefan had also grabbed hold. He was wearing brown leather gloves that were far too big for him. They belonged to Jürgen, who had lent them to him, because the tree's needles were so "pricky." Ludwig got on his knees and tightened the screws to secure the trunk. The tree slowly leaned toward the left. Edith watched and made fun of her husband, who was so talented in the kitchen but not much use elsewhere.

"He's all thumbs!" Stefan crowed.

"You have to unscrew it, Herr Bruhns. No, in the other direction . . ."

Ludwig turned the screw in the other direction and cursed.

"How do you expect the boy to turn out when he hears words like that coming from your mouth?" Edith scolded him.

"Oh, I'm a lost cause already," Jürgen teased.

"Mummy means me. But I already know much badder words. Want to hear?"

"No!" Edith and Ludwig answered at the same time, and everyone laughed.

No one noticed Eva, who was standing in the door. Her gaze fell upon a tray with four champagne flutes and an unopened bottle of Rüdesheim sparkling wine on the table. She felt dizzy. She knew what that meant.

"*Guten Tag,*" she said. Everyone looked at her, and Jürgen even blushed a little. He held onto the tree and smiled.

"There you are, finally. We have something to celebrate," her mother told her seriously. "Ludwig, the tree is fine!"

Ludwig stood up with a groan and grimaced as he straightened his back. He strode over to the table, seized the bottle of sparkling wine, and opened it swiftly, announcing, "Well, he did it. He's asked for your hand."

Eva had the impression he was fighting back tears. Jürgen took her hand and placed a small box in it. As Ludwig poured the wine, Stefan protested because he didn't get a taste, then crawled huffily under the table and allied himself with Purzel, who was also excluded from celebrations. Ludwig raised his glass and seemed thoroughly exhausted.

"In which case, you can call me Ludwig."

"Edith."

"Jürgen." The glasses clinked.

Under the table, Stefan griped, "Pff! That stuff is yucky, anyhow."

Eva took a big sip, and the sparkling wine tingled sweetly in her mouth. Her mother looked over and gave her a gentle nod, as if to say, *Forget that I was skeptical at first. It'll all work out just fine!* The small pendulum clock on the cupboard chimed once. Ping. Four thirty. Ludwig set down his glass.

"Unfortunately, we have to pause things here. But consider it a rain check for the engagement party."

Edith set her glass on the tray as well, stroked Eva's cheek, and smiled. "But by all means, you two should stay and make yourselves comfortable."

Her parents got ready to go out, to go downstairs and open their restaurant. They were in good spirits, despite the strenuous hours that lay ahead. Eva swallowed and smiled nonsensically.

"By the way," she said, "I went back to the prosecutor's office." Her parents froze in the doorway. Jürgen had been about to take another sip but paused. "I'm doing it. I mean, I told them that I'll translate. At the trial."

Jürgen took a big gulp of sparkling wine and swallowed, then pressed his lips together. The happiness vanished from Edith and Ludwig's faces. Everyone was silent, waiting for Eva to say more. Waiting for an explanation. But she remained silent, herself, because she couldn't explain it. She thought of that fellow David Miller, who had looked at her the same way: "And why now, all of a sudden, do you want to do it?" But he thought she was dim, regardless.

At that moment, Stefan squealed from under the table, "It's falling over!!" The tree was, in fact, listing dangerously to the side. Jürgen quickly lunged. He was just able to catch the tree before it fell, but its needles stabbed his hands painfully.

A little later, Eva and Jürgen sat across from one another at the living room table. They were alone. Even Purzel had scuttled out with his tail between his legs. A storm was brewing. Jürgen's expression was dark. He was silent. The little box from Krohmer Jewelry lay unopened between the betrothed on the Plauen lace tablecloth.

"We'd agreed to something different, Eva."

"All you said was that you didn't want me to do it."

"And I expect you to respect my opinions."

Jürgen's voice was cold and detached.

Eva was starting to feel scared. "Jürgen, by the time we're married, the trial will be long over."

"That's not the point. It's the principle of the thing. I mean, if it's already starting out this way—"

"Then what? What happens then?"

Jürgen stood up. "I've never made a secret of how I feel a marriage should work. I would like for you to quit on Monday."

Jürgen left. He was agitated, furious, and disappointed. The decision to marry had been a sizable step for him. He had overcome his own reluctance and risked everything. And for her to stab him in the back like this! He had to be able to trust his future wife. She had to do as he said.

Eva stayed at the table. She picked up the tiny box containing her engagement ring and turned it over in her hands. Then she sprang up and ran after Jürgen, out onto the street. He was by his car, brushing freshly fallen snow from the windshield with his bare hands. Eva marched up to him and held out the box combatively.

"Didn't you forget something?"

Jürgen took the box without hesitation and stuffed it in his coat pocket. Eva's stomach churned. She was overcome with fear of losing Jürgen. Or had she already lost him? She took his hand and held it tightly.

"How can I explain it to you? I have to do this. And it isn't forever!"

"Oh, yes, I think it is."

"What do you mean by that?"

Eva tried to read Jürgen's green eyes, but they appeared turned inward, and he avoided her gaze.

"You've got to ask yourself, Eva: How important to you is this job? And how important to you am I?"

Jürgen freed his hand from Eva's grasp. Then he got into his car. He started the engine and drove off without a good-bye.

Inside the restaurant, Edith stood by the window, a tray of empty beer glasses in her hands, and looked out onto the street. From the way Eva was standing there under the streetlight, Edith could tell that her daughter was crying.

AFTER MIDNIGHT THAT EVENING, Ludwig Bruhns opened the bedroom window. He gazed into the quiet inner courtyard, at the shadow of the tall, motionless fir tree. He had taken three more painkillers that evening, one every two hours. His stomach was upset; he'd have to ask Doctor Gorf to adjust the prescription. Edith's feet hurt more than normal too, and she massaged them with her special salve. The smell of camphor mixed with fresh night air helped cut through the kitchen odor that always clung to Ludwig, despite his lathering soap on his upper body every evening. Edith watched him look up at the stars through the window. He was wearing his tatty old pajamas—patterned with small dark blue diamonds on a light blue background—that he liked just a little too much. He simply couldn't throw them away, even after Edith had hemmed them several times. As a result, the sleeves and pants were both too short, and his ankles were bared. There was nothing Edith could do about the threadbare spots at his elbows, knees, and bottom. The fabric would soon tear there. Ludwig had honestly suggested she sew on patches. Edith had burst into laughter. Pajamas with patches? That didn't even exist during wartime. "At some point, they're just going to fall off your body. Turn to dust. And you'll be standing there like a fool," she had said. Ludwig closed the window and climbed into bed. Edith stepped over to the vanity and wiped her hands on a small towel, then opened a jar of yellowish paste and spread a thick layer over her face. Around her mouth and eyes she already had several wrinkles, which she tried to make disappear by application of various creams. As she got into bed beside Ludwig, he commented, "If you went out on the street like that, you'd be arrested."

"As would you, in those pajamas," Edith responded, as usual. They turned out their lights at the same time. Then they both stared into the darkness until their eyes had adjusted and they could make out the blurred shadow thrown onto the ceiling by the cross window. They had always found it comforting, but tonight, the cross felt threatening. Edith got up one more time. She closed the curtains.

"O HOW JOYFUL, O how blessed, O how cherished Christmastime." The organ in the Johanneskirche droned over Eva's head. The organist, Herr Belcher—"who had no say in his name," her father was quick to remind them—was clearly sober and playing decently well. Pastor Schrader, always rather disheveled, was in rapture over his joyful message, as he was every year on this day. Every last seat in the church was taken, despite there being so few

Protestants in this neighborhood. The Bruhns family had arrived a bit late. Stefan had to dress up for the Nativity play, and he'd put up a little fight. They hadn't managed to find a pew together and now sat scattered throughout the chapel—Annegret way up front, Eva wedged between strangers a few rows behind her parents. Still, she could see her mother, whom she knew must be grimacing with exertion. Edith teared up whenever she heard organ music, yet she was ashamed to cry in public, and, like a little girl who wants to be big and strong, she fought the tears unsuccessfully. Eva was always moved by it. It was usually contagious as a yawn, but she felt she had shed enough tears over the past few days. She'd had to listen to her mother's rebukes, although she herself had been against Jürgen at first. And to her sister's, who couldn't fathom how Eva could risk her "career as a businessman's wife" like that. All for some translation job! And from her father, who seemed to be trying to communicate, through strange looks of concern, *Eva, sweetheart, you're making a mistake.* Eva didn't consider herself especially strong-willed and self-assured, but her family's vehemence had sparked an unsuspected resistance within her. She hadn't contacted Jürgen. She hadn't quit on the prosecution. And now she sat there defiantly and watched the Nativity play being performed at the altar, which Pastor Schrader had rehearsed with the schoolchildren in the parish. As on every Christmas Eve, not a word either Joseph or Mary said could be heard. Only the innkeeper, who turned away the Holy Family, was audible. "No, there's no room for you! Move along now!" Stefan played the innkeeper. Edith had shown him how to project his voice. Although she hadn't been allowed to study acting, she knew these things intuitively. She had dressed him in a gray smock and dug out an old beige hat. Then Ludwig got involved, because he knew a little something about innkeeping, and put his chef's hat on Stefan's head. Edith argued against it: "A cook isn't necessarily the innkeeper! It will just confuse the audience. And it doesn't say anything in the Bible about a cook!" But Stefan had agreed with his father, and the hat now towered white over the other players' earth-toned costumes. The other mothers had sewn their children cloaks out of faded curtains or cinched belts around the fathers' old shirts. It looked like Mary was wearing her mother's shrunken, yellowed wedding dress. Several children's headdresses were too big, and kept slipping over their eyes. Some were presumably meant to be sheep, and had draped lambskins over their shoulders. *But isn't that what shepherds wear? Traditionally?* Eva thought. In her opinion, the Christmas story was never as confusing, long, and uninspiring as it was during the Nativity play, yet all of the threads came together at the altar by the end. The costumed children gathered in a circle around the homemade manger, knelt down on the cold church floor, and bowed deeply. Because there in the straw lay the Christ Child. A miracle.

The Bruhnses lingered outside the church for some time afterward, despite Stefan's begging that they go home. The German House owners were well known and loved in the neighborhood. To the steady sound of church bells ringing from the white onion dome above, they exchanged Christmas greetings with friends and acquaintances. The family then walked home. There was still snow on the street and in the corners of the recessed doorways, but it had gotten warmer, and the snow no longer crunched underfoot, but splashed. They had all linked arms, so that no one fell, "or so that if one goes, we all go!" as Ludwig had laughed. Except for Stefan, who was bubbling over and describing all the disasters that had happened backstage in the vestry, no one spoke another word.

Out of consideration for Stefan, they opened presents before dinner. The living room took on a golden glow from the many candles, the tree smelled of pitch and the deep forest, the tinsel shimmered, all four candles in the Christmas pyramid had been lit, and the shepherds and Three Kings hurried like never before. As usual, the Holy Family waited in vain. Stefan, on the other hand, was showered with gifts: both cheeks crammed with chocolate, he received an air rifle from his father, the book about the Swedish child detective from Annegret, and a dark blue seaman's sweater from his mother. "You look like Grandpa Bruhns. Like Grandpa Sea Lion." Eva had bought Stefan a Stabil construction set, and he planned to build the Schoormann warehouse the next day after nabbing a few sparrows in the courtyard with his gun. Lastly, Stefan opened the oblong package their grandmother had sent from Hamburg. Inside was a small uniformed doll wearing a knapsack that contained a cloth parachute—a paratrooper that Stefan now eagerly launched from every chair in the house. Purzel snapped at it in flight. Annegret was delighted to receive an elegant, burgundy leather wallet. Eva unwrapped a delicate silk scarf, blue with yellow polka dots. She would wear it in spring. When the sun began to warm things up. Some Sunday, when she took a stroll through the city in bloom. Without Jürgen. Eva stood up, because the image was hard to take, and began to pick up the wrapping paper and carefully fold each piece. Ludwig used this as an opportunity to apologize to Edith, because the washing machine hadn't been delivered on time. But it did have thirteen wash cycles. And you could set the water temperature. Edith replied that this wouldn't have happened if they'd ordered it from

Schoormann's. "They don't sell washing machines!" Eva said, placed the paper on the cupboard, and went to her room.

Eva turned on her reading lamp and sat down on the bed. It was the same as always, the rituals and timing, with just a few minutes' difference here and there, like earlier, when they'd arrived late at church. Even Purzel had already vomited, after he'd used a moment of distraction to go after the colorful plates underneath the tree. Everything was as it always had been. Eva lay down and closed her eyes. A recurring dream she hadn't had in some time began playing through her mind. She enters a long room with high ceilings, a blue floor, and light blue tiled walls. Spinning chairs are arranged along the walls, covered with a shiny, dark blue material, and hanging on the wall in front of every chair is a round mirror. There are two sinks on one of the short sides of the room. Waiting in a corner are three peculiar creatures that appear to be nodding at Eva with enormous, hollow heads. She takes a seat in one of the chairs and turns to face the mirror. But there's no one in the mirror. And then Eva feels a searing pain on her head. She screams.

Eva opened her eyes. The strange thing about this dream was that Eva had a scar on her scalp, a three centimeter-long bald spot above her left ear. Her mother always told her she had fallen as a small child. Eva heard someone call her name. It was her mother: sausages and potato salad were served.

AT THE SCHOORMANN ESTATE, Jürgen sat by himself in an armchair in the living room. The housekeeper, Frau Treuthardt, had been off since that afternoon. He hadn't eaten, he hadn't drunk, he had turned out all the lights and gazed out into the shimmering evening. He simply sat there and beheld the quiet picture, which hadn't changed in more than an hour. He looked like someone who had broken into the house, then sunk into a chair, overcome by the beauty of the garden. Jürgen's eyes, however, were blind to the charm the view was offering him. He was deliberating how to respond to Eva's disobedience. The Eva he had first met was much different—compliant, yielding, and prepared to accept that the man had the final word in a marriage. She was showing a whole new side of herself now, like one of those acerbic women who went to war alongside their husbands. Eva hadn't been in touch, and it was clear that she was determined not to budge. It was equally impossible for him. He couldn't lose face before they were even married. And while Jürgen ruminated on the traditional power dynamics in marriage, underneath it all he could sense his actual fear: he was afraid of the trial Eva was joining. He had fallen in love with Eva's innocence, with her purity, because he lacked it himself. What would this encounter with evil do to Eva? What would it do to him?

The standing clock in the hallway struck eleven. It ran fifteen minutes slow, and Jürgen realized that if he wanted to get a seat for midnight Mass at the Liebfrauenkirche, he would have to leave this minute. But he stayed seated.

AT MIDNIGHT, ANNEGRET ENTERED the first nursery, which was dimly lit. She had volunteered for the overnight shift and left her family after their meal of sausages and potato salad. A siren howled outside—maybe a Christmas tree had caught fire. Annegret liked the sound. It meant: *Help is on the way!* She paced between the bassinets and checked in on each little face. Most of the infants were sleeping soundly. Annegret stopped at one of the cradles. The name Henning Bartels was on the card at the end of the bed. Frau Bartels was housed in the maternity ward downstairs, battling childbed fever. Henning, on the other hand, was already a remarkably sturdy child, despite being just days old. Annegret bumped into the bassinet, as if by accident. Henning opened his eyes a crack, shook his little fists, and yawned toothlessly. Annegret gently stroked his cheek.

"Hm, you poor little nugget." Then she pulled something out of the pocket of her uniform: a reusable glass syringe without a needle. The barrel, which held ten milliliters, was filled with a brownish liquid. Annegret moved to the side of the bed, slipped her hand under Henning's head, and lifted it slightly. Then she stuck the syringe between the boy's lips, pushed it under the side of his tongue, and slowly emptied the contents into his mouth. Henning's eyes widened a little, and he began to smack.

"Tastes good, mmm, nice and sweet, right?" Henning sucked some more and swallowed. Some of the fluid ran out the sides of his mouth. Annegret pulled a cloth from her pocket and carefully dabbed his tiny face. "There we go, now you're all set."

IN THE APARTMENT ABOVE GERMAN HOUSE, Edith and Ludwig sat in the living room. The candles had burned out, and the floor lamp flickered tiredly. Eva's parents were both drunk, which they only allowed themselves on rare occasions. Midnight Mass at the Liebfrauenkirche was being broadcast on the radio. "For unto us a child is born, unto us a son is given; and the government shall be upon his shoulder, and his name shall be called . . ." Edith listened as the organ started to play and the priest made his auspicious proclamations—the Gloria—and she finally allowed herself to cry, shamelessly and unobserved. Ludwig sighed occasionally too, although he wasn't listening. He was reminiscing about childhood Christmases on his home island, the way Father Christmas would come riding through the darkness, over the frozen mudflats in a horse-drawn sledge. Blazing torches were affixed to the box seat, and Father Christmas heaved the bag of gifts for the Bruhnses from the sledge. One year, Ludwig jumped onto the skids in the back, held tight, and rode along to the next farm. Father Christmas discovered him there and gave him a mighty tongue-lashing. Ludwig recognized his voice as that of Ole Arndt, a hired hand at their neighbor's farm. Then he spotted the familiar bluish nose under his fake white beard. From that point onward, Ludwig had considered himself very grown up. But the First World War didn't start till a year later. Neither of his older brothers returned from France, and his mother died of grief. At age fourteen, Ludwig began to cook, after his father's spirit had failed and he'd stopped opening the grocery store. He cooked for his little sister and father. That's when he truly grew up. The doorbell rang. Edith wiped her nose and looked at Ludwig quizzically through misty eyes. He groaned as he struggled, like a beetle stuck on its back, to sit up. Not but yesterday, he'd been a young man. And now his back hurt. "It's twelve thirty?!"

EVA HAD FALLEN ASLEEP next to Stefan. She'd carried her brother to bed an hour earlier. He clutched the little paratrooper in one hand and his air rifle in the other. Eva started reading him a story about a young Swedish boy who wants to be a detective. But Stefan wanted her to sing something instead, his favorite Christmas carol, "Come, All Ye Shepherds!" He liked it "because the music bounces so nice." She hadn't needed to sing long and then snuggled up to her brother's small, comforting body.

She was now woken by the doorbell. Purzel was barking like mad. Someone was actually downstairs at the front door. Eva got up and padded into the hallway in her stockings. Her updo had come loose, and her hair fell long and disheveled down her back. She pressed the buzzer to unlock the entrance downstairs, and cracked open the door to the stairwell. Purzel slipped out and down the steps. Ludwig had also materialized in the hallway at this point. He was in his shirt and swaying a bit.

"Who the hell is it? Must be Father Christmas."

Eva heard the front door open and someone mount the stairs in big strides, while assuring Purzel, "You've met me already!"

Eva recognized the voice and quickly tried to fix her hair in the mirror. No use. Jürgen appeared in the doorway to the apartment, without a hat and his coat unbuttoned, out of breath, as though he had run the entire way from the Taunus hills. Ludwig gave him a quick, hard look, at once resigned and relieved, grunted something regarding a Merry Christmas, called "Purzel, come!" and with that, father and dog disappeared into the living room. Eva and Jürgen stood in the door and looked at each other in silence. Eva tried not to look happy. Finally she gave him a little smile. Jürgen touched her messy hair.

"Merry Christmas," he said earnestly.

At that, Eva grabbed Jürgen by the lapels and pulled him into the apartment.

"Merry Christmas."

And then they kissed in the corner by the coat rack, long and hard and without a hint of reverence.

PART
TWO

PART
TWO

I SWEAR TO TELL THE TRUTH, the whole truth, and nothing but the truth, so help me God."

It was the twenty-third day of the trial, and today the first testimonies from Polish-speaking witnesses would be heard. Eva was no longer seated in the outermost spot at the rear of the gallery, but now stood at the witness stand in the middle of the large auditorium. She was flanked by two older gentlemen in dark suits, the Czech translator and the English translator. Eva placed her left hand—which now bore a ring with a blue stone—on a heavy black book with a small stamped golden cross, and lifted up her right hand. Eva addressed the chief judge, who regarded her amiably, and his two associate judges. Her raised hand shook slightly. Her heart beat fast and hard, from her chest up into her throat.

"Please speak a little louder, Fräulein Bruhns."

Eva nodded, took a deep breath, and started over. She swore to translate carefully and faithfully all documents and testimonies delivered in Polish and examined in the trial. She would neither add nor omit any details. As Eva spoke, she thought she caught David Miller turning away in disdain, but the blond man

calmly watched her take the oath. Eva could feel the looks coming from her left. From the defendants' tables. Some of the men
and their attorneys regarded her with favor. Because she was a
healthy young woman with bright blond hair. Because she looked
decent and respectable in her high-collared, dark blue suit and
flat shoes.

". . . so help me God," Eva finished. The chief judge gave her
a tight nod. The two other interpreters were then sworn in. Eva's
nerves quieted some, and her gaze fell upon the large map behind
the bench. From this distance, she could make out the inscriptions. Block 11. Main Camp. Crematorium. Gas Chamber. *"Arbeit
macht frei"* was printed at the bottom. One of the other interpreters smelled strongly of alcohol. Probably the Czech. *O Lord, pre-
serve my judgments*, Eva thought sardonically. Her own breath was
undoubtedly stale and sour, because she had hardly managed
breakfast this morning. This morning—it seemed so long ago. Yet
only two hours had passed. At seven thirty, Eva sat at the kitchen
table with Annegret and Stefan and nervously stirred her coffee,
the spoon clinking inside the cup. Their mother came up from the
cellar with a jar of preserves labeled "Blackberry '63." She handed
the screw-top jar to Annegret, who opened it effortlessly, without so much as glancing up from her newspaper. A hiss escaped
from under the lid, and for several minutes Stefan tried to mimic
the sound. "Pfiiiiffffffff" was the closest approximation. Edith
scraped off the layer of greenish-white mold into the trash. She
joined her children at the table and spread jam on a piece of bread
for Stefan. Then they all recalled how late last summer, Edith had
ridden her bicycle up the local mountain, two tin pails hung from
either side of the handlebars, with another large bucket secured
to the rear rack. On the mountain, Edith filled the three pails

with jet-black, sun-ripened berries. The sisters were in the living room, watching the show *On Sundays, It's My Treat* when their mother returned from her outing, and they jumped up in horror as she entered. "Mummy! What happened? Did you have an accident?!" Eva ran to the phone to call the doctor, while Annegret tried to take Edith's pulse. Edith didn't understand what all the fuss was about, till she saw her face in the hallway mirror—she looked terrifying. Blackish-red berry juice was smeared over her lips and chin, and her pastel blouse was covered in dark stains. Edith had snacked as she picked, and the sticky juice ran down her chin. Patting her face with her handkerchief only worsened things. It looked like she'd fallen on her face and was bleeding heavily from the mouth. All three women had broken into laughter of relief that summer day. But no one laughed that morning at the breakfast table. A dark gray cardboard folder lay beside Eva's plate like a poisoned letter. It contained evidence the witness Jan Kral had provided to the prosecution's investigator two years earlier, which Eva would translate today in court. Eva had read through the documents twice the previous evening. If everything Herr Kral claimed to have experienced and seen was true, it was a miracle he was still alive. As she took a sip of coffee, she wondered what he must look like. Bent and full of sadness. At the same time, Stefan was whining about the sandwich his mother was making him for recess.

"I don't like crone beef. It's gross!"

"Mettwurst?"

"That's even grosser! Ew! That makes me sick to my stomach!"

"Well, I have to put something on it. Or do you just want butter?"

"Yuck, butter is gross!"

At that, Eva took her folder and lightly hit Stefan on the back of the head. "Stop being a baby!" Stefan looked at his sister in surprise, but she got up and left the room.

"Don't you want to take a sandwich, Eva?"

"I can eat there, Mum, there's a cafeteria."

Eva pulled on her wool coat in the hall. She looked at herself in the mirror. She was pale, her face almost white, and her knees felt like pudding, her stomach as though some furry creature were carving it out from the inside. As she listened to the quiet emanating from the kitchen, the silence of her mother and sister, she admitted to herself that what she'd felt creeping up inside her for days now was fear. She tried to puzzle out what it was she feared most: the fact that she would be speaking in front of all those people, or was it the responsibility she had to find the correct translation? Was it fear of not understanding the witnesses properly? Or, indeed, of understanding them exactly? Eva placed the folder in her leather briefcase, which she had given herself as a gift for earning her certification three years earlier. She put on her hat, called *"Auf Wiedersehen!"* toward the kitchen, but only received a response from Stefan.

"See you later, alligator!"

It was one of those days that has no weather, no sunrise and no sunset, a day that remains utterly gray, that turns neither warm nor cold. The snow was no more than a memory now. Eva walked all the way to the municipal building. With every step, her courage waned, seeping away like snowmelt in the gutter, and by the time she reached her destination it had vanished almost entirely. But the moment she entered the packed foyer and took in the countless reporters and two men with heavy cameras, recognized several defendants shaking hands, noticed policemen saluting the white-haired main defendant—the moment she witnessed the sense of self-evidence these men exuded and heard their strident voices, and then spotted individuals or small groups of tense, quiet, and knowing women and men standing round, Eva knew she was in the right place.

The hall never really brightened, even as midday approached, the foggy glass panes gleaming a soft gray. An attendant turned on the overhead lights, and the spherical fixtures floated over their heads like great glowing bubbles. Although several windows were cracked open, the air was thick. It smelled of damp wool, leather, and wet dog. Following their swearing-in, the interpreters were seated on the side of the prosecution. Eva took a seat directly behind David Miller. She pulled the dark folder from her briefcase and placed it on the table in front of her. She looked at the back of David's head, at his reddish hair that was just a little too long at the nape of his neck. He looked like a boy from behind. Like Stefan when he occasionally succumbed to childish brooding. David was reading through papers that he passed on to the blond man after a quick perusal. On the other side of the room, a tall man stood up. He fished through the folds of his robe and withdrew a silver pocket watch on a chain, which he popped open to check the time, somewhat absentmindedly. His long, soft features and white tie reminded Eva of the rabbit from *Alice in Wonderland*, a book neither she nor Stefan had liked because this wonderland was inhabited exclusively by unfriendly characters. The man was representing seven of the defendants. He made a motion to hear witness testimony from the wives of Defendant Number Four and the main defendant. Eva turned toward the gallery to look for the woman in the little hat, who smelled vaguely of roses, but couldn't spot her in the crowd. The blond man stood and stated that the prosecution rejected the motion. There was no knowledge to be gained from such testimony, he argued, as the wives were biased. They could also refuse to give evidence, should such details serve to incriminate the defendants. A clash ensued between the defense attorney and the lead prosecutor about the number of witnesses for the defense. Eva knew that the first witness to be called today was Jan Kral. She opened her folder and reflected that Jan Kral's wife, in any case, would not be called to the stand. The last time he had seen her was November 1, 1942.

The chief judge accepted the motion of the defense. Visibly pleased, the lawyer snapped shut his pocket watch. The blond man sat back down, took a drink of water, although he wasn't thirsty, and crossed his arms. His colleagues exchanged looks. David Miller leaned in and whispered something to him, but the blond man shook his head gruffly in response.

The chief judge then announced, "The court will now commence the hearing of evidence. Please call to the stand the witness Jan Kral!" The blond man turned to signal Eva, but she had already risen and was headed for the witness stand. A police officer led a dignified elderly man into the room. Kral came across as suave in his dark blue suit, as though he were an attorney himself, or even an American film star. Eva knew from his file that he worked as an architect in Krákow. Kral held himself remarkably erect. Eva watched him approach and tried to catch his eye. But Kral looked past her, through his angular eyeglasses, straight at the bench. He did not look at the tables of the defendants to the left, either. When he reached Eva, she expected him to shake her hand. But he didn't seem to notice her; his focus was now on the chief judge, who invited him to take a seat. Kral sat on the long side of the table, facing the judges. Eva did not sit beside him, but pulled up the chair at the end of the table, as she'd been instructed. On the table were two microphones, a simple carafe of water, and two glasses. The court began reviewing the witness's personal details: name, birth date, place of residence, profession. Kral knew some German and delivered curt responses to these simple questions in a loud voice. Eva didn't have anything to do yet. She pushed her notebook and pencil back and forth until perfectly positioned. She regarded the witness from the side, taking in his profile and distinctive eyeglasses. Kral had a slight tan and was clean-shaven, with a small nick on his strong chin. Eva noticed that he'd missed a bit of shaving cream beneath his right ear. She tried to breathe and smelled fresh soap.

David Miller observed Eva from where he sat, with a view of her in half profile from the back, of her feminine shoulders and tight chignon that just had to be real. Not padded with one of those strange round cushions that mostly older women used. Yet again, her appearance somehow infuriated him. He knit his eyebrows. He had a headache. He'd overdone it the night before with colleagues from the prosecution—only their boss and the blond man had not joined in the revelry. In the merry section of Berger Strasse, they had started with drinks at the Mokka Bar and watched the women slowly remove their clothing to the music. David then continued on his own and found his way into an establishment called Suzi's, where loud *Schlager* music played. Half-naked women sat at the bar, and after twenty minutes, David wandered into a back room with the one who reminded him least of his mother. The room—number six—was windowless and overly perfumed, and someone had carpeted the walls. The woman, who said her name was Sissi, quickly undressed and opened his pants. David had been with plenty of prostitutes in the past. It wasn't about desire. The act of intercourse was invariably mechanical and joyless. The women never smelled the way he hoped. But he could always tell himself afterward that he was a contemptible human being. His mother would be appalled. The thought pleased him in a strange way. The double bed had such a soft mattress, he thought he might sink into it and eventually emerge in Australia. Or, rather, what was the antipode of this German city? He thought of the globe he'd had in his bedroom as a kid, and how he had pierced it with a long knitting needle to see what was on the other side of the world. *Where will I come out if I dig a tunnel?* He recalled this as he lay down on top of Sissi: he'd have drowned in the Indian Ocean. Sissi smelled a bit musty and sweet, like raisins, which he didn't like and had fished out of desserts since he was a boy. As he penetrated her, he mused that she must have had at least one child. The review of personal details had now concluded in the auditorium. David turned his mind back to the trial.

"Herr Kral, when exactly did you arrive at the camp?"

Jan Kral now responded in Polish. He spoke rapidly, without any discernible pause for breath.

Thankfully, Eva thought, *he doesn't speak in a regional dialect*. She took notes. Ghetto, boxcar, bucket, straw, children, three days, son . . . Kral spoke faster and faster. Men. Officers. Trucks. What was that last word? Red Cross? He said that in German, didn't he? Eva could not keep up. She quietly addressed Kral in Polish.

"Please! Herr Kral. I'm sorry, you're speaking too fast. Please, you must take short breaks."

Jan Kral fell silent and turned to the side. He looked at Eva in confusion, as though he didn't understand who she was. Eva repeated her hushed plea, and the chief judge leaned in to his microphone.

"Is there a problem?"

Eva shook her head, but turned so red, it must have been visible to the spectators in the gallery. Some of the defendants, who all had a clear view of Eva's face, grinned and snorted—it was the less educated of the men, the stoker and the medical orderly. Kral had now realized what Eva's task was, and gave her a quick nod. He started from the beginning and spoke more slowly. Eva intently studied his lips, which blurred before her eyes. Her hands went cold. The blood began to roar so loudly in her ears, she could no longer hear Kral properly. *I can't do it. I've got to get out of here! I'm going to get up and leave. I've got to run . . . I'll run . . .* But then Eva noticed how, one after the other, small beads of sweat were appearing on Kral's forehead. His chin began to twitch. Only Eva could see it. She felt ashamed. What were her nerves compared to his hardships? She calmed down. Kral stopped speaking and looked at his hands, which rested on the tabletop. A drop of sweat ran down his right temple. Eva referred to her notes and translated what Jan Kral had said up to that point. She noticed that she was trying to mimic his tone.

"On October twenty-eighth, '42, I was deported from the Krákow ghetto with my wife and son. We traveled for three days by freight train. In a locked boxcar. There were no sanitation facilities. Just a bucket in the corner for eighty people. We had no food or water. People died along the way, at least ten. The elderly in particular. When we arrived, on November first, at the ramp, they pulled us out of the boxcar. Then the survivors were split up. Women, children, and the elderly to the left, men to the right. Two SS officers argued over whether my son—he was eleven, but already big—belonged on the left or the right. I thought that those on the left would be sent to a less strenuous camp. And I didn't want him to have to work. I got involved. I told one of them, my son is still too young, he can't work. He nodded, and my son climbed together with my wife into a truck. It was from the Red Cross, which reassured me. Then they drove away." Eva fell silent. The chief judge leaned forward to ask a question, but Kral started speaking again. It was only a few more sentences, and he spoke rapidly, his words tumbling out by the end. Then he stopped, as though he were finished. Eva looked at Kral from the side, at his Adam's apple above his starched white collar. She watched him swallow and swallow and swallow.

Eva whispered in Polish, "Could you please repeat the final sentence one more time?" Everyone was waiting, and someone drummed his knuckles impatiently on a tabletop. But Kral shook his head imperceptibly and looked over at Eva. Behind his glasses, his eyes were red. His chin was trembling. Eva sensed that it was impossible for him to continue. She paged through her dictionary and looked up two words, "slup" and "dym." Pillars and smoke. She leaned toward her microphone and stated what she believed to have heard at the very end. "At the camp later that evening, another prisoner pointed out a smokestack on the horizon. He said, 'Look. Your son and wife are climbing into the heavens.'"

Kral removed his glasses and pulled out a checkered handkerchief that was freshly pressed and folded. Eva thought, *He bought that for the trial.* Kral used it to wipe the sweat from his forehead. Then he hid his face in it.

For a moment, no one spoke in the hall, even among the defendants. A number of them had closed their eyes, as though dozing. The blond man jotted something down, then asked, "Herr Kral, why did you think your family would be sent to a less strenuous camp?"

Eva repeated the question in Polish. Jan Kral blew his nose, swallowed once more, and responded.

"One of the SS men on the ramp promised me it would happen," Eva translated.

"Who?" the blond man wanted to know. Kral didn't move. "Was it one of the defendants? Do you see him here?"

Kral put his glasses back on, then turned to face the defendants' tables. His gaze lingered briefly on Defendant Number Four's haggard face. Then he indicated Number Seventeen, the pharmacist in dark glasses. He snorted, practically amused, as though he'd been chosen to perform some prank in a parlor game. He stood calmly, and as he responded, Eva translated for Kral.

"That's a lie. The witness must be mistaking me for another person." The pharmacist sat back down.

His defense attorney, the White Rabbit, stood up. "Herr Kral, you claim to have arrived at the camp on November first, '42? The defendant was not even on site that day, as he was visiting Munich from November first through fifth. He underwent surgery there. We have documentation."

Eva translated. Kral replied, "It may have been October thirty-first when we arrived. One loses his sense of time when locked in a boxcar."

The chief judge addressed his associate judges. "Are death certificates available for the Kral family?" Head-shaking.

"Maybe the entire story is untrue. I doubt the witness's credibility," the defense attorney said, which Eva translated for Kral. He looked at Eva and went white in the face.

At the same time, the blond man countered sharply, "Many of the victims' names were not even known, as I am sure the defense is well aware! Your Honor, we have here the witness's registration at the camp." David Miller produced the document in question. The blond man quoted, "The witness was registered as prisoner number 20117 at the main camp on November first, '42. It was not uncommon for arrivals not to be processed until the following day. An arrival on October thirty-first is therefore entirely plausible."

Eva translated for Kral. The chief judge asked, "Herr Kral, do you remember when, exactly, you were registered after your arrival? Was it the same day? Or later?"

"I don't remember." Following a pause, he added, "To me, November first is the day my wife and son died."

The defense attorney declared, "I repeat: you therefore could not have seen my client on the ramp, Herr Kral."

Defendant Number Seventeen now took off his sunglasses and gave the witness almost a friendly nod. "I'm sorry, sir, but I was never on this so-called ramp."

Someone let out a cry of indignation from the gallery, and the crowd whispered. The chief judge called for order, then asked the witness to describe his arrival at the camp again, step by step, to allow for a better understanding of the timing. Eva translated for Kral. He gave her a quizzical look, and she repeated the request.

"Once more, from the beginning."

Kral began to shake; a giant invisible hand appeared to have seized him and was shaking every bone in his body. Eva turned toward the prosecution for help. The blond man saw that the witness needed a break, and motioned to the chief judge.

A windowless, low-ceilinged room behind the auditorium, which was normally used as a green room for performers, served as a waiting area for the witnesses. The lead prosecutor, together with David Miller, was there questioning Kral, who had declined to sit. He stood, swaying, with his back to an illuminated mirror and his face drained of color. His suit appeared to have become too big for him, his collar too wide. Any trace of his initial stateliness had vanished. Eva translated: his testimony was important, he had to try and remember. But Kral stated that he would no longer subject himself to this situation. He had realized that it would not bring his wife and son back to life. David grew more insistent and told Kral that he also had a responsibility. A responsibility to the other victims! He grabbed Kral by the shoulder, but the blond man pulled David back.

"You can't force me," Kral said. The blond man pulled out a pack of cigarettes and offered one to the witness. Kral took a cigarette. He and the blond man smoked. All four were silent. A few open-face sandwiches sat on a tray by one of the mirrors, left over from the day before. The slices of meat on top were sweating and had turned up at the edges. Like the others, the mirror was framed by a wreath of glowing white lightbulbs. One clearly had a loose connection and flickered alarmingly. Eva could see that David was fit to burst from impatience and aggravation. He had dark bags under his eyes, as though he had barely slept.

With strained self-control, he now said, "Herr Kral, you are not only an important witness with regard to the pharmacist. You are also critical in the case against Defendant Number Four, the Beast—"

"Herr Miller, I've already told you—" the blond man interrupted him.

David waved it off. "Yes, fine. Herr Kral, you are one of the few to have survived the tortures of Block Eleven. You must testify!" Then he barked at Eva, "Translate that!" Eva was about to speak when Kral's knees suddenly buckled and he fell like a marionette whose strings have been cut. Eva and David barely managed to catch him and helped him onto a chair. Eva took his half-smoked cigarette and stubbed it out in an ashtray.

The blond man gave David a long look and said, "We already had our doubts during the pre-trial interviews. I don't think we should insist any further if he's crumbling already. We're just wasting time." He addressed Eva, "You needn't translate that, Fräulein Bruhns!"

David started to respond, but the blond man looked at the clock, nodded at Kral, and exited the room. David followed him sulkily, without another glance at either Kral or Eva. He left the door open. Eva was outraged. How could those two simply leave this man sitting here like a broken appliance? She turned to Kral, who sat hunched over on the chair.

"Would you like something to drink, Herr Kral? A glass of water?"

He turned it down with a wave of his hand. "No, thank you."

Eva studied the man indecisively. He also seemed unsure of what came next. It looked like he was waiting for directions. Eva rested her hand on his lower arm, to her own surprise.

"Are you sure you wouldn't like to reconsider?"

Kral didn't look at Eva. "How old are you?" He didn't wait for an answer. "Such a young person shouldn't concern herself with the dead. She should live." With that, he struggled out of the chair, murmured a good-bye, and left the room. Eva watched the flickering lightbulb and wondered whom Kral blamed for the death of his son: the men out there or himself.

IN THE NURSERY, where—like in court—the electric lights had been on all day, Annegret prepared the infants for their second feeding. She placed the tiny bundles, which screeched with hunger, into small carts that she and Nurse Heide wheeled to the maternity ward. There Frau Bartels, a young mother, was already sitting up in bed in her private room—Herr Bartels had money—and waiting for her little Henning. Frau Bartels looked quite fresh again, after two weeks battling childbed fever. She and her boy were going to be released soon. Annegret lifted Henning from the carriage and laid him howling on his mother's bare breast. His cries quieted immediately and he began to suckle loudly. Annegret gazed at the back of his tiny, lightly bobbing head and smiled. Frau Bartels looked over her child at Annegret and decided that, although the nurse was a little too fat and wore too much makeup, she liked her. And that would be the case even if she hadn't saved her son's life. Frau Bartels had developed a high fever shortly after his birth, and breast-feeding was out of the question—the nurses had had to feed little Henning formula from a syringe. On Christmas Day, however, Henning suddenly began vomiting violently, and later developed diarrhea. He shed weight by the day, until his little arms were as thin and pliable as reeds. Every half hour, Annegret gave him a spoonful of sugar water, which immediately ran out the sides of his mouth. But she didn't give up. And after three days, Henning—more dead than alive, weighing just fifteen hundred grams—kept more of the solution down for the first time. Bit by bit from that moment on, things had started looking up. He now weighed almost as much as he had at birth. Frau Bartels was immensely grateful, which she repeated to Annegret yet again. As Annegret started for the door, however, Frau Bartels grabbed her arm and whispered, "There's something else I have to tell you, Nurse. My husband is suspicious and wonders whether Henning might have been given spoiled formula. He submitted a written complaint to the hospital. I just hope this won't cause you any trouble. I would be so sorry for that, after everything you've done for Henning." Frau Bartels looked at her apologetically. Annegret smiled in reassurance.

"That's perfectly all right. I would do the very same in your husband's position. I'll be back for Henning in half an hour." Annegret left the room. The moment she stepped into the corridor, the smile vanished from her face. *I have to stop doing this*, she thought, and not for the first time.

AT LUNCHTIME, most of the people involved in the trial went to the cafeteria in the municipal building. Members of the prosecution, spectators, witnesses, and family members chose between meatballs in caper gravy or goulash and ate at long tables in the impersonal, utilitarian space. Some of the defense attorneys, including the White Rabbit, also carried around their trays, searching for a spot. A group of defendants sat at a table to the side and satisfied their hunger like everyone else. People either ate in silence or spoke in low voices about the weather forecast, the terrible traffic, or the meat, which was generally considered dry or even rubbery. Eva took her tray to a table the other girls—the secretaries and stenotypists—had occupied. A rosy young lady in a pale suit, whom Eva had seen before at the public prosecutor's office, smiled at her in welcome. Eva sat down across from her and began to eat the meatballs, which her father would never have allowed to leave the kitchen, lukewarm as they were. Eva didn't have much of an appetite, anyway. Another two witnesses had testified before lunch, and both were from Poland. They had, however, spoken German well enough to testify without Eva's help. Still, Eva had sat by them, to provide assistance if needed. She'd only had to translate a single word: canes. Because that's what SS officers had carried on the ramp, instead of cudgels, to give new arrivals a sense of security when they stepped off the train. But if anyone spoke, asked a question, became defiant, or if children started crying—then the canes were used as clubs till quiet was restored. Both witnesses had seen Defendant Number Seventeen on the ramp. One of the witnesses also identified the main defendant, who denied as unequivocally as the pharmacist, ever having been at that place. Let alone having performed any of those so-called selections. Eva looked at the table across the cafeteria, enveloped by a cloud of cigarette smoke. She thought the defendants had all sounded like they were telling the truth. They all seemed surprised. Incredulous, almost incensed that one could think them capable of looking into people's mouths and squeezing their biceps, and separating the able-bodied individuals from their relatives, tearing families apart forever. They convincingly denied sending those deemed useless straight to the gas chambers. Eva set aside her silverware. Ten thousand people a day. That's what the witness Pavel Pirko, who'd been in a work unit responsible for cleanup on the ramp, said. Eva scanned the room for the mischievous little man, whose testimony was as animated as if he were recounting a boat tour on the Rhine. She couldn't find him. All she saw was David Miller at the other end of the room, quickly and carelessly shoveling food into his mouth and addressing a colleague with his mouth full. Eva tried to visualize it: ten thousand women, children, men. Ten thousand weakened humans, who climbed one after the other into trucks and were driven off. The only thing she could imagine, however, was their hope for a warm shower and a piece of bread.

ON BERGER STRASSE, Eva's mother, Edith, had gone downstairs to the laundry room, her arms laden with German House's dirty linens. She stood before the new machine in her blue checkered smock and watched the first wash cycle. The closed white box pumped and thumped, as if a big heart were beating inside. Edith couldn't break away from the sight, although she had plenty to get done in the kitchen. She had a vague sense that a new age was waltzing in. *Or better yet, lumbering in*, she thought, remembering how this monstrosity had required three men to carry into the cellar. Every Tuesday up till today, she had boiled aprons, tablecloths, dishtowels, and napkins in a large tub, stirred and churned them with a long wooden paddle, and finally drawn the soaking wet laundry from the lye, which made her eyes tear. Now she stood here and had nothing to do. She felt useless and sighed. Her hair was starting to thin and go gray, her body was losing its shape, becoming blurred, softer, weaker. Some nights, before putting on her face cream, Edith would sit in front of the mirror and pull her skin back, till her face appeared as smooth as it once had. She would sometimes skip dinner for days, to fit back into her velvet skirt. But then more creases would appear on her cheeks. *At a certain age, every woman's got to know whether it's a cow or a goat she wants to become!* Edith read that once in a women's magazine. Her mother had indisputably turned into a goat. Edith couldn't decide. She could be either onstage. And more: mistress, daughter, mother, grandmother. With makeup and a wig, she could play Lady Macbeth, Juliet, Schiller's Joan of Arc. . . . Her thoughts were interrupted by the sound of the cellar door opening, and Ludwig came in wearing his white chef's coat.

"What's keeping you, Mother?"

Edith didn't respond, and Ludwig could tell she was processing something inside. Just like the new washing machine.

"The whole point of that gadget there is to make use of your time elsewhere."

"I always liked doing the laundry, I liked stirring the vats, I liked scrubbing on the washboard, and I liked beating and wringing out the wash. I don't know if I'll ever get used to this thing."

"Sure you will. Now come on, you left me in the lurch up there with my potato salad."

Ludwig turned to go, but then Edith said, "Don't we need to talk to her?" Ludwig looked at his wife and shook his head.

"No."

Edith was silent for a moment while the drum inside the washing machine spun faster and faster on its axis. Whoom-whoom-whoom. "He lives in Hamburg now. He's a businessman and owns a really big company."

Ludwig knew immediately whom Edith meant. "How do you know that?"

"It's in the paper. And his wife, she's in the city too." The washing machine hissed loudly and then began to pump, gurgling. Husband and wife gazed at the appliance in silence.

AFTER ANOTHER EYEWITNESS HAD BEEN HEARD, who as a thirteen-year-old had seen her mother and grandmother for the last time ever on the ramp, the chief judge adjourned court for the day. Eva headed for the ladies' room, where she had to wait for an empty stall. There was a line of women, like at the end of a theater production. Missing today, though, was the lively

chatter all about how who had performed. The mood was restrained, and the women politely held the doors open, passed the
towel, and acknowledged one another with a nod. Eva felt dazed
herself. When a stall freed up, she locked the door and had to
pause for a moment to recall what she was doing there. Then
she opened her briefcase and pulled out a folded, pale-patterned
dress. She took off her dark skirt, her blazer. It was tight in the
little stall, and she kept bumping into the walls. As she pulled
the dress on over her head, she nearly fell over. She swore under
her breath and contorted her body reaching between her shoulders for the zipper, which she finally managed to zip up. The
restroom emptied out in the meantime, and silence fell outside
the stall door. Eva folded her work clothes and tried to fit them
into her briefcase. She couldn't get the clasp to fasten, though,
and left the bag open. She was about to leave the stall, when she
heard the restroom door open. Someone entered, sniffled, maybe
even cried. Then blew her nose. There was a faint smell of roses.
A tap was turned on, and the water rushed. Eva waited behind
the door, hugging her briefcase and holding her breath. But minutes passed, and the water was still running. Eva opened her stall
door and stepped out.

The wife of the main defendant stood at one of the sinks,
washing her hands. She was wearing her little felted hat again,
and her dark brown handbag was on the windowsill. The woman
dabbed her blotched face with dampened fingertips. Eva stepped
up to the second sink beside her. The woman didn't look up, but
her body stiffened. Evidently Eva was now her enemy. Side by
side, they washed their hands with curd soap that didn't foam.
Eva peeked out of the corner of her eye at the woman's wrinkled
hands and thin, worn-out wedding band. *I know this woman. She*

once slapped me. With that very hand, Eva thought, and was startled by the absurd idea. She shook it off, turned off the faucet, and turned to leave. The woman abruptly blocked Eva's way, while in the background the water continued streaming.

"You can't believe everything they're saying in there. My husband told me all they want is restitution—they want money. The worse the stories they tell, the more money they get."

The woman retrieved her purse from the windowsill and before Eva could say anything, she had left the ladies' room. The door closed with a snap. Eva looked at the running water and turned it off. She peered into the mirror and touched her cheek, as though feeling the memory of a blow she had received a long time ago.

After retrieving her coat, hat, and gloves from the coat check in the almost deserted foyer, Eva stepped out of the municipal building. It was just before five. The daytime gray had transitioned into the bluish gray of twilight. The headlights of passing cars threw long bands of light into the evening haze. The municipal building was on a busy street.

"You did well today, Fräulein Bruhns." Eva turned around. Standing behind her was David Miller; he was smoking and, like always, not wearing a hat. Eva smiled in surprise at the sound of praise coming from his mouth. "The lead prosecutor told me to tell you that."

David turned away and joined two other men from the prosecution, who had just left the building. Eva hung back, feeling somewhat snubbed. Why did this Miller fellow go out of his way to be rude to her? Was it because she was German? He didn't appear to take issue with anyone else, though—at least not his colleagues. Or the stenotypists.

EVA'S THOUGHTS WERE INTERRUPTED by the sounds of honking. Jürgen's yellow car had pulled up beside the row of parked vehicles. He left the engine running, jumped out, and opened the passenger door for her. Eva climbed in. In the car they kissed each other quickly and bashfully on the mouth. After all, they were engaged. Jürgen merged into traffic. Eva, who normally provided the lively, disjointed commentary of a child about what she saw to the left and right on the street as they drove, remained silent. She seemed blind to the people walking home at this hour, weighed down with shopping, dragging their children by the hand past the illuminated shopfronts that kept catching their attention. Jürgen looked over repeatedly, as though searching for a visible change, a mark that the day had left on her. But her appearance was unaltered. Then he asked, "So, you nervous?"

Eva turned to face him and couldn't help but smile. She nodded. "Yes." Because they had a plan that felt almost forbidden.

Twenty minutes later, Eva had the feeling the car was entering a different world. They passed through a tall, white metal gate that swung open and then closed behind them, as if by magic, and then followed the curves of an endless-seeming driveway dotted with squat lampposts. Eva squinted into the darkness, past the trees and bushes that were still bare, and detected an expanse of lawn beyond. She thought of how perfect it would be for Stefan to play soccer. And she thought of the two big flowerpots her father lugged up from the cellar every spring, which her mother filled with red geraniums and set outside to decorate the entrance to the restaurant. The house emerged suddenly in the darkness. It was long, modern, and white. It seemed as impersonal as a garage, which Eva found strangely comforting. Jürgen pulled up in front and briefly took her hand.

"Ready?"

"Ready."

They got out. Jürgen wanted to show her his house, which would soon be hers as well. Jürgen's father and Brigitte were still on their island in the North Sea. And as they took their daily seaside walk before dinner, bracing themselves against the gale, they never suspected that at the same time, their son was leading his blond fiancée through the rooms of the family estate. Jürgen even opened his father's austere but tastefully appointed bedroom for Eva. She was overwhelmed by the number of rooms, the liberality, the elegant colors. She gazed up at the high ceilings, which had been important to his father, Jürgen explained, because he needed space above his head to think. Eva's heels alternated between clicking brightly on the smooth marble floors and sinking deep into the thick, cream-colored wool carpet. The pictures on the walls also made a much different impression on Eva than the Friesian landscape at home. She studied the painting of a house composed of severe forms bordered in black, beside a weirdly erected lake, which had been painted wrong on purpose. That much was clear to Eva. She thought of her cows at home. When she was six or seven, she had given them all names. Eva tried to remember them and recited to Jürgen, "Gertrude, Fanni, Veronika. . . ."

"Good evening, Herr Schoormann. Fräulein. . . ." A buxom, middle-aged woman in a beige housedress had entered the room. She was carrying a tray with two filled flute glasses. Jürgen took the glasses and handed one to Eva.

"Frau Treuthardt, this is Eva Bruhns." Frau Treuthardt, with her slightly bulging eyes, stared openly at Eva.

"Welcome, Fräulein Bruhns."

Jürgen held a finger to his lips and said "Shhh" to her. "This remains a secret. Today is a first, unofficial visit."

Frau Treuthardt screwed up her eyes, which was probably meant to be a sly wink, and flashed a row of small, healthy teeth. "By all means! I won't make a peep. I'll tend to dinner now, if that's all right." Jürgen nodded, and Frau Treuthardt turned to leave.

"Is there anything I can do to help in the kitchen, Frau Treuthardt?" Eva asked courteously.

"That's all we need, our guests having to cook for themselves!" Frau Treuthardt left the room.

Jürgen, amused, told Eva, "She's a little rough around the edges, but she does her work very well."

The two clinked glasses and drank. The tingly cold liquid was dry and tasted of yeast to Eva.

"It's champagne," Jürgen said. "Now, how would you like to see the height of decadence? Bring your glass."

Eva was curious and followed Jürgen. They crossed a tiled corridor to the "west wing," as Jürgen sardonically called it. The unsettling odor, which Eva had noticed the entire time and thought was her imagination, grew stronger. Jürgen opened a door, turned on the ceiling lights, and Eva stepped into a huge room tiled in sky blue. The swimming pool. A long glass front made up the sidewall to the right and provided a view of the dark green lawn. A couple of scattered outdoor lamps created hazy coronas of light. *It looks like a poorly maintained aquarium*, Eva thought, *that hasn't held any fish in ages*. By contrast, the water in the pool seemed pristine. It sat there untouched, its surface gleaming.

"Would you like to take a dip?"

"No, no thank you."

Eva was in no mood to change her clothes and get wet. Jürgen seemed disappointed.

"Jürgen, I don't even have a swimsuit."

In response, Jürgen opened a cabinet that contained at least five options on hangers. "That shouldn't be a problem. I'll leave you alone too." Eva again tried to protest, but Jürgen continued, "To be honest, Eva, I've still got a call to make, which might take a while. You'll find swim caps in the shower over there."

Jürgen pulled a suit off its hanger, handed it to Eva, and left. Eva was alone. She noticed little bubbles floating to the surface from the bottom of the pool. Like the sparkling wine in her hand. *Oh, right, it's not sparkling wine. It's champagne.* Eva took another sip and shivered.

Ten minutes later, Eva—wearing the pale red swimsuit, which was a bit tight—climbed down the metal ladder into the pool. She had painstakingly stuffed her thick hair into the white rubber cap and obediently took one rung after the other. She created small waves, and the water surrounding her was warmer than she'd expected. When the water reached her breasts, she let go of the ladder and began swimming. She turned onto her back. Hopefully the swim cap would hold. When Eva's hair got wet, it took half an hour to blow-dry. Eva spread her arms and legs, lay at the surface, and gazed up at the humming tube lights on the ceiling. How odd, swimming in an unfamiliar house. With expensive champagne in her belly. In a bathing suit that wasn't hers. Eva had never felt less able to imagine leaving her old life to live here with Jürgen. But that was the way things worked. Eva thought of Jan Kral, who might already be on his way home. At this very moment, he might be flying away in an airplane high above the house with the swimming pool, going back to Poland. By way of Vienna.

Eva had taken this trip once herself, two years earlier, to an economic congress in Warsaw. That's where she had lost her virginity. Eva rolled onto her front and dove down into the water. She swam to the bottom of the pool and could feel the water slowly seeping into her swim cap. But she stayed under till she could no longer take it.

Jürgen paced silently on the thick carpet in his office. He wasn't on the phone—he had lied to Eva. He didn't have a call scheduled. Jürgen wanted to know what it felt like to have Eva here, next door, somewhere, in a different room, but not be able to see her. What would it feel like when she was living here with him? He had to admit, it was nice knowing Eva was in the house. Like a small new organ pumping fresh life into an old body.

Later, Eva and Jürgen sat together at the corner of the long dining table. "No, not across from each other, Eva. We're not royalty," Jürgen had joked. Eva had undone her hair, and it was still damp where it hung down her back. *There's something wicked about it*, Jürgen thought as he studied her out of the corner of his eye. *Something wild*. But he immediately suppressed his desire to kiss her. Not in his father's house, not before he knew about Eva. They ate a venison stew Frau Treuthardt had cooked. Jürgen was giving a detailed account of the renowned architect who had built the house eight years ago "as a meditation on early Mies van der Rohe." Eva thought of the doilies at home and tried to picture the architect in her living room. Then she asked Jürgen what the architect might say if he stopped by and found the furniture here suddenly covered in doilies. Jürgen looked at her blankly.

"I'm warning you, that's my dowry. Fifty-six doilies for all your needs."

Jürgen caught on and responded gravely, "Doilies too are

known to reflect the architectural principle of symmetry." Jürgen started laughing like a child who's played a naughty trick. Eva joined in, then laughed even harder when she heard the architect's name was Egon Eiermann. And how would Herr "Egg Man" react if he suddenly discovered the Friesian landscape, with its so very saturated sunset, hung over the mantel in his house? If he saw the cows? Amid the chuckles and giggles, though, Eva imagined her father and the way he sometimes gazed at the picture and sighed heavily. He felt homesick in those moments. And she saw the way her mother anxiously dusted the frame, because the painting had been expensive. And all it did was hang on the wall. Eva's mood turned serious, almost sad.

"I feel like I'm betraying my parents."

Jürgen stopped laughing too and took Eva's hand. "You don't need to be ashamed of them."

After dinner, they withdrew to Jürgen's office. Jürgen put on a record and sat down next to Eva on the wide gray sofa. It wasn't the first time Eva felt jazz was lost on her. She didn't know where one song ended and the other began. She didn't know what was happening in the middle, either. She liked music where she could tell what was coming before the next note was even played. That wasn't the case with jazz. Eva asked Jürgen for a little more wine, which comfortably clouded her mind and made everything in the room look even nicer—the warm light, tall bookcases, the endearingly messy desk and floor-to-ceiling windows behind it. Eva blinked drowsily and closed her eyes. An image of people with suitcases appeared before her. There was a lot of jostling, and men in uniform hissed terse orders. An old woman with a yellow star on her coat pulled something out of her pocket, thrust it into a younger woman's hand, and said, "Hold tight to your dignity!"

The old woman was then torn away, and the young woman looked in her hand. Eva opened her eyes and sat up on the sofa. She didn't want to think about what the witness had told them today, about the one thing of her grandmother's that had been left to her and that was then stolen in the camp.

"Which room do I get, anyway?"

Jürgen, who had tipped his head back and was listening to the music, smoking, responded distractedly, "The housekeeping room. Do you want to see it? And the kitchen? If nothing else, it's big—"

"That's not what I mean. I'll need a desk too!"

"You can use mine whenever you need to write a letter."

Jürgen stood up and flipped the record. Eva felt the onset of a stomachache. Game didn't agree with her. Frau Treuthardt had also overcooked the venison. The chunks of meat, which were dark as it was, had been almost black. They weighed down her stomach like coal. Or rather, she was like the wolf whose belly was filled with rocks instead of little goslings, a fairy tale Stefan had asked her to read to him earlier today, even though he was big now. Jürgen returned to Eva's side and placed a thick photo album on her lap.

"I'd like to show you pictures of my mother."

Eva tried to ignore her stomachache and paged through the album. Jürgen's mother was a delicate, black-haired woman who appeared blurry in almost every photo. There was one photo of his parents laughing and holding their little Jürgen between them. They were standing in front of a beer garden. Eva recognized Jürgen's stern expression. And she knew where the picture was taken.

"That's on the Lohrberg, in front of the tavern."

"Yes, that was the summer of '41, and two days later my father was arrested."

"Why?"

"He was a Communist. I didn't see him for another four years."

Jürgen fell silent and stubbed out his cigarette in a heavy glass ashtray. He evidently didn't want to linger on the subject. Eva got the feeling he regretted having handed her the album in the first place.

"Your mother was beautiful. And looks friendly. I would have liked to meet her."

Eva turned the page, but no more photos had been pasted there. A loose picture slid out. Eva caught it—it was a postcard depicting a mountainous landscape. She flipped it over, and the back was covered in writing. It was a child's scrawl. "Dearest Mummy . . ." Before Eva could read any further, Jürgen had snatched away the card.

"I was sent to the countryside, to the Allgäu region," Jürgen said, and after a pause, added, "I've hated the smell of cows and milk ever since."

"What was so awful about it?" Eva wanted to know. Jürgen placed the card back in the album, closed the book, and set it on the glass table.

"I wanted to stay with my mother. I felt I had to protect her. Like little boys do. Then she died."

Eva stroked Jürgen's cheek. Jürgen looked at her, and suddenly a small but unmistakable fart escaped her. That damned venison. Eva's face turned bright red. How embarrassing. Jürgen smiled gently. And kissed her anyway. They slid down onto the sofa, their breathing ragged, looked at each other, smiled shyly, then kissed again. Jürgen's hand wandered up Eva's bare arm.

Then he carefully grasped her hair, which was nearly dry and smelled faintly of chlorine. Eva pulled Jürgen's shirt out of his pants and slid her hands under it. He abruptly jerked back.

"Are you trying to seduce me?"

"Or is it the other way 'round?" Eva laughed.

But Jürgen growled, "I've told you where I stand on the matter. Not before we're married . . ."

"But isn't that a little old-fashioned?" Eva wanted to embrace Jürgen again. Not because she was overcome with desire—she just wanted to consummate the relationship already, to enter that final bond as a sort of vow of their commitment, as she saw it. But Jürgen gripped Eva's hand, and she was shocked by his dark expression. For a brief moment, Eva thought he might hit her. She sat up straight and did not speak. The music ended on a held note that slowly faded out. The record ended. Eva said, "I don't understand you."

"I'll give you a ride home."

AS EVA AND JÜRGEN DROVE through the late-night city streets, and Eva tried to stifle her worsening flatulence, the lights were still on in the offices of the prosecution. David Miller and the other clerks were in the conference room preparing the questions and documents for the following day of hearings. In the murky circle of light thrown by a desk lamp, the blond man sat smoking in his office with the attorney general, conferring quietly about rumors that the judges had received threats from old SS associates of the defendants. And at City Hospital, Annegret was finishing her shift. She crossed the front courtyard, straight into an icy wind. Was it going to frost again? The question had dominated break time conversation among Annegret's colleagues. The weather didn't interest her; she almost never got cold, and even today she hadn't bothered buttoning her tent-like, navy blue coat. She was headed left, toward the streetcar stop, but she noticed that someone appeared to be waiting for her: Doctor Küssner was leaning against his dark-colored car and pushed himself off as he saw her approaching. Annegret pretended not to see him at first. But he gave a small wave and even called quietly, "Nurse Annegret?"

Annegret walked over and waited silently in expectation, while the wind tore at her open coat. Küssner was sheepish, babbling something about "just happened to discover we live in the same direction" and "happy to bring you along." Annegret let him talk. She knew that this was the start of a new affair. She had sensed it coming for some time, registered his glances and intimations such as "My wife never has time for me." And for several days, the cards had spoken clearly, turning up the king of diamonds in the appointed position. It was always the same.

Annegret climbed into Doctor Küssner's car. "Would you like to go straight home? Or might you be interested in a little something to drink?" He did not wait for her response, but started driving and continued nervously, "I've got to tell you again how well you managed things with the Bartels boy. The father still wrote to management, though. They're hounding me now, but there's nothing more we can do but hygiene, hygiene, hygiene. . . . Or are we overlooking something?"

Rather than simply answering, however, something unusual happened to Annegret: she began to sob. She sounded like a sick cat caught in a drainpipe. Her round face turned pink as she grunted and wailed. It was not an especially attractive sight. Doctor Küssner slowed the car and kept looking at her. He finally pulled over and somewhat helplessly turned on the hazard lights. He had pictured this differently. But Annegret couldn't stop. Never had she felt so acutely what a mess her life was. Over before it began. Doctor Küssner handed her his unused handkerchief, which his wife had ironed, and said, "We're blocking traffic."

That made Annegret smile, and she calmed down. "It's okay. I'd be happy to get something to eat now. At the little wine bar."

JÜRGEN HAD BROUGHT EVA home in the meantime. As they said good-bye, they agreed to meet that weekend—they planned an outing to nowhere in particular, a drive to the Taunus hills, perhaps, to take a little walk. "If the weather cooperates," they said, almost in unison. Then they parted, both somber and skeptical. When Eva reached the darkened hallway of the apartment, she noticed light emerging from under the door to the living room. It was strangely quiet behind the door. Eva knocked gently but received no response. She entered the room and was alarmed by what she saw: her father lying flat on the floor, his feet and calves elevated on Edith's armchair. His eyes were closed.

"Daddy! What on earth happened?"

"My back will be the death of me. I haven't told your mother—she's already asleep."

Eva closed the door quietly behind her and moved over to him. "Don't you have any pills left?"

Ludwig opened his eyes, which were red and strained. "They do such a number on my system." Eva sat down on the sofa in her coat and regarded her father. She felt sorry for him. She almost felt the pain in her own back.

"Lenze suggested I do this. Her husband's got back problems

of his own. Lie down on the floor and elevate the legs . . . it's supposed to relieve the discs, those damned discs," Ludwig groaned. He didn't look at Eva, nor did he ask about her day, something he normally always would: *So? Anything major happen today?*

Eva thought of the two fathers she had encountered earlier. Unprompted, she said, "There were two men today who both lost their families."

For a moment, Ludwig lay there quietly. He pulled his legs off the chair and turned painfully to the side, got onto all fours, then to his knees. He cursed. He still didn't look at Eva. "Lots of people lost their families during the war—daughters and especially sons," he said.

"But this, this is something different. The people there were sorted . . ."

Ludwig got to his feet with a final lurch and stood up fully. "Yes, well, I am glad I was never sent east. Now, daughter, tell me: how many rooms do the Schoormanns have?" Ludwig asked, his tone suddenly playful. Eva frowned at her father, who turned off the floor lamp by pulling the chain twice. Once for each bulb. Click. Click. It was dark in the room. A hint of light came in from the street, and her father looked like a big, shadowy ghost.

"Daddy, thousands of people a day were killed in that camp." Eva was surprised to find her tone almost accusatory.

"Says who?"

"The witnesses."

"People's memories can fool them after all these years."

"Are you actually suggesting these people are lying?" Eva was shocked. She had rarely seen her father be so deprecating.

"I've already said my piece on whether you should even do that job." Ludwig turned to leave and opened the door.

Eva got up, followed him, and hissed, "But this has to be brought to light. And these criminals, they've got to be punished. They can't be allowed to just roam free!"

To Eva's complete bewilderment, Ludwig replied, "Yes, you're right." Then he left her where she stood in the darkened living room. Her father had never seemed so alien to her, she realized. It was a horrible feeling that she hoped would pass quickly. She heard a noise behind her, a sort of rhythmic brushing. Then a whimper. It was Purzel, sitting on the carpet and wagging.

"Purzy . . . do you need to go out again? Well, come on then."

Out in front of the house, Eva waited for Purzel to finish his business. Her stomachache had subsided. She took a deep breath and exhaled, following the cloud of air with her eyes, then breathed out again, blowing an even bigger cloud. Purzel was sniffing here and there, even around his lamp post, but he wouldn't relieve himself. *Something's wrong with him*, Eva thought. She pulled her coat more tightly around herself. It would freeze overnight. Frost was already forming on the parked cars, like a layer of powdered sugar. There was just one car there with a dark exterior untouched by the cold. Inside were two people, whose heads kept merging into one. Eva recognized her sister Annegret kissing someone. Eva turned away and yanked Purzel, ready or not, by the collar into the house. Another married man, no doubt.

It was already past two. Eva had put a second blanket on the bed, but she couldn't warm up. The images kept swirling in her mind's eye. Her father on his back—Jürgen spurning her—the witness sitting by the coat check, bent over like a bird that's flown into a window and is now listening to its body, trying to detect whether it will live or die—the young woman on the ramp, who opens her hand after her grandmother disappears, to find a piece of soap lying there—the wife of the main defendant in the ladies' room, washing her hands beside Eva. Eva tried to establish an order to her feelings, to the unknown, the love, the shock, the incredulity, the peculiar affinity. Like her parents and sister, she lay awake for a long time. Only Stefan slept soundly, sprawled diagonally in bed, an army of toppled soldiers and cake crumbs on the carpet. When she fell asleep at about four, Eva dreamed of Frau Treuthardt cooking venison stew in a massive pot in an outsize kitchen. Towering beside the pot was a pile of meat chunks almost as tall as Frau Treuthardt. "That's far too much for two people," Eva said to her. Frau Treuthardt glared at Eva impatiently and replied, "But I'm showing you right now. Just watch." Frau Treuthardt took a single piece of meat from the pile and dropped it into the big pot, then another and another. One after the other.

They didn't have another hard frost, although it had been widely anticipated. Winter was slipping off undetected, or "pulling a French good-bye," as her father said. Wide anticipation was now reserved for the proper arrival of spring. Eva went to the municipal building Tuesday through Thursday and spent Mondays in the office of the prosecution, where she translated written documents. She was dreaming with unusual frequency. At night, she encountered the people she had sat beside at the witness stand during the day. They would speak at her and not allow her any time to find her own words.

The camp was becoming incredibly familiar to her: the blocks, the departments, the procedures. There was no one at home she could talk to about it. Neither her parents nor Annegret wanted to hear a thing about the trial. They even paged past the articles that appeared in the newspaper almost daily. Eva began to record what she heard during the day in a blue school notebook at night. Her initial feeling that she had some connection to the camp—that she recognized people, the wife of the main defendant—passed. Eva became acquainted with the other girls at the trial, who worked as secretaries for the prosecution or stenotypists in court. They sat together at lunch and chatted about fashion and dance halls. What had been said in court was not discussed.

Eva and Jürgen spoke on the phone the evenings he didn't pick her up and take her out. His father and stepmother had returned from their island and hadn't discovered anything to betray Eva's presence in the house. Frau Treuthardt kept quiet and, as Jürgen told Eva, frequently screwed up her eyes at him and clearly relished being his accomplice. His father's condition had not worsened. On the contrary, the sea breeze had "blown away the cobwebs," Jürgen said he repeatedly declared. To his son's delight and dismay, he was meddling in the layout of the new catalog. Jürgen favored picturing a woman in mink on the cover. "We've got to start moving away from your cheapo Communist angle, Father!" But Walther Schoormann decided the cover would feature children playing in the snow. "Children are the future, something you clearly don't understand, Jürgen!" That had been the cutting exchange. Eva waited every day for Jürgen to introduce her to his father and his father's wife. But the invitation didn't come, and Eva didn't dare ask. They went dancing or to the movies, and they kissed when they knew no one would see. Sometimes Jürgen placed a hand on her hip or bust. But it seemed to Eva as though they didn't have much of a future planned as a couple. One evening they went to see a Swedish film everyone was talking about, from the stenotypists and secretaries in court to Annegret's colleagues in the nurses' lounge, their wide-eyed commentary whispered from behind shielding hands. The film was restricted to viewers eighteen and over; Eva had insisted they see it and watched with growing arousal as the woman onscreen demonstrated her lack of inhibition with regard to sexual matters. The second time the woman's naked breasts were displayed on the large screen, Jürgen stood and left the theater. Eva followed him angrily and cornered him in the dark entrance to Willi's Gun Shop.

"Is this still the priest inside you? You're a prude, Jürgen. Uptight!" Jürgen spat back that the sex in that movie had nothing to do with the intimacy and fulfillment he associated with the act. Nothing to do with love. "I thought what you needed was marriage, now suddenly it's love? In which case we could do it? Or maybe you just don't find me desirable?! I'd appreciate if you'd tell me the truth!" Eva fumed. Jürgen called her "lustish" in response. And although Eva knew the word didn't actually exist, she was outraged. She couldn't believe that she had to beg a man to sleep with her. "How could you humiliate me like this?"

"You're seeing to it yourself!"

When Eva got home from the movies that evening, she knocked on her sister's door. Annegret, with all her experience, ultimately concluded that Jürgen was gay and that Eva had to decide whether this was something she could live with. Eva cried a lot that night, but the next morning Jürgen showed up at the door with flowers and such an unhappy expression that she forgave him. She looked into his eyes and felt sure that he loved and desired her. Clearly there was something inhibiting him, but Eva dismissed the possibility that it could be any kind of otherness.

ONE EARLY MORNING, while the city was still dark, the first mild spring breeze blew in from the west. At the Sun Inn, Otto Cohn had been lying awake for some time; every few minutes, the elderly Hungarian man reached for the pocket watch he had set on the bedside table, opened it, and read its face. The gentlemen from the prosecution had kept putting him off, because everything was unfortunately taking longer than anticipated. Because something had been rearranged in the order of the hearings. He had waited patiently for many days. But today was the day. It was slowly brightening outside the orange curtains, and a bird began to chirp. The bird earnestly and persistently repeated the same three tones: *foo fa fee, foo fa fee.* When his watch read seven o'clock, the Hungarian man got up. Like every night, he had slept in his clothes. Like every morning, he put on his black hat with the narrow brim and took out a dark blue velvet bag embroidered with Hebrew characters from his suitcase. He looked in the mirror and was pleased to see that his beard had already grown past his shirt collar. When he walked through the lobby in his coat moments later, and wordlessly placed his heavy key on the counter as he passed, the proprietor didn't bother inviting him to the breakfast served in the small room behind reception. He had only tried the first few days: "Breakfast is included in the price." A waste of breath each time. After Cohn left the boardinghouse that day without eating, the owner said to his wife, as she stepped out of the kitchen with a fresh pot of coffee, that that kike was probably off to pray again. His wife quieted him. They had been through enough already, he didn't need to pile it on. She had read in the paper that the people had been "sectioned, or whatever it was called," upon arrival. Some to die and the others to work, which killed them soon enough. They really hadn't deserved that either. Her husband shrugged. He wasn't bothering the Jew. He was providing him with shelter, wasn't he? For weeks now! Even though he was certain they'd have to delouse the room after. "Deep down, you are really just a good person, Horst," his wife said and slipped into the breakfast room. The innkeeper wasn't sure if she was mocking him. It wasn't worth taking his time to find out, though. He had to review the quote from a plumber to install new sinks in four rooms. The man had named an outrageous price. And they were friends, no less.

The Hungarian man had reached the Westend Synagogue by this point. He gave the uniformed guard at the door a quick nod and entered the soaring, whitewashed sanctuary. More than a dozen older men were gathered here. The cantor, a small, energetic man in a black hat, prayed out loud to the congregation in Hebrew:

יִגְדַּל אֱלֹהִים חַי וְיִשְׁתַּבַּח
נִמְצָא וְאֵין עֵת אֶל מְצִיאוּתוֹ

אֶחָד וְאֵין יָחִיד כְּיִחוּדוֹ
נֶעְלָם וְגַם אֵין סוֹף לְאַחְדּוּתוֹ

אֵין לוֹ דְמוּת הַגּוּף וְאֵינוֹ גוּף
לֹא נַעֲרוֹךְ אֵלָיו קְדוּשָׁתוֹ

קַדְמוֹן לְכָל דָּבָר אֲשֶׁר נִבְרָא
רִאשׁוֹן וְאֵין רֵאשִׁית לְרֵאשִׁיתוֹ

הִנּוֹ אֲדוֹן עוֹלָם לְכָל נוֹצָר
יוֹרֶה גְדֻלָּתוֹ וּמַלְכוּתוֹ

One of the worshippers was a young man with an embroidered yarmulke resting on his red hair, which was just a little long in the back. The Hungarian man recognized him. It was one of the members of the prosecution. The redhead kept looking around, studying the other congregants' behavior. The Hungarian man removed his prayer shawl from the velvet pouch and uttered the appropriate verse as he wrapped it around himself. He murmured and his upper body fell into a gentle, rhythmic swaying. Today, though, he was not praying with the congregation. He was asking God's forgiveness for what he intended to do. What he had to do.

David Miller didn't notice the Hungarian man. He also wasn't following the cantor, who now recited, "Are not heroes as though nothing before you, and men of fame as though never born, and the wise as though without understanding, and intellectuals as though without reason? For their works are confused, the days of their lives vain before you, and man has nothing over the beast, for all is vain."

David Miller was not praying with the congregation, either. He prayed to God for gruesome vengeance upon the defendants. Especially upon the haggard man with the face of a ferret, Defendant Number Four. The Beast.

ALTHOUGH EVA WASN'T SCHEDULED until afternoon, she took her seat in the row behind the prosecutors' table half an hour before court was called to order. She enjoyed the almost reverent atmosphere in the hall. Not many people were there yet. And the few who were there, preparing for the day, placing documents and folders on the tables of the court, moved about cautiously and quietly, at most whispering to one another. Even the light seemed muted, like in church. The tall floodlights—which had been installed in every corner of the hall several days ago, to supplement the daylight and overhead fixtures and to help the judge spot nuances in the defendants' facial expressions—had not yet been turned on. Eva was wearing a new, pale gray suit made of a lightweight material that had cost nearly 100 marks. But she was earning 150 marks a week now, and her dark blue suit had made her sweat. The hall was usually overheated, and the many bodies in the room—there were always at least 200 people—further warmed the space and spent the oxygen. By midday, despite the high ceilings and cracked windows, and even after hall attendants turned off the heat, the room was stifling. Women sitting in the gallery had even fainted. *Although that may have been caused by the witnesses' horrific descriptions*, Eva thought as she pulled out the two dictionaries from her briefcase. She didn't understand why some of the spectators came to the hearings. The reporters, mostly young, unkempt men in dusty suits, could be identified by their notebooks and strangely impassive expressions, and Eva was by now familiar with the wives of the main defendant and of Defendants Number Four and Eleven, who never missed a day of proceedings. The other spectators must be relatives of the deceased. Or friends. They listened to the accounts with wide, horrified eyes, shook their heads, cried, and even exclaimed in rage when the defendants maintained, "I knew nothing! Saw nothing! Did nothing! That is beyond my knowledge!" Then there were the men who followed everything unresponsively but whose sympathies clearly lay with the defendants—men who gathered during the breaks and automatically clicked their heels when the main defendant passed. But there was also a group of spectators Eva couldn't classify. Some of them came every day and hung on every word. Eva had invited Jürgen to come listen sometime. He'd said he was too busy with the autumn/winter catalog. Eva knew it was an excuse. But she understood, and she even understood her family. Why should anyone voluntarily open themselves up to this chapter of history? *So why am I here?* Eva asked herself. She didn't know the answer. Why did she want to hear the testimony of the Hungarian man she had brought to his hotel that time? Why did she want to know—need to know—what had happened to him? Since the first day of the trial, Eva had repeatedly seen him in the foyer, with his big black hat and bearded face. As a witness, he was barred from following the trial. He often sat beside the door to the auditorium during proceedings, on a chair he had positioned there, as though he were keeping guard. He and Eva had exchanged glances a few times during the breaks, but he gave no indication as to whether he still knew who she was.

An attendant wheeled a cart into the hall with the help of one of the technicians. On the cart was a boxy device that had a short tube with a lens protruding from the front. It looked like a little tank without tracks. An episcope. Eva recognized it from her days in girls' school, when their geography teacher had projected photographs of alien worlds onto the wall. Usually naked savages standing before their smoking huts. "Is this race more ape or more human? Fräulein Bruhns?" Herr Brautlecht had loved that question. Sometimes, before he arrived, Eva and her classmates would turn on the machine and place pictures, which they had snipped from the papers, underneath of the stars they were currently swooning over. Young men in playful poses with pointy shoes. By contrast, Herr Brautlecht's painted Pygmies fell short of the mark. Eva smiled a little at the memory and watched the technician position the cart opposite a large white screen that had been hung beside the map of the camp. Holding the cord, he searched between the defendants' desks for an electrical outlet. They were probably hoping the device would help save time. Up till now, photographs and other pieces of evidence had been passed around and reviewed in turn by the court, defense, and prosecution, which was inconvenient. The technician turned on the machine. A quivering square of light appeared on the screen. At the technician's instruction, the hall attendant placed a sheet of paper on the projector's glass plate and closed the lid. Blurry words appeared on the screen. The technician turned the lens, and the letters grew more illegible.

"Don't we not need you till this afternoon?" David Miller walked past Eva to his table in the second row.

"Good morning, Herr Miller," she responded.

"We'll see if it turns into one."

Eva tried to craft a clever retort but couldn't think of anything. David took out several colorful folders from his briefcase and arranged them on the table in a specific order. A round, embroidered piece of fabric fell onto the table as he moved. A little cap, which David put back in his pocket.

"What is it you have against me, anyway?"

David did not turn around, but kept sorting his papers. "What makes you think I have anything against you?"

"You don't even say hello to me."

David still refused to look at Eva. "I didn't know you thought it so important: a very good day to you, Fräulein Bruhns."

The technician had finally managed to focus the projector: *Please do not flush sanitary napkins! Toilet will clog!* This sign hung over every ladies' room toilet in the building. The hall attendant and technician grinned.

The lead prosecutor, already suited up in his black robe, entered the auditorium and greeted Eva with a quick but friendly nod. His light-colored hair, which was as fine as an infant's— "angel hair," Annegret said it was called—shone damply. Had it started to rain? It was impossible to tell through the glass panes. David handed the blond man a folder.

"If we don't nail the pharmacist today . . . here's the arrest warrant. He's not waltzing out of here again! And if our man in the moon doesn't comply . . ."

The blond man waved a dismissive hand. "Then what? Then you'll arrest him yourself, is that it? I have repeatedly asked you to exercise greater discretion, Herr Miller. And yet you continue to behave as if you were the hero of a Western."

The blond man turned away from David and stalked across the room toward the chief judge, who had entered through a side door with the two associate judges. His face more closely resembled the full moon than ever, it was true. *"Our man in the moon"* was fitting, Eva thought. She smiled. David glanced at her over his shoulder.

"What are you looking at me like that for?"

He was clearly irked that she had witnessed the rebuke.

"I'm not looking at all."

"I'm not blind."

"I fear you may be suffering from delusions of grandeur, Herr Miller!" Eva had read an article about psychological disorders once that mentioned this term. David angrily opened a dossier. One of the stenotypists appeared in the entrance to the hall, Fräulein Schenke. She was wearing a new suit too, hers a tight fit and softly gleaming pink. She smiled at Eva as she took her seat. Eva flashed a quick smile in return. She didn't especially like Fräulein Schenke, who had a certain shiftiness about her—or "something Catholic," as her father would say. But Eva liked David Miller, she was surprised to realize at that moment. She looked at the back of his head as he bent deeply over the file. She regretted her comment and felt the need to place a hand on his shoulder. Like a friend.

A short time later, the spectators, followed by the prosecution, and then the defendants and their attorneys, flanked by eight policemen, had taken their seats. The last to enter were the judges, and everyone in the courtroom rose upon their appearance. The police lined up behind the defendants' tables, where they more closely resembled a guard of honor. As on every day of the trial, not a single open seat in the gallery remained. Otto Cohn stood rigidly at the witness stand and lightly braced himself against the tabletop with three fingers of his right hand. His big, jet-black hat with the narrow brim made him appear taller than he was. He had refused to take it off. He was wearing his thin leather shoes, no socks, as Eva could see, and his shabby coat. Cohn's beard reminded Eva of the Christmas tree her father and Stefan had carried up to the attic the day after Epiphany for keeping till spring, when they would burn it in the yard. *It looks like he hasn't washed since I spoke to him at the Christmas market. At the very least, why didn't he shave?* Eva thought. Eva was almost ashamed of the man's disheveled appearance, even though she scarcely knew him. Eva couldn't have known that Otto Cohn not only wanted to be heard and seen—no, he intended for those guilty men sitting at the defendants' tables to smell him too. Cohn spoke in German with a loud voice. Strongly accented, perhaps, but easily intelligible. He had insisted. "So that those people there hear me!" And he spoke fast. Fräulein Schenke and the other two girls could barely keep up on their little clicking stenotype machines. Like a mountain stream splashing over rocks, he recounted how he had been deported with his wife and their three young daughters in September '44 from the Romanian city of Hermannstadt, which had at that time belonged to Hungary. "When we arrived at the ramp, got out, there was a crush of people moving forward. I was with wife, three children—three daughters—and I said to them, 'Most important is that we five are together. Everything will be fine.' No sooner had I said that than a soldier stepped between us: 'Men to the right, women to the left!' They broke us from each other. I had not the time to embrace my wife. She screamed after me, 'Come kiss us!' Perhaps some womanly instinct told her the danger that threatened us. I ran to them, kissed my wife, my three children, and then I was pushed back to the other side, and we kept moving forward. Parallel but separated. Between the two platforms. Between the two trains. Suddenly I hear, 'Doctors and pharmacists gather here.' So I join this group. There were thirty-eight doctors from Hermannstadt, and several pharmacists. Suddenly two German officers turned to us. One of them, a high-ranking, handsome, young-looking man asked us nicely, 'Where did you gentlemen study? You, for example, you, for example?' I said, 'In Vienna,' the next said, 'In Wrocław,' and so on. The second officer we recognized immediately, and we whispered to each other, 'Why, that's the pharmacist.' He often worked with us doctors as a fill-in. I said to him, 'Sir, I have two twins, and they require closer care. If you would allow—I'll do whatever work you like, if you would only allow me to remain with my family.' Then he asked, 'Twins?' 'Yes.' 'Where are they?' I pointed and said, 'There they go.' 'Call them back,' he said to me. And then I call my wife and children loudly by their names. They turn around, they come back, and the pharmacist took them by the hand, my two daughters, and led them to another doctor. At his back, he says to me, 'Well, tell him.' I said, 'Captain, sir, I have two twins,' and was about to say more, but he said, 'Later. I don't have time now.'

He sent me off with a wave of his hand. The pharmacist said, 'In that case, they have to return to their side.' My wife and my three children went on their way. I began to sob, and he said to me in Hungarian, 'Ne sírjon. Don't cry. They're just going to bathe. You'll see them again in an hour.' So I went back to my group. I never saw them again. The pharmacist was Defendant Number Seventeen there. The one with the black glasses. At that second, I was grateful in my soul to the pharmacist. I thought he wanted to do something good for me. I only discovered later what it meant to hand over twins to that doctor for his experiments. I also got an explanation for why the doctor hadn't been interested in my girls. My twins were fraternal—they weren't identical. They were very different. One was just a delicate little thing and—"

The chief judge interrupted him. "Herr Cohn, are you certain that you recognize Defendant Number Seventeen as the pharmacist you spoke to on the ramp?"

Instead of answering, Otto Cohn reached into his coat pocket, searched around a little inside, then pulled something out. It was two photographs. He moved toward the bench and placed the pictures before the judge. The chief judge signaled the attendant who had been trained in operating the episcope. He approached earnestly and took the photographs. He turned on the episcope and solemnly placed the first picture on the glass plate. He briefly adjusted the lens, and the enlarged image appeared on the white screen for everyone in the auditorium to see. Eva had seen the photo before, for a fleeting moment, in the open suitcase in the small hotel room. She could study it properly now. Pictured was a family in a yard, gathered there on any other day in life. Just then, the school bell rang next door to the courtroom. The windows in the glass panes wall were open a crack, but the schoolyard behind the municipal building remained quiet. Eva knew that vacation had begun. Stefan had been put on the train to Hamburg to visit Grandma the day before, laden with admonitions and snacks enough for five trips.

Now, on the witness stand, Otto Cohn gazed at the picture and recalled how his oldest daughter, Miriam, hadn't wanted her photo taken. He and his wife had first implored her, then bribed her with hazelnut chocolate. It was clear in the image that her cheeks were still stuffed with it. Her lips were pressed together and all she could manage was a droll smile. Cohn thought that it was right, what he had planned.

The chief judge turned to the defendants' tables. "Does the defendant know this family?"

"No."

The pharmacist opened the daily paper and began to read, as if none of this applied to him. The attendant placed the second photograph into the device. Even in the blurry projection, one could identify Defendant Number Seventeen in the same yard. After the attendant focused the image, Otto Cohn and the pharmacist could be seen in the light of what was probably the setting sun. After a good day's work, with a good glass of wine. Beside each other.

"Does the defendant recognize this photograph? Do you admit to knowing the witness? Remove those sunglasses!" The pharmacist reluctantly took off his glasses and shrugged indifferently. He leaned toward his attorney. They whispered. Eva noticed that the White Rabbit seemed at a loss. He stood up.

"My client does not wish to comment on this matter."

At that, the blond man rose and read aloud the prepared arrest warrant.

"The statements provided by the witness are indubitable. The defendant's participation in the selections on the ramp has been attested . . ."

Eva could see the papers shaking in his hand, something David spotted as well, and he briefly turned around to Eva. They shared a look—they were equally tense.

"Your Honor, it is no longer in keeping with our laws that the defendant remain at liberty," the blond man continued. "We demand his transfer into custody!" Silence.

The chief judge withdrew to confer with his associate judges. Barely anyone used the quarter-hour break to visit the restroom or purchase refreshments in the foyer. Eva stayed in her seat too. In front of her, David was scribbling long rows of letters in a notebook. The people in the gallery either waited silently or whispered quietly among themselves. The blond man stood in the open doorway to the auditorium and spoke with the attorney general, who had been like the little man in a weather house during this trial, arriving on the scene periodically, then disappearing inside his little house for days on end, or so it seemed to Eva. Both men were looking at Otto Cohn, who had sat down at the witness stand. He had moved his chair to give himself a direct view of the defendants, who were using the break to doze or review documents. The pharmacist ignored Cohn and had turned around in his seat by extending an arm over the back of his neighbor's chair. He was saying something to the raptor-faced man, the main defendant, who—as during any short recess—sat motionless and erect while keeping a close watch on the people in the room. He now nodded at the pharmacist and said something in reply; both men appeared calm. Eva could not take her eyes off the pharmacist. He looked like a frog, a fat, happy frog ribbiting at his former boss. She was staring over at him when he suddenly turned back around and looked straight at her. The main defendant had also turned his attention toward her. They both studied Eva from across the room. She held her breath, as though someone else's foul breath were wafting over her. The pharmacist bowed ironically in her direction. Eva quickly grabbed at her general dictionary and began to page through it busily. She discovered what the word for "pedestrian crossing" was in Polish.

After the judges had returned and the courtroom had quieted back down, the chief judge announced that he would grant the prosecution's motion. Based on sufficient evidence regarding the charge of "aiding and abetting murder," Defendant Number Seventeen would be detained and transferred to custody at the conclusion of the day's proceedings. The pharmacist put on his sunglasses and crossed his arms across his expensive suit. He remained silent. Some of his fellow defendants protested, including the main defendant: "This lacks any basis whatsoever!" The blond man betrayed no emotion, but Eva caught him making a quick fist with his right hand under the table. A few people in the gallery applauded. David Miller impulsively spun around and whispered to Eva, "And this is just the beginning!" Eva nodded. She felt as happy as if it were her own victory. The chief judge then asked Otto Cohn, who had followed this development blankly, to detail his arrival at the camp and the following months. Cohn stood, again rested three fingers on the table, and described everything he had experienced. He spoke for more than an hour, and was only occasionally asked for quick clarifications. He had frequently seen the main defendant, the camp adjutant, who rode his bicycle from block to block, and he had heard about Defendant Number Four, whom everyone feared, and who had been dubbed the "Beast." He had seen the medical orderly, Defendant Number Ten, rest a cane over the throat of a prisoner lying on the ground, then place his feet on either end and thus strangle the man to death. "That's a dirty lie!" bellowed the man, whose patients lovingly called him "Papa" when he entered their hospital room, brought them breakfast, or changed a dressing. Eva was starting to feel nauseous. Cohn was now spouting on about everything they hadn't had at the camp: bread, warmth, protection, quiet, sleep, and friendship. And about what, by contrast, had existed in excess: dirt, roaring, pain, fear, and death. Cohn was sweating, and he took off his hat, revealing a partially bald head that made his beard appear all the more unruly.

"The day of liberation, I was naked, weighed thirty-four kilograms, was covered in a grayish black rash, and was coughing up pus. When I looked down at my body, it was like looking at an X-ray of myself. Just a skeleton. But I swore I'd survive, because I had to let people know what happened." Cohn placed his hat on the table and wiped the perspiration from his forehead with the threadbare sleeve of his coat. David thought that, although no longer gaunt, he still appeared doomed to die. Cohn looked at the defendants, as though expecting an answer. But the men kept quiet.

The medical orderly alone got to his feet, drew himself up, and brayed in all directions, "I strongly object! I have never done anything like that! I'm not even capable of such things! Ask my patients—they call me 'Papa,' because I'm so good to them! Ask them!" There was an outburst of indignation among the spectators, and the chief judge called forcibly for order. Eva was still fighting her nausea; she swallowed and swallowed, but her mouth was dry and her heart kept beating faster. The defense attorney stood and asked Cohn who this prisoner was, whom his client had allegedly killed with a cane. And when this had supposedly occurred. Cohn didn't know the name and could no longer remember the date, but he had seen it. The attorney, pleased with this response, took a seat, pulled out his pocket watch from the folds of his robe, and checked it.

"No further questions."

The prosecution had concluded their questioning as well, and the chief judge dismissed the witness. Eva was relieved that it was almost time for the lunch break; she was still swallowing and breathing through her mouth. But then Otto Cohn raised his hand.

"There's one final thing I must say. I know that all of the gentlemen here claim not to have known what was taking place in the camp. By the second day I was there, I knew everything. And I wasn't alone. There was this boy—he was sixteen. His name was Andreas Rapaport. He was in the eleventh barracks. He wrote in blood, on the wall, in Hungarian, 'Andreas Rapaport, lived sixteen years.' Two days later they came for him. He screamed to me, 'Uncle, I know that I'm going to die! Tell my mother I thought of her until the very last moment!' But I couldn't give her the message. The mother died too. This boy knew what was happening there!" Cohn took a few steps toward the defendants and shook both his fists at them. "This boy knew. And you didn't?! You didn't?!"

Cohn appeared to Eva like a figure from the Bible. Like the wrathful Lord. Were she one of the defendants, she'd have been frightened. But the men sitting there in their suits and tasteful neckties simply regarded Cohn with scorn, amusement, or indifference. Defendant Number Four, the "Beast" with the face of a ferret, even covered his nose with his hand, as though trying to block out a bad odor.

"Thank you, sir, the questioning has concluded. Herr Cohn, we no longer need you." The chief judge had leaned in, to the microphone. Cohn turned around and appeared confused, as though he'd suddenly forgotten where he was.

"You are dismissed."

At that, he gave a terse nod, turned, and walked toward the exit. Eva noticed immediately that Cohn had left his hat on the table. Without thinking, she stood up and headed for it while an associate judge announced the lunch break. She took the hat and followed Cohn into the foyer.

Several reporters were already queueing at the three small telephone booths that had been installed for the trial. People were speaking on the phones in the booths, one of which was white with cigarette smoke, entirely obscuring the smoking man inside. But as she passed, Eva overheard him saying, "Yes, that's what I've been explaining to you: the pharmacist has been arrested . . . he was part of the selection!" The air was stale and smelled of cafeteria food—potatoes and stuffed cabbage rolls, which were served almost daily. Eva still felt nauseous, which she forgot for the moment.

"Herr Cohn! Wait, you forgot your hat . . ." But Cohn did not seem to hear Eva. He strode toward the exit with the double glass doors, opened them effortlessly, and left the building. Through the window Eva could see Cohn march on without pause, straight ahead, step by step. She hurriedly wrenched open the heavy doors. She ran into the courtyard in front of the municipal building and was horrified to see that Cohn, without a glance to the left or right, was walking straight into the broad, busy street.

"Herr Cohn!! Stop right there! Stop!" Cohn did not respond, but continued moving like one of Stefan's colorful wind-up tin toys. A harlequin. Eva wished she could run faster, but her new skirt was so fitted that she couldn't take bigger steps. She stumbled forward. Cohn was between parked cars now. She had almost reached him. And then he stepped into the lane, into traffic, as though wading into a rushing river, one second before Eva could have grabbed him by the coat sleeve. Cohn immediately was struck by the hood of a white vehicle. Eva heard the collision. He staggered back, spun about, and fell forward like a sack. Eva swooned briefly, as if she were trying to fall with him, then she knelt down beside him and turned him onto his back with trembling hands. The car had braked a few meters on, tires screeching, while other cars honked and some drivers rolled down their windows to yell for having to swerve. They didn't see the man on the side of the road as they passed. Cohn was white in the face, his eyes were closed, and Eva stroked his forehead. "Herr Cohn, can you hear me? Hello, open your eyes. Can you hear me?" Eva took his hand and searched for his pulse, but all she could hear was her own heart. Someone crouched down beside her on the asphalt. David.

"What happened?" David lifted Cohn's head slightly. The driver of the white car had gotten out and approached them; he was a very young man, a new driver. He stared at the unconscious bearded man in terror.

"Is he dead? My God, what a sound! It wasn't my fault!" A rivulet of blood trickled out of the corner of Cohn's mouth and into his wild, filthy beard. Eva stood up, took a few steps to the side, braced herself against the back of a parked car with her right hand, and pressed her other hand, which still held the hat, against her belly. It looked like she was taking a bow after a performance, but instead she vomited onto the pavement in several small bursts. David appeared beside her and handed her a tissue. *A paper tissue! Typical Yank!* Eva thought in a daze. *No, wait, he's Canadian!* And for the first time, David looked at her warmly.

Twenty minutes later, an ambulance snaked its way through midday traffic, blue lights flashing and siren howling, toward the municipal building. A small cluster of people had formed around the man on the street. Several muttered about how horribly he reeked—he must be a tramp! Probably drunk too! A policeman with an absurdly small notepad was questioning the young driver, who kept shaking his head. A second officer was asking reporters, who had eagerly streamed out of the building, to refrain from taking photographs. Eva knelt down beside Cohn again and held his hand, which felt limp and cold. She didn't notice the main defendant standing directly behind her and scowling at Cohn with his raptor's face. "This street is too busy! There should be a crosswalk here!" he said to his wife, whose nose, poking out from under her little hat, looked even pointier than usual. The ambulance stopped beside them, the siren cut out, and Eva watched helplessly as Otto Cohn was quickly examined by a doctor, then loaded on a gurney into the ambulance by two paramedics.

"How bad is it?" she asked the doctor.

"We'll see."

"Can I ride with him?"

The doctor looked at Eva. "Who are you? His daughter?"

"No, I'm . . . I'm not related."

"I'm sorry, but in that case, no."

"Where are you bringing him?"

"City Hospital."

One of the medics slammed the doors shut. The ambulance

drove off and was soon out of sight, but the sound of its sirens lingered for some time. The crowd dissipated. David gave Cohn's name and home address to the policeman with the tiny notepad. Then the officer turned to Eva: "You were an eyewitness?" He took Eva's name, and she explained that Cohn was at fault for the accident. As she said it, a large truck hurtled past. The policeman didn't hear her, and she had to repeat, "He caused the accident himself." The officer thanked her and joined his colleague. Eva realized she was still holding the hat.

AFTER LUNCH, during which no one spoke about the accident, as if in secret agreement, Eva translated testimony provided by a Pole who had been a prisoner functionary in the storerooms. The old man described how everything was taken from people as soon as they arrived at the camp. The witness enumerated the foreign currencies, jewelry, furs, and securities that had accumulated over the camp's five years. He recalled most of the numbers exactly, and although this was what Eva had first mastered in the Polish language, she had to focus to avoid making a mistake. She forgot about Cohn for the moment. But when she reached the Berger Strasse apartment just before six that evening, she placed the black hat on the shelf above the coat rack and headed straight for the telephone, without taking off her coat or turning on the hallway light. In the half darkness, she dialed the number for the hospital. As she listened and waited to be connected, she spotted a small, reflective puddle on the floorboards by the door to the living room. Purzel was nowhere to be seen and hadn't come to greet her, as he normally did. A pleasant female voice sounded on the other end of the line: "City Hospital, reception?"

Eva asked about an old man—Otto Cohn, from Hungary—who had been admitted that afternoon. He'd had an accident, at the municipal building. How was he doing? The friendly lady on the other end of the line declined to provide Eva with any information. Eva then asked to be connected with the nursery, with her sister.

In the dusky examination room of the nursery, Doctor Küssner and Annegret were in the middle of an argument. They had only turned on the light above the examination table, typically used to illuminate their little patients. The empty table below looked sad and abandoned. They were both upset, but whispering, so that no one in the corridor outside could hear them fighting.

"I don't understand you, Annegret. This is such a rare opportunity!" Küssner's wife had taken their two children on an impromptu trip to visit relatives, yet Annegret refused to meet up with him that evening.

"I don't feel like it."

"It doesn't have to be at my house, although there would be nothing strange about a nurse visiting me at home to discuss something."

Annegret leaned against the cupboard that provided the base for their oversized scale—the most incorruptible of pediatric instruments, with its pitiless dial and cold metal pan. Annegret crossed her thick arms over her nurse's coat.

"Hartmut, I'm simply not interested in aligning my life to fit yours. We have plans for next Thursday. I'm not available before then."

"You are so miserably stubborn."

Doctor Küssner stepped toward Annegret and somewhat

helplessly stroked her blond hair, which she had recently dyed and appeared almost white.

"Don't you understand? I want to enjoy this brief moment of freedom. With you."

"Get a divorce. Then you'll be free forever." Annegret didn't really mean it, but she wanted to hear Küssner hedge and fall back on the old phrases she had so often heard from married men.

"I've told you, I just need a little more time." *Yes, that's one of their favorites*, Annegret thought, pleased. She smiled. Küssner pulled up her uniform and pressed his hand between her legs, where it then lingered, motionless. He was an inexperienced lover. Annegret pushed off his hand and moved away from him. He sat down on a metal swivel stool and suddenly looked very tired.

"I pictured this differently."

"What, having an affair? All you need is a little practice. People are machines, after all. Anyone can turn their feelings on or off. You just need to know which button to push."

Küssner stared at Annegret.

"I worry about you."

Annegret was about to make a funny face, but was alarmed to realize that Küssner was actually concerned. She went to the door.

"I need commitment from you, Hartmut, not feelings."

Küssner rose and threw up his hands in defeat.

"Fine, then I'll see you Thursday, as usual."

"And don't you dare fall in love with me!" Annegret warned him earnestly. Küssner laughed, as though he'd been found out, and was about to respond, when the door was torn open. Annegret and Doctor Küssner were standing at a harmless distance from one another, they were both relieved to see.

Nurse Heide peered in and said, with characteristic disapproval, "Your sister is on the line."

Küssner addressed Annegret in an overly businesslike tone, "Thank you, Nurse, I think that covers it."

Annegret crossed the hallway, where the night-light had already been turned on, and stepped up to reception. The phone receiver lay on the counter. She steeled herself for the conversation, because it was unusual for Eva to call her at work.

"Did something happen to Dad?"

"No, Annie, don't worry, I just need your help." Annegret leaned against the counter. Nurse Heide had sat down on the other side and was labeling forms and trying to look busy. Annegret was then astonished to hear that Eva wanted her to check on someone in emergency surgery.

"I don't understand a word of what you're saying, Eva. Who had an accident? Otto who? Who is that?"

"A witness. In the trial."

Annegret fell silent. Her eyes focused on the wall behind Nurse Heide, at next month's schedule hanging there. The days were clearly marked with colorful fields. Hers were light blue, like the armbands on the baby boys she liked so much. An especially sweet little nugget had been born two days ago and was now in the first nursery. Michael. He had weighed nearly three kilos at birth.

"I'll check," Annegret said into the receiver.

"Thank you. Please call me back as soon as you find out."

Annegret hung up. Nurse Heide looked at Annegret quizzically, her expression surly as ever. Annegret ignored her. She crossed the hallway and paused at the threshold of the first nursery. None of the children lying here in the dark was crying yet. Annegret still had half an hour before feeding. She crossed the room to Michael's bassinet and patted his little head; he was awake, and he stared past her with black eyes and shook his fists erratically.

AT THE BRUHNSES' APARTMENT, Eva fetched a bucket and cleaning rag from the storage closet off the kitchen. She wiped up the puddle Purzel had left in the hallway. They hadn't changed his walking schedule, but he had recently peed in the apartment a few times. He was already eleven, so it was probably a sign of old age. Eva tried not to think about the fit Stefan would throw if they had to put the dog to sleep. She washed and wrung out the rag in the kitchen sink, then looked at the clock. Her call with Annegret was half an hour ago. Did these inquiries really take that long? At that moment the phone rang. Eva dashed into the hallway and answered, "Eva Bruhns here?!" But it was Jürgen, calling from West Berlin. He was there for a few days on business, to visit a factory in East Berlin that manufactured bedclothes. Jürgen seemed cheerful. He told her he'd been positively surprised by the quality of the East German products. He hoped to get the linens for a good price. The Wall was an oppressive presence. He'd had an excellent *Tafelspitz* for dinner. He was staying at a hotel on Ku'damm, with a view of the destroyed Kaiser Wilhelm Memorial Church. He thought it was a mistake not to rebuild the church. "We don't need these memorials. People already carry them around within themselves. Within their souls."

But Eva didn't have the patience for one of Jürgen's philosophical diatribes. "Jürgen, I'm sorry, but I'm expecting a call."

"From whom?"

"I'll tell you in person when you get back. Okay?"

Jürgen was silent, but Eva could picture his face plainly, the way his eyes darkened in suspicion, yet he was too proud to ask any more questions. Jürgen was a jealous person, something Eva had noticed a few times while out together, when other men would ask her to dance. But it flattered her. After all, it meant she was important to him.

"Fine, I suppose we're hanging up now. Have a good night." He really was hurt.

"All right. Well, you know we'll see each other tomorrow. Sleep tight," Eva responded. She waited for him to hang up.

But then his voice buzzed out of the receiver, "By the way, my father and his wife want to meet you. We're going to dinner on Friday. To the InterConti. Agreed?"

Eva was stunned but answered happily, "Yes, of course! What did you tell them?"

"That I want to marry you." Jürgen's voice was strangely icy as he said it, but Eva didn't care.

"What? And? What did they say?"

"Like I said: they want to meet you." Jürgen hung up. Eva needed a moment to fully comprehend that the "breakthrough," as she'd dubbed it for herself, had finally come. The fear of Jürgen leaving her was finally banished. The Schoormanns knew that she existed. That she was their son's bride. Eva called loudly for Purzel, since there was no one else in the apartment she could hug with joy. But the dog didn't come. Eva went into the living room and squatted down. There was Purzel, a black spot with two shining eyes, in his usual spot under the sofa. Considering how sly he could be, and how painfully he would nip people when they least expected, he had a highly pronounced sense of shame.

"Come on out, I'm not going to rip your head off." Purzel didn't move, but she could see the whites of his eyes. Eva reached out and slowly pulled the dog out from under the sofa by his collar. Then she picked him up. The phone rang again, and Eva carried Purzel into the hallway and answered for a second time. It was Annegret. She had spoken to the chief physician in the emergency department.

"That Cohn fellow, he's doing fine."

Eva exhaled in relief. "How wonderful. It really did look bad—"

"It was just a concussion."

"Can I visit him? I have his hat—"

"He's already been discharged. It was his idea."

"What? Oh . . . thank you, Annie, I'm so happy. Thank you."

Click! Annegret hung up. Or the connection was cut. Eva squeezed Purzel, who struggled in protest. "What do you think about that?! Today's my lucky day!" Eva spun around the hallway with Purzel and kissed his short, wiry fur. "And I won't tell anyone what you did. I promise!" Purzel snapped at Eva's face in response. She dropped him. "You always were a little beast!"

AT THE HOSPITAL, Nurse Heide and a colleague wheeled the babies to their mothers in the maternity ward. Annegret was tending to Michael, whose mother was not yet lactating following the difficult delivery and was still too weak to bottle-feed him. Annegret was at the nurses' station, filling a glass bottle with four tablespoons of powdered milk and boiling water from the kettle. From the pocket of her uniform, she pulled out the glass syringe containing the brownish liquid. She slowly added the contents to the milk mixture, screwed the nipple into place, and shook the bottle vigorously. Then she entered the first nursery, plucked Michael from his bassinet, and sat down with him in a cozy chair by the window. Michael flailed his head about and pressed his mouth against Annegret's smock. She smiled—he was looking for his mother's breast. She tested the temperature of the baby formula by pressing the bottle to her cheek. Then she put the rubber nipple in the boy's mouth. He immediately began feeding hungrily and evenly. He made little chortling sounds as he did. Annegret looked down at him, and she felt the small, warm body and the trust it had in her. A great sense of peace spread through her body, a heavy, golden honey that flowed warmly into all of her limbs. She forgot everything—she forgot that she had just asked the head nurse in emergency surgery about Otto Cohn. She forgot that the older nurse, whom she knew casually, had taken her across the hallway to a special room. Her colleague described the imposition the patient had presented. His condition had been utterly squalid. He had smelled terribly. Annegret also forgot that the nurse had opened the door to that windowless room with a cross on the wall. There, covered by a white cloth, lay a figure on a gurney. The nurse explained that a rib had pierced his lung. He had already suffocated by the time the medics loaded him up. Annegret gazed at Michael suckling blissfully and no longer heard the nurse's question: "Did you know him?" Annegret forgot that she had stepped up to the gurney, and that beside the body's blanketed feet, she had seen the man's small collection of possessions. A shabby wallet with several new bills peeking out, a flattened pocket watch, whose hands had stopped at ten minutes to one, and two old photographs. She forgot that she lied to her sister about this troubled man.

LATER THAT EVENING, just as David was leaving the office, the lead prosecutor informed him that the witness had died as a result of the accident. The men stood facing each other in the office door and shared a silent look. The thrill of the pharmacist's arrest had taken on a bitter aftertaste. The blond man then asked that David tend to the formalities. Cohn had no one left in Budapest who would pay for his body to be brought back home. They would need to apply for a pauper's funeral with the authorities. David assured him that he would of course see to it. The blond man watched him walk down the corridor and disappear through the glass door at the end. He couldn't help it—he was starting to like the young man.

As David left the office building and stepped into the damp evening air, his legs felt unusually heavy. Cohn must have died as he and Fräulein Bruhns knelt beside him. His soul had slipped between them and climbed into the heavens. Or disappeared down a manhole. Depended on one's views of eternity. David was tired. But he wasn't ready to return to his room yet. He took a left, to visit Sissi. He knew that her shift at Suzi's didn't begin till ten, which would still give them a good hour together. He hadn't returned to the bar after their first encounter, but had instead tried other establishments and their ladies.

Not too long ago, though, he'd been in a chilly, cramped fruit and vegetable shop buying three oranges, because he had a cold and his mother's lectures about vitamins echoed in his mind. As the warmly bundled shopkeeper, who was wearing wool gloves with the fingertips missing, packed the fruit into a paper bag as carefully as if they were raw eggs, another woman—slender and somewhat pinched—entered the shop. She slowly took off her gloves and checked the potatoes in the crates by turning them over and over. She wore bright red nail polish, which didn't match her otherwise colorless appearance. "These caught some frost." "Now listen here! I only sell the best products!" The woman seemed strangely familiar to David. He stared at her while paying for his oranges and dug through his mind, trying to remember how he knew her. From the municipal building? From the prosecution? She didn't look like one of the older typists. Or was she a cleaner in the office? She sensed his gaze, turned to him, and pleasantly said, "*Guten Tag.*" At that moment, he picked up a vaguely sweet smell. It was Sissi, whom he had been in bed with. Whom he had been inside, and inside whom he had burst. David turned as red as his hair. Sissi smiled, and her face was transformed into a web of fine wrinkles David hadn't noticed in the darkened brothel room. He carried the potatoes home for her like a schoolboy hoping to earn a few pennies, and had visited her several times since. In her small apartment off a back courtyard, where she lived with her fourteen-year-old son—an "occupational mishap," as she said—they would sit at the kitchen table, talking and smoking. Sometimes they watched a show on Sissi's new television, which was her pride and joy. They were like two friendly dogs that liked each other and lay peacefully side by side. He hadn't slept with her a second time. It would have felt inappropriate, now that he knew Sissi in her real life. She wasn't interested in hearing about the trial. The war had been hard on her too. Especially after the war, when the Russians reached Baulitz, where she'd had a small farm with her husband. On the outskirts of town.

Tonight, Sissi noticed that David wasn't behaving as superior as usual. He seemed shaken and started talking as soon as the door opened: about traffic, the weather, the strange smell just now in the front building. While Sissi washed her stockings in the sink, her back toward him in the narrow kitchen, David sat up tall at the table and leaned against the wall and talked—not about Cohn, but about himself. Himself and his big brother. They had been deported to the camp from Berlin. His brother had been in the resistance and was sent to the political department. He was tortured to death in an interrogation. And they called him, the baby brother, to dispose of the body. He hadn't even recognized him anymore. The interrogation was performed by the head of the political department. Defendant Number Four. When David reached the end of his story, Sissi turned around and began hanging the wrung out, but still damp, stockings on a line she had stretched the length of the kitchen. David waited for her to say something in sympathy or outrage. But all she asked, without looking at him, was, "Have you told your boss yet?" David fell silent for a moment, snubbed, then snapped with disproportionate severity, "You really don't understand, do you? I'd be out on my ear!" He elaborated that having a personal stake would bar him from working on the trial. They called that conflict of interest! He'd had to make a decision. And he had decided not to be a witness, but to convict the perpetrators by law. Dramatic music swelled in the next room. Sissi's son was hunkered down in front of the television in the bed-sitter, watching a crime movie. David broke off. There were shots and someone screamed. Sissi continued hanging her stockings. David thought he must not have told the story properly. He cleared his throat and added that he'd never told this to anyone. Which was also a lie, because he had been out twice with Fräulein Schenke, the attractive stenotypist. He had confided in her the second time. And sworn her to absolute secrecy. Since then, Fräulein Schenke had sent him pitying looks from across the courtroom. And it wasn't just her—the other girls had been acting more solicitous toward him too, all except for Fräulein Bruhns. The story apparently hadn't reached her yet. Sissi had finished hanging her fourteen stockings. Several of the toes were dripping gently on the stone floor and David's thighs. Sissi said she had a headache. It wasn't good to think back on bad things. "You know," she said, as she opened David a bottle of beer, "I have this little chamber in here." She pointed at her belly, directly below her heart. "I piled everything in there and turned out the light and locked the door. The chamber aches sometimes, but then I just take a teaspoon of baking soda. I know it's there. But luckily I don't know what's inside anymore. Five Russians? Ten Russians? My dead husband? And how many dead children? No idea. Door's shut and light's out."

THE NEXT MORNING, right after breakfast, Eva packed the narrow-brimmed hat in a large paper bag and set out for the inn. The reception desk was deserted, and the murmur of voices and clatter of silverware emerged from a room behind it to the left. The guests were having breakfast, while the innkeeper's wife strolled between the tables with the coffeepot. The inn-keeper was nowhere to be seen. Eva remembered which room Cohn had booked. She climbed the stairs to the second floor and walked down the dark, carpeted corridor. She stopped outside the door bearing the number eight. She knocked softly. "Herr Cohn? I've brought you something." There was no response, and she knocked again, waited, and then tried the door handle. The room was empty, the window wide open, revealing a tall firewall, and the bright curtains moved in the breeze. Despite the fresh air from outdoors, a penetrating smell hung in the room. *Like gas or the chloroform they give you at the dentist to numb the pain*, Eva thought and involuntarily covered her nose and mouth with her hand. She drew back into the hallway.

"What are you snooping around for, Fräulein?" The innkeeper approached.

"I wanted to visit Herr Cohn."

He looked her over with his slightly puffy eyes. "Weren't you the one who first brought him here? Are you related to him?"

Eva shook her head. "No, I just have something of his . . ." Eva lifted the paper bag by way of explanation, but the man wasn't interested. He stepped into the room.

"He stayed in here for weeks," he noted and closed the window. "They just don't know the first thing about personal hygiene and care. So now I need to clear the lice out of all the cracks. And it's not like you can just ask nicely—you have to fumigate."

"Did he leave?"

The innkeeper turned to face Eva. "No, he was hit and killed by a car."

Eva gaped at the man and shook her head incredulously. "But . . . he was . . . I thought it was just a concussion."

"Beats me. One of the prosecutors, or something, already stopped by early this morning, red-headed guy—he picked up his suitcase. Everything's paid up. Except the fumigation. I've got to cough that up myself, of course. Unless you were planning to pay?" Eva turned and slowly made her way down the corridor without answering, the paper bag in her left hand. She brushed the wall with three fingers of her right hand. She felt she needed the support.

WHEN EVA GOT BACK to the Bruhnses' apartment half an hour later, she was surprised to hear noises coming from her room. Voices and laughter. Her mother and sister were standing at her opened wardrobe and rummaging through her clothing. They had already pulled out two of her best dresses and hung them side by side from the wardrobe door. Eva frowned at the two women. "What are you doing here?"

"We're trying to help you!" Annegret declared, without turning to face Eva.

"We're looking to see what you should wear tonight, child. You've got to look stunning for the Schoormanns," Edith added.

"But you can't just come into my room and go through my wardrobe—" Eva protested. They both ignored her objection. Instead, Annegret pointed out the dark blue sheath dress hanging from the door.

"I prefer this one, because it's so slimming, but Mum likes the light brown one. You know Mum's taste can be a bit common, though."

Edith playfully threatened Annegret with a raised hand. "You had better watch out!"

"Well, just look at you in that old sack." Annegret tugged at the blue checkered smock Edith wore whenever she wasn't working at the restaurant.

"How about that hair of yours? Like cotton candy. It defies the laws of nature—"

"Stop it!" Eva cried out so earnestly that Edith and Annegret immediately ceased their sparring. Eva placed the paper bag containing the hat on the bed and sat down heavily beside it. Edith eyed her searchingly and felt her forehead with the back of her hand.

"Are you getting sick?"

Annegret waved off her mother's concern. "Nonsense, Mum, she's just nervous. It'll be fine, Evie! You'll soon belong to high society yourself!" Annegret smiled somewhat spitefully and turned her attention back to the contents of the wardrobe. Eva looked at her sister's broad back.

"You told me that all Otto Cohn had was a concussion." Annegret, who was arranging a white cardigan over the dark blue dress to see if it matched, froze.

"I did what?"

"Who's Cohn?" Edith asked, confused.

"He's dead," Eva said in Annegret's direction, ignoring her mother. Annegret hung the white cardigan back up.

"All I did was pass along what the chief physician told me."

"His injuries must have been more serious. He must have died on the street somewhere, after leaving your hospital. How could you let him go?"

"How should I know? How the hell is this any of my concern, Eva?!" Annegret spun around and glared hotly at Eva, her expression slightly walleyed in her indignation. Eva recalled that Annegret had sometimes looked like this when they were younger. It happened whenever someone accused her of having eaten something from the pantry. Eva was shocked to realize her sister was lying.

"Now would someone please clue me in on who you're talking about?" Edith asked impatiently, as she ran a lint brush over the light brown suit.

"A witness from the trial, Mum. Yesterday he—"

"Oh, I see," Edith interrupted brusquely and raised the hand holding the brush to stop her. It was clear she didn't want to hear about it. Eva studied the two women, who had again turned their backs to her and were digging through her clothing, as if she weren't there. Eva suddenly felt like she was no longer at home in her own room. She stood up.

"Could you please leave?" They both turned and hesitated for a moment, then Edith handed Eva the light brown suit.

"Listen to me, wear this one—it's modest and tasteful, and you'll make a respectable impression. You're still going to wash your hair, aren't you?" Edith left without awaiting a reply. Annegret also headed for the door and shrugged regretfully.

"We just wanted to give you some advice. There's no helping some people." With that, she left too.

Once Eva was alone in the room, she hung the dresses back in the wardrobe and closed the doors. She took the hat out of the paper bag and turned it over in her hands. The jet-black velvet had rubbed off in a few spots, and the violet lining had come loose. The inside band, once blue-and-white-striped, was now a shiny, greasy black from sweat and dirt. The words *Lindmann Hats—Hermannstadt—Telephone 553* were embroidered in cursive on a cloth label sewn to the inside. Eva looked around the room. Then she pushed together a few books on her shelf and placed the hat on the spot she'd cleared.

SHORTLY BEFORE SEVEN THAT EVENING, Jürgen's car pulled up beneath the streetlight outside the house. Eva was not wearing either the dark blue dress or the light brown suit under her wool coat. She had opted for a maroon silk dress with a plunging neckline, as it was the most elegant piece she owned. She wasn't wearing a hat. She had styled her updo higher than usual. Her pumps made her seem even taller, which Jürgen was startled to discover as he opened the car door for her. He also noticed that Eva didn't seem nervous, and he made a joke about it. She did not respond. She had felt strangely numb since that morning. As though she were wrapped in thick cotton wool. Jürgen's nerves, meanwhile, were on edge, and he lit a cigarette and smoked as he drove, something Eva had never seen him do. They listened in silence to the news on the car radio. The announcer reported that demonstrations for racial equality had been held in several cities across the United States. A Sheraton hotel in San Francisco, in the state of California, had been occupied by protesters because hotel management discriminated against black job applicants. More than three hundred people were arrested. The weather forecast, which promised spring-like temperatures climbing over twelve degrees Celsius, was followed by a music show—*The Friday-Night Record Bin*, which Eva listened to whenever she stayed in. The young disc jockey's voice cracked as he announced that the Beatles had released a new single. Listeners were hearing it here first! "Can't buy me lo-ove! Lo-ove! Can't buy me lo-ove!" the singers screamed ardently, and without any musical introduction, from the little car speakers. At the fourth "love," Jürgen turned off the radio. They had argued about the Beatles before. Eva liked their songs. She thought their music was fun, and the four young Englishmen themselves cheeky and attractive. Jürgen had asserted that their music was little more than haphazard noise. Eva had replied that he was as uptight as her parents. She was not in the mood for another argument tonight and withheld comment. She secretly decided, though, to buy the new single in the music department at Hertie's on Monday. Those few measures had just helped lighten her subdued mood.

A short time later, the InterContinental Hotel appeared before them like an unscalable wall blocking out the dark red evening sky. "Have you ever been inside?" Jürgen asked. Eva had not. "Seven hundred rooms. And every last one has its own bathroom and television set." Jürgen turned the car directly toward

the building, and for a brief moment, Eva thought they were going to crash into it, when suddenly the vehicle dove down, and
they followed a ramp into the parking garage under the hotel. Eva
had never driven underground in a car. The ceiling appeared to be
sinking, a few dim lights glowed as they passed, and the colorful
symbols and lines on the concrete floor were indecipherable and
mysterious to her. She clung to the handle above her door. Jürgen
steered the car confidently through the labyrinth of columns and
parked by a steel door that read "Stairs to Hotel." Jürgen helped
Eva out of the car and held her for a moment, and she thought he
might want to kiss her. Instead, he said, "Please don't mention the
trial. It could upset my father. As you know, he was imprisoned
for years." Eva was stunned. Ever since she started going to the
municipal building regularly, Jürgen hadn't said a word about her
work. Evidently it was on his mind more than she'd thought. Eva
nodded. "Of course. Has he been doing all right?" Jürgen nodded,
but didn't look at her as he did. They stepped into the mirrored
elevator. The copper-colored panel beside the door had twenty-
two light-up buttons. Jürgen pressed the top one. As the elevator
climbed, Eva was captivated by their reflection as a couple, the way
they appeared over and over, in big boxes that grew smaller and
smaller, at once close then farther and farther away. Eva thought
they looked good together: Jürgen with his black hair and navy
blue wool coat, herself blond in pale checkers. Like husband and
wife. She caught Jürgen's eye in one of the reflections. They both
had to smile. The elevator stopped a few times, and other guests
entered. It got crowded. The elevator finally went *ping*, the uppermost light glowed, and the doors opened to the rooftop restaurant. Eva, Jürgen, and the remaining guests were all drawn first to
the panoramic window, where they took in the view. "The lights

in the houses look like fallen stars," Eva said softly. Jürgen stroked her cheek and said, "Don't worry, Eva. I think my father had a good day today." But it sounded as if he were saying it more to calm himself, than Eva. She squeezed his hand. In the vestibule outside the coatroom, they were greeted by an employee in a dark suit. Herr Schoormann and his wife were already waiting in the Manhattan Bar, he informed them. He helped Eva with her coat. Jürgen's eyes fell on her exposed cleavage. "Was that really necessary?" he hissed. Eva flinched; it felt as if he had slapped her. She laid her hand over her low-cut neckline. "Well, there's no changing it now." Jürgen offered her his arm, which she reluctantly took. The amicable mood was extinguished.

Walther Schoormann sat perched on a swivel stool at the luminous, ovoid chrome bar in the crowded lounge. Brigitte—in elegant, high-necked black—stood by him, dabbing a dampened napkin on a stain on the collar of his suit coat, which was too big for him these days. A man in a tuxedo played soft, cheery music on a black grand piano.

"Brigitte, leave it be!"

"It wasn't there back at the house. How did you manage it this time?"

Walther Schoormann saw his son enter. On his arm was an attractive, perhaps not overly elegant, but seemingly upright young woman. Her dress looked a bit cheap, the neckline too low for the occasion. But there was nothing calculating to her gaze, Walther was relieved to note. *Beautifully thick hair,* Brigitte Schoormann thought, *but what a horribly old-fashioned updo. But that neckline. Daring. Interesting contradiction.* Eva sensed the couple's penetrating, appraising looks. She formed her own first impression as she approached: she liked the Schoormanns. There was no doubt he was moody and gruff, the way he had just pushed off his wife. He seemed funny, though, alert and approachable. Not at all unwell. His wife kept a straight face—she didn't immediately betray her opinion. But to Eva, she looked like someone who made an effort to be fair. "I'm pleased to meet you, Fräulein Bruhns." And Eva knew Brigitte meant it. They shook hands. Eva hadn't noticed the music till now. The pianist was playing "Moon River," from the film *Breakfast at Tiffany's*, which Eva had seen in theaters with Annegret a year ago. The sisters had cried through the entire final half hour.

Eva sighed involuntarily. The tension she had felt subsided. The bartender filled four glasses with what Eva assumed was champagne, and they clinked glasses where they stood. Eva took a large swig, and sure enough, it had the same dry flavor she had illicitly tasted for the first time at Jürgen's house. She glanced at Jürgen, who was staring at her neckline. She covered her bare skin with her hand. Then they went to a private, wood-paneled room, where their table had been festively set. Eva was immediately taken in by the room's warm atmosphere and gentle orange lighting, whose source she could not locate. The city lights glittered in the distance beyond the windows. Brigitte told them that a six-course French meal was planned. Walther Schoormann pulled out a chair for Eva. "Take the seat to my left. I can hear better on that side. Jürgen, you'd better sit on the right." He grinned at his son, who jokingly bared his teeth and sat down opposite Eva.

NEARLY EVERY SEAT WAS TAKEN at German House that Friday evening. They were hosting no fewer than two groups of regulars, including the neighborhood Carnival planning association.

Ludwig cooked, stewed, and roasted with the support of Frau Lenze, whose finger had more or less healed after all these weeks, and a newly hired young worker, who did nothing but wash dishes and chew gum. Edith was waiting tables together with the perpetually grim but competent server Fräulein Wittkopp, who was still unmarried at forty-eight and would stay that way. Herr Paten, a longtime employee, tended the bar. There was no chance to catch their breath, no time for a private moment between the Bruhnses, although they both needed it more than ever. Edith chanced upon Ludwig alone just once, when she came into the kitchen laden with dishes. The dishwasher was out back, chewing away and having a smoke, and Frau Lenze had slipped off to use the toilet. Edith hovered beside Ludwig, who was breading schnitzel cutlets with remarkable speed and arranging them in a large pan of sizzling oil. "Almost ready, give me six minutes. Five." Edith did not respond. Ludwig looked over and was shocked to discover that she was crying. He turned to her and somewhat helplessly brushed a floury hand across her cheek. Then he took a dishtowel to wipe both the tears and flour from his wife's face.

"What is it, Mother?"

"Soon we won't be good enough for her anymore."

"Oh, baloney! Our daughter won't let herself get carried away."

Frau Lenze returned to the kitchen. Her finger hurt, she said, it just hadn't been the same since the accident. Edith choked back her tears, balanced five plates of cucumber salad, and carried them out to the dining room. Ludwig flipped the schnitzels and swore. They'd come out a bit dark. "Oh, they're still fine. Not meant for girls, anyhow!" he boomed.

In the dining room, Edith delivered the plates of salad and took new orders. An elegantly dressed gentleman and equally refined woman emerged from behind the felted curtain hung at the entrance. Edith glanced over and immediately recognized them. She turned her back to the couple and grasped Fräulein Wittkopp by the arm as she carried a tray past.

"Please let those folks know there are no tables available."

"But table two is about to—"

"It's been reserved for nine!"

Fräulein Wittkopp frowned at Edith for a moment, because that wasn't true, then approached the newcomers, tried to make her dour face look apologetic, and told them, "I'm sorry, we're full."

"We've heard how excellent your schnitzel is. How unfortunate," the raptor-faced man replied pleasantly. Leading his companion out the door, he said, "We'll come back another time, Mother." They vanished behind the heavy curtain. None of the diners had recognized the man, although his photograph had frequently appeared in the newspaper over the past few months—he was the main defendant, after all.

At the InterContinental, the third course had arrived: *coq au citron*. Eva had never eaten chicken that tasted like lemon. The flavor reminded her of dish soap, but she chewed on bravely. Conversation had initially revolved around the catalog. Brigitte had admonished Walther and Jürgen to find a topic of conversation that would also interest the women. So they talked about the increase in traffic on the roads. Brigitte was currently working toward her license, and she described driving practice as "unspeakably infernal drills." Eva said she didn't know if she would ever need a license. Jürgen didn't think so. Eva's defiance stirred, and she was about to announce that maybe she would sign up at a driving school, when Walther Schoormann unexpectedly touched her forearm. "Excuse me, my dear girl, but who did you say you were again?" Eva stiffened, and a wave of heat cascaded down her body. Jürgen set down his silverware in alarm, but Brigitte remained calm and said to Walther, "This is Fräulein Bruhns, your son's girlfriend." Walther Schoormann looked bewildered. "My name is Eva Bruhns." He looked at her with unseeing eyes and repeated her name.

"Do you have a husband? Children? A job?"

"I am a translator from the Polish."

Jürgen caught Eva's eye and shook his head faintly in warning. But at that moment, Walther Schoormann nodded. He edged in his chair and tapped his index finger repeatedly on the table as he spoke: "Of course. I asked after you. You're translating in the trial at the municipal building."

Eva looked at Jürgen helplessly, then responded, "Yes."

"What's the trial about?" Walther Schoormann asked. Eva looked at him incredulously. Did he really not know what it was about? Or was he testing her? Jürgen fixed her with an urgent stare. Brigitte also flashed Eva a small, pleading smile. Eva tried to take on a breezy tone: "Oh, it's against a few men, well, war criminals, who worked at that camp . . . at a camp . . . so, who committed crimes in Poland. It was a long time ago and people . . ." Eva dropped off in the middle of the sentence. It felt wrong to speak about the trial so lightly. The little old man had thankfully turned his attention back to his lemon chicken. He seemed to have forgotten his question. Eva and Jürgen abashedly began eating again too. "Yes, the war was terrible. But now it's time we went back to talking about nice things. Were you maybe planning to take Fräulein Bruhns to the island over Easter?" Brigitte said. She turned to Eva affably. "I think it's the most beautiful time of the year, when everything starts to blossom and—" Walther Schoormann suddenly burst out, "You'll never get me to talk—never!" He got up from his chair. "Brigitte, I need to use the washroom." Eva looked down Walther Schoormann's body. A dark spot was spreading over the middle of his trousers. Brigitte stood up. "Come, Walli, come with me, everything's fine." Brigitte rounded the table and led her husband out of the room. Jürgen glanced at the empty chair, but the silk upholstery did not appear to have been touched. Eva sat there, rigid and helpless. The maître d' entered soundlessly and bowed slightly. "May we clear this course?" "Yes, please," Jürgen gestured. "And would we like to wait a moment before the main course?" Jürgen eyed the man. "Please bring me the bill." The maître d' seemed vexed but did not ask further. He nodded and withdrew. Eva sought Jürgen's gaze. "I'm sorry, but I couldn't lie." "Eva, in no way is this your fault."

They went to the coat check, then happened upon Walther and Brigitte at the elevator. They were also wearing their coats. The four stepped into the little mirrored compartment together, going down. "Are you also in the garage?" Brigitte responded, "No, we're parked outside." Jürgen pressed the button beside the *L* and the button beside the *P*. The elevator jolted, then descended smoothly. Eva didn't look in the mirrors this time, but at the carpeted floor. *What a sad way to end the evening.* Walther Schoormann regarded Eva at that moment and said, "I'm sick, miss. That's why these things happen to me."

"Yes, I understand, Herr Schoormann."

"It might have been a better idea to invite you over to ours. I'd have a pair of replacement pants, then." Eva smiled uncertainly. "Yes, that's true." When the doors opened to the lobby, they shook hands. Their good-byes were brief, and Eva and Jürgen continued down into the garage.

Back in the car, Jürgen made no move to start the engine. He sat there, bent forward and gazing at the speedometer; the needle was stationary. He began to talk about his father, about how he'd always been unpredictable and how his illness hadn't actually changed anything other than his control over bodily functions. When he was a child, his father encouraged him, praised him, spent hours fishing with him at the pond, then out of nowhere, humiliated and struck him. He could always go to him with questions, no matter how outlandish. But he had occasionally earned himself a solid cuffing, just because he had described a storm trooper uniform as "neat." His mother loved him reliably, whereas his father repeatedly let him down. But he survived the war. He had to live with him. Jürgen turned to Eva, and his eyes shone black in the cold gloom of the parking garage. Jürgen said that he could tell his father had liked Eva. And that in spite of everything, the evening had been a success. And to be perfectly honest, had his father found fault with her, he wouldn't have been able to marry her. Eva saw Jürgen's eyes begin to glint. A sob escaped him, and he covered his face with his hands. Men didn't cry. And as he turned away from Eva bashfully, yet so clearly full of relief, she thought that although she didn't understand Jürgen, she did love him. She drew his hand, damp with tears, away from his face and stroked it. It seemed she would soon be living together with Walther and Brigitte Schoormann in that house that smelled of chlorine. Eva tried to imagine sitting at breakfast with the Schoormanns, sorting laundry with Brigitte, or arguing with Frau Treuthardt in the kitchen. It was impossible. But when she pictured what had always been her home, the stuffy apartment above the restaurant, her family, she was not filled with the usual sense of sleepy security. Eva held Jürgen's hand and gazed at a concrete wall. She was sitting underground, under a twenty-one-story building with seven hundred rooms and as many bathrooms, in a car that wasn't moving, yet she felt as though she were on a distant journey.

IN THE MIDDLE OF THE NIGHT, Eva was driven from bed by sheer hunger. She had starved herself all day in anticipation of an evening spent at a luxury restaurant, and those few appetizers were now long digested. She padded barefoot into the kitchen, spread some butter on a slice of bread, and poured herself a glass of milk. She returned to the window in her room and ate by the glow of the streetlight. Every now and then, she took a sip of milk. On the ceiling behind her, the shadow cast by the streetlight trembled. Don Quixote wielded his lance, as he did every night. Sitting on the shelf, like a new house pet getting used to its surroundings, was the hat. The street was quiet—not a single car drove by, and only two windows in the apartment buildings opposite were lit. Maybe someone was sick. Her mother had always been fanatical in caring for them, even when it was no more than a slight cold they had. Fevers sent Edith into a panic, and Doctor Gorf had been summoned in the middle of the night before, to check whether the death of her children was imminent. Eva had always enjoyed that, seeing as she'd only been dangerously sick once, when she was five. She liked seeing her mother so concerned and distraught. And Edith's relief, when they felt ready to eat or get up again, was absolute. "Those days are over," Eva said out loud. She swallowed her final bite and took the last sip of milk. Her feet had gotten cold. She wanted to get back into bed, under the two blankets she'd needed lately to keep warm, and turned away from the window. Out of the corner of her eye, she saw another light appear. In the apartment building diagonally across the street—a new, three-story structure—someone had turned on the hallway light. An unfamiliar orange glow appeared behind the frosted glass of the front door. She thought that the light fixture must be new. New and already broken, because the light was flickering, as if it had a loose connection. Eva watched for someone to leave the building. But no one came out. Meanwhile, the light was growing brighter and turning yellow. It was moving. It took Eva a few more seconds to grasp what the flickering meant. Fire. There was a fire in the downstairs entryway of the building across the street. Eva froze for a moment, then stumbled out of her room toward the telephone in the hallway. She screamed, "Daddy!! Fire! Over at number fourteen!" Eva dialed 112, and, gasping, repeated the address twice before the emergency dispatcher on the other end understood her. The doors to her parents' and Stefan's bedrooms opened, but Annegret's remained closed—she must not have returned yet from the night shift. Ludwig, wide awake, barked, "Where?!"

"Across the street, at Penschuks'!"

Ludwig bolted from the apartment as he was. Stefan, shadowed by an anxiously yipping Purzel, tried to follow, but Edith caught her son by the collar of his pajamas. "You stay put!" Eva hung up the receiver. "They're coming! The fire department is coming!" Edith nodded, threw on her robe, strode toward the door, then had a thought and came back, opened the hall cupboard, pulled out an armful of folded blankets, and followed her husband onto the street. Purzel darted out the door as well.

Stefan again tried to go after them. "Mummy, I want to come!" Eva had to restrain him with all her strength. "Let me go!" he bawled. Eva picked him up, and he struggled and kicked her painfully in the thigh. He didn't calm until Eva carried him to her bedroom window. "There, now you can see everything."

From the window, Eva and Stefan then watched their father run across the street as fast as he could in his threadbare pajamas and slippers—which he nearly lost—bellowing, "Fire!! Fire!!" They watched him ring all of the doorbells by the front entrance at once, then pound on the door, then ring again. One by one, the lights turned on in the apartments. Edith crossed the street with the blankets in her arms. She said something to Ludwig at the front door. He pointed toward an archway that led to the back courtyard. Edith hurried back through the little front yard and disappeared behind the house. The flickering behind the front door now filled the entire glass pane. Windows opened upstairs. Someone leaned out. Ludwig yelled something that Eva and Stefan couldn't hear; the person vanished from the window, then reappeared and tossed something down that landed in the yard. Ludwig bent over and looked for it. Then he picked it up and returned to the door. He unlocked it. "What's Daddy doing?" Stefan cried in terror. Eva didn't answer and watched in disbelief as her father pushed open the front door. The fire was unmistakable now, blazing, white; black smoke billowed above and streamed toward the door. Eva watched helplessly as her father hesitated for a moment, then charged into the house and was swallowed by smoke. "God, what is he doing?" she whispered. A shapeless form emerged from the darkness on the street below: Annegret. She stopped in her tracks and looked at the open door and black clouds pouring out. Three tenants wrapped in blankets ran through the archway onto the street and joined Annegret. Everyone stared at the open door. Their father was nowhere to be seen.

"The fire department is coming!" Stefan was shaking with fear in Eva's arms. She listened but couldn't hear anything. She opened the window and smelled the smoke. Burning fabric. Singed lambskin. Her father remained hidden, somewhere inside the burning hallway. "Daddy!" Stefan shrieked. "Daddy!!"

Half an hour later, the Bruhns family—Annegret holding Stefan on her lap—had gathered in the German House dining room with the tenants from five out of six of the apartments in the building opposite (the elderly Penschuks were fortunately out of town, visiting their daughter in Königstein). Everyone was in pajamas and nightshirts under the blankets Eva's mother had brought them. A small child was whining, half asleep. "It looks like you were bombed," Edith concluded. She and Eva, both in their robes, had prepared tea for the grown-ups and cocoa for the children. Ludwig was being celebrated as a hero. Even before the fire trucks arrived, he had "put his life on the line," as people kept saying, and thrust the blazing baby carriage out of the building and onto the street. He was now sitting at the table; Edith had laid a blanket over his shoulders as well, and he was soaking his hands in a bowl of ice water. But the burns were just superficial. "As a cook, I'm used to much worse temperatures!" Ludwig repeated yet again. Eva could tell, though, based on how white his nose was, that the intervention had not been without danger. The fire department had arrived just moments later, and a fireman jumped from the truck as it was still moving, to extinguish the fire devouring the stroller, which was rolling slowly toward German House. The stroller then stood abandoned in the middle of the street, a bizarrely twisted conveyance whose dangling metal parts were still aglow. It belonged to a young family Eva hadn't met before; the dark-haired wife had thanked her for the tea in broken German. The baby was now fast asleep in her arms. Her husband, a gentle man, sighed anxiously. He was probably worrying about how he would manage to pay for a new stroller. Edith told Eva that these were the Giordanos, migrant workers from Italy—Naples—who were still new to the city. "Am I pronouncing your name right?" Edith asked, and Frau Giordano smiled. Someone stepped through the felted curtains into the dining room. It was the fire marshal in his dark blue uniform. Stefan sat up in Annegret's lap and stared at him reverently. Everyone else's conversations—largely speculation about who might have set the fire—fell silent. Hoodlums? A lunatic? The man in uniform coughed tersely and informed them, with a certain accusatory tone, that the fire had spread to the wall covering in the hallway. Which was a disgrace, by the way, because it flouted every last aspect of the fire code! They all looked at him remorsefully, although not one of them could be held responsible for the decisions the landlord from across the street had made. The fire marshal paused dramatically, then told them that the danger had been contained. It was safe to go back home. The apartments did, however, need to be aired out thoroughly. Frau Giordano translated in a whisper for Herr Giordano. He sighed so deeply that everyone laughed. Then they applauded. Ludwig pulled his hands out of the ice water, threw off the blanket, headed behind the bar in his favorite pajamas, and passed out generous pours of schnapps—cheers to the fright they'd had. The women also joined in the drinking; only the fire marshal declined. Eva threw back her schnapps, shuddered, and murmured, "God, am I relieved nothing happened to anyone." And Eva could see how pleased her father was with this positive outcome for the neighbors from across the street. Although they were free to return to the house, Ludwig poured a second round of schnapps. After refilling the glasses on the table, he made a toast to the rescued folks, positively beaming. Eva stood and gave her father a quick hug, to his surprise. She gave her mother, who'd observed the embrace with a smile, two kisses on the cheek. Annegret sneered. Eva gave her sister a defiant look. She knew her exuberance came from drinking schnapps on a nighttime belly. But it also came from love.

ONLY A FEW DAYS LATER, something happened that shook Eva deeply. It was a Thursday, a day in court. Spring had long since arrived in the city, and the silhouettes of the trees outside the glass panes shimmered green. There was a certain drowsiness in the auditorium that morning. Even the most combative of the defendants seemed unusually withdrawn. The chief judge's moonish face hung low. David rested his head heavily in his hand and looked half asleep. Even the children in the schoolyard behind the municipal building seemed muted during recess, their voices drawn out like a slowed record. Eva was translating testimony from a Polish Jew, Anna Masur, a dark-haired woman only a few years younger than Eva's mother, but who looked like an old woman. She had greeted Eva with a friendly smile at the witness stand, and from the first, she nodded in gratitude for every sentence Eva translated. Eva liked this woman with the shrunken face and dull eyes; she seemed modest, intelligent, and polite. The chief judge asked for her name, age, profession. Then he wanted to know her prisoner number, which they had been unable to find in their documents. Eva translated the question. Instead of answering, Anna Masur pulled up the sleeve of her gray suit jacket, which fit her loosely, then her light blouse. She turned her forearm toward Eva so that she could read and translate the number there. As the number appeared, digit by digit, out from under the sleeve, Eva was overcome by a profound feeling that grew from the depths of her belly. *I've seen this before. I have experienced this exact moment before.* Another déjà vu. But this time it didn't pass. On the contrary, it grew stronger. As Eva read the numbers out in German, she began to shrink like Alice, after biting into the magic mushroom in the children's book that both she and Stefan had disliked and soon abandoned. Eva turned into a little girl, and standing beside her was a man in a white coat who pulled up his sleeve and showed her a number on his forearm. He spoke amiably to little Eva. She was sitting in a chair that you could spin. It smelled like soap and burned hair. The man in the coat recited the numbers for her: 24981. Eva could see his mouth before her, his brownish teeth, the little mustache, the way his lips formed the words. In Polish. The man stood before her, as clear as day and beyond question, and suddenly a pain above her left ear seared so intensely she could have screamed, and at that moment she knew: this had really happened. "My dear girl, are you all right?" someone asked her in a quiet voice. It was not until Anna Masur lightly placed a hand on Eva's arm that she came back around. Eva searched Anna's questioning look, which radiated a sorrowful friendliness. The judge also interjected, "Do you need a break, Fräulein Bruhns?" Eva looked over at David, who had half risen from his seat, at once concerned and impatient, as though he expected her to faint at any moment. But Eva collected herself and spoke into the microphone, "No, thank you. I'm fine." She began to translate Anna's statement regarding her work as a clerk in the camp registry office. The main defendant was her boss. She had to write death certificates, sometimes hundreds a day. And that was only for the people who died in the camp. Those sent into the gas—no one recorded their names. She was required to write "heart failure" or "typhus" for the cause of death, although the people had been shot or beaten or tortured to death. "There was just once I refused to enter 'heart failure' as one woman's cause of death. I argued with my boss about it. With him, sitting right there." "What was it about this one woman?" the chief judge wanted to know. Eva translated the witness's response. "She was my sister, and another woman, who'd been with her in the women's hospital block, told me how she died." Eva listened to Anna's account of her sister's martyrdom, then translated it as gently as possible, Anna Masur nodding thankfully after each sentence. "The doctors were looking for cheap ways to sterilize women."

At the end of the day's proceedings, Eva stayed in her seat as the room around her slowly emptied. She had a headache, and the small oblong scar above her left ear was burning, which it hadn't done in years. She sat in her chair and gathered her courage without knowing exactly what for. When everyone had left, save the two hall attendants scanning the rows for forgotten umbrellas or gloves, Eva stood and walked to the front of the room, where the deserted judges' bench stood. It smelled different here—more serious, like stone—although that may have been the dust in the thick, pale blue curtains that concealed the stage behind the bench. Eva moved closer than she ever had before to the huge map of the camp, which wouldn't have fit in her hands had she stretched her arms all the way out. She read the familiar script above the gateway. She followed the camp road with her eyes and studied each of the brick-red buildings, one after the other, the blocks, every bar-

racks in the surrounding area, she wandered down every path, past
the watchtowers to the gas chambers and crematorium, then back
again, as though searching for the answer to a question that had
not yet crossed her lips. In the upper left-hand corner, outside the
camp's exterior fence, five houses were drawn in—two-story and
box-like, they stood in a tight row. The drawings had a sketchy
quality and weren't colored in like the rest of the map. Eva knew
that the main defendant had lived in the largest house there with
his wife, the raptor-faced man and his wife in the little hat. Several weeks ago, the court had been interested in mapping his daily
route into the camp, which witnesses said he went by bicycle. The
blond prosecutor wanted to prove to the main defendant that he
would have had to pass the crematorium on his way. Twice a day.
That it would have been impossible for him not to know about
the gas chambers. The main defendant remained impassive, as
usual, and simply stated that the map was inaccurate. Eva stared
at the smaller house next door to the main defendant's home.
She was reminded of something—not the building itself, but the
style of the drawing, how pointed the roof was, and how crooked
the door and disproportionately large the windows appeared. Eva
saw a girl of about eight, sitting at a table and drawing a picture
like that with a thick pencil. Was it a friend? Her sister? Herself?
When children draw houses, don't they all look alike? Eva did not
notice that David Miller had come back. He silently crossed the
auditorium, wearing a light-colored coat that was wrinkled, like
everything he owned. He glanced at Eva, perplexed, and went to
his seat. He picked up the two statute books lying there, flipped
through them hastily, then dropped to his knees and checked under the chairs. David hated wallets and carried his cash and identification papers loose in his pockets. He had been headed to Sissi's

and wanted to buy the season's first strawberries at the little fruit and vegetable shop along the way. When he went to pay, however, the twenty-mark bill he was certain he'd had that morning was gone. The last of his money for the month. David couldn't find the bill now, either. He got back up and looked over at Eva, who stood motionless before the map, as though she expected to be absorbed into it. He eyed her blond updo and rounded back, the soft shapes under her pale suit. *I wouldn't touch her with a pole. Funny girl. What the hell is she up to, anyhow?* David thought. Then he called out, "Any chance you could float me twenty marks, Eva?"

EVA NEEDED TO HELP in the restaurant that evening. Herr Paten went to night classes at the adult education center every Thursday to learn Spanish. He was planning to move to Majorca with his wife when he retired. Ludwig didn't like either aspect: that Herr Paten was out every Thursday, or that he would need to find a new bartender in three years. In their fifteen years of working together, Ludwig and Herr Paten had scarcely ever shared a personal word. The remaining exchanges ("Everyone's been asking for dark pils, Herr Bruhns." "It's a fad. I'll order just four kegs to start.") could be counted on two hands. They got along wordlessly and trusted each other blindly. Eva wore a dark blue smock that was impervious to splashed beer and alternated between pouring pils and soft drinks behind the heavy counter. She was practiced in pulling the shiny taps, washing the glasses, rinsing, and drying. She smiled at the guests, chatted a bit about the fire in the house across the street, which could have cost fourteen people—including five children—their lives. Could you imagine! If Eva's father hadn't so fearlessly, and so on. She was only half

listening. She kept looking at the clock, but the minutes till closing were passing as though caught in pine pitch. Eva wanted to
be alone to think. About the man in the white coat who had addressed her. About the child's drawing. She wanted to write down
in her blue notebook what Anna Masur had said about her sister,
so she could stop thinking about it. Edith came up, face glowing as it always did at this hour and earrings dangling as she
swung her round tray onto the bar. Eva removed the dirty glasses
and loaded the tray with freshly filled ones. She thought of the
abdominal pain she herself experienced every four weeks. And
about how, before the operation she'd had last year, her mother
would withdraw into her darkened bedroom for a full day every
month. How she would curl up in bed with a hot water bottle
on her belly and whimper, how she would vomit into a metal
bucket. Despite the painkillers, Edith had suffered terribly.
And she hadn't had chemists blend a liquid that doctors then in-
jected into her uterus. A liquid that slowly set inside her till it was
hard as concrete. Eva pursed her lips. Edith studied Eva, who did
not look at her mother. "Is everything all right between you and
Jürgen?" Eva nodded noncommittally. "They invited me to their
island over Pentecost. For four days." "And have you decided
on a date for the wedding?" Eva shrugged and saw her father
come out of the kitchen, slightly stooped in pain and his face
red. He stepped up to one of the tables, where a raucous, larger
group was sitting. The Stauch family were regulars. Eva saw her
father shake the Stauchs' daughter's hand and say something,
and everyone laughed. The young woman flushed. The family
was probably celebrating her twenty-first birthday. Edith lifted
the loaded tray from the counter. "Don't worry, Evie, he's not
going anywhere. His father likes you." She carried the tray over

to the Stauchs' table and handed out the glasses. Now she was talking too, likely commenting ironically on whatever her husband was saying. No doubt some joke about how trying it was to have grown daughters in the house. More laughter. A toast. Eva plunged the dirty glasses in the sink. She felt a chilly draft on her cheek. New guests had opened the front door and emerged from behind the burgundy felted curtains. It was the main defendant and his wife. Eva froze, while they stood at the door and scanned the room for an open table. The dining room was not "packed to bursting," as Eva's father would say, and as it had been on their last visit, but instead there were tables to choose from. Fräulein Wittkopp, who was cleaning off a table that had just opened up by the window, looked over. She did not remember the pair and walked up to them, dirty plates balanced on her arm. "Two in your party? Please, have a seat over there. I'll be right back with menus." Fräulein Wittkopp went into the kitchen. From her spot behind the bar, Eva watched helplessly as the main defendant led his wife to the table. He helped her with her coat, she sat down in the chair he pulled out for her, and he walked over to the coat rack to the left of the bar without noticing Eva. She observed his sharp profile and quiet movements as he reached for a hanger and hung up first his wife's coat, followed by his own. He looked much older up close—his skin was like crinkled parchment. One of the two drinkers sitting at the bar knocked on the wood countertop and called for a refill, but Eva was paralyzed. The main defendant returned to his table and sat down across from his wife. He sat with his back to the window and had a view of the entire dining room. Eva's parents were still standing at the Stauchs' table. Herr Stauch was telling an involved story, and they couldn't get away. Neither had noticed the new guests. Fräulein

Wittkopp came back out of the kitchen and handed them two of the dark green menus. As she dispassionately recited the day's specials—"We've got fresh kidneys today"—the main defendant suddenly lifted his gaze and looked Eva square in the face. The very same way he had caught her eye from across the courtroom. Eva felt nauseous. She wanted to turn away, disappear—but then she realized he didn't recognize her. She was an unfamiliar face for him in this different setting. Eva exhaled in relief and, her hands shaking, she began to pour fresh beers, holding the glass at an angle and turning it slightly to create the perfect head. She did it the way she always did, the way she had learned as a twelve-year-old, the way she could practically do in her sleep. "Excuse me! Fräulein, do you have a wine menu?" The main defendant was addressing her mother, who had just broken away from the family party after tousling the youngest Stauch child's hair. Edith approached the table by the window and put on her friendly, yet firm, work face. Eva knew she would now tell them that their guests were always highly satisfied with their selection of five house wines. But then Eva saw her mother falter and stiffen strangely as she neared them. The main defendant and his wife appeared stupefied at the sight of Edith Bruhns. Edith stopped at their table and automatically responded, "We don't have a wine menu. In the regular menu, you will find—" At that moment, the raptor-faced man stood up so tall and menacingly before her mother that for a split second Eva expected him to leave the ground, spread his wings, and fly off. He did something different instead: he sucked in his cheeks, pursed his lips, and spat at Edith Bruhns's feet. His wife rose as well and pulled on her gloves, shaking with indignation or rage. Eva heard her hiss, "We are leaving at once. Robert, at once!" Ludwig had also finally managed to pry himself away from the Stauchs and was headed for the kitchen when he noticed the three strangely poised figures. Like dogs on the prowl, the quieter and more concentrated, the crueler the attack. Eva saw the color drain from her father's face. There was no doubt that he too recognized their guest and his wife.

PART THREE

THE SCRAWNY BOY, wearing a uniform several sizes too big for him, trips over an endless carpet. The orange sky is so low, the boy can almost touch it. But he's looking down. The carpet arches and ensnares his feet, but the boy breaks free and tumbles onward, his weapon at the ready. He's not alone. Other children run alongside him, wheezing, falling, getting up. They all carry weapons. The boy's ears prick up—there's a rumbling and rattling approaching in the distance. He freezes and stares at the sweeping horizon. A row of black silhouettes appears before the fiery heavens, creeping slowly and inexorably toward him. Tanks, mighty and faceless, crawling over the carpet, hundreds, thousands of them, in one endless row toward the children. "Retreat!" the boy screams, but the other children continue on, as though deaf and blind. The boy watches as the first tank runs over two children. It swallows them noiselessly. "Retreat! I said retreat!!" the boy screams more loudly. He seizes one of the children walking past him toward the tanks, and the boy briefly turns his face to him. It's Thomas Preisgau, his best friend. "We have to retreat, Thomas!" But Thomas breaks away from him and strides toward one of the tanks. It devours him. The scrawny boy cries in despair, "No! No!!"

"Hey there, little one, wake up. Stefan . . ." Stefan opened his eyes and blinked. Someone was bent over him with a worried look. "You're dreaming." Stefan felt relief at the sound of his father's voice. He looked around—he was lying in his bed, in his room. Light fell in through the open door. Purzel sat panting at the foot of the bed, as if he had just been trudging through the swamp alongside Stefan. Ludwig swatted the dog on the snout and Purzel growled, but Ludwig was unimpressed and shooed him from the bed. "You've got no business being in here, you pest!" Purzel jumped reluctantly to the floor. Ludwig stroked Stefan's sweaty hair.

"You were having a nightmare."

"Daddy, I was yelling, but they wouldn't listen to me!"

"Sometimes we dream about terrible things. But everything is okay now. You're safe at home."

"Do you sometimes dream about terrible things too?"

His father did not respond. He straightened out the twisted bedspread and tucked it in tightly around his son. Then he said, "I'll leave the door open. You sleep well now," and stepped over Purzel, who was still out of breath, and the toys littering the carpet, and left the room. Stefan heard him shuffling back to bed. He left the hallway light on. Toppled soldiers lay in the small band of light that shone on the carpet. Stefan had thrown no small number of them into a pile. Perhaps he had pretended those were the dead.

Next door, Eva lay awake in bed, on her back with her hands folded. "Retreat!" she had heard her brother calling. She had been about to get up, when their parents' bedroom door opened and someone went over to Stefan. She heard her father and Stefan talking through the wall. It was just before four. Eva hadn't fallen asleep yet. The incident from the night before played in an endless loop in her mind, like a short, grotesque film. In the restaurant earlier, after Edith locked the door behind Fräulein Wittkopp and Frau Lenze, Eva, who was wiping down the tables, turned to her parents and asked the question. Though it made her heart race and she was terrified of the answer, she summoned the courage she needed.

"How do you know that man?"

Her father, who was flushing out the beer taps behind the bar, shot her mother a look. Edith took Eva's washrag, turned, and replied as she walked away that they didn't know why he had behaved so strangely. They had never seen him or his companion before. Ludwig nodded, dried out the sink, and turned off the light. They filed out the door to the stairwell. They left their daughter behind in the dining room.

Eva began to sweat and threw off the two blankets. She could not recall a time when her parents had lied to her so blatantly. She stared at the shadow of Don Quixote, whose lance quivered threateningly. He was poised to attack. For the first time ever, he was against her. Her teeth began to chatter and she pulled the covers back on. It was five thirty before Eva fell into a light, feverish half sleep. *He spat at Mum's feet. He doesn't like her. That's a good thing. It's good. Jürgen would also say that's a good sign. Then why are they lying?* Eva opened her eyes again. It was getting light out. Don Quixote had disappeared from her ceiling. Otto Cohn's dark hat sat on the shelf.

"THIS CAN'T BE." Annegret, wearing her white uniform in the nurses' lounge, stepped over to the window overlooking the inner courtyard. She pulled the green curtain around herself like a blanket, as if she wanted to wrap herself up in it, as if she wanted to disappear into it like a child hiding from the world. Doctor Küssner came over to her and tried to gently loose her from the curtain, which was threatening to tear from the rod above. He spoke to her reassuringly. About how they were sometimes powerless, about how they could do everything humanly possible but couldn't work miracles. About how Annegret had done everything she could. He said more along those lines, till Annegret suddenly and soberly uncoiled herself from the curtain and told him to "quit it with the bullshit blather." She sat down at the Formica table in the middle of the room; there was a plate of cookies that had probably gone soft and stale overnight. "'Everything humanly possible'? That sounds so pathetic," she said bitterly. She covered her ears with her hands, as though she couldn't stand to hear any more. Küssner looked at the back of Annegret's head, at the little nurse's cap and her white-blond hair like surgical cotton. "Will you come?" She did not respond. He gently pulled her hands from her ears. "Will you come back to see him?" Annegret did not look at Küssner but said softly, "I'm sorry, Hartmut, but I can't be witness to that." He lingered for a moment, then went out to the child dying in room five. Annegret began to eat the cookies.

Küssner crossed the hallway. He was also upset by this case. Two weeks earlier, the nine-month-old Martin Fasse had undergone surgery performed by a veteran specialist—it was a complicated but critical procedure to reverse a congenital stricture of the esophagus, which the undernourished boy had withstood remarkably well. For ten days, they could positively watch him gain weight. Four days ago, though, he had unexpectedly developed diarrhea and begun vomiting. Penicillin did nothing, antiviral agents did nothing, and he couldn't keep their tonics down. Martin steadily declined, and even Annegret, the master of nursing children back to health, had looked uncharacteristically fearful. Last night, she stayed with the boy almost without pause, dabbing his little, bluish mouth by turns with milk and water, and ultimately she picked up the whimpering, rapidly cooling child and carried him close to her body, to warm him up. Martin went very still at about four in the morning, and Küssner had to search for a pulse, moving his stethoscope across the child's sunken chest. Stepping into the room now, which held just three bassinets for especially critical cases, he could see from the door that Martin had lost the battle. Küssner stepped up to him and performed a final examination of the tiny body, which had already gone cold. He looked at the clock and recorded five thirty as the time of death in the medical chart. As he wrote, he thought about the fact that in just a few hours, he would have to account for another case of infant diarrhea to the hospital director. Enhanced hygiene measures—boiling all bottles and nipples twice before use, changing bed linens daily, medical staff washing their hands before and after every patient contact—had not brought about any improvement. Küssner was at a loss. When he returned to the nurses' lounge moments later, the plate of cookies was empty. Annegret stood at a cupboard, preparing the morning meal for the children who could not yet be nursed. She dispensed powdered milk among the bottles. Water boiled in a kettle. "Would you like to see him one more time?" Annegret shook her head. Küssner came up to Annegret, turned her around to face him, and hugged her. She stiffened but did not resist. Küssner said he would wait till seven, then call the parents. Why wake them now with news like this? Annegret pulled away from him, drew herself up, stroked his cheek briefly, firmly, and replied that she had a good connection with Frau Fasse. She would call.

She turned her back to Küssner and poured the boiling water. He looked at her back and thought, *Today's the day*.

After Küssner stood before the hospital director for three quarters of an hour, trying to radiate competence and optimism regarding what had happened, when all he felt was helpless and sad, he went home, exhausted, to his recently constructed, single-family house on the outskirts of town. He paused in the front hallway and listened to the noises in the house. The kids were at school, their colorful slippers stowed under the coatrack. Ingrid was busy upstairs with the radio on. A *Schlager* pop song played, and Ingrid joined in the refrain, "All of Paris is dreaming of love." Küssner thought of Annegret and her disdain for any form of sentimentality, the way she sneered the time he suggested they take a trip to said city of love. "Romance is dishonesty in disguise," she said. He turned to the mirror and saw a tired man who appeared much older than he was. His hair had long since taken its leave. Soon enough, he would start gaining weight and develop blocked arteries and suffer a heart attack at forty-five, like his father. He had not been happy in his marriage. As Küssner still stood there, Ingrid came downstairs, carrying a heap of used bedclothes, cheery tangles of flowers printed on white. She moved jauntily, energetically. She smiled at the sight of her husband. As always, he was struck by what a unique, timeless beauty she possessed, and what a miracle it was that she had chosen as average a man as he was. He did not smile back, and she also turned serious.

"Did something happen?"

"I have to speak with you, Ingrid." Ingrid dropped the laundry by the door to the basement and turned to him expectantly. She waited.

"Let's go to the living room."

"I'm starting to get scared. What have you got cooked up this time? We are not moving again, though! I like living here! The children like living here—"

"Yes, I know."

Doctor Hartmut Küssner followed his unsuspecting wife into the living room.

EVA DID SOMETHING UNUSUAL that morning too. She was not needed in court, so she visited Jürgen unannounced at his office at the Schoormann warehouse. She had been there only once before, late one evening when he led her through the many stories of puzzling passageways, and she peeked into deserted rooms packed floor to ceiling with products and into a gloomy hall containing endlessly long tables and conveyor belts, where shipping started every morning at four. "This place starts humming like a beehive," Jürgen said. They climbed the stairs to the roof, where they kissed under a ledge, because it had started raining. The sound of the rain hitting the window façade in Jürgen's office grew louder and louder as Eva spun around in his executive chair, pulling up her skirt as if by accident till her thighs and underwear were fully exposed. Jürgen abruptly crouched before her on the carpet, collapsed between her knees, and pressed his face so forcefully into her lap that it hurt. She held her breath and waited. Only seconds later, Jürgen stood back up and said that they were leaving. She had come at an inconvenient time today, she could tell. He greeted her distractedly and helped her with her transitional coat—bright red and brand new—and said, with a slight edge to his voice, "Aren't we seeing each other this evening?" Eva sat down in one of the visitor chairs. "What's so urgent?" Jürgen continued.

His curt tone threw her off. "I needed someone to talk to, Jür-gen." "Do you want something to drink? A cup of coffee? I do have a meeting in five minutes." Eva watched the way Jürgen took a seat behind his big, shiny black desk, as though behind a bar-ricade. She noted how deep-set his eyes were, and how dismissive he seemed with his arms crossed like that. He was almost alien to her at that moment, and she saw him through her parents' eyes: shadowy, black-haired, rich. Jürgen could sense her skepticism, and he spread out his arms and smiled with a sigh. "Eva, spit it out, since you're here."

Eva haltingly began to tell him, first about the encounter in the ladies' room at the municipal building months earlier and the feeling she had, that she knew the main defendant's wife from somewhere. About her clear memory of the man in the white coat, who showed her the number tattooed on his arm, and about how, even as a child, she had been able to count from one to ten in Polish. About her recurring suspicions that she was somehow connected to the camp. Finally, she told him about the incident in the restaurant. About her parents, who had lied to her. That they had not been able to look her in the eye at break-fast that morning.

"Wait a minute." Jürgen had not once interrupted Eva, but now he lifted his hand. "Why don't you believe your parents?"

"Jürgen, what other explanation can there be for this man's behavior? They know each other from the past!"

Jürgen got up and went over to the wall, where a long line of draft catalog pages hung from a panel of clips. "Fine, but they clearly don't want to talk about it."

"And I should just leave it at that?"

Jürgen pulled down one of the pages. There were white boxes

pictured on it. He had clearly taken Edith's advice and added washing machines to their selection.

"Maybe they experienced something similar to my father and don't want to be reminded of their pain."

"But my parents weren't Communists."

"Maybe they were in the resistance?"

Eva almost laughed at the notion. "Not a chance, Jürgen!"

Jürgen clipped the page to a different open spot along the panel. "If they don't talk about it, how can you be sure?"

"Because they always say, 'Leave politics to the powers that be, and we'll just suffer the consequences.' I know my parents!"

Jürgen went back behind his desk. "The Fourth Commandment states, 'Honor thy father and thy mother, that thy days may be long upon the land which the Lord thy God giveth thee.'"

"Why would you say that right now?!"

Jürgen didn't answer. He sat down. When he heard the Ten Commandments for the first time as a young boy, listening as his mother read to him from the Bible, he pictured how he would honor his parents: adorning them with wreaths of flowers, kneeling before them, and giving them all the chocolate he had gotten from Aunt Anni. He'd thought it a bit much, but if God said so? Eva stood up and came over to him. She looked furious. And he could understand why.

"What does this have to do with the Ten Commandments? I want to know what happened between this person and my parents! Can't you understand that?"

Eva didn't wait for him to respond, but continued, "No. How could you? You don't know the first thing about what I know, what I've heard, the unthinkable things that happened. The crimes these men committed!"

"I can imagine it." Jürgen's face hardened. He glowered at Eva and turned away. For a moment, she thought, *That's what he'll look like when he's old.* She despised him.

"It's not something you can imagine! Not once have you come, not once have you listened. And not once have you asked me what these people experienced. Do you think they want to be reminded of their pain? Yet they still come! And they get up and stand there, in that room that's always too hot, under the glare of those floodlights. And they've got those pigs breathing down the back of their neck, sitting there in their suits with their legs splayed, and they laugh and turn away and say, 'You're lying! That's not true! It's all slander!' Or, worst of all"—Eva stood up tall and mimicked the main defendant's icy tone—"'That is beyond my knowledge.' And despite all of that, the witnesses, they stand there and describe how they were treated like animals, like cattle for the slaughter, like the scum of the earth. They suffered pain like you can't imagine, and neither can I. Doctors did experiments on prisoners, medical experiments—"

Jürgen stood. "Eva, I think that's enough now! I'm not as ignorant as you think, but this isn't the time or place, and now I have a—"

But Eva could not be contained. "You listen to me, Jürgen! Even though they were tortured! And there was nothing to eat! Even though everything in the camp was full of shit—"

Jürgen waved off Eva's outburst and tried to adopt a scornful tone. "And now you're forgetting your manners too. Would you mind toning it down. . . ." He gestured toward the door, his secretary on the other side.

But Eva continued, "Even though there were dead bodies everywhere and the stench and the shit, the people still wanted

to live!" Eva rubbed her face with both hands and let out something resembling a wail. She had flown into a rage unlike one
she had ever known. She stood in the middle of Jürgen's huge office on the pale woolen carpet, breathing heavily.

Jürgen took a step toward her. "I knew that this would happen. Your nerves can't handle it."

Eva recoiled. She looked at him and tried to speak quietly. It
was difficult, though. Nerves. What a ridiculous word! "The day
before yesterday, there was a woman from Krakow who described a
Gypsy camp that was going to be broken up. The prisoners found
out about it and made themselves weapons out of sheet metal.
They sharpened pieces of metal into knife blades. They gathered
sticks and boards. That's what they used to defend themselves
when the SS men came. Women, old and young, men, and children all fought for their lives with all their might. Because they
knew they were bound for the gas chambers. They were all shot
dead with machine guns."

In the office outside the padded door, Fräulein Junghänel—a
plain, gray-haired woman nearing her twentieth work anniversary, who had performed many years of good service for Jürgen's
father—sat at her desk, typing a personal letter. She was writing
to her landlord, informing him that the young man who had recently moved into the first-floor apartment of her building could
no longer be tolerated. He tossed his rubbish in the courtyard and
urinated in the front garden. Loud music could be heard from
his open windows until late at night. The smell was atrocious. He
had once tried luring a child into his apartment. She was writing on behalf of all of the tenants in the building and wished to
remain anonymous, for fear of possible retaliation by the man.
Fräulein Junghänel pulled the sheet out of the typewriter and

scanned it one last time. Besides having twice heard some quiet music coming from the first-floor apartment, nothing she had written was true. But the man, whose language she didn't understand, scared her. She had to pass by his apartment several times a day. She didn't want him in her building anymore. As Fräulein Junghänel folded the letter, she thought she heard a scream coming from her employer's office. She paused. Surely that wasn't possible, what with the thick door padding? Fräulein Junghänel stood and stepped up close to the door. She listened, her mouth open slightly, but heard nothing. She must have imagined it. She returned to her desk and slid the letter into an envelope on which she had already typed her landlord's address. She had almost made the mistake of addressing it by hand. In her own writing. She placed the letter in her purse. She would stamp it that evening at home—she would never steal a stamp from her boss—and then, once it was dark, toss it in the mailbox two streets over.

It was silent in Jürgen's office. Eva sat hunched over in the visitor chair. She had broken into a crying fit, and Jürgen had slapped her across the face twice. It had helped. Jürgen had turned to the window. They did not speak. Then Eva asked quietly, "Why won't you even listen?"

"Because that's where evil lurks." Jürgen said it soberly, without any recognizable emotion. He gazed over the city; his office was on the eleventh floor, and beyond the high-rises, he could make out the rippled green band of the Taunus hills along the horizon. Eva dried her face with the handkerchief Jürgen had handed her, wiped her nose, and got up. She retrieved her purse, which she had set on the leather sofa beside the door when she arrived. She draped her coat over her arm. She swallowed the phlegm that had formed, and the final salty tears that passed through her nose ran into the back of her throat and burned. She approached Jürgen by the window and said, "That isn't true, Jürgen. That's not where evil lurks. Or some devil. It's just humans. And that's what's so horrible." Eva turned to go. She left the door open, nodded to Fräulein Junghänel, who eyed her with curiosity, and exited the front office. Jürgen remained where he stood by the window. He looked down at the front courtyard, where people moved about like flies. He waited to catch sight of Eva in her bright red coat. She appeared and crossed quickly to the left, toward the streetcar. He had expected her to appear much smaller. She looked tall, though, upright. Fräulein Junghänel appeared in the door and reminded him of his meeting with the head of the fashion department. He was already five minutes late. Jürgen replied that she should say he wasn't coming at all. She stared uncomprehendingly at his back and waited. He corrected himself: "In twenty minutes." Fräulein Junghänel closed the door. Jürgen went to his desk and opened a drawer. He pulled out a heavy black book, the back cover of which was stamped in gold with his name and the date of his First Communion. Jürgen simply held the Bible in his hand. He did not flip through it. He thought of Jesus in the desert, and how thrice he was led into temptation and how thrice he resisted. He thought of the fact that he hadn't managed the same, that he'd been too weak. That something alien had taken control over him. He had smelled it on himself as he stood there in the middle of the field and looked into the eyes of the dying man: cloying sulfur and the acrid smell of burning. His hands had become claws. Jürgen smiled in exasperation. Of course that was a childish image of the devil. Not that that made it any less real. After all, that experience had inspired him to become a priest, close to God and out of harm's way.

THAT MORNING, LUDWIG BRUHNS was in an office at Henninger Brewery, busy negotiating keg prices for the upcoming season, as he did every year at about this time. Seated across from him was Klaus Belcher, whose name no one dared mock. They'd known each other for years, always reached an agreement, and polished off a fair amount of schnapps during their ritual haggling. At a certain point, Herr Belcher's mood would turn gloomy and he'd bemoan the city's ban, years ago, on horse-drawn conveyances— "Boy, those were the days, and were those handsome steeds, or what!" Today, however, Ludwig turned down the very first schnapps. Herr Belcher was genuinely shocked. Was Ludwig seriously ill? What on earth was wrong? Everything all right with the family? Ludwig nodded vaguely and blamed his gut, which had been acting up recently.

Meanwhile, Edith lay in a dental chair with her mouth open wide for Doctor Kasper, an ageless, austere man. He was inspecting Edith's teeth with a mirror and poked her gums here and there with a small hook. Then he inserted his thumb and index finger into her mouth and wiggled each tooth, one after the other. The room was silent, except for a hose gurgling somewhere. When Doctor Kasper finished, he leaned back a little on his stool. "Frau Bruhns, you have periodontitis," he told her gravely.

"And what is that?"

"Inflammation of the gums, hence the bleeding when you brush. Several candidates are already loose."

"Candidates?"

"Unfortunately."

Edith sat up. "But how can that be? I always brush. Do I need vitamins? I eat plenty of fruit."

"It's your age. Menopause." Edith stared at Doctor Kasper.

Her family doctor, Doctor Gorf, had used the word before too. When he said it, though, it sounded like little more than a passing cold without lasting consequences. Coming from Doctor Kasper's mouth, by contrast, it reverberated like a death sentence.

"Is there nothing I can do, Doctor?"

"Rinse with antiseptic mouthwash. And at some point they'll need to come out."

Edith leaned back into the chair and gazed at the ceiling. "The candidates."

"Yes. But there are really decent replacements these days. Nothing like the old chattering teeth from before the war. The only place you'll find those is in the haunted house ride at the fair. . . . Now, Frau Bruhns, there really is no reason to lose your composure."

Edith couldn't help it. Though she felt ashamed and covered her face with her hands, she began to weep piteously.

In the apartment above German House, Eva knocked carefully on Annegret's door and then peeked into the room. Annegret was asleep in the dim light the yellowish blinds let through, as always rolled up on her side like an embryo. It smelled like beer and potatoes in there. Eva didn't want to know why and slowly closed the door. She went into the living room, Purzel prancing about her feet, and walked up to the heavy, tall cupboard. As a child she had often pretended she was a princess, the cupboard her castle, complete with parapets, windows, and turrets. Now, opening its doors and drawers, one after the other, she was met with the familiar smell of dry cigars, sweet liqueur, and dust. Every last white tablecloth and cloth napkin was familiar to her, the half-burned red Christmas tree candles in a box, the case containing the silver-plated cutlery that both her parents proudly thought "fit for a king" and therefore never used. Eva dropped to her knees. Her parents stored documents and albums in one of the lower compartments. Eva paged through a ring binder containing bills and warranty certificates. The oldest receipt was from December 8, 1949, shortly after her parents had opened German House. It was the proof of purchase and warranty for an appliance from Schneider Electrics on Wiesbadener Strasse. A dish heater. Eva recalled how it hung above the bathtub. Whenever she went to the bathroom, she would pull the chain to turn on the heater. As she sat there and took care of her business, she watched in fascination as the thick gray filaments inside the metal dish slowly turned pink, then began to glow bright red. At a certain point the heater disappeared from the wall. Eva never addressed its absence, because she was convinced she had broken the appliance by turning it on too often. There were also five photo albums in the compartment. Three were from recent years, with pale, patterned cloth covers, whereas the other two were made of black and dark green cardboard. Eva pulled out one of the older two albums, the dark green one. It contained photographs of a group trip her father had taken as a youth. Heligoland in 1925. Her father had freckles and a huge smile on his face. It was his first time away from home. In one picture, he stood outside by a fire and stirred a pot hung over the flames. The steam from the pot obscured his face, but one could tell it was Ludwig by the shorts and undershirt he was wearing in the other photos as well. Ludwig loved telling the story about how for ten days he had cooked for thirty boys. At the end, they'd awarded him a medal made of tinfoil, naming him "Master Chef of Heligoland." The rosette was also in the photo album, flattened and dulled with time, the writing barely legible. Eva sat on the carpet, Purzel lying beside her, and opened the black album. On the first page, in painstakingly ornamental script, her mother had written, "Ludwig and Edith, 24 April 1935," with a white pencil on the black cardboard. Their wedding picture was pasted on the following page. Eva's parents stood before velvet drapes, a low pillar beside them, out of which flowers appeared to be cascading. Her mother had linked arms with her father and both were smiling, Ludwig incredulously, Edith in relief. She was wearing a flowy white dress that did not quite conceal her little belly. Annegret had pointed out this part of the photograph so many times in the past, that the photo paper around Edith's midsection had been rubbed off. "And that's me!" Eva turned the pages, mechanically stroking the dog at her side, and studied the familiar, silent images. The reception had taken place in a restaurant in Hamburg. It was easy to distinguish Edith's family of refined city folk from the ruddy island dwellers on the Bruhns side. Edith's parents had not agreed with their daughter's choice in partner. Nevertheless, the young couple occupied two rooms in their apartment in Rahlstedt after the wedding. Ludwig found seasonal employment, working summers by the sea, winters in the mountains. He was earning good money, but struggled to find a permanent position. The couple would be separated for months at a time, which neither liked. Shortly after Eva was born in the spring of 1939—arriving within twenty minutes on her grandparents' most valuable carpet—they finally got the chance to lease a restaurant near Cuxhaven and live there as a family. Ludwig was nearly thirty years old, Edith in her mid-twenties. "But then war broke out and everything changed." It was a line Eva had often heard repeated by both parents. Ludwig was conscripted for the field kitchen shortly after the war began, serving first in Poland and later in France. He was lucky, because he was never sent to the front line; sometimes pots went flying by his head, but he was never seriously injured. Edith initially stayed with the girls at her parents' in Hamburg. They managed fine, had enough to eat. When the English began bombarding the city, though, Edith sent her daughters—ages eight and four—to relatives on Juist, Aunt Ellen and Grandpa Sea Lion. That was what little Eva had called him. She didn't remember it. The only memory she had of her grandfather with the walrus mustache was from the wedding photos. He looked like he was crying in every picture. Eva had nearly reached the end of the album. The final photos were of Edith and Ludwig dancing. Her mother's veil had been traded for a nightcap, and her father was now wearing a long, pointed nightcap as well, an old tradition, as her mother had explained: at midnight, the bride's veil was removed, the couple was given nightcaps, and a poem was read aloud. The poem was printed on a sheet that lay folded up in the album:

> *Hear the bells toll far away,*
> *that mark the end of this wedding day.*
> *But tomorrow the sun once more shall rise*
> *on you, the happy groom and bride.*
> *Beautiful bride, allow me this,*
> *at this hour, at this place:*
> *remove your veil, that splendid treasure,*
> *that all day long has brought such pleasure.*
> *Take this cap, this humble crown,*
> *Beneath whose many frills are found*
> *Contentedness and gaiety*
> *from now to all eternity.*
> *To you as well, the new husband,*

I do not come with empty hands.
I present you with this here chapeau,
That you might remain a faithful beau,
Who shows no tendency to carouse,
But instead heads to his house.
From now on, avoid the sirens' cries,
And pull this cap o'er ears and eyes.

The guests stood in a circle around the couple and clapped with blurred hands, their faces gleaming white, some merrily cockeyed. Eva's parents alone appeared sober and clear, as though cutouts, in a firm embrace and looking into each other's eyes.

"HE'S GETTING OLD." Annegret stood in the doorway in her dressing gown, a glass of milk in her hand, and pointed at Purzel, whose tongue was lolling out. "Definitely has heart problems."

"Nonsense," Eva responded, although she had thought the same for some time. She pet Purzel's head, and he snapped at her hand.

"Annie, do you remember the time we spent on Juist?"

"Sure, but not exactly—"

"Why do we have so few photographs? And none that were taken during the war?"

"People tended to have concerns other than taking pictures in those days."

"Did we ever swim in the ocean?" Eva didn't want to let Annegret go, but she turned in the door and muttered, "I had a terrible night." She left. Eva closed the album and returned it to the cupboard. Finally, she took out a manila folder wedged in to the right of the albums. It was where their parents kept some of their childhood drawings. Eva opened the folder. Right on top was a drawing of the smaller house next door to the main defendant's house. It had a pointed roof, crooked door, and disproportionately large windows. Next to the house were two girls—both had braids sticking out of their heads, a big girl and little girl holding hands. Two yellowish-red stripes had been colored in thick behind the house, soaring into the sky. One might have thought they were the product of a child's imagination. But Eva knew what they were meant to represent. She leaned back against the cupboard that had once been her castle.

LATE THAT AFTERNOON Eva went to the public prosecutor's office. She was hoping that most of the staff would have left for the weekend, so that no one would catch her in the act. There was a list of names of officers who had served at the camp. It included more than eight thousand names and was kept in two hefty ring binders Eva had often seen when the chief judge was cross-referencing witness testimony. Had this or that officer been working at the camp at the time of a given event? This incorruptible list had often proven statements wrong. It was a demoralizing moment for the witnesses every time. They stood before the court as liars simply because they could no longer recall the month or season their suffering had taken place. Eva had grown to fear these two binders. The idea that her own life could be tied to this list, however, would never have occurred to her. She walked to the end of the deserted, infinite-seeming hallway, where the file room was located. She paused outside the door and thought of the many forbidden doors in fairy tales, which Stefan had been losing interest in for some time. She entered the room and closed the door behind her. She oriented herself in the windowless space, walked among the racks, and discovered the two gray binders more quickly than she would have liked. She pulled out the one labeled "Personnel SS/Camp, A–N" and carried it cautiously, as though it might explode in her hands at any moment, to one of the tables that had been pushed together in the middle of the room. Then she set it down. It was still quiet outside the door to the file room. Eva wondered whether it wouldn't be better to simply put the binder back as carefully as she'd taken it out, leave the room, go home, have a bath, and get dressed up to go see *The Treasure of Silver Lake* at the movies with Jürgen. Muffled laughter came through the wall. There was a kitchenette next door. Fräulein Lehmkuhl, one of the secretaries, was probably in there flirting with David Miller or another one of the clerks. Eva listened—more laughter. It was Fräulein Lehmkuhl, a rosy, carefree woman who had already earned a bad reputation. The office girls certainly did talk. . . . Eva opened the binder. She scanned the index with her forefinger, starting at the letters B–Br. She turned the pages and read through the names. From top to bottom: Brose. Brossmann. Brosthaus. Brücke. Brucker. Bruckner. Brückner. Brüggemann. Brügger. *Bruhns.*

The door burst open and two people stumbled in, pushing and pulling at each other, kissing loudly. David Miller fumbled with the buttons on Fräulein Lehmkuhl's blouse, and she laughed again, this time loud and clear. David pushed her onto the table—and discovered Eva. She stood frozen on the other side, a ring binder open in front of her, a look of pure horror on her face. David slowly righted himself, pulled Fräulein Lehmkuhl up, and grinned sheepishly.

"Sorry, the kitchenette was too cramped."

"We were just coming to get a file—" Fräulein Lehmkuhl lied poorly.

Eva closed the binder. "I was on my way out," she said softly. She returned it to its spot on the shelf, and David followed her with his eyes.

"But you're not going to tell anyone, are you, Eva?" Fräulein Lehmkuhl nervously called after her. "It was just a bit of fun . . ."

Eva left without responding and closed the door behind her. Fräulein Lehmkuhl shrugged and looked at David. "Now, where were we?"

But David turned away from her. He strode over to the shelf and pulled out the binder, whose contents had so rattled Eva.

MONDAY WAS THE BRUHNSES' DAY OFF. That meant the family ate dinner together. Even Annegret attempted to schedule her shifts at the hospital so that she was free Monday evenings. The Bruhns family ate at six thirty in the kitchen. They had bread with sausage and cheese. Sometimes canned fish. Their mother would open a jar of Stefan's favorite, mustard pickles, and their father prepared a large bowl of his famous egg salad with mayonnaise and capers, which was also on the menu at German House. It was only for his family that Ludwig used fresh dill, however, "whatever the cost." That evening, they had opened the window to the back courtyard, because the weather was unusually mild for early May. The song of a lone blackbird floated in. They were all gathered at the table. Only Stefan's spot was empty. Edith called, "Stefan, dinner!" Annegret spooned egg salad onto her plate and told her father about a doctor at the hospital, an older surgeon, who for years had suffered the same back problems as Ludwig, and who'd been saved by a corset. He was practically pain-free now. Her father joked about how hard it would be for him, as a man, to wear a corset, but he thanked her for the new information. Maybe one of those things would help him beat his pain, and allow him to start lunch service again. Edith, who was eating just two pieces of crisp bread, since she'd been putting on weight, smiled and said she would lace him up every morning and unlace him at night. As a young girl, she'd had to help her grandmother on with her corset. She was sure she'd still know how to do it. "The things you learn as a young girl, you never forget. Although I never would've dreamed I'd have reason to do that again." Everyone laughed but Eva, who mutely observed the amusement her parents and sister found in picturing Ludwig in a corset.

Her father had not looked at Eva once today. Her mother, on the other hand, occasionally gave her a quick, concerned glance. She reached over now and stroked her hair. "It's the Italian mettwurst you like so much." Eva jerked back her head like a petulant child and felt annoyed with herself. What should she say to them? What should she ask? She was sitting with her family in the kitchen, the most familiar place on earth, and couldn't express a single clear thought.

"Mummy." Stefan appeared in the doorway. He looked different than usual, his face blotchy and eyes open wide in horror. "Mummy," he said again, miserably. All four instantly saw that something bad must have happened. They rose, one after the other, as if in slow motion. Stefan said, "He won't get up."

Moments later, they all stood among the soldiers on the carpet in Stefan's room, gazing at the dead dog by the bed. Stefan was crying and attempting to tell them what had happened, between sobs. "He went number two on the floor, and I yelled at him and hit him a little, and then he fell over and was kind of shaking all funny, and then . . . and then . . ." The rest was drowned out by his bawling, impossible to be understood. Ludwig pulled Stefan toward him, and Stefan pressed his face into his father's comforting belly. His cries sounded quieter, but no less frantic. Edith left the room. Annegret crouched down beside Purzel with a grunt and examined his black, furry little body, as she was accustomed to doing. Breathing, pulse, reflexes. She got back up.

"It was probably his heart."

Stefan wailed, and Eva stroked the top of his head. "Purzel is in dog heaven now. There's a big meadow there just for dogs . . ."

"Where he can play all day long with other dogs. . . ." her father added. Annegret rolled her eyes but kept quiet. Edith returned to the room with a piece of newspaper, which she used to clean up Purzel's final little pile.

After wrapping Purzel in an old blanket, they laid him to rest in a biggish box Ludwig had fetched, with the words "Pronto Thickener—For Clump-Free Gravies and Sauces" printed on the side. The family placed an array of "grave goods" in the box: their mother contributed a slice of Italian mettwurst, while Annegret donated a handful of fruit candies—the green ones she didn't like, and had therefore picked out. Eva dug out Purzel's favorite toy, a gnawed-up tennis ball, from under the sofa in the living room. Stefan deliberated for a long time, still hiccupping and whimpering, whether to put his wind-up tank in the box, but then decided on ten of his best soldiers to protect Purzel—just in case there were bad dogs in dog heaven too. Stefan then got to choose who he wanted to sleep in his room that night. "Everyone," he said. The family discussed, and ultimately Eva lay down beside Stefan. She held the little boy's body tight, as he sniffled and cried himself to sleep. The tied-up box sat by the bed. In dark blue colored pencil, Edith had written "Purzel—1953 to 1964" on top. Eva buried her nose in Stefan's hair; he smelled of grass. She closed her eyes and saw the list before her, the ring binder lying open in the window-less room. Following "Anton Brügger," the next name had been "Ludwig Bruhns, SS Noncommissioned Officer, Cook, Served in Auschwitz 9/14/1940–1/15/1945."

In the bathroom, Edith brushed her teeth at the sink. She kept her eyes closed to her face in the mirror. The foam she spit out was bloody. At the same time, Ludwig sat in the living room, in his corner on the sofa, with the television on. The crocheted coverlet had been folded back. A talent show highlighting strange acts and hobbies was on, but Ludwig wasn't watching as a man, who had filled his basement from floor to ceiling with all sorts of fake owls, was introduced onscreen. Ludwig was thinking about his daughter Eva, who had sat at the table that evening like a stranger.

Early the next morning, before even the lonesome blackbird had woken, they buried Purzel under the black fir tree in the courtyard. Ludwig dug a hole and had to fight a few roots, which he severed with forceful blows of the spade. He paused a few times to clutch his back. Stefan didn't want to let go of the box, but with gentle force, Eva managed to wrest it from him. Their father quietly struck up a tune. "Now take this little doggy, who was so true and good." The others hummed along, although they didn't rec-ognize the melody Ludwig had chosen. As they walked back into the house, Edith put her arm around Stefan's shoulder and said he would get a new dog. Stefan replied earnestly that he would never want a dog other than Purzel. Eva hung back and was the last to go inside. She didn't want anyone in her family to see how hard she was crying about the dog's death, a dog that had lived such a thoroughly satisfactory life. A dog that had been forgiven everything.

AN ORDINARY FACE. He sat between the Beast and the medical orderly but never spoke to anyone. It looked like he had slipped down, deep into his dark suit—Defendant Number Six was the least conspicuous of all the men seated at the defendants' tables. On the seventy-eighth day of the trial, the day after Purzel's passing, the focus turned to his function at the camp. He removed his horn-rimmed glasses and wiped them lazily with a white handkerchief while Eva translated the testimony from a Polish witness named Andrzej Wilk, a man in his late forties with an ashen face and who smelled of liquor. They sat at right angles to each other, the two water glasses and carafe set before them, along with Eva's dictionaries and notepad. Wilk reported on how the defendant had killed prisoners in the so-called medical building. The prisoners were led into an examination room. They had to sit down on a stool. They had to lift their left arm and cover their mouth with their hand, both to muffle the anticipated scream and give the defendant access to his victims' hearts with the syringe. The witness said, in German, "'*Abspritzen*,' that's what we called it." Then he switched back to Polish and Eva continued translating, "I worked first as an orderly, then I moved corpses. That is, it was my duty to dispose of the murdered bodies. We carried the dead from the room where they were killed, across the hallway to the washroom in the cellar. In the evening, we then loaded them onto the truck and took them to the crematorium."

The chief judge leaned forward. "Herr Wilk, were you present in the same room in which the defendant performed these injections?"

"Yes, I stood about a half meter or meter away from him."

"Who else was in the room, besides you and the defendant?"

"The other prisoner who helped carry the bodies."

"How many people were killed in your presence, in this manner?"

"I never counted, but it could be anywhere between seven hundred and a thousand. They sometimes did it daily, Monday through Saturday, sometimes three times a week, sometimes twice."

"Where did the people come from, who were killed there?"

"They were from Block Twenty-eight at the camp. And one time, seventy-five children were brought. They were from somewhere in Poland, between eight and fourteen years old."

"And who killed the children?"

"The defendant right there. Together with Defendant Number Eighteen. The children were given a ball beforehand, and they played with it in the courtyard between Blocks Eleven and Twelve."

A pause followed; everyone involuntarily listened for noise coming from the schoolyard behind the municipal building. The children were in class at this hour, though. The shadow of a tree swaying gently was all that moved beyond the glass panes. The accused had put his polished glasses back on. The lenses reflected the glare of the floodlights. Andrzej Wilk sat there very quietly. Eva waited for the next question from the judge, who was paging through a folder. A young associate judge pointed out something in one of the documents. Eva noticed that she was starting to sweat. It was always stifling in the auditorium, but today she had the feeling the oxygen had been depleted once and for all. She took a sip of water from the glass on the table, which somehow made her mouth feel even drier. The chief judge was now formulating his next question and turned his kind, moonish face toward Eva.

"Was your father at the camp too?"

Eva stared at the judge and felt the blood drain from her face. The witness beside her understood the question and responded, in German, "Yes. That he was." Eva took another sip of water, which she barely got down. The figure of the chief judge grew hazy before her eyes, as though he were disappearing behind the wall of glass. She blinked.

"And how did your father fare?"

The witness responded in Polish. "The defendant murdered him before my eyes. It was September twenty-ninth, 1942. They were giving injections daily at that point." Wilk spoke on, while Eva stared at his mouth and attempted to understand the words. But then his mouth dissolved as well and the words poured out.

"I was in the examination room . . . defendants, we waited . . . the door . . . my father . . . Take a seat. You'll be getting a shot . . . against typhus . . ."

Eva laid a hand on Andrzej Wilk's arm, as if she were trying to hang on to him. "Could you please repeat what you just said?" she asked quietly. The witness said something. But it wasn't Polish. Eva had never heard this language, and she turned to the chief judge, who had by now completely evaporated. "I don't understand him. Your Honor, I don't understand him . . ." Eva stood up and the hall began to spin around her, hundreds of faces circling, and in the same flash, she saw the linoleum floor racing up toward her. Then everything went black.

When Eva opened her eyes again, she was lying on a small couch in the room behind the auditorium, the dim green room with its illuminated mirrors. Someone had opened the top buttons on her blouse. Fräulein Schenke placed a wet cloth on her forehead. She hadn't squeezed it out enough, and water seeped into Eva's eyes. Fräulein Lehmkuhl stood beside Eva, fanning her face with a folder. "The air in there is just hellish," she said. David leaned in the open door and looked truly concerned. Eva sat up and said she was already feeling better. David gestured for her to stay seated. "The witness will continue his testimony in German. He speaks it well enough," he told her. A hall attendant appeared in the door and told them that the recess had ended. Fräulein Schenke and Fräulein Lehmkuhl both nodded encouragingly at Eva and scurried out. Eva tried to get up and follow them, but her knees buckled, as if she had the joints of a child attempting to carry an adult. She took a deep breath. David came into the room and took the last open-faced ham sandwich from one of the plates set out by the mirrors.

"Ludwig Bruhns. That's your father, isn't it?" Eva thought she had misheard, but David continued. "He worked as a cook in the officers' mess at the camp. How old were you then?"

Eva was silent. She'd been found out. She searched for the right response. Then she gave up and spoke the words heard so often in the courtroom: "I didn't know." She continued, "I had no memory of it. How else could I have taken on this job? I didn't even know my father was in the SS."

David chewed stoically. Eva looked at him and detected a sense of satisfaction. She felt a rush of anger and stood up. "You feel vindicated, don't you, Herr Miller?! You've always said that every last one of us in this country had something to do with it. Except maybe your colleagues in the prosecution—"

"Yes, I do believe that," David interrupted. "That so-called *Reich* could never have functioned so seamlessly had the large majority of people not been involved."

Eva laughed bitterly. "I don't know what my father did there, other than fry eggs and make soup!" She added softly, "But I will hand in my resignation."

David put the sandwich, with bite marks, back on the plate and looked at Eva in the mirror. "Pull yourself together, Fräulein Bruhns. We need you." He turned and came up close to her. "I won't tell a soul."

Eva looked at David and noticed his differently sized pupils, which she had only ever seen up close that one time, months ago in the German House dining room. It had appeared strange back then, but this peculiar part of his face now struck her as strangely familiar. Eva finally nodded uncertainly. Then she said, "Andrzej Wilk told me this morning that speaking German is torture to him. I will continue translating."

SEVERAL DAYS LATER, the Saturday morning before Pentecost, four people crossed an airfield under pale blue skies. A baggage cart rolled past, and the driver, a white-uniformed steward, pulled up beside a small silver plane, a Cessna that belonged to Walther Schoormann.

"Perfect flying weather," Jürgen said to Eva, whose colorful head scarf had loosened around her updo and flapped in the wind. Brigitte had linked arms with Walther Schoormann, who looked around in wonder, smiling like an excited child. He hadn't recognized Eva, but greeted her happily with the words, "I wear diapers now!" The four climbed into the aircraft, one after the other, and the steward loaded the suitcases from the cart into the small hold beneath the cabin. In the cockpit was a man whose face was unrecognizable behind his mirrored sunglasses and enormous headphones. He shook hands with Jürgen and Walther Schoormann, then carried on checking the displays, levers, and controls. Eva nervously took her seat in the narrow cabin. She had flown to Warsaw once, on business. She hadn't had any issue putting her trust in such a big, bulky airplane. But this dinky little thing seemed like a model, and it didn't feel safe. Eva told Jürgen, who was buckling his seat belt beside her, that she didn't love the designation "single engine." What if that single engine failed? Jürgen responded, very businesslike, that the plane had just been thoroughly serviced. The door was shut and locked, but the pilot didn't start. Walther Schoormann asked from the back why they weren't going yet. Jürgen explained that they were still waiting for clearance to take off. The pilot held up three fingers to Jürgen, who gave a thumbs-up back. Eva knew that they'd be waiting for another half hour. Half an hour to allow the sleeping pills Brigitte had mixed into her husband's breakfast tea to take effect. Jürgen had told Eva that on the last trip from Frankfurt to the island, his father had tried to get out somewhere over Hamburg. He had tried opening the door, which wasn't exactly safe. As a result, Brigitte and Jürgen had hatched this plan. As Eva's fear grew, Walther Schoormann fell asleep behind her. When his head finally tipped back, the pilot got clearance over the radio and engaged the engine. They taxied to the runway. Eva clutched her armrests with both hands as the small airplane accelerated. And as the engine's howling grew louder and the markers on the runway began to zip by beneath them, she'd have liked nothing better than to scream. At that moment, Jürgen took her hand from the armrest, and the wheels left the asphalt; they lifted off, they were flying. They left behind the houses, traffic, and people in the city and climbed ever higher into the pale blue.

The flight lasted just under three hours. The engine noise in the cabin was so loud that conversation was completely out of the question. Walther Schoormann was asleep with his mouth open, and with a handkerchief Brigitte wiped away the drool that leaked from the corner of his mouth. Jürgen was reading work documents, marking things occasionally in pencil or writing a note. Eva could see that they were contracts written in English. Brigitte pulled an illustrated newsmagazine out of her bag—*Quick*—and began to read. Eva looked out the window, into the tremendous depths; she followed the dark lines that were rivers, counted the green patches, the woods, and imagined herself walking among the trees, small and insignificant, and looking up through the branches at the silver dot creeping silently across the sky. Eva reflected that dying now would not be amiss. *I lived there, and my sister lived there. My father walked through the gate every day on his way to work. My mother closed our windows. She kept our house free of soot from the smokestacks.* David Miller was the only one who knew so far. And the main defendant's wife. She had recognized Eva behind the bar at German House. Their eyes met two days ago at the municipal building, and she regarded Eva with undisguised contempt. Then the woman in the little hat made a hand gesture, as if to say, "You'd best watch out, girl, or I'll do it again!" And with that, Eva remembered. She was small. Everything itched. She had bug bites on her arms and legs, and she was standing in a walled yard and scratching herself till she bled. The air smelled sweetly scorched. There was a bed of roses in the garden, and the bushes were in full bloom. Yellow and white. A big girl in a striped linen dress stood in the middle of the bed, decapitating the roses. It was Annegret, and she was laughing, and Eva laughed with her. She started tearing off the blossoms as well. It was hard at first, but she got the hang of it. They pelted each other with blossoms, and then went after the buds. But then Annegret abruptly stopped and gaped at something behind Eva. She sprang from the bed like a rabbit, bolted across the yard, and vanished in a bush. Eva slowly turned around. A woman wearing a smock was approaching, and she had the face of a mouse—a furious mouse. She grabbed Eva's upper arm and slapped her forcefully. Then again and again. That was when Eva noticed the scent of the torn roses beneath the smell of burning. She had been four years old at the time.

IN THE SCHOORMANNS' THATCHED BRICK HOUSE, with a forged sign reading "1868" hung over the front door, Brigitte showed Eva to her room beneath the roof, a small, wind-warped space with flowered curtains, polka-dot wallpaper, and a single bed.

Brigitte smiled wryly. "You're not married yet, after all." She then added, in confidence, "Jürgen's crazy, but otherwise he's all right."

She left to see to her husband, whom they had guided, still half asleep, out of the aircraft with their combined forces, but who was now waking up in earnest and crying out fearfully for his wife. She left the door open. Eva had a view of the dunes through the window, outlandishly barren and covered in reddish weeds. She spotted a strip of the North Sea, which was wild and rough on this side of the island. Jürgen carried in Eva's little suitcase and came over to her at the window. She leaned against him, and he put his arm around her shoulders. She could feel his heartbeat, hard and fierce, as though he'd been running.

"Jürgen, should we go to the beach? Do you think we can already swim?"

"I'm sorry, Eva, I'm not finished with the contracts yet. And I've got to return them by telex today."

"On a Saturday?"

Jürgen ignored the question and dropped his arm. "I'm happy you're here," he said, although he seemed almost angry as he looked at her.

"Jürgen, isn't this a bit ridiculous, with the separate bedrooms? We're adults. And engaged."

"I'm not discussing this with you again. I'll see you later." Jürgen left. Eva thought about how he'd picked her up at the municipal building the day before. How he stood at his car and waved. How he slowly lowered his hand when he saw David walking beside her. She and David weren't speaking, looking at each other, touching. Nevertheless, Jürgen must have sensed there was something that connected them, something he was excluded from. Eva saw how insecure it made him. Sad and jealous. Then why did he remain so unavailable? Jürgen continued to mystify her.

Eva went to the beach by herself. She had her towel and underwear in a floral cloth bag Brigitte had given her. Eva had put on her bathing suit under her dress. It was almost summery. A few white clouds billowed above, the blue of the sky saturated and heavy. The air smelled of little blossoms, and there was buzzing in the grasses. When Eva came out between the tall dunes and onto the wide beach, she took off her shoes. She wasn't wearing stockings and walked barefoot through the sand to the water. She had never been on such a big beach. Although no small number of people were sitting or lying in the sand, running through the retreating waves, and some even throwing themselves in the water, Eva felt alone. She stopped and observed the formation and fall of the waves for a while, how the water piled up, how it approached and kept growing, till it finally collapsed, how it retreated, bright and glittering as it seeped away in the sand. Her father had grown up so close to these waters. And he was always telling stories about the dead, the drowned, those who had fallen victim to "Blanker Hans," the turbulent North Sea. About the fathers of schoolmates who had been fishermen and never returned from the job, about the two children next door who had swum out too far. Once, when Eva was fifteen, they went to Juist on vacation; Grandpa Sea Lion had already been dead for some time, and they stayed with Aunt Ellen, her father's sister. A few days before they arrived, a sudden storm capsized a pleasure craft. Eight people drowned, and all were recovered but a six-year-old boy. Eva, who had always loved swimming, didn't want to go in the sea. She was afraid that something might touch her in the deep waters, that this boy might get caught between her legs, that his bloated face might appear before her in a wave. Her father responded that that wouldn't be a bad thing, because then those poor parents could finally bury their child. Eva had been ashamed of herself for being so self-centered. Her father was a good person.

Eva kept walking till the first wave washed up around her feet. The water was cold as snow. She decided not to swim, but instead to walk. She went far and stayed by the water for a long time, the sun beating down on her face; at some point she headed into the dunes and followed the little rabbit trails here and there. She enjoyed wandering through this moonscape, when she was suddenly startled: a few meters farther on, there was something pale lying in the dark dune grass, a motionless body, and beside it a second, then another and another, like corpses, but then she saw them move. It was people exposing their naked bodies to the sun. Eva froze, spun around in embarrassment, and ran toward the sea. As she fled, she bumped into yet another person, this one dripping wet and coming up the dune from the water, his member bouncing merrily in all directions as he jogged. Eva burned with shame, and she covered her eyes as she stumbled past the man.

Brigitte was setting the table for dinner back at the house. A large window façade behind the dining area opened onto the dunes and the sea. Dark beams held up the low ceiling. In a red-brick fireplace, its inside blackened with soot, a little fire was burning—not for warmth, since the house had central heating, but for atmosphere. Eva was out of breath as she entered, and she gaped at Brigitte for a moment without saying anything. Brigitte looked at her quizzically.

"What happened?"

Eva stammered, half amused and half embarrassed, that there were people down on the beach who weren't wearing any clothes or bathing suits. Brigitte waved her hand dismissively and continued arranging plates. Oh, that. It was the new fashion. Luckily you didn't have to join in if you didn't want to. Romy Schneider, the actress—surely Eva knew who she was? Well, she'd been here just once and had later said that it was just awful. That there was a naked ass floating in every wave. Eva and Brigitte looked at each other and laughed. Walther Schoormann entered in his undershirt; his chest appeared sunken. He carried a shirt that was clearly giving him some trouble, and he needed Brigitte. It wasn't till she saw him up close that Eva noticed the pale red lines covering his shoulders like a net. Scars.

"What are you laughing about?"

"The nudists. Eva had an explicit encounter."

"I apologize, Fräulein," Walther Schoormann said. "Already active in May now, are they? Brigitte, that is cause enough for me to sell the house."

Brigitte helped her husband into his shirt and responded, "Walli, we'll discuss that later. After all, you're walking around the place half naked yourself."

Walther Schoormann ignored the comment and addressed Eva. "They say it's because there's nothing indecent about showing the world how God made them. Meanwhile, most of them are damn atheists."

Brigitte buttoned up his shirt. "So are you!"

Eva couldn't help but smile, and suddenly Walther Schoormann looked at her warily.

"Don't you own a pub? A pub on Berger Strasse?"

Eva swallowed. "My parents do, yes, but farther up the street. Not by the train station."

The old man narrowed his eyes. He did not appear reassured.

"It's a restaurant, Walli," Brigitte interjected.

Walther Schoormann considered this, then he nodded. "A person's got to eat."

That night, Eva lay on the narrow bed in her tiny room, listened to the sea, and thought about the naked man in the dunes. She had to admit that she'd been aroused by the sight—the man was attractive, healthy, and lighthearted. Eva thought about how badly she yearned to be in bed with Jürgen right now. She felt pleasant little waves rising from her vagina—as she respectfully referred to her privates in her mind—and she pushed her hand between her legs and closed her eyes. She saw the sea rolling toward her, gently murmuring. Jürgen embraced her, the water rose up her body, nice and warm . . . Suddenly Eva sensed that she was not alone. She opened her eyes. A dark figure stood in the middle of the room before the open door to the hallway. Motionless.

"Jürgen?" Eva asked quietly.

"You'll never get me to talk!"

It was Walther Schoormann's penetrating voice. He repeated the line. Eva shot up in bed and fumbled for the switch on her bedside table. Then the light went on in the hallway, though, and Brigitte appeared in the doorway.

"Walli, you went to the wrong room by mistake." She gently led her husband out and closed the door. In the meantime, Eva had found the switch. Click. She turned on the light and stared at the slanted ceiling for a while. She turned over and studied the picture hanging on the opposite wall. A seascape. A ship was fighting its way through monstrous waves. Fish flew through the air. *It's obvious that won't end well.* Eva turned the light back out. She couldn't sleep. She was thirsty. She had probably eaten too much of the "unspeakably delicious herring salad" Brigitte had raved about. She listened for movement in the house, then got up. She put on her fashionable new dressing gown, which she had bought specially for this trip, and tiptoed down the stairs to the kitchen, where she came upon Brigitte. She was sitting in the white-and-blue-tiled room on a wooden bench at the table, illuminated by the soft circle of light thrown by the hanging lamp, a half-drunk bottle of beer before her. She was not made up and her eyes were puffy, as though she'd been crying. Eva was about to leave, but Brigitte waved her over.

"Have a seat. Would you like a beer? We don't use glasses at this hour, is all."

"Agreed."

Moments later, the women were clinking bottles. Brigitte said how much she liked Eva's dressing gown. Then she unexpectedly began telling her about losing her entire family in an air strike on Dresden—her father, who had been home on R & R at the time, her mother, and her brother. She was twelve years old. Walther had been her father, mother, brother, companion, and lover, all in one. These days, though, he was often no more than a child. It felt as if she were losing her family all over again.

"It's even worse for him. I try not to let it show, but he can tell how sad I am. For as long as I've known him, he's wanted only one thing: to make me happy. Now he makes me a little unhappier every day. And he's powerless against it. All that damn money, and it doesn't do him a lick of good."

Brigitte finished her beer and fell silent. Eva cleared her throat and asked why Walther Schoormann always repeated that same sentence. Brigitte replied that she knew almost nothing about his time in prison. But that he had been tortured. Brigitte got up and cleared the empty bottles into a little pantry off the kitchen. *I was at that camp with my parents as a child*, Eva wanted to say. She would have liked to tell Brigitte that for as long as she could remember, the smell of burning had nauseated her mother. To tell her about the incident at German House. About the destroyed roses. That they couldn't possibly be the reason the main defendant, after all these years, was still so irate that he would spit at her mother's feet. Eva would have liked to ask Brigitte what she should do. Whether she should talk or keep quiet. But Eva kept quiet now and got up from the table. The women said good night to each other in the front passage. Eva slowly climbed the stairs. With every step, it became clearer: she didn't need any advice. For months, she had sat in a room with people who had lived and worked at the camp. For months, she had heard what happened at that camp, day and night. More and more words poured out of the witnesses' mouths, their voices entered Eva and formed a choir inside her: it was a hell created and run by humans. And for months, she had heard the defendants assert that they hadn't known a thing. Eva didn't believe them. No one in their right mind believed them. Eva's fear that her parents would make the very same claim—"We didn't know a thing"—was debilitating. Because if they did, she would have to part ways with her father and mother.

Eva walked along the upstairs hallway toward her room, the floorboards creaking under her bare feet. When she reached the door, behind which Jürgen was sleeping, she stopped. She didn't think it over, but knocked softly and entered the room. She could make out the contour of the bed beneath the open window. The sky glowed dark blue outside. She sat down on the edge of the bed. Jürgen was sleeping on his stomach, and she couldn't see his face under his black hair.

"Jürgen?"

Eva stroked the back of his head, and he woke up, gasped, and asked sleepily, "Is it my father?" He turned over onto his back.

"No, but I don't want to be alone right now."

Silence. The curtain moved gently in the night breeze. Eva chuckled and almost laughed, because she could positively hear Jürgen thinking. Finally he lifted the blanket. Eva crawled in beside him. He put his arm around her. Jürgen smelled of resin, soap, and sweat. He felt around with his right hand for her braid, which she plaited every evening. Eva could feel his heartbeat even more forcefully now, almost as if his heart were beating in her chest. Something outside in the dunes shrieked. A bird?

"Was that a bird?" Eva asked.

Instead of answering, Jürgen leaned over, kissed her quickly and hard on the mouth, then lay down on top of her, tore her dressing gown open with both hands, pushed up her nightgown, pulled down her underwear, his pajama pants, thrust himself deeper between her legs, which she opened; he gripped his stiff member, maneuvered with it, swore, couldn't find her, then did and furiously entered her. Eva held her breath. He moved a few times inside her, and it hurt her, then he groaned frantically, whimpered, and collapsed on top of her. For a moment he lay there heavily, sobbing quietly. Eva caressed the back of his head. He slid off her then and sat up on the edge of the bed. He rubbed his face with both hands.

"Forgive me, Eva."

He was like a boy, brutal and helpless at once. She rubbed his back as she felt his semen trickle warmly out of her. As though her vagina were crying.

SISSI WAS COAXED INTO accompanying David. They strolled, almost like a couple, through the deserted holiday streets toward the Westend Synagogue, while David pontificated about the significance of Shavuot, the Feast of Weeks. Sissi linked arms with him; she was wearing her tasteful rust-red suit and a new hat, whose violet hue didn't quite match. David often spoke about his

Jewish faith as if he were reading from a book. Sissi wasn't listening. She was calculating whether she could afford to send her son to middle school. He wanted to stay in school for another two years, so he could later apprentice as a travel agent. Meanwhile, Sissi could arrange an apprenticeship at the slaughterhouse for him immediately—and with eighty marks pay per month, at that. "I will never become a butcher! Over my dead body!" he had exclaimed in disgust. He wanted to sit in an office and sell trips to faraway lands—not wear a rubber apron and slop around in animal carcasses. Sissi could see where her son was coming from, but things would get tight financially. Her johns weren't exactly increasing in number, although her experience did help offset the aging process. But how much longer would that last? David was explaining that Shavuot celebrated the day the Torah was presented to the Jewish people at Mount Sinai. By reading the Ten Commandments, one renewed one's ties to the ineffable. Infants, small children, the elderly—anyone who was able to, should participate in this celebration. The faithful traditionally drank milk and ate dairy and honey.

"Because the Torah is like milk, Sissi! Milk that the nation of Israel drinks as eagerly as an innocent child!"

"Oh," Sissi said. She finished her calculations and concluded that she would give it a try, even if it meant she'd need about a hundred marks extra every month. If necessary, she could pour drinks at Mokka Bar. She didn't need much sleep.

In the temple vestibule, a throng of worshippers gathered for services. The walls were decorated with birch branches and colorful bands of fabric. The men wore festive yarmulkes, the women their best dresses and silk head scarves. It seemed the kids barely dared breathe, for all their finery. The mood was social and cheery.

Rabbi Riesbaum, a serious man with sincere eyes who had helped David work through his many questions concerning faith over the past few months, greeted him warmly. He took quick stock of Sissi, then gave her a nod. David secured his purple yarmulke in place, and Sissi smiled and pointed at her hat and said that now they looked like twins. She moved toward the sanctuary, but David told her to take the stairs to the side. Women had to sit in a separate gallery. Sissi climbed a few steps and peeked into the space upstairs, where several women, girls, and young children were already seated. She hurried back to David and hissed, "You mean to say I'm supposed to go up there and stare at the wall?"

"It's tradition."

"That's too much for me. I'm leaving." Sissi turned and headed for the exit. David grabbed her arm.

"Please stay. You'll like it. And there's food afterward. Pancakes with yogurt. And cheesecake."

Sissi paused. "Cheesecake?"

David smiled. "Cheesecake and the Ten Commandments. That's what this is all about."

Sissi hesitated, then turned and somewhat reluctantly climbed the stairs. David entered the sanctuary, which was now so familiar. A few men nodded amiably in greeting. But he still felt like a fraud.

Upstairs, behind the wall, Sissi listened to the prayers and songs and reading from the Torah with the other women. She listened to the foreign language. The cantor sang in Aramaic,

God shall prepare a meal for the righteous.
May you faithful,
who hear this praise in song,

receive invitation to this communion.
May you be found worthy
to sit in this hall,
because you have heard these ten words
that resound in glory.

To Sissi, the melody sparked an image of a withdrawn child singing to himself as he played. She didn't understand the words, but she was well acquainted with the Ten Commandments. She thought every last one was right. Sissi had an uncomplicated relationship with God—he left her alone, as she did him. She had observed nearly all of the commandments her entire life. Only she hadn't been able to honor her parents. She had never met them.

"YOU'RE GETTING A DIVORCE?!"

Annegret almost choked on her meringue cake. She was sitting with Doctor Küssner in the Hausberg Schänke beer garden outside the city; every last seat was taken. They had driven there in Küssner's car, because Annegret wouldn't dream of lifting a finger in her free time. Their table was loaded with cups and small coffeepots as well as two plates of cake, although Doctor Küssner didn't like sweets. The neighboring tables were occupied by howling or hungrily snacking children, courting couples, and sweaty, thirsty hikers. They were surrounded by lively Sunday afternoon activity, but Annegret had frozen.

Küssner regarded her and said, "I've already spoken several times with Ingrid. She is starting to accept it. She'll stay in our house with the children. You know I've never liked this ugly city. And it keeps getting uglier. I've been offered the opportunity to take over a practice in Wiesbaden. It's a beautiful old house. Art Nouveau, with a big yard. Nice area, only cultivated people. Well-behaved children, friendly parents. I'd like to live and work there together with you."

Annegret chewed and swallowed, then set down her cake fork and stood. "Excuse me for a moment."

She maneuvered her way among tables and chairs. She entered the dim taproom, where just a few older guests had come to escape the sun. She followed the sign pointing the way to the restrooms, along an unventilated hallway, across a small courtyard, and down a long flight of stairs into the basement. The restroom had three stalls, one of which was luckily unoccupied. Annegret went in, lifted the toilet seat, and abruptly vomited half-chewed meringue and cream into the bowl. She yanked the toilet chain and the water gurgled, but the meringue remained afloat, and she flushed again. The white chunks hung in the water like little icebergs. In the meantime, a woman had come out of one of the other stalls.

"Can I help?"

"No, thank you."

Annegret wiped her mouth with a handkerchief, standing before the spotted mirror. She took her lipstick out of her purse and redid her lips in a slightly garish shade of orange. She began to tease her hair with a comb. She poked around her hair with the handle of the comb for a long time. Finally she let her hand fall.

Hartmut Küssner sat upstairs in the beer garden and regretted nothing. He had been afraid of this conversation, almost more than of that with his wife. He worried it would feel wrong to map out their shared future. But that hadn't been the case. On the contrary. As he watched Annegret return—luminous lipstick reapplied, her white-blond hair more cottony than ever, fat and combative in her spring dress with the large floral print, yet her eyes so full of fear and vulnerability—he knew at that moment that he loved her. That he wanted to provide for her and take care of her for the rest of his life. Annegret sat down across from him and began to eat her cake again almost immediately.

"I'm sorry," she said, with her mouth full. "You've made a mistake, Hartmut. I won't be going anywhere with you."

"It's in Wiesbaden-Bierstadt."

"Doesn't matter where. Or living with you. I've never been anything but clear with you. We're having an affair, and that's it."

"It's true, you've never said anything to the contrary. But I don't care."

Annegret looked up. She couldn't help but laugh at this unassuming, balding man without a single wrinkle, who was demonstrating such unexpected power. Annegret put down her fork.

"I already have a family."

"Where you'll die an old maid?"

"Well, not so sure about the 'maid' bit." Annegret smiled wryly. "No is my answer. So what are you going to do, Doctor Küssner? Kidnap me and lock me in the basement of this sensational Art Nouveau house in Wiesbaden-Bierstadt?"

Doctor Küssner pulled a pair of sunglasses Annegret had never seen out of the breast pocket of his jacket and put them on. "Maybe."

Annegret laughed, but it didn't sound genuine.

THE FLIGHT BACK FROM the island was, as Brigitte put it, "unspeakably bad." They had taken off into black clouds, because the pilot initially saw it as an exciting challenge, then flown through heavy rains that turned into a storm. The little airplane shook so badly that even Jürgen discreetly clutched his seat a few times. Furthermore, Walther Schoormann's morning sedatives weren't working, which did not become clear till they were already in the air. He feared for his life, but thankfully did not start thrashing about; instead, he babbled incessantly. They could only catch the occasional fragment or word, but the topic was clear: communism as the sole enduring humanist social system. Eva listened and gave in to the shaking; she was the only passenger who wasn't scared, as though all feeling inside her had died.

When Eva opened the door to the apartment above German House later, she instinctively expected Purzel to jump up around her as she entered. Instead, Edith came out of the kitchen. She took her daughter's wet coat. "What's this weather you've brought with you?" she asked in greeting. She usually reserved this line for strangers. She didn't await a response, either, but immediately started telling Eva that Stefan had dug Purzel up again the day before. Her father, who wandered out of the living room and looked like he'd been sleeping, explained that Stefan had discovered he was missing two of his best soldiers, which he needed to maintain "sufficient troop strength" against his friend Thomas Preisgau. Stefan hadn't considered this at Purzel's burial. Stefan was sitting at the kitchen table, doing his homework. He hugged Eva and reported at length about Purzel's current condition—about his eyes, which were just gone, and about the "beastly" smell. Stefan held his nose at the thought of it, while their mother returned to the stove, where she was preparing lunch, a stew of vegetable and meat leftovers thrown together from Ludwig's kitchen. Eva liked this dish—"big pot in a little'n," Ludwig called it—but didn't have much of an appetite and just poked at her food. She told them about the sprawling beach on the northernmost island in the North Sea, prompting gruff commentary from Ludwig, ever the Juist patriot. That beach was man-made. "They dump sand there from China when the tourists aren't looking!" Over coffee after lunch, Eva gave them their presents. She had bought Annegret some East Frisian tea and a big bag of rock candy, which she set aside for later that evening. Her parents unwrapped a blue-and-white tile, which depicted a young couple ice-skating, painted in delicate brushstrokes. They were overjoyed, and Eva noticed how tired they both looked. Stefan got a blue captain's hat with a pom-pom plunked on his head by Eva. He beamed and dashed into the hallway. He saluted before the mirror and marched back and forth.

"Left, right, left, right, attention!"

"Stefan, it's a captain's hat!" Eva called to him.

Stefan took a moment, then cried out, "All hands on deck! Pull in the lines! She's taking on water at the stern!"

And as a ship threatened to sink in the front hallway, Eva and her parents sat in silence at the kitchen table, Edith and Ludwig both resting their hands on the waxed cotton tablecloth. The rain Eva had brought with her from the island beat against the kitchen window. Eva took another sip of her coffee, which had gone cold and tasted stale. She placed her hands on the table as well. *Don't speak. Don't move. Hold your breath till it passes and no one will come to any harm.*

DAVID WAS NERVOUS. He had slept poorly and looked unwell. The blond man noticed it the moment they said good morning in the auditorium. He would have liked to put a hand on his shoulder. Instead, he remarked snidely that David's big day had finally come. They had finally reached Defendant Number Four. David responded so earnestly, however, that the blond man regretted his comment. He still hadn't managed to figure out what connected David to this defendant—the Beast. To the prosecution's dismay, the defendant was still at liberty. His request for deferred arrest had been renewed three times for health reasons. Over the next few days, fifteen former prisoners were scheduled to speak about what had occurred in Block Eleven. Six came from Poland and would be dependent on Fräulein Bruhns's interpreting. Eva showed up at the municipal building that day as if nothing had happened. She greeted Fräulein Schenke and Fräulein Lehmkuhl, and they commiserated over the dearth of fashionable weatherproof clothing. It was still raining outside, as the cold snap dug in its heels. Inside the overheated foyer with its foggy windows, the reporters seemed agitated, besieging the attorney general, prosecutors, and defense attorneys, eavesdropping on each other, and fighting loudly over the use of the pay phones. Two even started tussling and had to be separated by a hall attendant. The reporters felt certain that new atrocities would come to light, which meant good numbers. Seats in the gallery were hard-won too. Defendant Number Four's wife, the faded beauty, had taken her spot in the front row, her bearing even more erect than usual. She wore a strikingly elegant suit and had carefully done her hair and makeup. Eva regarded the woman from across the auditorium and mused that she was like a one-time opera singer who had played all the major roles— Ophelia, Leonora, Kriemhild—without ever feeling a thing in her heart.

Silence fell in the room, the judges entered, and the first witness was called: Nadia Wasserstrom, who had worked as the personal secretary to Defendant Number Four at the camp. The ferret face remained impassive as the woman, on crutches, slowly approached the witness stand. Eva helped her into the chair and then translated what the woman could remember. As Nadia Wasserstrom began to speak in a clear Polish, without hesitation, without searching for words—and Eva reproduced the sentences in the same rhythm, without the help of her two dictionaries, detecting meaning and placing pauses—Eva sensed that something had changed. She tried to discern what it was, while she translated testimony that the defendant, who led the camp's political department with the rank of SS-Oberscharführer, had arbitrarily ordered people shot—and shot them himself—at the Death Wall, men, women, and children. He invented a type of swing, from which prisoners were hung upside down from the backs of their knees. The defendant then questioned them in this defenseless position and beat them with rods and whips, many to death. During these descriptions, Defendant Number Four tilted his head occasionally to the left or to the right. He waved at his wife once, who gave him a quick smile. The chief judge rebuked him and asked what he had to say about the accusations; his attorney—the White Rabbit—replied, after rising, "My client denies these accusations without exception. He was simply performing interrogations as ordered."

During the lunch break, Eva stayed seated in the hall. Was she getting sick? She was sweating and wiped a handkerchief over her brow. She took a small bottle out of her briefcase and unscrewed the top. Peppermint water, which she had kept among her things since her fainting spell, and which had helped her stave off nausea on a number of occasions already. She sniffed at it, expecting the sharp, refreshing scent, but she couldn't smell anything. Her nose must be stuffed. Maybe she really was coming down with the flu. David hadn't left his post, either. He stared over at the empty defendants' tables, at the seat of the defendant, who was currently sitting with the other defendants at a table on the far side of the cafeteria next door to the auditorium, protected from spectators and reporters by a police guard, eating his lunch.

Nadia Wasserstrom's testimony continued after the break. Eva translated. "A very young man, a German Jew, was once beaten to death by the defendant. It was September ninth, '44. I recall it so clearly because he fainted in my office before the interrogation. From hunger. One of the female wardens had given me a piece of cake. I gave it to him. Then the defendant called him into his office for the interrogation. Two hours later, the door opened. The young man was hanging from the swing. He no longer looked like a human being. His clothes were gone. His buttocks, his genitals—everything was swollen, bloody, open. He was just a sack, a bloody sack. Another prisoner came in then and dragged him out. I had to mop up the blood." Eva could see the image before her eyes, she was standing in that outside office, registering every detail, the facial features of the deceased, the open door to the office, the red trail leading to the swing. She caught every last detail, yet still felt blind. She looked around the courtroom as though searching for something, and met the blank gaze of the defendant's wife. Eva started, because it was like looking in a mirror. She now knew what was different about today: she no longer felt anything.

David stood up and leaned over to the blond man's microphone. He spoke into it, which wasn't actually allowed, and asked, "It was his brother who had to carry him out. His younger brother, wasn't it?"

Eva glanced at the blond man, who gave her a terse nod. She turned to Nadia Wasserstrom.

"Was it his brother?"

"That, I don't remember."

"I present you with the following, ma'am!" David insisted, holding up a document. "You stated as much on January tenth, two years ago, at your first interview with the prosecution's investigator!"

Eva spoke softly to Nadia, who shook her head.

"She must remember!" David exploded. "Ask her again!"

"David, sit down!" the blond man hissed.

The chief judge spoke into his microphone at the same time. "I do not consider the question material to the witness's testimony."

The blond man grasped David by the shoulder and pushed him back into his seat. David sat down reluctantly and ran his hands through his hair, then stood up and charged across the auditorium, through the seated spectators, up the steps to the double doors, and out of the room. Eva noticed that even the defendant was watching David's departure. Then he said something to his attorney, who rose: his client wished to make a statement. The chief judge turned toward the ferret face and made a gesture. Granted.

The defendant stood and stated, in a soft voice, "I was not even at my office that day. We were celebrating our commandant's birthday. He had invited approximately twenty officers on a boat tour of the Soła, followed by lunch in the officers' mess. You may ask my wife, right over there. She joined me that day too. Or the adjutant here. He was there that day with his wife as well."

The chief judge turned to his associate judges. They conferred briefly. The defendant's wife was then called forward. She introduced herself and began to describe the day in question, slowly and exhaustively. Eva and Nadia Wasserstrom had moved to sit on the prosecutors' side. She translated quietly for the witness, who listened carefully and never took her eyes off the defendant's wife. The faded beauty remembered many details, but mainly recalled the shared lunch in the officers' mess. They'd had roast pork. With mashed potatoes and cucumber salad. Finally, the wife opened her purse and pulled something out.

"This photograph was taken over dessert. Would you like to see it?"

Nadia, meanwhile, said to Eva, "Then it happened on a different day. A different date. But it happened. Just on a different day."

But Eva didn't hear her, although the witness was speaking directly into her ear. Eva looked at the photograph in the wife's hand. She was certain her father was pictured there. Laughing among the sated officers and their wives. But Eva didn't care.

WHEN ANNEGRET LEFT City Hospital that afternoon and hurried through the rain toward the streetcar stop, Doctor Küssner was waiting for her. As on their first evening together, he'd been leaning against his dark vehicle, then stepped into her way as she passed. His coat was soaked—he'd clearly been waiting for some time. She had been avoiding him in the ward for the past few days. He now grabbed her arm and steered her toward his car so forcefully it would have attracted attention had Annegret attempted to free herself from his grip. He put her in the passenger seat, slammed the door shut, and sat down behind the wheel. Annegret feigned scorn and asked if he was following through with his plans to abduct her. Doctor Küssner ignored the question and informed her that he had moved out of his house. "How is that any of my concern?" Annegret snarled. He retorted that it was high time she shook the unhealthy attitude that nothing ever concerned her. Outside the car, Nurse Heide walked past in her shapeless raincoat and heard loud voices. She glanced through the windows, which were beginning to fog up, and recognized the two quarreling. She considered her long-held suspicions confirmed and happily made her way home. Human depravity had proven itself yet again!

Doctor Küssner had started crying in the car, awkwardly but authentically, which Annegret could barely stand.

"What the hell is this? Do you think you can pressure me like this? Or are you bawling because you regret it? I told you from the start—"

"Shut your trap!" Küssner hissed, uncharacteristically uncouth. He wiped away his tears and stared at the rain streaming down the windshield. "I'm sad because I'm hurting my wife. I'm sad because I won't be living with my children anymore. Yet it's still the right thing to do." Doctor Küssner sat up, turned the key, and started the engine. He turned on the wipers, which cleared their view of the street, passersby, and other cars' headlights. "We're driving to Wiesbaden. I'd like to show you the house."

Annegret reached for the door handle. "I don't want to!"

But Doctor Küssner turned on his blinker to enter traffic. "I love you." It was the first time anyone had ever said that to Annegret.

"You don't know me."

"What do knowing someone and loving them have to do with each other?" Küssner stepped on the gas, and at the same time, Annegret opened her door. She heaved herself out of the moving car. Küssner hit the brakes.

"Are you insane?!"

Annegret rolled her ankle and roared that he was a selfish pig, just like every other man, and threw the door shut. She limped away in outrage. Doctor Küssner honked twice, loudly, then sped off. He was furious too. He soon calmed down, though, and drove by himself to Wiesbaden, where he signed the lease agreement for the thriving pediatric clinic, the rental contract for the Art Nouveau mansion with its overgrown lawn, and dreamed of a shared future with Annegret.

Annegret entered the apartment above German House. Her ankle barely hurt anymore. She was tough.

"Anyone home?" There was no reply. Annegret hung her wet raincoat on a hook and headed straight for Eva's room. She went to her desk, opened the second drawer from the top, and pulled out one of the blue notebooks inside. She lay down on Eva's bed, fumbled in the pocket of her black stirrup pants for a fruit candy, which she popped into her mouth, and began to read: *Women and children were first led into the "Showers," followed by the men. In order to trick the victims and prevent panic from breaking out, signs were mounted, indicating the way to the "Bathroom" or "Disinfection Room." Five to seven hundred adults and children in a given arrival group would be forced into a space barely a hundred meters square. Zyklon B was dumped into a wire mesh contraption, then released into a wire mesh column through a hatch in the roof. Screams could be heard outside the gas chambers at first, then the sound of the voices changed into a buzzing, like in a beehive, till everything went quiet. They all died within five to fifteen minutes. After airing out the gas chamber for thirty to forty minutes, the Sonderkommando, a special prisoner work unit, had to clear out the corpses. They had to collect the dead people's jewelry, cut off their hair and extract their gold teeth, separate babies from their mothers . . .*

Annegret closed her eyes. She thought of little Martin Fasse. She had managed to control herself since his death. She didn't even carry around the syringe anymore. The one filled with the brownish liquid that made the children weak, feeble, and fatigued. Annegret fell asleep, and her half-finished candy slipped out of her mouth and onto the pillow. The opened notebook fell onto her belly. This was how Eva found her when she got home. She gaped at her sleeping sister, grabbed the notebook, and shook her by the shoulder.

"What do you think you're doing in here?!" Annegret blinked and came to, then sat up. Eva was fuming. "What were you thinking, prying through my things?!"

"I'm not prying, I'm reading."

"Annegret, what's the big idea? Why would you do that?"

With a wave of her hand, Annegret got out of bed, the mattress creaking, and stepped over to Eva's wardrobe, which had a mirror on its middle door. She fixed up her white-blond hair, picking at it with her thumb and index finger. "I find it engaging."

Eva looked at her sister in the mirror. She must have misheard. Annegret continued, "You know, it's like at the hospital. Patients are always trying to outdo each other with their stories."

"These aren't stories! This happened." Eva was aghast.

"Everybody wants to be the one closest to death. Among our parents, those whose child is sickest are the most revered. And if the kid dies, well, they get the gold crown."

"What the hell are you saying?!" Eva felt dizzy, as if she were in the middle of a bad dream where trusted people did atrocious things. Annegret turned and stepped up close to Eva. Her breath smelled of sticky raspberry candy.

"I mean, Eva, you're not exactly dumb yourself. It's just common sense that they're all lying through their teeth. It was a labor camp—"

"Hundreds of thousands of people were systematically murdered there." Eva looked at her sister, whom she had known her entire life.

"They were criminals, so of course they wouldn't get kid-glove treatment," Annegret continued, unimpressed. "But the numbers that are being thrown around, those are nonsense. I did a rough calculation, myself, once. I happen to know a little bit about chemistry, after all. Do you know how much of this Zyklon B stuff they would have needed to kill all those people? They would've had to receive four truckloads every day—"

Eva walked out on Annegret midsentence. Annegret followed on her heels and continued to explain that this alleged mass extermination wasn't even logically possible. Eva went into the living room and opened the cupboard. She pulled out the manila folder and opened it. She thrust the top sheet in Annegret's face.

"You drew this."

Annegret fell silent and looked at the pointed roof, the slanted door and disproportionately large windows, at the two girls in braids and the smokestacks in the background. She shrugged, but Eva could clearly see little beads of sweat form on her sister's brow and her face turn white.

"Those two," Eva said. "That's us. We were there, Annegret. All of those people died right next door to us. We were there, and you know it." The sisters looked each other in the eye. Eva began to cry, then to sob. Annegret looked increasingly perturbed, as though someone had woken her from a long, comatose slumber. She took a step toward Eva, like she wanted to hug her. Then the front door opened and they heard their father come in.

"Man, oh, man, is it coming down out there. I'm ready for you, Noah!"

Annegret yanked the drawing out of Eva's hand and began to rip it up. Ludwig and Edith appeared in the door. Ludwig was standing up straighter than usual.

"Notice anything different about me?" he asked jovially.

Edith, on the other hand, immediately sensed something was amiss. Her eyes wandered from Annegret, who was tearing the paper into smaller and smaller bits, to Eva, who was rubbing her face. Her cheeks were blotchy, and her updo had come loose. Then Stefan burst into the room.

"Daddy's wearing a crosset!"

"It's called a 'corset,' little one. And I could get used to this. I think it's already helping!"

"Hush, Ludwig," Edith interjected. "As for you, sweetheart, off to your room now."

"Why?! Were you crying, Eva?"

"Yes, because of Purzel." Eva swallowed and pulled herself together.

Edith pushed Stefan out the doorway. "Time to practice your dictation. Scoot! Otherwise no pudding later." Stefan puffed out his cheeks and shuffled to his room. The other four didn't move. Even Ludwig was getting worried now.

"What on earth is going on? I have to be in the kitchen in half an hour."

There's nothing left to lose, Eva thought, and she said, "What was it like, Daddy, to serve up full bellies and happy hearts to those murderers?"

At that, Annegret pointedly let the scraps of paper flutter to the floor and left the room.

Ludwig sat down at the dining room table. The room was silent but for a gentle knocking on the window whenever the wind blew rain against the panes. Edith crouched down on the carpet and gathered the scraps into her cupped hand. Eva looked at the painting on the wall and tried to remember the cows' names.

"What would you like to know, Eva?" Ludwig asked.

"A VISITT TO THEE ZOOO is some-thhhingg for thee whole fam-i-lee. We lookk att thee an-i-malss andd fen-ses pro-tecctt us from the dayn-ger-ouss an-i-malss." In Stefan's room next door, Annegret was practicing a dictation with her brother. She stood beside him and read the practice text out loud, excessively enunciating each word. Stefan was stooped over his notebook, writing slowly and making lots of mistakes.

"Fen*ces*, sweetie. Fences with a 'c.' Next sentence: 'We can see goats or horses anywhere, but where else can we see the lion's impressive mane or the tiger's bright fur?' Question mark."

"IT WAS A HAPPY TIME," her father had said. This sentence echoed in Eva's mind as she stood in the streetcar and held onto one of the hanging straps with her right hand. She was on her way to the public prosecutor's office. Her parents had still been talking about their time at the camp when the phone in the front hallway rang. It was Fräulein Schenke. There was an urgent telex from Poland that needed translating. Despite the late hour, the streetcar was crowded. Eva stood hedged among the breathing bodies and didn't feel their touch. She saw her father sitting before her at the table, his posture better than usual. Her mother, hands clasped behind her back, leaning against the cupboard. "It was a happy time," her father had said. Because this position was the first where he was allowed to bring his wife and daughters with him. They lived together as a family for the first time, in a big house, provided for and protected. It wasn't till some time had passed that they began to understand what was going on at the camp. The guests in the mess were officers, upstanding folks. Not all of them, of course—some drank too much. The director of the political department? The one with the ferret face? Polite and unassuming. He sometimes asked for leftovers. For the prisoners who worked in his department. No, they didn't know what he did during office hours. No, the SS people didn't talk about their work at lunch. Eva's mother had said that she never even went into the camp. She tended to the household, did laundry, and cooked. She took care of her daughters. Yes, she had to close the windows. It smelled awful when the east wind was blowing. Yes, they knew that bodies were being burned there. But they didn't learn till afterward that people were being killed in gas chambers. Not till after the war. Why didn't he request a transfer? He tried twice. No luck. Yes, well, he did indeed join the SS, even before the war. But only because he felt alone, because he was so often separated from his family. Not because of personal conviction. Eva had asked why the main defendant spat at her mother's feet.

"And why was his wife so hostile? What have they got against you?"

Edith had replied that they didn't know, and Eva's father had repeated the line. "We don't know."

The telephone had rung in the hallway. When Eva returned to the living room after the short call, and explained that she had to go to the office, her father had looked at her and said, as though making his final point, "We had no choice, child."

Eva got out at the stop near the office building. She could not remember ever having been so tired in her life. It was all she could do not to sit down on a park bench, never to rise again. Eva took the elevator to the ninth floor, rang at the glass door, and Fräulein Schenke appeared on the other side to let her in.

"So, are you going to join us later at Boogie's?" Eva shook her head, but Fräulein Schenke continued. "Lehmkuhl's coming, Miller, and that other clerk . . . what's his name again, the one with those unbelievably long lashes?"

"Herr Wettke," Eva replied.

"Right."

At that moment, the light blond-haired man appeared in the hallway, and he rushed toward Eva, his face visibly tense. He handed her a thin piece of paper, the printing slightly smeared. A telex. Eva skimmed the brief message and translated its content.

"The journey has been approved by the highest authority. Visas are being issued for all individuals requested."

For a moment, the blond man looked as if he wanted to embrace Eva, but then he gave her a quick nod and shook her hand with unaccustomed warmth.

"Thank you."

"Was that it?"

"Yes, that was it. But it was important. It's in regard to the on-site inspection. We're going to Poland."

Eva understood then. After various defendants first claimed that they couldn't have seen or known this or that, because their office was located elsewhere, and after recurring assertions that the map of the camp was flawed, the prosecution—led by the blond man—had made a motion for a visual inspection of the camp. The defense had been against it, arguing that there were no reliable diplomatic ties between Germany and Poland, and that organizing a trip of this nature behind the Iron Curtain would be too involved. The blond man had persisted, though, and appealed to the highest levels of government in Bonn and Poland. To him, today's telex represented the greatest success in the trial thus far. He looked happy.

"Will I be joining?" Eva asked quietly. "Or is there someone there who can translate for you?"

The blond man then gave her a look, as if just recognizing her now. "Could I have a quick word, Fräulein Bruhns?"

Eva was surprised by his familiar tone. She followed him down the corridor to his office. He offered her a chair and stood by the window, his back to the courtyard below, out of which the city's next new high-rise was climbing into the night sky.

"Your fiancé came to see me."

Eva sat down.

The morning after their return from the island, Jürgen had turned up at the public prosecutor's office. David Miller had opened the door for him, and they'd given each other a once-over. Their dislike was mutual.

"Fräulein Bruhns isn't here today," David said.

"I know; I'd like to speak with the lead prosecutor."

David hesitated, then made an exaggeratedly servile hand gesture. "If the gentleman would care to follow me."

David went first, and Jürgen followed him down the hallway. He eyed David's hair, which was too long in the back, his wrinkled suit coat, and his inappropriate footwear, which looked like athletic shoes. *What a slovenly fellow*, he thought. At the same time, he had to acknowledge that there were surely plenty of young women impressed by David. Eva, for example. David knocked on the open door to one of the offices and waved Jürgen in. The blond man, in shirtsleeves, was crouched on the floor by the wall; sunlight was beating in through the window, and he had taken off his jacket. He was sorting documents into different-colored folders. Order forms and delivery slips for Zyklon B.

"The people who signed these are all dead. We're still missing those damn driving permits!" the blond man said to David as he entered.

"You have company," David responded and left.

The blond man offered Jürgen a seat and waited expectantly. Jürgen removed his hat and explained.

"I am Fräulein Bruhns's fiancé."

"I see." The blond man had been searching for his cigarettes under the papers on his desk. He offered Jürgen one from the pack. "What is this regarding, Herr Schoormann?"

Jürgen had felt badly. But it was too late.

EVA SAT OPPOSITE the blond man and listened as he told her, "He said that the work is taking too great a toll on your nerves, and that your nerves are not terribly stable as it is. He requested that we release you from your duties."

Eva felt as if she were falling to indefinable depths. She was stunned. "He never discussed this with me. And I'm not going to stop! I'm a part of this trial! I provide the voice for these people."

The blond man made a placating hand gesture. "Unfortunately, he holds the decision-making power in this case. As a governing authority, we would be liable to prosecution, ourselves, if we continued to employ you against the wishes of your future husband. I am sorry."

Eva looked at the blond man and wanted to say something, but she just shook her head mutely. She felt nauseous. She stood up and left the office without a word. She rushed down the hallway, which seemed to go on endlessly, and ducked into the ladies' room. Fräulein Schenke and Fräulein Lehmkuhl were both standing at the mirror, getting ready for an evening at the Boogie Bar. They glanced at Eva, who looked miserable.

"What happened?"

Eva fished the little bottle of peppermint oil out of her purse and opened it. This time the sharp smell shot straight into her forehead, her eyes teared up, and she coughed.

"That pig!" she finally said.

"Which one?" Fräulein Schenke snorted, penciling in her eyebrows.

"Your fiancé? Schoormann?" Fräulein Lehmkuhl asked. "If you don't want him anymore, let me know."

Eva stepped up beside the young women and looked at herself in the mirror, at her friendly face crowned with the prim hairstyle. Then she plunged both of her hands into her updo, pulled out the bobby pins one by one, undid the hairband, and shook out her tresses. She let out a desperate, enraged howl, like a battle cry by someone who's still practicing. The two girls exchanged a bewildered look, then Fräulein Lehmkuhl grinned.

"So you *are* coming with us?"

Three hours later, Eva was dancing in the middle of an enormous black metal bucket where someone was stirring powerfully and relentlessly with a big metal spoon. Someone who—Pastor

Schrader was convinced—made all the decisions. It was so loud that Eva couldn't think. It was so full that she didn't know where her body ended and another began. The air she breathed in was the air others had breathed out. Her breath was breathed in by them. *She loves you, yeah, yeah, yeah! She loves you, yeah, yeah, yeah! She loves you, yeah, yeah, yeah. With a love like that, you know you should be glad! Yeah, yeah, yeah. Yeah, yeah, yeah, yeeahh.* Eva was drunk and loved the feeling of Herr Wettke spinning her around this cauldron filled with colorful black people and white people. Eva occasionally caught a glimpse of David Miller, who was sitting on an elevated bench along the wall of the metal bucket, necking with Fräulein Lehmkuhl. Then Eva herself was sitting beside him, without knowing how or when she got there. Or what had become of Fräulein Lehmkuhl. "Where's Fräulein Lehmkuhl?" she yelled into David's ear. David shrugged—he was drunk too. He was celebrating his big day, after all. The Beast had been arrested earlier! The court had finally lifted the "deferred detention for health concerns." He sadly hadn't gotten to see the ferret's face. After fleeing the courtroom, he raced to the synagogue. He sat down in the sanctuary, which was empty at that hour. He waited for Rabbi Riesbaum. He might have been able to confide the truth to him. The truth about himself, about his brother. About his family. But after a little while, he'd caught his breath, calmed down, and left. David watched the dancing people, the American soldiers, the civilians, and bellowed into the din, "That was my brother the Beast beat to death! And I had to carry him out! They had gassed my parents as soon as we arrived!" Then he felt Eva's head fall heavily on his shoulder. She had fallen asleep. Or fainted. He sighed and lifted her off the bench.

Eva came to in the summery evening air outside the Boogie Bar. David had her coat draped over his left arm and held her up with his right.

"I'll hail a cab for you."

David led her to the edge of the street and kept an eye out for a glowing yellow roof sign among the passing cars.

"Thank you," Eva said weakly. Then she remembered something. "What were you just saying about your brother?" Eva lifted her head and tried to find David's face, but everything was spinning, and she couldn't catch it.

Then David threw up his arm and waved. "Taxi!"

The car pulled over, and David deposited Eva on the backseat. He placed her purse in her lap, tossed her coat on the seat beside her, and told the driver, "Three-eighteen Berger Strasse." David shut the door before Eva could even say thank you. He watched the taillights as the taxi drove off and thought that Eva had looked different today. He couldn't put his finger on it, though. Then he popped up the collar of his jacket and trudged off. To Sissi's.

The taxi driver, an older man, wanted to have a conversation with Eva. He tried making eye contact in the rearview mirror.

"You want to go to German House? They close soon. In any case, the kitchen is already closed." Eva looked at her watch but couldn't make out the time. The driver continued, "Is that place worth visiting, the Boogie Bar? Full of Negroes, isn't it? You girls need to be careful around them."

Eva leaned forward then and said she wanted to go somewhere else. She gave the driver the address. The driver repeated it, puzzled, then switched on the blinker, turned the car, and didn't ask any more questions. The fancy address had silenced him.

THE DOCTOR WAS PAYING Walther Schoormann a visit. He'd had a seizure. He and Jürgen had been talking about their new range of products over dinner, in particular about the washing machines. Should they offer installation packages or not? Would it be worth partnering with plumbing companies and charging a percentage? Walther Schoormann resisted the idea of making money off the workers. He spoke out against it. There was no argument—on the contrary, Jürgen agreed with his father. Walther Schoormann then toppled from his chair, like a candle from its holder. He began to convulse on the carpet, kicking forcefully in all directions. It looked as if he were possessed by a demon. Jürgen couldn't bear the sight and had to leave the room. Brigitte, together with an astoundingly calm Frau Treuthardt, cleared away everything that might injure her husband and waited for the fit to end. The doctor had prepared her for something like this. After three minutes, it was over. Walther Schoormann was now lying, exhausted, in the expansive bed in his room. He looked fearful but alert, and was discussing with the doctor whether he should spend the night in the hospital. They ultimately decided that the doctor would stay at the house a little while longer.

"But a word of warning: I charge by the minute, Herr Schoormann." Everyone laughed. Then the doorbell rang, and they all looked around in surprise. Who could that be, at this hour? Jürgen went to see.

He could immediately tell that Eva had been drinking, and as he steered her quickly down the hallway, he called toward the master bedroom, "It's Eva. She . . . she was in the area."

Jürgen closed the door to his room behind them and studied Eva—who stood swaying slightly before him, her hair down, makeup smeared, and eyes glazed—with a mixture of revulsion and desire. "Sit down. Would you like something to drink?"

"Got any gin?"

"I think you've had enough."

Eva collapsed on the wide sofa. "You're right, I have had enough. Jürgen, I'm breaking up with you."

Jürgen instantly felt sick. He tried hard not to let it show. "I see. And what has brought about this decision?"

"You! You've brought it about! How could you go the office behind my back like that? I will not be treated like a child. I decide for myself, where, when, and how I'm going to work. I'm in charge of myself, and myself alone!"

Not everything came out clearly—Eva was slurring slightly and stumbled over some of her words. But she was very serious. Jürgen could see that.

"You've fallen in love with that Canadian."

Eva looked at Jürgen and swore indistinctly. "That's the only reason you would get, isn't it?" she said. "You're so shortsighted!" She struggled with the word "shortsighted," which came out sounding more like "shoresighed." But she was furious, sad, and absolutely decided. "You know, Jürgen, what I need is a friend. And I've realized that you aren't one."

"Well, I am your future husband."

"Which means what? My lord? My master? I have to do your bidding?"

"When we met, you told me you were happy to be led."

"Depends on who's doing the leading. It would have to be someone who's mature and knows himself. Not a boy like you!"

"Eva, where is this insolence coming from?"

Eva did not respond, but instead pulled the engagement ring

off her finger, with some effort. She set it on the glass coffee table with a distinct click and got up.

"Besides, I could never live in a house that reeks of chlorine like this!"

Jürgen was afraid now. He approached her and tried to take her hand. She dodged him.

"Is this because of what happened the other night?"

Eva almost laughed, then growled, "Please, I've experienced worse."

Jürgen flinched, and Eva almost felt badly for him, but she did not take back what she'd said. Jürgen made one final, fittingly pathetic attempt.

"I just wanted to protect you. I can see how this trial has changed you."

"Yes, thankfully."

Eva took her purse from the sofa, her raincoat from the back of the chair, and teetered slightly as she left the room. Jürgen followed her to the front door. He was quiet, then suddenly dashed in front of her in the hallway and blocked her way, his back to the door.

"You're not leaving!"

Eva looked into Jürgen's eyes, dark green and flashing deep in their sockets. She looked at his black hair, which by this hour was a bit mussed—he had two devil horns. He had once come close to hitting her. Today, though, all she sensed was his desperate fear of being left. She could have cried, but instead she said, "I wish your father all the best. And please give Brigitte my warm regards."

Eva reached past Jürgen for the front door handle. Jürgen looked at the floor, then stepped aside and let her pass. The door snapped shut. Brigitte appeared in the hallway and looked at Jürgen curiously.

"What did she want?"

But he went to his room without answering.

ONE DAY IN LATE SUMMER, when especially fat black flies were buzzing against the closed windows, the little girl and her big sister were allowed to join their mother at the hairdresser's for the first time ever. The big sister didn't want to go, though. She stamped her foot, and when her mother tried pulling her out of the house, she clung to the door frame with both hands. She was screaming like a small child, although she was nearly nine years old. Then she bit her mother's hand, and her mother slapped her. But she also no longer insisted she come along. The little girl turned around in the doorway one last time and tapped her temple at her sister. She couldn't begin to understand her behavior. After all, they were going to get their hair curled and would smell like flowers afterward, like fancy ladies did. The little girl was excited as she walked down a dusty road, holding her mother's hand. The apples were turning red on the trees, but would still give you a bellyache if you ate one. A group of men in striped suits came walking from the other direction. They were led by three soldiers. One of them greeted her mother by lifting the cane he was carrying. The men in the suits were thin, with big eyes and funny haircuts under their hats. *They need to go to the hairdresser's too*, the girl thought.

"Don't look over there," her mother said. The girl was spooked by the men, who wouldn't look at her and moved as if there were no one at home inside. The girl and her mother reached a red-and-white gate. Her mother had to show a piece of paper with a small picture of herself glued on it, then she had to sign something. The girl craned her neck and looked down the endless fence. She wondered why there wasn't a single bird sitting on the wire. They passed through the gate and walked toward an archway that had something written on it. The girl already knew the letters A and E, because they were in her name.

"A-e-a-e," she spelled out loud. They passed under the archway.

The light blue room smelled of soap. A man in a white coat lifted the girl into a chair and spun her around a few times. Like a merry-go-round. And like a magician, the man made a comb and pair of scissors appear in his hands.

"I want curls," the girl said.

The man responded in a foreign language and pointed at a sink. The girl was scared, because having her hair washed hurt her eyes. But the man led her to the sink. He turned on the warm water and let it run through the girl's hair; he rinsed and lathered and rinsed. He was careful. Not a single drop of water touched the girl's face, but she kept her eyes shut tight the entire time.

His name was Jaschinsky. Eva remembered now. Standing at the shattered sink in the camp's former hair salon, Eva remembered him. He'd been a prisoner—once, during a later visit there, the sleeve of his white coat had ridden up, and Eva had noticed the tattooed number. She pointed at it, and he read her the numbers out loud in Polish. Eva repeated them, in order not to forget. At her next visit, she wanted to show Herr Jaschinsky that she had memorized the numbers. But he wasn't as friendly as usual that time. He normally had two helpers, two young women, who swept up the clippings and put ladies' hair in curlers. One of them had a funny face, a nose that swooped upward. She wasn't there that day, though. Herr Jaschinsky washed Eva's hair and got soap in her left eye. He didn't notice. Eva typically would have cried at that, but for some reason, she kept quiet. Later, though, when it was time to crimp her hair with the curling iron, he pressed the hot metal against her scalp. It hissed and smelled of burned hair and skin. Eva shrieked. Her mother yelled, and Herr Jaschinsky apologized. With tears in his eyes. Eva's mother never took her back.

Eva involuntarily touched her fingertips to the spot above her ear, where the oblong scar was covered by her hair. She was ashamed of her childish bawling. What was that momentary pain compared to everything those people had been forced to endure here? A figure appeared in the open doorway to the salon.

"Where have you been? We need you outside. We're at Block Eleven."

Eva followed David Miller out onto the camp street.

The day before, Eva had been the one woman among twenty-four men to arrive there by way of Warsaw. The group included six representatives of the defense, the chief judge and his two associate judges, the lead prosecutor, five other prosecutors, David Miller, and two reporters, among others. From the airport, the travelers rode seven hours in a rickety bus on poorly constructed roads. By the time they reached the town that had given the camp its name, it was already dark. They retired to their rooms in a simple lodge on the outskirts. There was very little talking. They were all tired and watchful at once. Eva moved into her small, sparsely appointed room. On the narrow bed was a folded towel of an indistinct pale color and so threadbare that one could almost see through it. *That towel's probably been in use since the camp was running,* Eva thought. She got into bed, turned out the light, and tried to comprehend where she was. On location. She listened to the brave ticking of her travel clock and assumed she wouldn't sleep a wink. But she soon drifted off and the night passed in dreamless sleep. A rooster crowing woke her the next morning, even before her alarm. She went to the window and looked out at the yard behind the inn, where the rooster was bustling about with his hens. Beyond the fence was a marshy meadow, and the horizon was lined with rows of trees—poplars—whose leaves glowed yellow in the morning sunshine. At breakfast, where the whitewashed chill of the dining room suggested a newly built clubhouse more readily than an inn, the men from the defense sat together. The White Rabbit was opening and snapping shut his pocket watch even more than usual. On the other side of the room, members of the prosecution were gathered around the light blond-haired man. David sat there quietly, withdrawn, and didn't touch his food. The chief judge sat alone at a table and paged through documents as he ate his bread. *They look human without their robes, like fathers and sons, husbands and friends and lovers*, Eva thought as she sipped the weak coffee. After breakfast they walked to the entrance of the main camp, past single-family homes, where children wearing knapsacks came out on their way to school, and past workshops busy with activity. Conversation, lively at first, quieted and then petered out entirely. They met three Poles at the gate, older gentlemen in dark coats; one was a representative of the Polish government; the other two, employees at the camp memorial site, who would be guiding their tour. Eva translated for the chief judge, whose face no longer looked like the man in the moon from up close, but ordinary. "We would like to gain a comprehensive understanding of the conditions at Auschwitz-Birkenau, the concentration and extermination camp." The guides looked at them almost pityingly at this request. Together with the delegation, Eva walked under the lettering of the archway and into the camp. Many photos were taken, both by the two reporters and one of the prosecutors. The White Rabbit was busy with a tape measure, pacing off the space between individual blocks with one of his colleagues. He noted distances and vantage points. He hoped to prove the courtroom map of the camp unusable. Eva translated the guides' remarks and looked around without recognizing anything. Until they entered one of the two-story brick buildings on the camp street.

"The camp registry office was located in these rooms. And here was a barber shop. SS men and their wives had their hair cut here for free by inmate hairdressers."

The men took a brief look around the light-blue-tiled room. Eva, though, stayed behind, studied the clouded mirrors and dusty swivel chairs and remembered Herr Jaschinsky.

She now followed David toward Block Eleven. He was practically sprinting, and Eva could barely keep up. The group had disappeared around a corner, and for a moment they were alone on the camp street.

"David, wait . . ." Eva caught up and linked arms with him. He gave her a quick sidelong glance.

"How do you feel about the fact, Eva, that we can just walk down this street? As free individuals?" He didn't wait for a response. "What did we, of all people, do to deserve this? I think it's obscene."

He freed himself from her, turned to the right, and disappeared between two brick buildings. Eva followed him. The men from the delegation were standing there before a brick wall. They appeared ashamed, at a loss. Eva approached, and the blond man turned to her. He asked her to please explain to their guides that unfortunately, no one had thought to bring a wreath. Eva saw that a few flowers and grave candles had been placed by the wall, as well as two wreaths, one of which had a Star of David on its ribbon. Eva translated, and one of the guides made an indistinct gesture. The chief judge announced that they would observe a moment of silence. Eva noticed the White Rabbit discussing briefly with his colleagues. Ultimately, however, they too bowed their heads, folded their arms, or clasped their hands, and recalled everything they had heard from the witnesses over the past months, about what those people saw with their own eyes. They were silent and thought about the people who were forced to stand before this wall, whose naked bodies were marked with large numbers, to aid in the identification of the executed at the crematorium. They were silent and thought about the twenty thousand men, women, and children who were shot here for no reason.

Although the visitors began speaking again as they walked on—through Block Eleven, through the Beast's interrogation room, through the infirmary, where the experiments were performed, across the grounds where people lined up for roll call, where people were broken, shot, and beaten, to the barracks, where the people were penned, and where they died of sickness and hunger— the moment of silence continued within them. Not one remained unmoved. The sky was cloudless, as though nothing should go unseen. "Beach weather," one of the reporters said, and took more photos. One of the guides led them into a wooden barracks. They slowly walked down the long middle passage, flanked to the left and right by the three-level wooden bunks on which the people tried to sleep, find a little peace, gain strength, lying there in turns, tightly packed beside each other, on top of each other. By one of the beds in the back, the guide crouched down and pointed to the niche above the lowest bunk. They all leaned in and looked over his shoulder. At first, Eva didn't understand what there was to see, other than a rough wooden wall, which must have let in the freezing cold during the winter. But then she peered at where the guide was pointing and noticed the faded writing on the wood. Someone had written on the wall, in Hungarian, "Andreas Rapaport, lived 16 years." The guide read aloud the inscription, and the visitors, who had clustered around the bunk bed, softly repeated the name and remembered how the witness had told them about Andreas Rapaport, who wrote his name in blood on the wall—and who lived only sixteen years.

Eva left the barracks and began to cry. She couldn't stop. The guide came to her and said, "I've seen this many times. You can know every last thing about Auschwitz, but being here is something different altogether."

David hung back in the barracks by himself. He stood by the plank bed where Andreas Rapaport had lain. Then he knelt on the floor and placed his hand on the wood.

That afternoon, after a lunch break that Eva would later find impossible to recall, they toured the extermination camp, which was two kilometers from the main camp. Eva had packed one of her blue notebooks, to record her impressions that night, back at the lodge, in an effort to get them out of her head. But after she and the others spent hours walking the grounds, along the rambling gatehouse with its distinctive tower in the middle, straddling the train tracks; after they followed the same final path the people took from the ramp; after they stood under the same trees in the birch forest where the people spent the final moments of their lives; after they, like those people, heard the birds singing in the treetops, under a cloudless sky; after they saw the entrance to the chamber, after they grasped the irreversibility; when Eva saw David and the blond man standing close to one another, motionless; when she saw the defense attorney, the White Rabbit—who, like the rest of them, had been utterly humbled—help the chief judge sit down on a tree stump; when she saw the men cry, Eva knew that there were no words for this.

PART
FOUR

A T DUSK, as the men gathered in the dining room, Eva left the inn. She wanted to look for the house where she had lived with her parents for four years. There were no streetlights, and Eva stumbled through the darkening evening. She reached the outer boundary of the camp and followed it toward the west. Every fifty meters, a sign with a skull hung from the fence. *Danger— High Voltage.* Although Eva knew the wire was no longer live, she could hear it humming. The path was unpaved, and she tripped once. The fence turned into a concrete wall. She started to think she was headed in the wrong direction, when lights appeared before her and as she approached, she could make out a row of houses. One of the smaller ones had a markedly pointed roof. Eva stopped by the low hedge that bordered the front yard and peered through a big window into a lit room. Three people were sitting at a table, eating dinner. A man, a woman, and a child. A family. Eva walked a little farther, to the neighboring house, where the main defendant and his wife had lived. It was dark. Beside the house, where the rose bed had been, a car was parked on a paved surface. "Hello? You out there. Are you looking for someone?" a voice called in Polish. Eva turned and saw that the man, who had just been sitting at the table, had come to the door. He sounded wary. Eva moved in a bit closer and answered that she was from Germany, here with a delegation. She was about to say more, but the man interrupted her. Yes. They'd heard about the visitors from West Germany. His voice now sounded curious. His wife appeared in the doorway beside him. Eva saw that she was pregnant. The woman asked if Eva wouldn't like to come in. Eva declined, but the couple was persistent and displayed the proverbial Polish hospitality. Eventually Eva crossed the threshold into the house, and the first thing she saw was the date chiseled into a stone in the floor: *1937*. She remembered tracing the numbers with her finger as a child. And how cold the floor had been under her knees. Even in summer. This was the right house.

The Polish child came to the door, a piece of bread in hand, and stared at Eva curiously. The child had longish hair, and Eva couldn't say whether it was a girl or a boy. She nodded warmly at the child before being led into the living room. She was given a plate and a large helping of stew. She ate out of politeness. Potatoes with bacon and cabbage. The child dug toys out of a crate under the window: building blocks, a colorful rag doll, and wooden beads that thundered across the floor. The man explained that he was a restorer. He'd been working here for half a year. It was his job to conserve evidentiary material for court. It wasn't easy: hair remains were devoured by mites, there was rust gnawing away at glasses frames, and shoes were decaying, attacked by mold or the salts typical of human sweat. The woman swatted jokingly at her husband and told him that this wasn't appropriate dinner conversation. The man apologized. Eva looked around but didn't recognize anything.

"Did you renovate?"

The man nodded and told her, with poorly concealed pride, that nothing was like it used to be. He had torn down walls, put in new floors and windows, hung wallpaper, painted. His wife rolled her eyes, recalling the chaos. She asked Eva to tell them about West Germany, whether it really was so golden, whether everyone really was so rich. The man asked about the trial and whether those SS men would get the death penalty. Eva told him that the death penalty didn't exist in Germany anymore.

"Too bad," the woman said and began clearing the table. Eva stood up to leave. Back in the front hallway, Eva wasn't sure it really was the right house. There must be others built the same year, with that date. She shook the couple's hands, wished them all the best, and thanked them. At that moment, the child came running and held a balled fist up to Eva. Eva hesitated, then held out her hand. The child let something drop into it. Something small and red. The man looked at it.

"What is that?"

His wife shrugged. "No idea where it came from. I think it's a present for you." She smiled.

Eva swallowed. "Thank you," she said to the child.

In her hand was the missing piece of the Christmas pyramid, the Moorish king's offering, the little red wooden package.

THE DINING ROOM WAS WHITE with cigarette smoke, and there was a voice coming from an unseen radio that no one was listening to. It smelled of beer, schnapps, and men's sweat. The prosecutors had joined the defense attorneys at a table—the White Rabbit was the only one missing. The chief judge had also retired already.

They were telling jokes and sharing funny stories about the town that lay just outside the dingy windowpanes. The blond man had read that the Arab League had imposed a boycott on imports from the London-based raincoat company Burberry because one of the board members was a Jew. In a statement, the company had responded that it barely ever rained in Arab countries, anyway—and as such, they exported so few raincoats to the region that they could live with the boycott. Everyone laughed heartily. David sat with the men but wasn't listening. A picture on the wall had caught his eye. It depicted a four-in-hand sleigh being pulled over an icy plain. The driver was cracking his whip, the horses rearing. It was unsettling to see the steamy breath from their massive nostrils. They had a destination to reach. David closed his eyes and yearned for Sissi's embrace, for her bony breast, the subtly sweet, musty smell of raisins she had, even though he'd never liked them as a kid. The blond man regarded him, then clinked his beer glass against David's. He opened his eyes and drank. Eva appeared in the doorway. She hesitated, then started for her room, but one of the young reporters spotted her and waved her in.

"Fräulein Bruhns! Come keep us company!"

Eva stepped into the dining room, into its familiar smell. She glanced at the bar to the right and for a moment, saw her mother standing there smiling, wearing her "sugar face," as Stefan called it, her eyes tired but yearning. And her father poking his ruddy face out of the kitchen and scanning the room. Everyone satisfied?

Eva joined the men, who eagerly made room for her at the table. She took a seat and found herself sitting opposite David. They looked at each other. In the midst of the noise meant to dispel the memories of the day, they recognized themselves in the other's helplessness. They both smiled, happy they were no longer alone.

The White Rabbit came into the dining room and approached the table. He looked despondent, *as if he were hanging his long ears,* Eva thought. The group looked up at him, and he told them his pocket watch was missing. He set it on the edge of the sink in the communal bathroom and forgot it there. And once he realized it half an hour later, the watch had vanished. The White Rabbit looked around the table: had one of the gentlemen, or perhaps the lady, taken the watch? They all shook their heads. He turned to Eva: could she please speak to the innkeepers and ask about the watch? Eva got up and went to the bar. The innkeeper and his wife merely shrugged. They didn't know anything about any watch. "A likely story!" the attorney said and dropped heavily into the chair beside Eva. One of the reporters cracked a joke about Poles—everyone knew they'd rob you blind if given half a chance. The storytelling continued. The White Rabbit didn't laugh, but kept fingering his vest pocket in disbelief. He turned to Eva beside him: his mother gave him that watch after he passed his law exams. A simple woman, who had sold her jewelry to afford it. Her son needed a watch that wouldn't fail him in court, she said. Eva could see tears in the White Rabbit's eyes. The blond man ordered another round of pils. Plus vodka. He clinked glasses with David again. Eva nipped at her glass, then she too shot back the harsh liquid. Two older men in dark sweaters entered the dining room. They sat down at the bar, but when they detected German being spoken at Eva's table, one of them sidled over. He had a wide head and looked strong despite his age. He asked what they were doing there. Eva translated. He was offered a seat by her side. He sat down, while the other man leaned against the bar. The Pole said that he didn't believe the Germans—of all people—could administer justice.

"The whole thing is just a show trial to ease your conscience."

The men at the table were first dumbfounded, then felt affronted and all began speaking at once. Eva wasn't sure whose response to translate first. The Pole continued: he had been a prisoner himself, and there was no avenging that suffering.

"I'm a Jew!" David interjected, his voice inappropriately loud.

The Pole, who understood him even without Eva's help, shrugged and asked in broken German, "Were you at camp?" David blanched, and the blond man sat up and watched him attentively. David remained silent, and the Pole went on, "No? Did you lose family?" David began to sweat. The blond man tried to interject something, but the Pole said, "Also no? Then you have no idea!"

At that, David jumped up and struck the Pole in the chest with the flat of his hand; the man was thrown backward in his chair, and only just managed to catch himself. Several of the men at the table rose in alarm, as did Eva. The man at the bar sauntered over, rolling up his sleeves. The Pole planted himself in front of David threateningly.

"What do you want? A thrashing? That can be arranged!"

The blond man placed a hand on the Pole's arm. "Please. I apologize for my colleague. Please calm down. We're sorry!"

Eva translated, and added, in Polish, "You're right. We can't make amends for anything."

The Pole looked at Eva and hesitated. David, on the other hand, was ready to fight. "Come on, what are you waiting for?! Hit me!"

The blond man grabbed his arm. "Stop it, David! Apologize to the gentleman!"

But David yanked his arm free, turned, and bolted out of the room. Eva exchanged a look with the blond man, who had impulsively started to follow. He forced himself to stay where he was.

"You go."

The matte light of the full moon illuminated the street outside the lodge. Eva looked around for David. He seemed to have disappeared. Then she heard a thud, followed by a whimper in the stillness. She followed the sounds behind the building. David was standing by a wall, and as Eva approached, he rammed his forehead against the stones a second time. He howled.

"David! What are you doing?!"

Eva seized David's shoulders and head and tried to restrain him, but he elbowed her off, leaned his head back, and slammed it into the wall a third time. He groaned in pain. Eva tried to get between him and the wall, but he screamed at her to leave him alone and slapped her, sending her sprawling. She lay on the cold ground for a moment, her cheek on fire, and suddenly she didn't care anymore. She got up, brushed off her skirt, and watched as David again drove his head into the stones with all his might, then crumpled over sideways like a sack. Eva crouched beside him and turned him onto his back. His face was dark with blood.

"David? Say something! Can you hear me?!"

David blinked. "I have a headache."

Eva pulled a handkerchief from her skirt pocket, cushioned David's head in her lap, and wiped off the blood as best she could. David saw the dark outline of her head, and over her shoulder the full moon, which looked down on him like the chief judge. David chuckled.

"I don't even have a brother. I've got two older sisters. They live in Canada, just like my parents and the rest of my family." Eva listened as David told her that the Müllers immigrated to

Canada in '37 without any difficulty, and even managed to save their fortune. He didn't even have relatives affected by the extermination. David sat up and leaned his back against the wall. Eva kneeled beside him and said that it was lucky he and his family were spared. But David responded that she would never understand the guilt one felt. He was a Jew because his parents were Jewish. But he wasn't raised with religion. It wasn't till he reached Germany that he tried to lead a faithful existence. But this God had ignored him. "And I know why too. I don't belong."

As daybreak neared and the rooster climbed out of the coop to prepare for his morning crowing, Eva brought David to his room, which was as small as hers. She helped him into bed and took his threadbare towel. She dampened it in the bathroom and used it to cool his swollen face. She sat on the edge of the bed and thought about what he had told her, about the fact that even those who escaped, even their children and children's children, had to suffer the existence of this place. Eva stroked David's hand. He pulled her close on the narrow bed. And then they did the one thing that might possibly be done to counteract it all: they made love.

The delegation was ready to leave and stood outside the lodge in a light drizzle. When Eva came out the door with her suitcase, bleary-eyed but coiffed and wearing a fresh blouse, the blond man approached her. "Where's David?" Eva wasn't sure. When the activity outside the door had woken her, David was no longer beside her. She had expected to see him outside. The blond man checked his watch. The bus was coming in twenty minutes. Time passed, and no David. Eva went back to his room. A chambermaid was stripping the bed. She looked at Eva with indifference. Eva was already no longer a guest she had to be polite to. Eva looked around and opened the warped armoire. No suitcase, no clothes. She asked the chambermaid if she had found anything. The young woman just shrugged. The bus pulled up outside and waited, its engine idling. The driver was loading suitcases into the luggage compartment. The men boarded, one after the other. The blond man stood by the bus and looked at Eva. She shook her head, at a loss. "He's gone. His things too." The White Rabbit, who was the last to hurry out, because he insisted on a proper breakfast, overheard Eva and grumbled, "The Poles stole him too." He handed his suitcase to the driver and boarded the bus. The blond man followed him, and Eva saw him speaking to the chief judge, who looked at his watch and said something. The blond man came back out to Eva and said that the longest they could wait was half an hour. They had to catch their flight before their visas expired. He sounded worried. He offered Eva a cigarette, which she declined, and lit one for himself. The bus driver turned off the engine. The weather turned pleasant, and the rooster strutted across the street with a few chickens and disappeared into a bush on the other side. Eva lifted her face toward the sky. The drizzle was like a gentle touch on her skin. They waited.

Eva dozed on the flight back. She knew where David was: in a canoe on an expansive lake in Canada that reflected the entire sky. Eva woke up and gazed out at the clouds. She thought of Toker, the first dachshund her family had ever had. She was eleven and just starting middle school. She was having a hard time making friends, so one day she brought Toker with her to school, to break the ice. It worked. On the way home, however, Toker was hit by a car. He wasn't even a year old. In confirmation class, Eva asked Pastor Schrader, "How can the good Lord allow something like that to happen?"

The pastor looked at her and responded, "God isn't responsible for the suffering on earth. Humans are. How could you allow that to happen?"

Eva hadn't liked the pastor after that; she imitated his limping gait behind his back and told people that he didn't wash. Which they believed too, because he always looked a bit unkempt.

Eva turned away from the window and decided that she would apologize to him that very week. She suddenly understood why none of the defendants acknowledged their guilt. Why they only admitted to individual crimes, if that. How could one human possibly bear the responsibility for the deaths of thousands?

Sissi stood outside the gate at the airport and waited. The first thing she wanted to tell David—she could hardly contain herself—was that her son had gotten a C on his first German assignment in middle school. She always knew he was smart. Sissi was wearing her modest suit under a new, parrot-colored coat. It was a little big, since she'd gotten it from a friend, but Sissi felt pretty in it. Pretty and sophisticated. *Perfect for the airport!* she thought. The first travelers passed through the electric sliding doors, almost all men in dark overcoats. Married. Well-to-do. They were followed by a young woman with an outdated hairstyle—she was probably from a good home—and a face that appeared as if she were straining to hear something deep within herself. Maybe she also had a bolted chamber inside. She passed by Sissi without a glance. Only a few more people came out the sliding doors. The arrivals hall emptied as travelers, reunited families, friends, and couples ambled, arms interlocked, out to the parking lot. Sissi stared at the door that had stopped opening.

A yellow car was waiting outside the airport. *Jürgen,* Eva thought, and realized it made her happy. Then she recognized the gnarled figure of the attorney general in the backseat. A chauf-

feur sat at the wheel. The blond man approached and offered Eva
a ride into the city. He let her sit in front, whereas he took a seat
in the back, to report to his boss. The car drove off. The blond man
explained that some witness testimony was refuted, given certain
distances or vantage points. Most, however, were confirmed. They
also received credible new documentation from Polish authorities.
Driving permits signed by the main defendant. The blond man
handed the attorney general a folder, which he looked through.
Eva watched her city's worsening traffic through the windshield.
She was afraid of seeing her parents again and was grateful for
every red light. As they turned onto Berger Strasse, the blond man
reported on another unexpected occurrence: they lost one of their
travel companions. The attorney general immediately knew who.
That Canadian Jew.

"What the hell got into him this time?"

The blond man told him that they informed the Polish security police in Warsaw before their departure. The police would be
launching a search of the area.

Eva got out of the car at German House and couldn't believe
her eyes. Through the windows of the restaurant she could see
people—guests—sitting at the tables. She checked her watch. It
was just before two. Lunchtime. She spotted her mother standing at one of the windows; Edith had stopped there, a few plates
balanced on her arm, and was peering out at Eva. She looked anxious, as if she feared Eva wouldn't say hello. Eva waved halfheartedly. Then she decided to get the reunion over with and entered
the dining room, suitcase in hand. Edith was serving the plates.
Eva lingered by the door. There was a pink porcelain pig on the
bar, which was new. Edith came up to her.

"Hello, Mum."

Edith moved in for a hug, but Eva deflected, holding out her right hand. They shook. Edith then took the suitcase and carried it to the door to the stairs. Eva followed. She noticed a little sign stuck to the piggy bank as she passed: *Giordano family.*

"Yes, your father made that," Edith said, turning back to address Eva. "I tried talking him out of it, but you know how stubborn he can be."

They stopped at the door. Edith stepped toward Eva and whispered, "And look around. Look how well it's been received already. There's an insurance company around the corner now. That's those three tables right there. I'm working the bar myself, by the way." Eva still didn't speak. "Have you eaten? There's beef roulade. The meat is so . . ." Her mother formed an oval with her thumb and index finger and kissed her fingertips. It made her earrings swing.

"I'll go say hello to him first," Eva said. She went into the kitchen, her mother following on her heels, as though she were afraid she might reconsider along the way and run off. Eva's father was standing at the stove, his back straighter than usual, shaking a big pot in which he was browning the roulade. He periodically stirred the gravy bubbling in an oval saucepan. Steam rose and enveloped her father. Frau Lenze rapidly spooned mashed potatoes onto six plates that had been lined up on the sideboard and then heaped several small dishes with cucumber salad.

"Hi, Frau Lenze. Hi, Daddy."

Frau Lenze looked up. "There's our girl! Was it nice? Feeling better after some time in the sun?"

Eva frowned at her in confusion.

"Frau Lenze means by the sea," Edith hastily explained.

Eva's father removed the pot from the flame and came over.

He looked bad, his eyes bloodshot and his face reddish blue. Nonetheless, he did his best to beam proudly.

"Well, I took the plunge! This corset is worth its weight in gold. Did you see how busy we are? We've already sent out eighteen orders of roulade."

Eva just looked at her father. She didn't know what to say.

"But I've got one set aside for you!" he continued. "Take a seat out there. You get the nicest one of all! Coming right up, browned to perfection." He turned quickly back to the stove.

Eva took a seat at one of the back tables in the dining room. Her mother wiped the dark wooden tabletop with her dishtowel.

"I'll bring you a glass of white." It was a statement, not a question. Eva didn't respond. Her mother went to the bar, taking a few new orders along the way. Eva observed the cheery guests, their bellies full and hearts happy, thanks to her father. She suddenly recalled that she had eaten lunch in the former officers' mess during their tour of the camp. She remembered that none of them ate much. As they were leaving, David quietly and earnestly asked whether she didn't at least want to peek into the kitchen. Eva had shaken her head and rushed outside, only to find her anxiety grow even greater there. Her mother returned with the wine and her plate.

"The mashed potatoes are made with extra butter, Daddy told me to tell you," Edith said.

Eva looked at the plate, at the roulade lying there in a thick gravy, a heap of light yellow mash beside it. Her father appeared in the kitchen doorway and watched Eva. Her mother stood behind the bar, pouring beers and keeping an eye on her too. Eva picked up her fork in her left hand, the knife in her right. She plunged the fork into the mashed potatoes. The tines disappeared in the puree, which glistened with butter. She pulled the fork out again. She cut a piece of roulade, which began to steam from the inside like a living body. Eva brought the skewered bite up to her mouth. The smell of the meat penetrated all the way into her forehead. Something crept out of her stomach and slowly made its way up into her throat. Eva put down her silverware and took a sip of wine, which tasted like vinegar. She swallowed and swallowed. Out of the corner of her eye she could see her father in the doorway, trying to catch her attention. He wanted to know how it tasted. Her mother started making her way over. Eva felt as though the guests at the other tables had stopped speaking and eating and were also looking at her expectantly. "I'm sorry!" she wanted to cry. But her mouth had filled with saliva, which she couldn't get down. At that moment, the felted curtain at the entrance was thrown open and Stefan burst in. He wore his schoolbag on his back, and he looked around, spotted Eva, and dashed toward her table.

"We're serving luuuunch againnnn!" he yelled as he ran, as if the family had won the lottery. Edith snagged him and held a finger to her lips.

"Shh!" She then led him to Eva's table and took his knapsack. "Have you finally gotten your dictation back?"

But Stefan just bared his teeth and ignored the question as he hung on Eva's shoulder.

"How was your vacation? Did you bring me anything?"

Eva shook her head. "Not this time."

Edith looked at Eva's plate. She was normally horrified when guests left a lot uneaten—"Was there something wrong with your meal?"—but she kept quiet this time, helpless.

"Stefan can eat it," Eva said. "I'm not hungry."

"No," Stefan protested. "I get to have pudding today!"

Eva got up and opened the private door to the stairwell. "I'm going to go lie down." She took her suitcase and left the dining room.

Stefan turned to his mother. "You said this morning that I could have pudding at lunch if I hurried!"

Edith didn't respond. She took Eva's plate and went into the kitchen. Ludwig was waiting there behind the door. He too saw that Eva hadn't eaten anything. With the cutlery Edith scraped the food into the big metal trash can. Frau Lenze looked at her in surprise but didn't ask. Ludwig was silent and returned to the stove. He pushed pots back and forth, stirring and turning things busily. But Edith saw that his shoulders were twitching—that he was crying.

Edith knocked on Eva's bedroom door later. She entered and sat down on Eva's bed and avoided looking at the hat on the shelf. Eva, lying on the bedspread, hadn't slept. She didn't look at Edith, who placed a hand on her shoulder.

"You can't do this to your father." Eva remained silent, and Edith continued, "It was twenty years ago. By the time we realized what was happening there, it was too late. And we're no heroes, Eva. We were afraid—we had young children. People didn't speak up in those days. It can't be compared to how things are now." Eva still didn't move. Edith took her hand off Eva's shoulder and said, "We never hurt anyone."

It sounded like a question. Eva regarded her mother out of the corner of her eye. She looked small sitting there on the edge of the bed, and she smelled of flour and the expensive perfume from Paris Ludwig gave her every year for their anniversary. Eva detected wrinkles around her upper lip that hadn't been there before. She thought of her mother's dream role, Schiller's *Maid of Orleans*. Feisty, but ultimately lacking her own will.

Edith tried to smile. "Your Jürgen called twice while you were gone. What's going on between you two?"

Eva normally would have wanted to tell her mother about David, her strange friend, who had just vanished. And about Jürgen, whom she didn't want to live with, but whom she probably loved. She had always confided in her mother. Her mother was the person she was closest to. Eva studied her mother's hands, the fingers that were too short for playing the violin, the worn wedding band. Eva saw that the hands were trembling slightly. She knew that her mother wanted her to do what she had always done when they'd fought in the past—take her hand and say, "Everything's fine, Mummy." But she didn't move.

AT THE HOSPITAL, Annegret had picked up her "naughty habit" again, as she called it. She had battled with her conscience. But Doctor Küssner, who had given his notice, pushed her over the edge, and her sister, with her lies, also pushed her over the edge. It was all quite clear to Annegret: she needed those pitifully fussy newborns who convalesced under her care. She had to save lives and receive the thanks for it. It was the only thing that quieted her heart and gave her the strength to endure everything else. Annegret had taken to carrying the reusable syringe again, its glass barrel filled with a brownish liquid contaminated with E. coli, which she either mixed into the children's milk or administered directly. Annegret acquired this solution by means that disgusted even her. But it was the easiest way. Annegret wandered among the bassinets, assessing the little creatures cradled there. She stopped at one of the beds and looked at the boy pedaling his legs and gazing at her trustingly. Annegret listened for noise in the hallway—her colleagues had all gone to the cafeteria for lunch. A sunbeam stole through the window and threw a white spotlight on Annegret as she pulled the syringe from her pocket, stepped up to the head of the bassinet, and opened the boy's tiny pink mouth with the index finger of her left hand and inserted the syringe with her right.

"You'll be rid of me in three weeks. Just spoke with the boss." Doctor Küssner entered the room and walked over. He looked at Annegret's hand by the baby's mouth, first in curiosity, then alarm. She pulled out the syringe and tried to stuff it back in her pocket, but Doctor Küssner seized her wrist.

"What is that? What are you doing?"

THE TRIAL CONTINUED. The days repeated themselves. In the mornings, children played in the schoolyard beyond the auditorium. The autumnal trees swayed outside the glass panes, their movement familiar. The defendants remained steadfast, while the public hungered for new bombshells. And the witnesses remained those who had to muster the most courage to enter the courtroom. Nothing appeared to have changed. In the same way that floodlights were installed after a certain amount of time to better see the defendants' faces, however, the tour of the site turned the imagined into certainty. Auschwitz was real. The chair diagonally in front of Eva's spot remained empty. Fräulein Lehmkuhl and Fräulein Schenke were stunned to learn from Eva that David had disappeared and the Polish police hadn't yet located him. "He must have gotten lost," Fräulein Lehmkuhl said in distress. The blond man also glanced at the empty seat from time to time. Someone else noticed David's absence as well. The White Rabbit approached Eva during a break one day. Defendant Number Four wanted a word. Eva reluctantly followed him to the other side and finally saw the haggard-looking face up close. He asked her about the young man with the red hair. He had gone missing? Well, when was he last seen? Where? What efforts were undertaken to locate him? Eva could easily picture how this man had led his interrogations. She looked at him furiously.

"That's none of your business!" she hissed.

She turned to leave, but the Beast caught her arm and said, "He's a hotheaded young man. Just like I used to be. I'm worried about him."

Eva would have liked nothing better than to spit in his face. Instead she replied, her voice strained, "I don't think David would like it for you, of all people, to concern yourself with him!"

She freed herself and returned to her seat, thinking, *He's a criminal. A mass murderer.* She couldn't forgive him for that. Then what were her parents? What did she have to forgive them? Did she have to? Eva was floating, as though in a bubble—she could see her parents outside it, indistinct, their voices muffled. She wished the bubble would burst. But she didn't know how to make it.

At the end of another day of proceedings, which had limped along in the tedious review of papers and petitions, and by the time most people in the hall had their minds set on dinner, the light blond-haired man presented the court with the documents he had acquired from Polish authorities. They were driving permits for the delivery of Zyklon B, signed by the main defendant. The forms were marked, "Materials for Jewish resettlement," which served as a cover-up.

"Does the defendant still wish to claim he had no knowledge of the gas chambers?!" the chief judge snarled into his microphone.

The main defendant turned his raptor head to his attorney, and they exchanged a few words. It then appeared as if they were both stealing a glance at Eva. But she must be imagining things. The White Rabbit stood up. He pushed up the sleeve of his robe with his right hand and checked his shiny new wristwatch. He stated that his client had always been against what happened at the camp. He had wanted to leave and had volunteered for the front—in vain.

"Trying to portray him as a resistance fighter now, are we?" the blond man interjected sardonically. The attorney was not deterred and added that he wished to call a witness to attest to his client's disposition.

"The defense wishes to call the witness Priess to the stand."

"Priess? There's a different name in your written request," the chief judge said.

"Just a moment . . ." The White Rabbit searched one of his documents for the name. "Yes, Priess is her maiden name."

Maiden name, Priess. Eva felt as if someone had pulled the chair out from under her, the floor, the entire world. The defense attorney's voice sounded over the loudspeakers.

"The defense wishes to call the witness Edith Bruhns to the stand."

Eva stood up and clutched the side of the table. Everything was spinning. The blond man turned to her, his brow furrowed. Eva's mind was racing: David must have said something! Given her away! But why as a witness for the defense? It couldn't be! Eva sank back into her chair and caught someone's eye in the crowd— the wife of the main defendant was watching her, squinting out from under her little hat like a mouse, a triumphant mouse.

"The court grants the request of the defense," the chief judge now declared.

The blond man leaned over to Eva. "Bruhns? Is she in any way connected to you?"

But Eva just stared at the double doors being opened by the bailiff.

"MY NAME IS EDITH BRUHNS, née Priess. I live at three-eighteen Berger Strasse. I am a restaurant server by profession."

"Frau Bruhns, when did you arrive at the camp?"

"September 1940."

"And in what capacity?"

"I was accompanying my husband, who served as the cook in the officers' mess."

"How much did you know about the camp?"

"Only that prisoners of war were held there."

"And what more did you discover on location?"

Edith remained silent. Someone called out from the gallery. Eva thought she heard the words "Nazi whore." But maybe she was just hysterical. Up there at the witness stand, not three meters away, sat her mother. She wasn't wearing any jewelry. She had put on her black suit, which she only wore to funerals. She was serious and pale. She bore herself as if she were onstage, but Eva could see she wasn't acting—she was making an effort to be honest. She had placed her handbag in front of her, the handbag Eva had emptied so many times as a child and the contents of which she knew by heart: a comb, a handkerchief, eucalyptus lozenges, hand cream, and a wallet with the most recent photos of her children. Eva's heart raced. Her mother's voice reverberated throughout the hall. "I discovered that normal people were imprisoned there too. I mean, who weren't criminals."

"Did you not wish to leave, then? You had two young daughters."

"Oh, I did," Edith responded. "I told my husband that he should request a transfer. But then they would have conscripted him. They were desperate for soldiers at that point, you see. He feared for his life, and I stopped trying to persuade him." She once witnessed a woman being shot, because it happened directly beyond her yard. She figured the woman was trying to flee. Eva could see the yard, the neighbors' rose bed, the fence, the woman crumpling. She looked at her mother, here in the auditorium, and recalled the last time they'd visited the municipal building together. The play *The General's Trousers* had consisted of little more than lewd one-liners, but they couldn't help laughing and kept egging each other on. That was an entirely different lifetime. Edith was now telling the court that she first learned about the gas chambers from the main defendant's wife. They were neighbors. She called her attention to the smell.

"Does that mean you were also acquainted with the main defendant?" the chief judge asked.

"Yes, we encountered each other from time to time. Outside the house or at social events."

The defense attorney now stood and fumbled in the folds of his robe for the pocket watch he no longer possessed. Then he glanced at his wristwatch.

"Ma'am, did you encounter each other at the camp officers' Christmas party?"

"Yes."

"Do you recall a specific incident from around that time?"

Eva saw her mother duck her head, trying to shrink like a child who doesn't want to be seen, but knows: I've been spotted.

"I'm not sure what you mean." Edith grimaced. She looked like Stefan when he was lying.

"Is it not true that on the following day, you filed a complaint with the Reich Main Security Office against the main defendant?"

"I don't remember."

Edith stared straight ahead. She hadn't looked at Eva once. The room filled with whispers. The hands on the large wall clock ticked audibly. Five o'clock. Normally at this hour the chief judge would adjourn proceedings till the next day. Instead, he asked incredulously, "Frau Bruhns, you don't remember? Surely you are aware of what such a complaint could mean at that time."

The blond man leaned over to Eva and whispered, "Are you related to the witness?" He looked at her intently. Eva blanched and shook her head repeatedly.

The chief judge, the man in the moon, asked loudly, "Why did you denounce the main defendant, Frau Bruhns?"

At that, Edith Bruhns turned to face her daughter, as though taking her leave.

EVA RAN DOWN THE SIDEWALK, the evening commuter traffic beside her flowing like a dirty river of metal. Everyone in the auditorium that day now knew that in December '44 her mother denounced the main defendant after he criticized the speech the propaganda minister had delivered to the *Volkssturm* militia in Berlin. Among other things, the main defendant said, "That firebrand is contributing to Germany's demise." Her mother had quoted this line in court. She composed the letter together with her husband and sent it off, although it could have meant a death sentence for the main defendant. An investigation followed, and the defendant with the raptor's face was demoted, but then came peace. Peace! Eva was thrown backward—she started crossing the street, but now stood face-to-face with the hood of the car that had just hit her. She checked her body, which appeared unscathed, then looked at the furiously gesticulating driver behind the windshield. The man tapped his temple at her madly with one hand while repeatedly honking with the other. Then he leaped from the vehicle and rounded the front threateningly.

"I'll turn you in! I'll turn you in if there's a single scratch!"

Eva watched the way he feverishly examined the car's pristine body, the way he checked the paint from every imaginable angle above and below, smoothing his hand over it. He was wearing a checkered hat that was too small for him. Eva recovered from her shock and began to laugh.

"I don't know what's so funny, miss. This car just came from the factory!"

Eva couldn't stop. She walked away laughing, covering her mouth with her hand as her eyes filled with tears and she struggled for air. She didn't calm down till she reached German House. She stopped out front. On the other side of the street, a dark-haired woman was pushing a stroller over the sidewalk, then maneuvered it into the entrance of the apartment building there. Before the door closed, the woman noticed Eva in the distance and waved warmly. It was Frau Giordano. It seemed the family had managed to buy a new stroller with the money collected at German House. Eva entered the stairwell.

Inside the apartment, Eva went to her room and hauled her big suitcase out of the wardrobe. She fetched her toiletries bag from the bathroom and packed clothing, her dictionaries, a few favorite books, the folder containing her identification papers, and a photo she took from the wall above her desk. It was a picture of Stefan balancing Purzel on his head. Purzel looked unhappy.

There was a knock on the door. Ludwig, wearing his white chef's coat, came in; he was out of breath, as if he had charged upstairs from the kitchen, and he looked at the suitcase.

"I told your mother she should tell you beforehand. But she said it wasn't even certain the court would call on her. And then she would have caused an unnecessary commotion."

Eva noticed a little fleck of green stuck to her father's cheek. Probably parsley. She turned her back on him and didn't respond. She added the hat and her blue notebooks to the suitcase and closed it.

"Where on earth are you going to go?"

Eva passed by her father wordlessly. As she stepped into the hallway, the front door opened, and her mother entered. She was in miserable condition and had clearly been crying. Her eyes fell on the suitcase in Eva's hand.

"Let's talk, Eva."

Eva shook her head and went for the door.

"Please," her father said.

Eva set down her suitcase. "I don't want to live with you anymore."

Edith stepped up to Eva. "Because I testified for the main defendant?" she asked in despair. "But they just arrested him! My testimony didn't even help. And I had to respond to the summons."

Eva looked at her mother in disbelief; she was playing dumb, refusing to comprehend.

"Child! You're acting so . . ." Ludwig started. "You're making it seem like we're murderers," he stammered.

Eva gazed at her father, at his white jacket and soft red face above it. "Why didn't you do anything, Father? You should have poisoned every last one of those officers!"

Edith reached for Eva's arm, but she recoiled.

"Eva, they would have shot him then. And me. And you and Annegret."

"And child," her father said, "it wouldn't have made a difference. They would have just sent new ones to replace them. You wouldn't believe how many of them there were. They were everywhere."

Eva lost control. "'They'? Who's 'they'? And you, what were you? You were a part of the whole. You were 'them' too! You made it all possible. You may not have murdered anyone, but you allowed it. I don't know which is worse. Tell me which is worse!"

Eva looked at her parents standing there so pathetically and waited for an answer. Edith just shook her head, turned, and went into the kitchen. Ludwig searched for words but found none. Eva picked up her suitcase, effortlessly pushed past her father, and opened the door. She left the apartment and stumbled down the polished staircase, through the lower entranceway, and out of the building. Two boys were approaching on the sidewalk, Stefan and his best friend, Thomas Preisgau.

"Eva, where are you going?" Stefan asked.

Eva gave Stefan a quick squeeze. "I'm going on a trip."

"For how long?"

Eva didn't answer, but grabbed her suitcase and hurried away as fast as she could. Stefan watched her in alarm.

Annegret had been lying on her bed, a bag of pretzel sticks on her belly, and listening to everything as she chewed. When she heard the door close, she got up, the nearly empty bag slipping to the floor, and went to the window. She watched Eva leave. Her pretty little sister. She started to cry, then angrily pounded the windowpane once with the palms of her hands. "Just go, then!"

Annegret pressed her forehead against the cool glass, sniffed, and thought, *It's better that she go, she wouldn't leave us alone, making such a fuss about the past, playing the great moralizer, clearly clueless about the shortcomings of human nature!* Annegret couldn't see Eva anymore, and she turned away from the window and picked up the pretzel bag. She dumped the remaining crumbs into her cupped hand. She slowly licked them up and thought about her conversation with Hartmut Küssner after he caught her in the act. They went into one of the examination rooms, and Annegret confessed that in the past five years, she had employed various means to infect nineteen male newborns and babies with E. coli to nurse them back to health. Doctor Küssner's face was ashen with horror and disgust. She had killed a child! But Annegret swore that she had nothing to do with Martin Fasse's death. She hadn't given him anything. She had only ever chosen babies she knew were stable enough. He had to believe her! Annegret begged him, pulled her hair, and threw herself at him as he turned to go report her to the director. She would go with him, she stammered. To Wiesbaden or wherever he wanted. Live with him, bear his children. But he couldn't destroy her life. Doctor Küssner shook her off and left the room, but he took a left down the hallway, rather than a right toward administration. Annegret had been consumed with fear since, but so far, she hadn't been called in. She knew that Hartmut wanted nothing more than to believe she didn't have a child on her conscience.

The light blond-haired man sat in his office with his colleagues. They were working on the criminal charges. Dirty coffee cups perched atop towers of file folders, their saucers overflowing with stubbed cigarette butts. The enormous skeleton of the new building next door was visible through the windows. Tarps flapped in the wind. The construction site appeared deserted, as though the owners had unexpectedly run out of money. The blond man observed one of the younger lawyers, who was searching assiduously through a statute book, and thought of David Miller, who had vehemently declared at the start of the trial that nothing short of a life sentence could be sought for each defendant. Every last one of them had committed murder! The young prosecutor was now saying that the most they could likely prove was complicity in murder—according to German law, the main perpetrators were the uppermost commanders of the Reich. Furthermore, the defendants would all plea superior orders, which was difficult to repudiate. Several in the office nodded, and the blond man said yes, requesting life sentences would not be possible in all cases. He waited, but no one challenged him. David had left a void. There was a knock on the door, and then Eva peeked in.

"I don't mean to interrupt."

The blond man stood and waved her in. "Come in, Fräulein Bruhns, we're finished for the day."

His staff rose and filed out of the office, every last one greeting Eva warmly as they passed. The blond man gestured toward a chair. Eva sat down and said that she was sorry, but she would no longer be able to continue working in the trial.

"Your fiancé again?"

"No, it's because of my parents." Eva then confirmed the suspicions the blond man had expressed during Edith Bruhns's testimony. Eva confided that she could no longer meet anyone's eye in the courtroom. She carried her parents' guilt within her. The blond man said that, from a legal stance, that was nonsense. One couldn't view an entire nation guilty by association. Besides, it would be difficult to find a replacement for her. Eva remained resolute and got to her feet. The blond man didn't push her any further. All he could do, then, was to thank her sincerely for her good work. Eva said that she had just one final request. She wondered whether he could find anything out about a certain prisoner. His name was Jaschinsky. His number had been 24981. The blond man jotted down a note and said that he would be in touch.

Eva took the elevator down. As she crossed the foyer, she noticed a thin woman in a strikingly bright coat outside the glass door, running her finger down the doorbell nameplates. Eva had seen this woman before, outside the municipal building. She had been standing outside at the end of proceedings one day, clearly waiting for someone. Eva stepped outside and asked the woman if she could help. Sissi looked up.

"Where is the public prosecutor's office?"

"Who are you looking for?" But Eva already knew the answer; she could see the concern in Sissi's eyes.

The two women walked through a park set back from the street. The first yellow leaves of the season spiraled down around them. Eva told her about the trip. That she was with David that night, that he was distraught, and that she stayed by his side. She didn't include that she slept with him, but after a quick sidelong glance at Sissi, she realized that there was no hiding it from her.

"We're not a couple," Sissi said. "But I'm very fond of him, and he likes me. And my son doesn't mind him. That counts for a lot." After a pause, she added, "Do you think he took his life out there somewhere? Or will he come back?"

Eva was silent and thought of the telex that had arrived two weeks earlier from the local police in Poland, which she had translated: a male body was found in a swamp not far from the camp. The condition of the body, however, was such that identification

of the deceased was impossible. One of the authorities even suggested it had been lying there for years. Eva refused to believe it
was David. The blond man also had his doubts. Eva told Sissi that
David lost himself to that place. But that he would come back
someday.

When they arrived back at the entrance of the park, Eva smiled.
"You know, the thing is, he's got to come back! He still owes me
twenty marks."

But Sissi remained solemn and opened her purse. She pulled
out her wallet and said, "I can pay it off."

"No, thank you, that wasn't what I meant," Eva insisted, refusing the offer.

The women shook hands good-bye. Eva watched Sissi walk
down the street. It took a long time for the colorful coat to disappear. Like a bouquet of flowers upon the ocean, it rocked up and
down, up and down, till a wave came and washed over it.

AUTUMN ARRIVED. Eva had rented a room in a boardinghouse
run by two older women. One of the women, Frau Demuth, was
never around, whereas the other, Frau Armbrecht, was all the more
curious about this unmarried young woman. The furnishings in
her room were tossed together carelessly, and the window opened
onto nothing more than a whitewashed firewall. That didn't
bother Eva, though. She started working for Herr Körting at the
agency again. Of the girls who had worked there a year earlier, the
only one left was Christel Adomat, who had a crooked nose and
smelled bad. All of the others had gotten married in the meantime.
Eva interpreted in meetings and business discussions, and back in
her room, she translated contracts and instruction manuals at her

narrow desk. There was a job for her once at Schoormann's, but she asked Christel to take it. Eva tried not to think of Jürgen anymore. She continued to follow the trial; she bought the daily papers and read that the evidentiary hearing had concluded. Following closing arguments, the prosecution sought life sentences for fourteen of the defendants, including the Beast, the "Injector," the medical orderly, the pharmacist, and the main defendant. The defense then requested acquittals, in particular for those who had engaged in the selections. Eva had to reread the passage several times to understand what it was the White Rabbit argued: that these men had clearly acted in opposition to extermination orders and saved a great many lives by virtue of their selections. He also entered the plea of superior orders, stating that the accused had been soldiers acting according to prevailing law. In the boardinghouse common room, crowded with furniture, Eva watched a televised interview with the attorney general. "For months, prosecutors, witnesses, and spectators have awaited a humane word from the defendants," he said. "It would cleanse the air, if a single humane word were finally uttered—but it has not been uttered, and it will not be uttered."

On the day of sentencing, Eva stood at the mirror in her room and slowly buttoned her suit jacket. Behind her, Frau Armbrecht was nervously brushing off the furniture with her favorite feather duster and asking, "So what do you think? What'll they get? Surely nothing short of life?! Life in prison! Don't you think?" Frau Armbrecht stopped talking and looked at Eva in the mirror, concerned. She had asked Eva, shortly after she moved in, about the black hat she had placed on one of her shelves. "Did it belong to your father?" And Eva had told her about Otto Cohn and the others. She now turned to Frau Armbrecht and replied that she, too, hoped for a just verdict.

In front of the municipal building, where the whole city, if not the whole world, appeared to be flocking today, Eva paced up and down the sidewalk a little off to the side. She didn't want to run into anyone. She looked at her watch: nine fifty. Just ten more minutes till the chief judge called the final day of proceedings to order. Eva recognized many of the people entering the building: the wife of the main defendant, the wife of the Beast, and Andrzej Wilk, the witness who was forced to watch his own father's murder. At one minute to ten, Eva approached the entrance. The foyer was crowded with reporters and spectators who didn't get a spot in the gallery. The double doors to the auditorium were already closed. The sentencing would be announced over the loudspeakers; the gray box mounted beside the door sputtered. Eva stayed back, in an alcove by the glass entryway. One of the hall attendants recognized her and beckoned her over to the auditorium door, which he opened a crack. Eva declined with a wave of her hand. The attendant appeared vexed, then pointed at a chair by the door. It was where Otto Cohn had so often sat, as if keeping watch over what transpired inside the hall. Eva hesitated, then walked over and sat down. The speaker above her head crackled: "The High Court." A scraping and rustling droned out of the box. For the last time, everyone in the auditorium got to their feet, the defendants, defense attorneys, prosecutors, joint plaintiffs, and spectators. Eva involuntarily stood up with them. The voice spoke: "Please be seated." Again, the sound of murmuring and chairs moving. A tense silence followed, even in the foyer. The speaker static provided the only noise. Outside the big windows, a few children scurried across the front courtyard. Eva realized then that vacation had started, and that Stefan had probably gone to see their grandmother in Hamburg. The chief judge's voice then began to buzz over the speakers: "Over the many months of this trial, the court has experienced vicariously all of the pain and suffering that the people endured there and that will forever be tied to the name Auschwitz. There are undoubtedly those among us who will for some time find themselves unable to gaze into the happy, believing eyes of a child . . ." The voice that had—for all those months—remained so firm began to tremble as he continued, "without recalling the hollow, questioning and uncomprehending, frightened eyes of the children who took their final steps there in Auschwitz." His voice broke. Even out in the foyer, several people bowed their heads or hid their faces in their hands. Eva pictured his familiar face, the man in the moon, who was only human, himself. A son. A husband. A father. What a difficult task he had taken on. After a pause, the chief judge continued, composed: culpability for crimes committed during the Nazi era was subject to the laws existing at the time.

"What was lawful then cannot be considered unlawful today," a reporter beside Eva quoted.

The voice continued, "It is according to these precepts that those involved in the Holocaust will be sentenced. Only those perpetrators who acted in excess, who killed contrary to orders or of their own accord, may be sentenced to lifelong imprisonment for murder. Those who simply carried out orders are deemed accessories. I shall now impose sentencing."

Eva had disappeared from her spot by the door by the time the floodlights were extinguished in the auditorium. Hall attendants rolled up the map of the camp, while technicians dismantled the microphones. The blond man was the last to leave, gathering his papers together and lingering for just a little while longer in the hall. He smoked a cigarette, which wasn't allowed. Today, though, no one said a thing.

Eva wandered the streets. She wasn't in any hurry to get back to the boardinghouse, and she took several detours. Suddenly it seemed as though David were walking beside her. He was beside himself and spat at her, "When in doubt, for the accused?! I can't believe it! Take the pharmacist—accounts of his involvement in selections on the ramp and of his managing the toxic gas were corroborated by dozens of witnesses! But he's found guilty only of being an accessory to murder?! Defendant Number Eighteen and the medical orderly, who single-handedly killed their victims with a shot in the back of the neck, or the men who administered the gas in the gas chambers—you're telling me they're nothing more than accessories?!"

Eva got the feeling she had to hold David's head still, look into his uneven eyes, and say, "At least Defendant Number Four got a life sentence."

But there was no calming him, it seemed. "Shooting and gassing thousands of defenseless victims is punished with four to five years?!"

Eva nodded. "You're right, David, you've got to appeal!"

But David wasn't there anymore. Eva walked on alone. She, too, felt disappointed and empty.

That evening, Walther Schoormann sat slumped in a chair in the living room of his mansion, staring blankly at the television. They were covering the sentencing on the late news. In the next room, Frau Treuthardt was clearing the dinner table and whistling a *Schlager* pop tune, "You Aren't Alone." The anchor read the verdict: six sentences of lifelong penal servitude, including for the defendant known as the Beast, who had an instrument of torture named after him. The formal main defendant, the commander's adjutant, was given fourteen years for aiding and abetting murder. Three defendants were acquitted for lack of evidence. The rulings had triggered widespread outrage, the newscaster reported. Jürgen came in from outside, and Frau Treuthardt met him in the front hallway, where she took his coat and briefcase. What would he like for dinner? But Jürgen declined; he had eaten in the cafeteria. He went in to his father and dropped a catalog in his lap. On the cover was a woman changing bedclothes with gusto. A child was playing with a doll in the foreground.

"Our special edition, 'Laundry' catalog. Hot off the press. And with a kid on the cover."

Walther Schoormann mechanically turned the pages without looking at them. Jürgen went to the television and turned it off. "Our circulation has reached a hundred thousand," he added.

"Everything hurts today," his father answered. He rubbed both hands on his chest, then his shoulders, and grimaced. Then he began tearing pages out of the catalog, crumpling them into balls, and rubbing his torso with them, as if trying to remove a stain. Or blood. Jürgen stepped over and took away the catalog.

"I'm sorry to hear that. Would you like a pill?"

Walther Schoormann looked at his son. "Why doesn't that young woman come by anymore?"

"You ask me that a hundred times a day," Jürgen griped.

"Why doesn't she come by anymore?"

"She called off the engagement, Father!"

"Why?"

"Because our house reeks of chlorine!"

"That's true."

Jürgen left the room. He met Brigitte coming through the

doorway, wearing a fashionable new dressing gown and a towel twisted into a turban on her head. She had clearly been swimming.

"And my wife reeks of chlorine too," Walther Schoormann said. Brigitte went over to her husband and stroked the top of his head.

"Someone's very charming today."

"I'd like a pill."

Brigitte studied him. "I'll go get you one."

THAT SAME EVENING, Doctor Hartmut Küssner showed Annegret their new home together. They paced through the empty rooms of the Art Nouveau mansion. Bare bulbs dangled, illuminated, from the ceilings. Their steps echoed, and the yard outside the windows was hidden in the dark. Annegret pointed out that they had barely any furniture, and asked how they were going to fill all these rooms. She suggested leaving the upstairs empty. Küssner agreed. The pediatric practice at the front of the house was out-fitted with white steel furniture. It smelled strongly of camphor and rubber. Annegret said that the space felt too clinical and that they should paint the walls in color. "Whatever you say," Doctor Küssner repeated. He was happy. A few days earlier, he had gone to the nurses' lounge to take his leave. But then he refused to let go of Annegret's hand and asked her, right in front of Nurse Heide, whether she would come with him. Not once had he brought up "Annegret's misconduct," as he secretly referred to it. And they both knew: they never would speak of it. They would marry the following year. Annegret would stay fat. Hartmut would love her unfailingly. She would get pregnant and give birth to a baby boy in her early thirties, under life-threatening conditions.

The parents would spoil and neglect their son in turns. When he reached adolescence, he would dye his hair green and then one night, with his friends, sneak into the tennis club where his father was an active member—his mother a passive member—and take a pickax to the courts, tear through the fencing, and set fire to the nets. Against the establishment!

Dear Eva, there's something I have to tell you, because you don't know who I truly am . . .

That's where he got stuck. Jürgen couldn't count the number of times he had started this letter. He never managed to get past the opening sentences. He crumpled the paper and threw it in the trash. It was almost midnight. Jürgen sat at the desk in his room. He, too, had heard about the sentencing in the car on the way home. He could imagine how Eva was taking it. He wanted to write to her. He took out a new sheet. *Dear Eva, I heard about the verdict on the radio and . . .* There was a knock on the door. Brigitte poked her head in.

"Jürgen, I can't get him into bed."

Jürgen stood up and followed Brigitte into the dimly lit living room, where Walther Schoormann was still in front of the television, sitting rigidly in his chair. He looked like a worn-out doll.

"Come on, Father, it's late."

Jürgen tried to help his father up, but Walther gripped the armrests with both hands. Brigitte tried to loose his fingers, while Jürgen took hold of his father under the arms from behind, to lift him from the chair.

"On three," he said quietly and counted. Brigitte then pulled on Walther Schoormann's hands, and Jürgen hoisted him up. But the old man howled so wretchedly, as if they'd inflicted terrible pain on him, that they both let go, and he dropped back into the chair.

"What's wrong with him?" Jürgen asked Brigitte over his father's head. She shook her head helplessly. "Father, are you in pain?"

"You'll never get me to talk!" Walther Schoormann said.

Brigitte looked at Jürgen. "I already gave him two pills. I don't know. I don't know," she repeated. Then she placed a hand before her face and said, from the bottom of her heart, "I can't do this anymore, Jürgen."

"Go sleep. I'll stay with him."

Brigitte regained her composure, nodded, assumed her near-proverbial optimism, and left the room. Jürgen looked at his father, who stared straight ahead, at the television.

Then he walked over to the sweeping panoramic window and peered out. Several of the trees in the yard were recently attacked by a fungus and had to be felled. *It looks like the yard has cavities*, Jürgen thought.

"Why doesn't that young woman come around anymore?" his father asked.

Jürgen shook his head in exasperation. "Do you know who I am?" he asked in response.

"It's so dark in here. Are you my brother?"

Jürgen took a step closer to the window. As he spoke, his breath appeared on the glass. "I killed a person. It was a week after I learned of Mother's death. I ran away from the farm. I wanted to find my way to you and rescue you. It got dark. I was in a field, and then these low-flying aircraft flew over, Yanks on their way toward Kempten. The sirens started howling, and I saw the flak firing on the horizon, and one of them turns back, burning in the air. I see a man fall out. A parachute opens, and the Yank lands right at my feet. He lay before me and couldn't get up. 'Help me, boy.' There was blood running out of his mouth. And I kicked him, first in the legs, then in the stomach. And finally in the face. I was screaming with a voice I didn't recognize, kicking with all my strength, and it was fun, hellishly fun. I ejaculated. It was my first time. And then the man was dead. I ran away and holed up somewhere. I went back the next day. I always thought, I didn't do that—evil did." Jürgen listened to his father's silence, then continued. "But that was my powerlessness, my revenge, and my hatred. It was all me, and only me."

Jürgen fell silent. The room stayed quiet behind him for some time, and then a voice said, "My boy." Jürgen turned around. Walther Schoormann had gotten out of his chair and was reaching a hand toward Jürgen. "Help me."

Jürgen went to his father and placed an arm around his shoulders. He guided him slowly toward the door. Walther Schoormann stopped suddenly.

"That's why you wanted to become a priest."

"I think so, yes."

Outside his bedroom door, Walther Schoormann looked up at Jürgen. "It's hard being human." Then he opened the door and disappeared inside.

In late November, Eva came across a postcard-size ad in the paper: *Christmastime is Time for Goose! German House, Your Destination for Good Home Cooking for Family and Business Gatherings. Also Serving Lunch. Reservations Required. Proprietors: Edith & Ludwig Bruhns, 318 Berger Strasse, Tel: 0611–4702.*

Eva cut out the ad, then didn't know where to put the slip of paper. She placed it on the narrow table she had pushed up to the window as a work space. A few days later, the clipping was gone. Maybe Frau Armbrecht had cleared it away or a draft had pulled it out the window. The first Sunday of Advent was approaching, and Eva thought about decorating her room for Christmas. Ultimately, Frau Armbrecht made the decision for her and placed a pine arrangement with a yellow candle on Eva's table. Now, when Eva translated her instruction manuals (*This machine to be operated by trained professionals only! Keep area around master switch free of foreign objects!*), the light flickered and gave off the delicate scent of beeswax. Sometimes she had to blow out the flame, because it made her too sad. In those moments, Eva cursed the decoration and Frau Armbrecht and Christmas as a whole. One afternoon, there was a knock on the door. Frau Armbrecht poked her head in and trilled that there was a "gentleman" here to see her. For a moment, Eva hoped it was Jürgen. But then a small figure in an orange hat appeared in the doorway. Eva opened her arms, and Stefan ran in. She squeezed him tightly and breathed in his boyish smell, which reminded her of grass, even in winter.

"This is my brother," Eva explained to a curious Frau Armbrecht. She waved and withdrew. Stefan wandered around the room, taking everything in, but he wasn't interested in anything he saw, beyond the picture of himself and Purzel.

"All that's left of him now is bones, isn't it?"

Eva took Stefan's jacket and hung it on a hook behind the door. Stefan sat down in her only chair and stretched his legs out. He looked at Eva.

"You're so skinny," he said.

"It's true, I haven't been very hungry lately."

"Do you think it's going to snow soon?"

"Definitely." Eva smiled. She asked if their parents knew he was visiting her. Stefan shrugged. They thought he was at Thomas Preisgau's. But he wasn't even his best friend anymore.

"How come?" Eva asked.

"He told me his parents don't want him playing with me anymore. Herr Paten quit too."

"Herr Paten . . ." Eva repeated pensively. She didn't ask any further, and Stefan had already changed the subject.

"Mummy hit me."

Eva looked at Stefan in shock—that had never happened before. "Why on earth did she do that?"

Stefan hemmed and hawed, then admitted, "Because I called her a toothless granny. She has teeth she can take out now."

Stefan got up to climb on the bed. Eva grabbed hold of him. "Stefan, you can't say things like that. It hurts her feelings."

"Yeah, I know that now!" he responded impatiently, then jumped onto the bed.

Stefan bobbed up and down. "I'm getting a bike for Christmas. And a dog from Annegret. I already know everything. Annegret is coming with her new husband. She has a husband now and you don't. Weird, huh?"

"Yes. Do you want some cookies?"

Stefan's mouth twitched halfheartedly, but then he nodded. Eva took a tin off the shelf, where she kept the cookies. She bought them a few weeks earlier, when Fräulein Adomat and their new co-worker came over for coffee. They discussed getting a work anniversary gift for their boss, Herr Körting, and settled on a wicker rocking chair. Since both of her colleagues were dieting, there were lots of cookies left over. Stefan chewed listlessly on one of the dried-out treats but reached for a second. To be polite. Eva looked at her brother and was surprised to realize that he had matured.

"How are you doing, Stefan?" she asked.

"Daddy hasn't been singing any Christmas songs this year," he replied.

"He always sang them wrong, anyway." Eva began to sing, "While shepherds watched their clocks at night," but she got a lump in her throat. She swallowed.

Stefan didn't laugh either, and slid off the bed. He stood before her on the cheap rug and asked her bluntly, "What did Mummy and Daddy even do?"

"Nothing."

How could she explain to her brother just how true that answer was?

When Eva brought Stefan to the front door and pulled the orange hat back over his ears, he said, "I don't want the bike or the dog. I don't want any presents. I just want you to come home for Christmas."

Eva gave Stefan a quick hug and quickly opened the door to the stairwell. He went out and trotted down the steps. Eva watched the orange hat slowly disappear.

A few days before Christmas, Eva received a piece of official mail: her visa for a four-day trip to the Polish capital had been approved. Eva went straight to a travel agency; the older woman, who also had a pine arrangement with a lit beeswax candle on her desk, shook her head incessantly as she paged through tables and made phone calls. It was impossible, she said. Too short notice. And certainly not by way of Vienna; those flights had been booked for weeks already. Was she not aware it was Christmas? Eva didn't respond to her stupid questions. But ultimately the woman managed to cobble together a connection that was inconvenient but doable. Eva packed her bags, which also proved a challenge. Nothing fit anymore. The skirts slid off her hips, the jackets hung in loose folds around her torso. Wearing her pale plaid wool coat was like standing inside a tent. But Eva liked her slow disappearance, she liked running her hands over her back and feeling every last rib. She thought it only appropriate.

Eva flew to Berlin-Tempelhof on a full flight. The woman innkeeper at the Auguste, a hotel on a cross street to Kurfürstendamm, eyed Eva warily: she mistrusted all women traveling solo. Eva ignored the look. She lay down on the bed in her room and listened to the distinct voices coming from next door. ("If you don't want to buy me the stole, that's your decision. But this one time I really hoped you wouldn't let me down!" a woman's voice yelled.) Eva got back up and left the hotel. She mindlessly followed the people and lights on the street and ended up at the Christmas market set up in the shadows of the ravaged Kaiser Wilhelm Memorial Church. Strains of "O Du Fröhliche" could be heard. It smelled like food everywhere. Grilled sausages, candied almonds, chicken. Greasy. Eva forced herself to eat a bratwurst at one of the stands. She thought of Schipper's sausages at the Christmas market back home. Every year she ate one of those with Annegret, enjoying the delightful feeling of doing something forbidden, because their father was convinced that Schipper the butcher was a swindler. Eva stood opposite two tiny old people—they barely reached the top of the standing table. They were not speaking, each concentrating instead on their food, although they did bite down and chew their sausages in unison. When the woman finished her mustard, the man held out his paper plate, which still had mustard on it. *He's done that a hundred times before*, Eva thought. Not far from them, a brass band began playing "Unto Us a Time Has Come."

"This is the most beautiful Christmas carol," the woman commented.

The man looked at her and smiled. "You don't say."

The ensemble played well, with far fewer slips than the group Eva and Jürgen had once laughed at so uncontrollably. Then the woman began to sing in a quiet, unsteady voice.

Unto us a time has come,
And with it brought an awesome joy.
O'er the snow-covered field we wander,
We wander o'er the wide, white world.
'Neath the ice sleep stream and sea,
Whilst the wood in deep repose doth dream.
Through the softly falling snow, we wander,
We wander o'er the wide, white world.
From on high, a radiant silence fills hearts with joy,
While under astral cover, we wander,
We wander o'er the wide, white world.

And her husband watched her as she sang, and listened.

Eva suddenly knew what to do. She had passed by a phone booth earlier. She retraced her steps, entered, picked up the receiver, tossed coins into the slot, and dialed a number she knew by heart. It crackled and tooted. She waited. Tooot-tooot-tooot. And then finally, "Schoormann residence."

It was Frau Treuthardt's self-assured voice.

"Good evening. This is Eva Bruhns . . ."

"How may I help you?"

"I would like to speak with Jürgen, please."

"Herr Schoormann is away on business. He won't return until tomorrow. Would you like to speak with Frau Schoormann?"

"No. No, thank you. But where is he? Is he reachable elsewhere?" A lengthy pause followed. "I . . . I was his fiancée."

"He's in Vienna, at the Hotel Ambassador." She sounded affronted.

"Thank you, and—"

But Frau Treuthardt had already hung up. Eva leaned against the glass wall; the booth stank of urine and damp ash. She counted her change, then asked the operator to connect her with the Hotel Ambassador. The front desk suggested she try reaching Herr Schoormann in his room. The phone crackled and tooted again. The coins dropped. Eva was about to hang up, the receiver suspended above the cradle, when she heard Jürgen's voice. "Yes?"

Eva still hesitated.

"Hello? Who's there? Brigitte?" Jürgen asked.

Eva brought the receiver back up to her ear, her heart pounding heavily. "It's Eva." Jürgen didn't respond. "I'm in Berlin, on my way to Warsaw, and I was just at the Christmas market, and I just wanted to talk to you," she continued rapidly. The final coin clattered, and Eva inserted a mark.

"What are you doing in Warsaw?"

"There's someone I want to look for, a prisoner from the camp. The lead prosecutor found him and called me."

"And why? Why . . . ?" The connection sputtered and began to echo. *Why? Why?*

Eva remained silent and added another mark. "I don't have much change left."

"Can I call you back?"

Eva examined the pay phone and found a metal plate engraved with the number at the bottom. "That must be it." She read off the numbers for Jürgen, then they both fell silent. "We can still talk," Eva said. "I already paid."

But they both waited and listened to the clicking over the line. The final coin tumbled, and Eva quickly said, "Wouldn't you like to come to Warsaw?"

Click. Tooot. Eva hung up and waited. She watched the lights of passing cars through the streaked glass of the phone booth. The headlights turned into stars, then burned out. At last the phone made a strange buzzing noise. Eva answered. "Hello?"

"It'll be tricky with the visa," she heard Jürgen's voice say. Eva was silent. Outside it began to snow.

EVA WAS UP by five o'clock the next morning. The border crossing, the woman at the travel agency had told her, would take at least two hours. The train to Warsaw departed from Ostbahnhof at ten thirty-five. Eva got out of the subway at Friedrich Strasse. Armed border guards patrolled the station, scrutinizing everyone they passed. Eva walked up to a booth and pushed her documents through a narrow opening. The young uniformed man behind the glass studied her identification, visa, and passport photo for an unnecessarily long time, only to wave her through impatiently. Eva walked down tiled passageways that seemed to have no end. It smelled like the zoo back home. Like the hippo area, where the hippos emerged from their "poop soup," as Stefan called it, an expansive mass surfacing and just as slowly opening their enormous mouths, as though they wanted to devour the entire Bruhns family.

Eva came out of the catacombs on the eastern side and blinked in the winter glare, as if she had been underground for weeks. She had never been to East Germany. She was curious about life there, about the people's earnest activity. Everyday life existed here too. For its citizens, the GDR was normal. Eva recalled the two lawyers from the East who had represented joint plaintiffs in the trial. It always seemed to her that they behaved as if they had a handicap, as if they especially had to prove themselves. They always spoke a bit more loudly, more insistently, than the other lawyers. An hour later, the train was clattering its way out of East Berlin. Eva looked out the window and tried not to think about the other trains. Cranes twirled on the horizon, as though the wind was carefully playing with them.

After they crossed the border into Poland, the snowy fields grew larger, the forests endless. Later, in the dining car, Eva drank a beer that was so flat, bitter, and lukewarm that her father would've thrown it in the waiter's face. The waiter was exceptionally friendly, though, bowing to Eva with a flourish of his white napkin. When he discovered that she spoke Polish, he couldn't contain his delight. And by the time they pulled into the capital's central station, Eva knew his whole life story and even more about his brother, who'd had a lot of rotten luck in life. The ladies were his bane.

The hotel was a modern high-rise. Eva had stayed here before, two years ago, when she traveled with the executive board of a machinery company as their interpreter. She and the director's secretary were the only women. The secretary warned Eva about her boss: he made a pass at everyone. And sure enough, that evening at the bar, the man took a seat beside Eva and launched into his jokes. He was entertaining and told such funny stories that Eva couldn't help but laugh. Suddenly his tongue was in her mouth. She was in such high spirits and drunk. She wanted to finally experience it for herself, and took the company director up to her room. He'd been her first.

Now, Eva couldn't sleep. Her room was on the third floor, right above the lobby. She could hear muffled dance music coming from the neighboring bar. She thought of Herr Jaschinsky and of how he had lost his daughter, the girl with the funny nose. The Beast had summoned her for interrogation, because she was supposedly passing on secrets. She was shot three days later at the Death Wall. Eva stared at the gray nighttime ceiling and missed her Don Quixote. To be perfectly honest, she didn't know what she was doing in this city. The closer she came to her goal, the less she understood the purpose of this trip.

The next morning, Eva walked down a lively street with many small businesses, lined up like a string of beads: shoes, potatoes, coal, milk. It was cold, the air a hazy gray, and people wrapped their faces with scarves and hid them under fur hats. *It's snowdusting*, Eva thought, as she scanned the numbers on the doors. She knew it wasn't flakes of ice floating through the air, though, but rather bits of soot belched out of the countless chimneys dotting the rooftops. The hairdresser's was number seventy-three. Eva spotted it on the other side of the street and froze. Her heart was pounding. She hadn't managed to eat any breakfast, and now she had a knot in her stomach. The words "Salon Jaschinsky" were written in blue above the door. It was a small shop, and hanging in the front window were two pastel photographs of a woman and a man with hairstyles like cast metal. Like helmets. Two figures moved inside the salon, one a younger woman with towering teased hair who was serving a client. The other was an older, gray-haired man sweeping. Herr Jaschinsky. Eva crossed the street.

A little bell tinkled above the door. The young woman, who was shaving the back of her client's neck with a straight razor, didn't look up as Eva entered. In practiced motions, Herr Jaschinsky took her coat and hat and led her to one of the chairs. A numbing smell of soap and hair tonic pervaded the room; the shop was utterly spotless. Eva sat down, and in the mirror, she could see a little girl bouncing excitedly in a chair, Herr Jaschinsky watching her with a smile. She turned to him. He returned her gaze languidly, his eyes magnified behind his thick lenses.

"What will it be today?"

Eva began haltingly: she was from Germany. Herr Jaschinsky started, then took out Eva's updo. He began to brush her hair in practiced motions.

"Shampoo and trim the ends?"

Eva felt naked. But she was determined and continued, "We've met. I was still a child, and my mother brought me along. To the salon. At the camp."

Herr Jaschinsky slowly kept brushing her hair. Then he paused and looked at the oblong scar above Eva's ear, where the hair didn't grow. He lowered the brush, his face ashen, and for a moment Eva feared he might faint. The young woman looked over. Eva turned her gaze up toward Herr Jaschinsky.

"I want to ask your forgiveness," she said quietly. "For what we did to you. You and your daughter."

Herr Jaschinsky peered down at Eva, but she couldn't tell what was going on inside him. Then he regained his composure, shook his head. He started brushing her hair again, more vigorously than before, and said, "You must be confusing me for someone else. I was never at any camp. So, what will it be today?"

"I'd like for you to cut off all my hair and shave my head. Please."

Herr Jaschinsky's expression hardened. He set aside the brush. The young woman, whose client had left the shop, came up and asked something Eva didn't catch. Herr Jaschinsky waved her off.

"I won't do that," he then said to Eva. "It isn't right."

He strode over to the coat rack and retrieved Eva's coat and hat. He came back to Eva, who was still sitting in the chair, and held out her things. He looked at her resolutely. She nodded, twisted up her hair, and stood. The little bell above the door tinkled.

Inside the shop, the young woman stepped up to Herr Jaschinsky. He stood by the window, watching Eva in her pale plaid coat disappear in the haze. He looked agitated, and tears welled up in his eyes. The young woman had never seen her boss like this. Perplexed, she asked who that woman was. He didn't respond.

"What did that woman want?" She put a hand on his arm. Herr Jaschinsky calmed down some. "What did she want from you?"

He turned away from the window. "Consolation. They want us to console them."

Eva ran down the street; everything around her seemed louder and more garish than before. The city seemed adversarial to her. She ran faster. She was out of breath, kept running. Her feet hurt, and her hair came undone beneath her hat. She wheezed, her pulse hammering. She ran and ran, as if running away from something. She eventually had to stop. She struggled for breath where she stood, in front of a monument apparently honoring some Polish national hero. Her chest ached, and she coughed, then gagged and swallowed. She sobbed suddenly in despair and forced herself to admit what Herr Jaschinsky had truly said to her, which was not, "It isn't right." What he'd meant was, "It isn't your right." Eva stared, breathing heavily, up at the stone figure covered in a thin layer of snow like icing. Its eyes looked back coldly. Eva realized now that she truly didn't have any concept of the life, love, and pain of others. The people who had been on the right side of the fence would never comprehend what it meant to be imprisoned at that camp. Eva felt ineffable shame. She wanted to cry, but couldn't. An ugly wheezing was all that crept out of her throat. *I have no right to cry, either.* Hours later, when Eva finally found her way back to the hotel, the concierge had a message for her.

The next morning, Eva waited in terminal two at the airport for the delayed flight from Vienna. She walked back and forth outside the barrier and wasn't sure whether to be excited or nervous. Whether what she had blurted out so spontaneously was a good idea. But when the board registered that the flight had landed and the first passengers emerged from behind the light blue wall, and when she glimpsed Jürgen—his tall, dark figure—he appeared so familiar to her that she broke into a smile of relief. Jürgen was also moved by the sight of her, something she could tell the moment they spotted one another from across the barrier. And as he stood facing her, she discovered something new in his eyes: openness. They didn't know how to greet each other after such a long time. They ended up shaking hands.

The childlike roundness in her face has gone, Jürgen thought. Then he asked, "Don't you eat anymore?"

They waited at the carousel together for his suitcase. A little hatch in the wall industriously discharged pieces of luggage that then twirled onto the belt as though being displayed on a cake plate. Jürgen's suitcase never appeared. They went to one of the counters, where they were told to go have a cup of coffee and come back in an hour.

Eva and Jürgen stepped into a futuristic café of chrome and glass that overlooked the airfield. They sat down beside each other on a bench upholstered in silver leatherette and took in the view. Pale clouds were gathering on the horizon, the skies above promising snowfall. Jürgen told her that during his flight he had read in the paper that the people setting fire to baby carriages in Eva's neighborhood were caught. It was a group of students, brothers in a fraternity apparently. They stated that they did it to draw attention to the threat foreigners and migrant workers posed, and to the imminence of miscegenation.

"And were they arrested?" Eva asked. They had to pay damages, Jürgen responded. There wouldn't be any trial, though. The whole thing was being written off as a boyish prank. Eva looked at Jürgen incredulously. Yes, he said, and it seemed the students' influential families played some role in it too. Eva took a sip of her coffee, which looked blue in the café lighting.

"That's terrible." Then she told Jürgen about her visit to Jaschinsky, what he had said, and what she had realized.

"Don't be so hard on yourself, Eva," Jürgen said. "You're very brave."

Eva looked at him and again; it seemed like he had changed. He seemed vulnerable, like he'd set aside some heavy armor. Jürgen briefly stroked her cheek, then her hair.

"I, for one, am quite pleased that Herr Jaschinsky reacted the way he did."

"How long does your visa last?" Eva asked.

"I fly back tomorrow morning. It might be the last Christmas Eve I have with my father. He and Brigitte didn't go to their island this year, for the very first time."

"How *is* your father doing?"

"He can't speak anymore. No, that's not quite true. There are two sentences he still says: 'Please help me' and 'You'll never get me to talk.' Like in a spy movie." Jürgen laughed cheerlessly. Eva was silent. He looked at her. "What about you? You don't want to see your family?"

"Stefan visited me and said that he would give up all his presents if I came. My return ticket is for Friday."

"Christmas will be over by then. We could ask if there are any seats available in the flight tomorrow. Then we'd fly home together."

Instead of answering, Eva dug through her coat pocket, pulled something out, and placed it on the glinting chrome tabletop. It was the little package of red-painted wood.

"What is that?"

"The gift brought by the Moorish king."

"Myrrh," Jürgen said, taking the little red cube and turning it around in his fingers. Eva told him the story behind it. As she did, she could see her mother before her, setting up the Christmas pyramid on the cupboard in the living room. Fitting it with four red candles. Going through the motions silently this year, for the first time ever failing to recount the story of the missing package. Eva saw her father sweating in his kitchen, preparing the best goose for his family, all the while knowing that his daughter would not be coming to share in it. She saw her family leaving church on Christmas Eve, skidding over the icy streets in a row, their arms all linked. She was missing. That evening, her parents would sit in the living room till her father said, "I'm sure she'll come next year." Her mother would remain silent, wondering whether her life was actually over.

"What is myrrh used for?" Eva asked.

"It's a resin. It was once used for embalming dead bodies. And it represents human nature. For the earthly realm. It is both bitter and healing."

Eva put the little package away. She took Jürgen's hands firmly in hers. If nothing else, she knew this much was good. "There's no shaking this feeling of love inside me."

It was time to check on the lost suitcase, but they sat close for a while longer in the futuristic café. They looked at each other from time to time and thought that they really would be good together, while planes descended onto the airfield and others climbed calmly into skies heavy with snow.

AUTHOR'S NOTE

I would like to express my gratitude to the staff at the Fritz Bauer Institut in Frankfurt. Their remarkable work, and in particular, the extensive archive of materials from the first Auschwitz trial were indispensable to my research. Over the years, the transcripts and sound recordings of witness testimony (https://www.fritz-bauer-institut.de/mitschnitt-auschwitz-prozess.html) became the springboard and source of meaning for my artistic work. The fictitious witnesses who appear in the novel exemplify the fate of survivors in my mind. To create them I sometimes quoted excerpts from original testimony. In other cases I merged statements; this creative consolidation represents an effort to provide a platform for as many voices as possible. I bow to those individuals in the trial who revisited their traumatic experiences and confronted the perpetrators. They provided the world with comprehensive, lasting testimony of what Auschwitz was.

The following participants in the trial were quoted directly:

Mauritius Berner
Josef Glück
Jan Weis
Hans Hofmeyer (chief judge)
Fritz Bauer (attorney general)
Hildegard Bischoff (witness for the defense)

A NOTE FROM THE TRANSLATOR

Translating Annette Hess's *The German House* presented a range of linguistic, stylistic, and thematic challenges, as the story moves from past to present, between characters representing different ages, backgrounds, sensibilities, and intentions, and from internal thought processes to external actions. Like Eva, I felt a deep sense of responsibility to do justice to this story, to translate faithfully and thoughtfully the testimonies of Auschwitz survivors and the process of this young woman's coming-of-age and crisis of identity, as she discovers the truth of her family's past and must question her own role within it. Eva's painful personal reckoning parallels the slow thawing of widespread reluctance among her fellow Germans to account for the crimes of the Nazi era—crimes of such magnitude that, indeed, they could never have come to pass, had only a tiny sliver of the population been complicit.

The quick pacing of the narrative demanded nimble, colorful language that contributes to the novel's page-turning quality and reflects the dynamism that characterized the economic boom in post-war West Germany. This energy carries over into the many passages of dialogue, where my task was not only to convey the content of conversation, but to stay true to each character's distinct voice while maintaining the tone of mid-century speech.

The kinetic world that Hess creates for readers in *The German*

House—from the noisy and rapidly changing cityscape of Frankfurt to the ways her characters love, fight, negotiate, tease, or sing—is counterbalanced by moments of recollection that may be quieter, but are no less powerful. Memory plays a central role in this story. Defendants claim not to remember what happened at Auschwitz, while survivors recall their trauma before a public audience that expects their memories to be flawless. Eva realizes that what she has always accepted as her childhood memories can no longer be trusted. Memories are often fragmented, incomplete, illogical in the way the mind stitches them together, yet they help define who we are. It was critical to reflect this sense of both distance and immediacy in the language of their telling.

—Elisabeth Lauffer